Marsali grew up near Edinburgh, Scotland. Her family holidays were spent in a remote cottage in the West Highlands, the region where her detective Gavin Macrae lives. Like her sailing heroine, Cass, she has always been used to boats, and spent her gap-year earnings on her first sailing dinghy, *Lady Blue*. She studied English at Dundee University, did a year of teacher training and took up her first post, teaching English and French to secondary-school children in Aith, Shetland. Gradually her role expanded to doing drama too, and both primary- and secondary-school pupils have won prizes performing her plays at the local Drama Festival. Some of these plays were in Shetlandic, the local dialect.

A Shetland Winter Mystery is the tenth novel in her much-loved Shetland Mysteries series.

By Marsali Taylor and available from Headline Accent

The Shetland Mysteries

MARSALI
TAYLOR

A
SHETLAND
WINTER
MYSTERY

ACCENT

First published in 2021 by Headline Accent
An imprint of HEADLINE PUBLISHING GROUP

1

Cataloguing in Publication Data is available from the British Library

ISBN 978 1 4722 9206 3

Typeset in 11/13.5pt Bembo Std by Jouve (UK), Milton Keynes

Printed and bound in Great Britain by Clays Ltd, Elcograf S.p.A.

HEADLINE PUBLISHING GROUP
An Hachette UK Company
Carmelite House
50 Victoria Embankment
London EC4Y 0DZ

www.headline.co.uk
www.hachette.co.uk

Contents

To the committee of Sustainable Shetland, who led the fight.

Tulya's E'en

Wednesday, 16th December

Tide times at Aith:
LW 03.05 (0.7m);
HW 09.21 (2.2m);
LW 15.37 (0.5m);
HW 22.07 (2.0m)

Sunrise 09.07, moonrise 09.58; sunset 14.58, moonset 17.44.

Waxing crescent moon

Chapter One

trow: The trows were Shetland's 'little people', who lived in mounds in the hill, and could only come out after dark. They liked bright colours, feasting and music (there are tales of human fiddlers being kidnapped and taken underground for a trowie wedding), and were known for working mischief about the croft; sometimes their actions were more sinister, like substituting a baby of their own for a human child (Old Norse, troll)

There was the sound of children giggling, stifled quickly as if they were up to mischief; a group of trainees planning some devilment. Kitten growled and jumped down from the bed. Whoever was on watch would deal with it, I thought, hunching into the bedcovers, and the thought jerked me awake. I wasn't in my cabin aboard *Sørlandet* but in Gavin's cottage in Shetland. Our nearest neighbour was a mile away over the hill, and they didn't have children.

I eased my nose out from under the downie and listened. Cat stirred and sat up. Nothing; silence, that dead silence after snow had fallen. There had been the first few flakes as Gavin had driven me back from the airport, followed by a rattle of haily puckles that had covered the ground in white; a good base for snow to lie on. I tilted my head up to look out of the window. Yes, more had fallen while I'd slept. The low hill of Papa Little was blue-white in the moonlight, and the stars sparkled with cold light.

3

I reached for my watch and pressed the button to light up the face. Half past eleven. Naturally the youngsters of the ship's watch would be up at that hour, but I wasn't on board ship now. All good land children were tucked up in their beds, sleeping peacefully, or illicitly playing on their computers or texting their friends. They weren't wandering round a cottage miles from anywhere.

I was thoroughly awake now. *Sørlandet* had spent the last two months exploring the eastern seaboard of the States, and my body clock was telling me it was six in the evening. I'd had a short nap to refresh me, and now I could get up and party. Beside me, Gavin was curved over on his side, back towards me, his breathing deep and even.

I slid out of bed and padded over to the window. The sliver of crescent moon had gone down, but the clear sky gave a pale light over the snowy hills and stars gleamed in the depths of the coal-black water. There was no sign of movement anywhere, yet I had this sense of something stirring in the darkness. Kitten looked downwards from the sill, growled again, then jumped down and trotted downstairs. I heard the clack of the catflap.

Whatever it was, I supposed I'd better investigate. Maybe the ponies in the field behind the house had broken into the garden. I lifted up my bundle of clothes from the chair, and was tiptoeing out of the bedroom when I heard a car start up, way in the distance. I wouldn't have heard it at all if I hadn't been awake, if the back skylight hadn't been open, if it hadn't been such a still night. I reached the window just as the sound died away, and thought I saw a brief flash of headlights move across the starry sky. The silence closed in again.

I went slowly downstairs, not switching the light on. The ground shifted disconcertingly under me, as if the land had become fluid. It would take a couple of days before my balance adjusted. Freezing lino under my feet, the air icy on my skin.

I scrambled into my clothes and hauled on my boots, then eased the back door open.

People had been here. Several sets of footprints came down from the end of the garden, between the vegetable beds, spread out a bit as if they were looking at the house, and then joined again to come right to the briggistanes. One set came right up to the door and ended in a scuffle by the catflap: tiny bare feet, shorter than my hand. There were no prints going back.

A cold shudder went down my spine. While we'd been lying asleep upstairs, someone had come into our house.

It should have made it less scary that Gavin was sleeping so peacefully, but somehow it made it worse. I felt like I was the only human awake while something sinister was stirring in the darkness.

I didn't want to show a light just yet. I reached for the blinkie by the door and held it in my hand as I leapt over the doorstep, landing clear of the footprints. After they'd looked, after one had gone in and not come out, the others had set off around the house. There were several sets of footprints; the moon made sharp shadows of them. I made a print of my own for comparison. Yes, even the largest of them was no bigger than my size four. Child-sized. Little-people sized.

Suddenly I remembered the date: the sixteenth of December. It was Tulya's E'en, the day when the trows started their Yule patrol around the houses. A long-forgotten primary-school project surfaced in my mind. Trows didn't come near human houses normally, but in the dark days of midwinter they could come out and work mischief around the crofts. The old folk *sained* their houses against them with straw crosses and holy water, to keep them from stealing gear, animals or children. They'd make a plait with a hair from every animal in the byre, and hang it above the byre door, and they'd go round the outhouses with a burning peat on a shovel. The school jannie had done that bit, and we'd followed with our straw crosses.

5

We'd hung the thin braid of all our hair above the classroom door, and on the last day of term we'd baked sun biscuits, pointed all around and with a hole in the middle to thread a ribbon through. The boys had eaten theirs, but my best friend Inga and I had saved ours to hang on our Christmas trees.

There was a snick behind me. I jumped, heart pounding, and spun around to find Cat had come out of the catflap behind me and was sniffing at the tracks. I began to walk round the house, listening intently and pausing at the corner, as if I expected something to leap out at me. Nothing. Cat was going on ahead, plumed tail upright. Kitten pounced out at him from around the corner, and there was a scuffle which ended in them both charging across the snow, tails fluffed out. I found I'd been holding my breath, and let it out. There was nothing strange about when the cats were acting normally. All the same, I didn't want to follow the prints round the corner, where the house's deep shadow jutted out on the white snow.

'Everything okay?' Gavin asked from behind me. I jerked round, heart pounding. He was dressed in kilt and jumper, auburn hair tousled. He reached for his jacket then jumped over the doorstep to join me, kilt pleats flying. 'Hobbits?' He bent down, looking at the footprints closely. 'Four of them.'

'Not hobbits,' I said. 'Trows. It's the sixteenth. St Tulya's E'en.'

Gavin began strolling along the line of prints. 'Is she in the Roman Calendar of Saints?'

'I think it's a he,' I said. 'It's a corruption of St Thorlak. He was Icelandic.'

'Oh yes?' Gavin linked his arm through mine and we went on together, following the line of little footprints around the corner of the house. The snow had come from this direction and piled up against the wall of the house, so the prints were deeper here, clearer.

'Three of them here,' Gavin said. 'The other one went through the catflap.' He sounded remarkably unworried about it. 'One's lagging a bit, see, trudging footprints, as if it's carrying something heavy.'

'Hawkeye Macrae,' I said, impressed.

'Have I never told you I spent my teenage summers helping my grandfather stalk deer?' The next corner brought us to the front of the house, facing the sea. The kelp at the water's edge was glazed over with ice, and the rocks of the dyke below the house had snow sticking to the face of each stone, with the crevices between making a black crazy-paving pattern. 'Here we are.' He stopped at the sit-ootery door, facing out over the sound. 'He went in through the catflap and came out again here.'

I looked at the prints on the windowsill, neatly together, facing out from the house, and the pair of footprints, deeper and together, where it had jumped down.

'Four again,' Gavin said. 'All together. One of the bigger ones dragging the little one by the hand. He's getting a bit tired.'

'Past even a trow's bedtime. Or since trows are nocturnal maybe he was complaining about it being too early.'

'A tidy trow. He locked the window behind him.'

I looked at the window. It was one of those old-fashioned ones with a holed shaft that fitted over pins along the inner sill. The shaft was lying snugly in its place, and I didn't see how you could do that from outside.

'So,' Gavin said, starting to move again, 'what has your improbable saint got to do with an invasion of trows in the night?'

'They live underground, but when the nights are at their darkest, then they can come out from their trowie mounds and wander among the houses. The dark nights start at Tulya's E'en.'

'Ah,' Gavin said, entirely unruffled. His breath smoked in the cold air. 'Well, let's see where they wandered to.'

We followed the tracks along the front of the house, along the byre joined to it and around the corner. Back on the landwards side of the house, the tracks curved upwards to rejoin the trail leading down to the garden. The ponies were awake, standing above the rocky knowe at the far side of their park, heads turned to watch us. One gave a friendly whicker, and they both moved over towards us, manes damp and back fur spiked with snow.

'Care to tell us what's going on?' Gavin asked them, and fished out a packet of polo mints from his pocket, which they crunched with relish and a bit of head-nodding.

We paused at the foot of the slope and looked. The only marks in the icing-smooth snow were that double track and the neat hooves and dragging tailmarks of the ponies leading from their usual sleeping place behind the garden wall to the knowe where the tracks ended.

We went on upwards, the cats bounding around us.

The rocky mound was waist-high, an outcrop of boulders that had once been a Neolithic tomb, long since robbed of usable stones; a *trowie hadd*, the sort of place where trows were supposed to live in underground burrows. The tracks of feet came out of a dark gap between two larger stones, and went back in there.

We walked right around the mound, just to be sure. There were no other footprints, just a few sheep tracks and the stampled place where the ponies had stood. The only footprints in that smooth snow around the circumference of the mound were our own.

Sow Day

Thursday 17th December

Tide times at Aith:
LW 04.15 (0.8m);
HW 10.31 (2.3m);
LW 16.47 (0.5m);
HW 23.17 (2.1m)

Sunrise 09.05, moonrise 10.44; sunset 14.56, moonset 18.53.

Waxing crescent moon

Chapter Two

jookerie-packerie: *trickery, mischevious behaviour (Old Scots* jouk-erie: *deceit, trickery* + pauk(erie): *a trick)*

Gavin was up before me. I woke to the rattle of the kitchen Rayburn being riddled, followed by the clank of an ashbucket and the crackling of flames in kindling. I hauled on jeans and jumper and went downstairs. He was picking up the cats' plates now, dressed for work, in his everyday green kilt and leather sporran, and a rather baggy green jumper over his shirt and tie. The overhead light glinted on his russet hair, the colour of a stag's ruff. He lifted his head and smiled as I came in, grey eyes warm with welcome. 'It's good to have you home.'

I went over to put my arms round his waist, feeling the strength of his back muscles under my hand. 'It's good to be together again.'

Impatient with this delay to his breakfast, Cat stretched up against my leg with his soundless meow, and Kitten leapt onto the worktop.

Cat was a spectacularly beautiful long-haired grey with fainter silver stripes and as plumed a tail as any squirrel. Kitten had grown in the last couple of months, but she was still going to be a small cat, and (as she was well aware) a very pretty one. She was a tortoiseshell, with a coat the colours of several different spice jars shaken together over a worktop. Like Cat, she had neat white paws and a white bib, and her tail ended in a pale apricot tip. She was already spoiled rotten; even my redoubtable Maman had failed to resist such an avalanche of cuteness. I set her bowl of kitten food pointedly down in front of her, then called Cat to the other side of the kitchen for his. Her little head was butting his out of the way in seconds. I lifted his to the work surface and put her back to her own. 'I'll catch you some fish later,' I promised.

'Yes, you need to try the boat under power,' Gavin said. 'I'm pleased with it. It's fine for a day's fishing.' His sea-grey eyes smiled at me. 'You'll be heading up to Brae?'

'To check on *Khalida*,' I agreed. *Khalida* was my own yacht, an Offshore 8m, and had been my home until this new venture of living ashore with Gavin.

We went together to the door and stood for a moment, looking out. I'd forgotten how beautiful Shetland was under snow, how strange, a world turned monochrome, with the hills white against the grey sky. Several centimetres had fallen, enough to smooth over the rough heather of the hill as if it had been iced. Above us, the blue peat smoke scented the air.

The little footprints from last night were crisped into the clean snow. Now it was half-light I could see them better. They were bare feet, the toes clearly marked, with the big toe out of proportion, and a fuzziness about the outline.

'Tulya's E'en,' Gavin said. 'So today must be St Tulya's Day?'

'It ought to be.' I frowned. 'Except that I think it's Sow Day, the day the pig was killed ready for the Yule feast. I've a vague memory of not quite getting it at school either. It didn't make sense. You had Halloween, then All Saints, Christmas Eve and Christmas Day, so Tulya's E'en then Sow Day didn't work for me.'

'I wonder whether they stayed up late, and came with parental help, or sneaked out in the middle of the night and were brought here by a complicit sibling.'

His Highland accent made music of the phrase. I tucked my hand into his. 'I love your vocabulary.' I tried to imitate the lilt, and lingering 's' sounds. 'Complicit siblings.'

'An ingenious lot, the local bairns.'

'Definitely,' I said. 'I like the furry feet. Cut-out soles on the bottom of socks, would you say?'

'I hope there was a layer of wadding too. Even the hardiest trow would be getting chilblains in this frost. I wonder if we're the only ones they've visited?' He looked at the ponies, and smiled, then turned back towards the house. 'Now, *mo chridhe*, breakfast, then I must go. A million forms are waiting for me. I'll be back for lunch, then we'll have the whole weekend.' His arm closed round my shoulders again. 'I didn't feel I could go completely rearranging the schedules just to suit me. I'm still feeling my way.'

'Can't be helped,' I said. 'Besides, I'm feeling jet-lagged, from flying over the Atlantic instead of sailing it, in a civilised fashion. And the floor's rocking about as if it was water.'

'I got meat in for a stew, and we can have an early night.'

He served up the porridge and we ate, with Kitten installed on Gavin's kilted lap, and Cat condescending to sit by my chair, then I left Gavin to get ready and sauntered to the gate, ready to wave him off. Cat came bounding after me, tail high. Kitten followed him in a series of leaps, then picked her way disdainfully along the path, belly arched against the cold snow.

We had four weeks. The entire crew had; we'd left our beautiful ship in Bermuda and flown back for Christmas, leaving another crew to fill her with people escaping a northern winter. This, I reflected, would be Gavin's and my second Christmas together. Last year had been at his home in the Highlands, while we were still tentatively finding our way to a relationship, with Midnight Mass in Gaelic. This year we'd be here, in the cottage. Maman and Dad were coming over. We could have all the things I remembered from my childhood: a crib, and a tree, and stems of holly along the tops of the pictures.

At my feet, Cat froze, whiskers twitching. He turned his head to the hill, obviously hearing something; then a black 4x4 scrunched over the crown of the hill and began making its cautious way down the road to the house. It was too early for Maman, wanting to tell me what she'd organised for Christmas, and Dad's driving was more confident. Visitors, at this hour?

Cat had decided he didn't like the look of them; he slid, belly low, into the shelter of the sycamore trees that bounded the back yard. Kitten dithered for a moment, then followed him. I waited at the gate to see what they wanted.

The car ignored the turning space where Gavin's Land Rover was parked, and came right down to me. It stopped in the middle of the track, and the driver switched the engine off. It had tinted windows which stopped me from looking into it, and the sudden silence was sinister. It seemed to last for ever; then the doors opened together, as if the movement had been rehearsed, and a man got out from each side of the cab.

They were an implausible, frightening pair of apparitions in the middle of the snowy hills. A pair of goons, I'd have said, if it had been a gangster movie. Muscle-men. They were like twins, tall and broad-shouldered, shaven-headed, wearing identical black suits and reflective dark glasses, so that all I saw was myself in their eyes: dark curls, eyes big above French cheekbones, scar on one cheek, mouth slightly open in surprise.

The near one took one step, the far one three, so that they were standing right on the other side of the gate, much closer than I liked. I refused to let my feet move backwards.

'We've come to talk to you,' the first one said, in an unmistakably cod New York tough-guy accent.

'Just talk,' the other one chimed in. 'We can see you're going to be sensible.'

14

If they hadn't been so intimidating I'd have wanted to laugh at them. Even as one of them moved to block the first rays of the sun from my face part of me was wondering if this was a welcome-home wind-up from my friends at the boating club, members of Ronas Drama Group having fun being gangsters. I kept my face calm, and tried not to let the flimsiness of the gate between us, the way they towered over me and the confident menace in their voices frighten me. 'What are you wanting me to be sensible about?' I was pleased to hear my voice made it sound quite ordinary.

They looked at each other and shook their heads, then turned back towards me. 'Lady, you know better than that,' the first one said. 'We think you should retract your testimony.'

'Plenty of other witnesses,' his doppelganger corroborated. 'There's no need for you to stick your neck out.'

'Especially when sticking your neck out's liable to get your head chopped off.'

Now I really didn't have a clue what they were talking about. I'd managed so far to avoid being a trial witness in any of the cases I'd been involved in, but maybe one where my testimony was crucial was coming up, and I'd been subpoena'd.

They were too close for me to be able to look at them both at once, and that was disconcerting too. I went for the one who'd driven the car and looked my reflection straight in the eyes. 'I really don't understand what you're talking about.'

He sneered and looked at his mate. 'She *really* doesn't understand what we're talking about.'

'Short memory,' the other one responded, shaking his head.

The driver turned his attention back to me. 'I don't need to mention names. Just forget the testimony. Don't turn up in court.'

'You won't lose by it,' his twin rumbled. His head tilted towards the house. 'You could pay for a new roof, maybe.'

'Or a new car.' The other one smirked up at Gavin's Land Rover. The cheerful cross-talk when they were still leaning over me was somehow more sinister than the threats.

Then both heads shifted together and stilled. They were looking over my shoulder. Gavin's voice came from behind me: 'Everything all right, Cass?'

The heads turned to each other, then to me. 'Cass?' said the passenger.

Gavin joined me at the gate, neat and trim as if he'd spent an hour dressing. He spoke in a brisk, matter-of-fact voice. 'Can I help you, gentlemen?'

'Sorry to disturb you,' said the driver. 'Case of mistaken identity. We'll be on our way.'

I kept quiet. They were going, that was the main thing. If there was a confrontation Gavin would come off worse.

The goons nodded and turned away. The driver took the car cautiously down to the jetty, did a six-try turn and revved up to take the hill at speed. The black 4x4 snarled past us, jolted to the brow of the hill and was gone. Only the noise of the engine still hung in the air, gradually diminishing.

'Well,' Gavin said, 'what was that about?' He fished out his phone and tapped the car's number plate into it.

I shook my head. 'They said they wanted me to retract my testimony.'

'Testimony for what?'

I quoted the driver. '*I don't need to mention names. Just forget the testimony. Don't turn up in court.*'

'As a witness.' Gavin frowned, thinking. 'You haven't mentioned a subpoena letter.'

'I haven't had one. Then the other one said I wouldn't lose by it.'

'Threats and bribery.'

'But I think it really might have been a case of mistaken

16

identity. The way they reacted when you said my name – they turned to each other, then looked at me, and repeated it.'

'If they were relying on Google satellite to find you – or whoever – they'd have lost it coming out of Aith,' Gavin agreed. 'I'll try and get an owner for the car.' He made a face. 'Ah well, it's been an interesting day so far. See you later, *mo chridhe*. Have fun in the boat.'

Chapter Three

trigg: neat, orderly (Old Norse, trygg: *faithful, secure*)

I went back into the kitchen and looked around. My heart sank. It didn't feel like home: the gleaming new work surfaces, the pine table and matching chairs, the gingham curtains. I washed the porridge dishes and pan, but needed to open cupboard after cupboard before I found where they lived. I caught myself longing for my *Khalida*'s wooden walls and faded navy cushions, for lockers where I knew exactly where to find what I needed, and straightened myself up. I was glad to be back with Gavin, but being with him meant living on land. I'd soon feel at home here.

It was no good hanging around making myself gloomy. My *Khalida* was securely tied up in the marina up at Brae, but Gavin had bought a small motorboat of indeterminate race, a fibreglass 15-footer with a little wheelhouse and an electric motor, which I hadn't had a chance to try out yet. I went into the spare room for my old overalls, and that almost set me off again, for one bed was piled with *Khalida*'s cushions, her curtains, the books from her shelf in a box, and the other had the plastic boxes with my spare clothes. I picked up one cushion and hugged it to me, breathing in the smell of damp and diesel fumes, then put it down quickly. Enough. I pulled on a jumper and my old sailing overalls and left the room, closing the door firmly behind me.

I'd barely scrunched halfway down the gravel track to the pier when the catflap at the house rattled twice, the sound travelling clearly through the still air, and Cat and Kitten came charging after me. They were aboard the motorboat before I was, leaping neatly from jetty to thwart, where they sat and looked pointedly at the roll-up canvas that covered her doorway. I clambered after them and fitted the battery to the outboard, then rolled the canvas up for the cats. I wasn't surprised to see a two-cat-size wooden box with pre-arranged blanket secured on the floor, and Cat's lifejacket lying ready. No doubt they'd been happy to join Gavin on fishing expeditions, especially if some of the catch came their way. Kitten headed straight for the box; Cat stayed on the thwart, shaking the snow from his paws disdainfully. I cleared both cockpit seats with my gloved hands, chucking the snow overboard, and was just unclipping the mooring lines when I spotted four unken birds bobbing along the opposite shoreline, chestnut, with a darker head and white throat. Gavin would know what they were.

I put Cat's lifevest on, then rowed out from the jetty. The oars dipped with a satisfying swirl; the water rattled along the motorboat's sides. Once I was far enough out I lowered the outboard shaft into the water, put the kill cord from the magnetic key round my wrist and pressed the button.

The engine came to life with a gentle throbbing noise that would be inaudible twenty metres away. The otter patrolling the point lifted its head, stared for a moment, then went back to its fishing; the strange ducks ignored me. 'Well!' I thought, impressed. I suspected there would be drawbacks to this new technology, but at the moment I couldn't see any. No juggling with flammable petrol, no yanking at recalcitrant cords, no noise waking everyone for miles – what was not to like? I pulled the telescopic handle to a comfortable length for sitting in the lee of the cabin bulkhead and opened up. The throb speeded up, but the motor sound was easily drowned by the crunch as the boat bounced off the waves in Cole Deep. The computer panel told me I was going at six knots, better than my old Volvo Penta would achieve with *Khalida*.

It took me less than twenty minutes to get to Brae. By that time my nose and cheeks were frozen, and I was glad of my scarf and gloves. Hot chocolate aboard *Khalida*, I promised myself as I curved around the end of the marina and slowed to a potter, looking for a space.

Naturally my friend Magnie had spotted me coming out of Houbansetter and up the voe. As I came through the marina entrance his mustard-yellow Fiat came crunching down the boating club drive, turned with a skidding of gravel and led the way along to the far pontoon, where most of the sailing boats were moored. They looked strange and small without their masts, those 32- and 35-footers who spent their summers heading for Norway, Faroe or Orkney. My 26-foot *Khalida* was tucked in neatly between the two largest. By the time I'd reached the pontoon, Magnie was at the end of it, waving me around to the far side of it. 'Third berth down, lass, you can go in there.'

He was as trigg as if he was going visiting. His reddish fair hair had been combed with water; his ruddy cheeks were freshly shaved. Instead of a boiler suit and yellow boots, he was wearing cloth trousers and his second-best gansey, the one with stripes of brown pattern on a white ground, knitted two winters before she died by his late mother. He had to be well through his seventies now, for he was already retired when he'd first been my sailing teacher twenty years ago, but his movements on the pontoon were as sure and spry as a teenager's. He caught the bow as I nosed into the berth, and reached across for the clip, looking approvingly at the spliced rope. 'Your man's been busy while you were away.'

'A neat job,' I agreed. 'Come and have a cuppa aboard *Khalida* and tell me all the news.'

I felt a pang to the heart at the sight of my *Khalida*, bare and empty without her cushions, the forepeak curtain, or the books on their shelf. Her varnish was dulled by the cold, and the little horsebrass fish had lost its brightness. Magnie's hand clapped my shoulder. 'Perk up, lass. Come spring she'll be like herself, and in the meantime just think how much sounder you'll sleep without worrying about what's happening to your mast in every winter gale.' He gave my face a shrewd look. 'Put you that kettle on, and let me tell you all about the trowie visits here in Brae. Man, this bairns have fairly got the place in an uproar.'

He settled himself down on a thwart while I boiled the kettle. Cat investigated *Khalida*'s bare interior, whiskers forward disapprovingly; Kitten squirmed straight into the exposed lockers whose hardboard tops were normally barred to her by cushions and came up trying to sneeze off the smear of oil on her nose. I checked my bilges, set the engine running, made two mugs of tea and came up to join him. I'd just set the mugs down when a movement at the marina mouth caught my attention: a pair of the unken ducks sculling past the marina opening. 'Magnie, those deuks, what are they?'

He turned his whole body round to look at them, and got a glimpse before they disappeared under the water. 'Herald deuks. Are you no' seen them afore?'

'No' that I've noticed. Heralding what?'

'Christmas, likely.'

I glanced across at the little motorboat. 'Gavin was wanting a name for his boat. I'll see what he thinks to *Herald Deuk*.'

'You're all set for Christmas then.'

'Haven't had a chance to think about it. I arrived from the States last night.'

'Ah,' Magnie said. 'Headlight and the land swaying under your feet?'

21

'That's about the size of it.' I made a face. 'Aeroplanes. What's with these trows?'

'They're been out in force. Brae, Voe, Nesting. A couple of houses up in Hillswick too.'

'And us at the Ladie.' I gave a moment's thought to the geography of it. 'We're the odd man out. Otherwise it's the Brae school catchment area.'

Magnie put on a chilling voice. 'Mysterious footprints that just stop and start. In gardens, over the roofs of sheds, a set going into a drainpipe and coming out o' the other end, or a few along the top o' a wall, but none either side o' it.' He reverted to normal. 'Braaly ingenious.'

I thought of our tracks, vanishing into the trowie mound, and the little one who'd gone through the catflap and come out of a locked window. 'Did anyone catch them at it?'

Magnie chuckled. 'Catch them? No' they. It's these mobile phones they all have. One sees a car coming, and lets the ones ahead ken, and by the time it arrives they're all gone to ground behind the nearest shed. All the same . . .'

He paused, thinking. His mouth turned down. 'I dinna like it, Cass. I have a feeling in me puddings that there's trouble coming o' this. The old folk are up to high doh about it, particularly Auld Tirval. He was on the phone first thing this morning. He's no' happy, and he kent I ken you. He'd like to have a speak wi' you. So I thought, when I saw you heading up the voe, well, maybe no time like the present, if you're no' busy.'

I gave him a blank look. 'Do I ken Auld Tirval?'

'You might no', at that,' Magnie conceded. 'He bides down on the south side o' Voe. The last house along the Grobsness peninsula. It's opposite Weathersta, you ken, where the old whaling station used to be, and the refuelling station for the cruisers in the war.'

I nodded.

'Just as the voe narrows. Kurkigarth, it's called, on the hill of the Sneugie. If you went from the Ladie straight over the hill on the back of the Loch o' Gonfirth, you'd be at Kurkigarth.'

'Pedigree?' I asked.

Magnie paused to think about it. 'Berwin, that comes to the sailing, Tirval's his great-grandfather. Tirval Marvin Smith. The Marvin was after some Yank that saved his dad's life in the first war. He was only fifteen when he signed up, and this Yank was a surgeon who saved his life in the last days o' it, at Verdun. He was one o' the last folk to bide at the Hams o' Roe, the two old crofthouses on the hill. They moved out o' there when Tirval was, oh, no' school age yet, and came to Kurkigarth.'

'But what's Tirval got to do wi' the price o' fish, and how can I help?'

'Well, no' help, exactly,' Magnie conceded. 'It's more that he wants to talk to your father.' He finished his drinking chocolate and set the mug down. 'I thought you could maybe be a go-between, so to speak. He says the reason there's trows out all over the place is because of the diggings for your father's company's wind turbines.'

Since Kurkigarth was halfway homewards for me, Magnie phoned Auld Tirval and arranged a lift back with him when he came into Brae to do his messages. I shut *Khalida* up again, collected Cat and Kitten and the four of us set off back southwards, around into Olna Firth, the long inlet leading down to the village of Voe.

'The whole family lives here,' Magnie said, indicating the long, low hill we were heading for. 'They croft the whole headland. That first house, that's Kurkigarth.'

I'd vaguely known it was there, a white-painted two-storey dwelling set up a bit from the banks, with a pontoon jetty in the cleared landing space at the beach.

'Then the next one along, that crofthouse by the shore, Tirval's daughter married a Callahan man, Irish, and they bade there. Helge bides there now, his grandson's wife. Well, his first wife, but when the marriage broke up she moved in with his mother, and lookit after her till she died.'

Helge's crofthouse was set in the next beach to Tirval's, with a track leading up to Kurkigarth. Blue peat smoke curled up from the chimney. I wondered what that had felt like, to go from being mistress of a household to being a daughter again. I loved my parents, but I'd live aboard my *Khalida* in the coldest of winters rather than move in with them again. And to move in with a mother-in-law . . . for a moment I was selfishly grateful that Gavin's brother lived with their mother. If ever we moved south, it would be to our own cottage.

'She goes up and down to look to Tirval too,' Magnie added. 'She has a son who's a painter, and he bides in the next one along.' His house looked like a converted byre, another field along and halfway up between the sea and the road leading along the hill to the houses.

'And that cluster o' houses, further along again, that's Tirval's grandson's house, where he bides wi' his new wife. Berwin, from the sailing, he's from that marriage.'

'Too complicated,' I said. 'Let's focus on trows.' I nosed our new boat in alongside Tirval's navy double-ender (kept shining with paint and varnish, and well secured against the winter gales), tied her up, let Kitten out of the cabin, and followed Magnie up the track to the house.

Auld Tirval'd had visitors too. There was only one set of footprints on the track, a man in rubber boots checking his boat, but once we got to the house we found it circled by barefoot tracks. I put my booted foot beside one print. The largest of these was a much bigger foot than mine, and the foot seemed to be smooth rather than hairy, as if older trows had hardskinned feet. These tracks had come from somewhere further left on the hill, circled around the house against the sun, and gone in a slightly different direction upwards.

Tirval had kept up the traditions, with a plaited straw cross hung prominently on the door. I was just looking at it when there was a bark from inside and the door opened.

The name Auld Tirval and the suggestion that he believed in trows had misled me. Old he most certainly was, with beard and hair snow-white, and he leaned on a wooden staff, but both hair and beard were clipped naval-fashion, and he wore a navy gansey over a shirt and tie. His wrinkled face was weathered brown, but the skin had a softened air, as if he was no longer outside much. A grey-muzzled collie stood behind him.

'Thorvald,' he said, shaking my hand. His voice was Shetland overlaid with BBC English. 'Pleased to meet you, Cass. I don't think we've met, but I've enjoyed watching your comings and goings in the voe. Come in, come in.'

I hesitated, indicating behind me, where Cat was sniffing at a rabbit hole. 'May the cats come in too? Or would your dog not approve?'

'Oh, Floss is long past chasing cats. Bring them in.'

I called to Cat and he came trotting up, with Kitten bounding behind him. He went stiff-legged as he saw Floss by the door, and Kitten copied him, making a bottle-brush of her tail and pouncing sideways. A moment's assessment and Cat decided this dog was no threat, unlike some of the ones he'd met in harbours. He came forward cautiously, sniffed at Floss from a metre's distance, and followed me into the house. Kitten bounced after him and began eyeing up the curtain at the back of the door. I grabbed her before she could climb it.

Tirval showed us into the front room, a snug space with a squashy couch and a flame-effect electric stove blazing away in the fireplace. There were shelves in the recess on each side of the pushed-forward chimney, packed solid with antique machines. In pride of place on the mantelpiece was an old radio with gold and white mesh over the loudspeaker, a scale marked Luxembourg, London, Light, West, Scottish and two dials for volume and tuning. There was a machine with two silver reels, like an old film projector: ReVox Stereo Tape Recorder, it said, in neat lettering. Another one in a neat pale blue case sat beside it, lid open to show the reels horizontal instead of vertical. There was a ham 'whisker' radio with headphones attached, and a Sony record player with a perspex lid and an extra arm for stacking up records. The fire was flanked by hip-height speakers on little legs with three sizes of circular speaker cones, and there was a table with a mixing desk that had as many switches and sliders as the bridge of a modern tug.

'Coffee?' Tirval said. He gestured us to sit down, and returned in two minutes with a coffee percolater, three cups, milk in a jug and sugar in a bowl. 'Milk, sugar?' He set my cup on a little glass-topped table. 'A ship wireless operator I was, in South Georgia first, which was where I met Magnie here, and after that in the Merchant Service. When I retired I volunteered for the summers aboard a tall ship. I was even aboard your *Sørlandet* for a couple of seasons.'

He shook his head reminiscently, and settled back in his armchair. 'Well, I'm obliged to you for coming along. You saw the footprints, so you ken what it's about.'

I gave Magnie a doubtful look, wondering if he'd been winding me up. 'Trows,' I said.

Tirval nodded. 'Exactly. Now, I thought about speaking to your father direct, but he's not a seaman, he's a businessman. If he can't see it, it's not there.'

I nodded, warily. Magnie hadn't been having me on. This sane-seeming, neat, organised old man was about to talk seriously about trows.

'Well, the trows have had centuries to get good at hiding from us, so of course he's not going to see them. It's taken me three decades to get in tune with them, but even I rarely see one, and then it's only a glimpse from the corner of my eye, at dawn or dusk. Naturally I wouldn't dream of interfering with them at night.'

'Naturally,' I agreed, feeling rather as if I'd stepped through a looking-glass.

He gestured towards the hill behind the house. 'Now the Sneugie here, there's a tribe of them live there. When I say a tribe, I couldn't give you an exact number. A large family, more like. Robin, my great-grandson, he reckons to have seen as many as a dozen.'

I wondered what this Robin was up to, that he was encouraging his great-grandfather in trowie fantasies.

'Then in the valley,' Tirval continued, 'there's a larger group. That area there's never had houses, too far from the sea, so they colonised it.' His voice was perfectly sensible. 'These tracks came from towards the Kames, where the turbines will be, and went around the house then up to the trowie mound, and went in there. Cousins of my ones, maybe, asking their kin for shelter. There are no tracks coming back out again.'

At our house too, the tracks had come from the trowie mound and gone back in there. I felt a cold shiver down my spine and tried to shove it away. I leaned forwards, hands out. 'Thorvald, I'm not sure what you think I can do.' I made an impotent gesture. 'I don't talk about the windfarm to my dad, because feelings run so high, you know that, and I'm not sure I agree with it.' I imagined myself trying to ask Dad to stop the windfarm because he was upsetting the local trows. I knew it wouldn't work. 'My father really does believe he's helping Shetland. I don't think he'd be willing to stop the work because of – ' I chose my words carefully – 'what he'll think is a mythical creature.'

Tirval gave me a sideways look from shrewd eyes. 'You ask him what he has to say about the problems his contractors are having. Sabotage, they're calling it, but they're had a man on

27

watch night after night, and caught nobody yet. You tell him there's a good reason for that.' He paused for a moment, then sighed. 'I ken they're no' going to stop this turbines. But they could leave this side of the valley alone. Iceland, the first thing they do when they're thinking of a new road, is to check with the elves.'

I didn't see Dad liking that analogy. 'I will try, really. But I don't think he'll listen.'

'Do your best, lass.' He nodded towards the housing estate in Voe, framed in his window. 'They were out in force last night. If things don't improve for them, there'll be trouble.'

Chapter Four

slestery: messy, a right slester is a guttery, muddy mess (Norse, sluska: to splash)

Gavin had arrived home when I got back, and came down to take the lines. 'We need to give this boat a name.'

'*Herald Deuk*,' I said promptly. 'Those birds over by the Blade there, with the darker heads.'

He looked. 'Oh, the mergansers?'

'Is that the English name? According to Magnie, they're herald deuks. Heralding Christmas.'

'Magnie can't be wrong. *Herald Deuk* she is.'

'How was your morning?'

'The phone ringing off the hook. Trow prints all over the north mainland.' He sounded more amused than concerned. 'Someone's been finding out about the Devil's Hoofprints. It was a Victorian mystery, down in Devon. Snow like this, and overnight hoofprints appeared all round the houses, and on roofs, and going through drainpipes, and over walls. 1855. It's in Wiki, nice and accessible for getting ideas from. How d'you fancy a trip into Voe?'

'By land? I've already been there by sea.' I took the battery out of the motor. 'I do like this electric thing. What are the snags?'

'I'm waiting to find out. What were you doing by sea in Voe?'

'Visiting a friend of Magnie's. An apparently perfectly sane elderly seaman who assured me that the trows are upset by Dad's windfarm. I hadn't realised they'd already started digging.'

'Aye. It's taking up a lot of our time right now. There were a good few protests, oh, nothing unpleasant, but you ken what it's like, if you get enough people gathered together there's always one to go out of line. The anti-folk are trying to keep a permanent picket on it, so we have to keep an eye there too.'

'Magnie's pal, Tirval – '

'Tirval?' Gavin repeated, disbelievingly.

'It's an old Shetland name. Thorvald. He was talking about sabotage.'

Gavin frowned. 'I hope not. There's been nothing so far – posters put on the office door overnight, that sort of thing, but no damage. They've got a compound for the plant, to bring it off the hill at night.'

'It's not like Shetland, damaging things. We don't even have graffiti.'

'Feelings are running high over it. It's a pity your council never held any kind of referendum to give it more legitimacy.'

'Perhaps they knew it would go against them, and they wanted the money,' I suggested.

'As a public servant I couldn't possibly comment. We could go the long way round, if you wanted, and take a look at it.'

'Yes, let's. What are we going to Voe for anyway?'

Gavin tilted his chin towards Kitten, who had finished her bowl of kitten food, and was washing her whiskers. 'There's a pet shop there, they might have a kitten harness to fit her. If we don't get her used to a lead soon she'll never go on one.'

We set out straight after lunch, over the hill onto the single-track road towards Aith. The crust of snow had barely lain on the heather, and the hills were coloured auburn by the red moor grass growing between the old stems. Further on, past Bixter, the auburn turned to russet with a green sheen to it, like the verdigris on old cannon. The paths of burns meandered emerald through it, the water glinting silver in the low sun.

The first sign of works was a red placard at the height of Weisdale Hill: WORKS ACCESS AHEAD. Just past it was a road gouged straight up the hill, then a trampled track to the mast. There was a flat piece, concreted over, then a third track, gravelled, with two wheel ruts outlined white with lying snow.

We came around the bend, and I looked across towards the Kames, the long north-south hill ridges that made the spine of central Shetland.

'Draw a long line south from these and you'd reach the banks of Loch Ness,' Gavin said. 'It's all part of the same fault-line.'

There was something wistful about his voice. I hoped he wasn't missing his own hills. Maybe he too felt an alien among pine furniture and gingham curtains.

Ahead, the track through the Kames wound towards the main road north. There was a widened road being created to the side of the current one, with scarlet diggers busy on it. Orange lights flashed. A green truck turned into where they were working, and drew up by a pile of rubble. The digger pivoted and raised its elbow, then its clawed hand. A shower of dirt fell into the back of the truck.

'The turbine blades have to be in one piece,' Gavin said, 'and they couldn't get them around that bend at the top of the hill, even with special raised tilting trucks and the like, so they're having to make a straight piece of road for them.'

He drew in to the side of the road. My first feeling was surprised relief. From here, the bit of road they'd completed didn't look too bad: a smooth grey ribbon winding up the hill with the heather growing undamaged to either side. I tried to envisage the turbines sticking up from the hill. One hundred and fifty metres . . . the telegraph poles in the valley were about the height of my *Khalida*'s mast, thirty feet. I tried to count up fifteen times that size looming from the top of the hill, but the half-sky height I was getting seemed implausibly huge. Surely they couldn't be that big.

At the far end of the track, more diggers were working, yellow ones this time, half a dozen of them shunting back and fore in a welter of broken hill, shovels rising and falling relentlessly. Another truck made its way along the road towards them.

'Oh!' I said. 'There's a house there!' I'd never noticed it before, set well off the curve of the road and right below where they were digging, a square, white house, backed by trees, and set in its own green space of farmland. Until now, it had looked only at the hills around it, in a peace of wind and birdsong. 'How awful for them.'

'Yes.' His voice sparked briefly into anger. 'They don't even get compensation. You've no "right" to the amenities of hill and sky. I'm not sure they even get disturbance money for two years of constant building beside them – that is, if the project keeps to its timescale, which I don't expect it will. And their house, the most valuable thing they own, will become worthless. Who'd want to buy it once it's surrounded by turbines? No compensation for that either. The other end of the valley too. You know, where Rainbow that owns the ponies lives.'

I nodded. Rainbow was a horsey child who also came to the sailing, because she was best pals with my schoolfriend Inga's oldest, Vaila. Rainbow generally crewed for her, unless I forced them to swap roles.

'Her father's a special constable,' Gavin said. 'He was talking about it. The diggers are above their house now. They'll get this last Christmas in peace, while the workers are on holiday. This time next year the turbine shafts will be up. And this –'

32

he waved a hand across the fertile green farmland in the valley floor, where sheep were grazing peaceably, ignoring the trucks rumbling past – 'this rich soil is where the interconnector building is going to go.'

He put the Land Rover into gear and drove on. There were two groups of people clustered at the entrance to the site office, with yellow containers set like giant building blocks and a mesh compound, like a school multicourt, where more bulldozers were parked. They were protesters holding a vigil, half a dozen of them at each side, with placards, photographs and slogans printed in colour and mounted on thin board. *What's green about this?* one placard shouted, above photos of children working by a grey-mud mine. *Peat is our planet's lungs* said another, with a picture of one of the bulldozers in a deep peat trench. *Calculate the cost* the next one advised, with figures that were too small for me to read below it. *Not cheap, not clean, not green*, shouted another, next to one with a picture of a lone turbine: *242 tons of CO_2 to build one turbine.* Another *What's green about this?* was an aerial photo of a row of turbine blades being buried as landfill. To one side of the protesters, a couple of police officers stood uneasily in front of their squad car.

'We were asked to keep an officer presence,' Gavin said. 'Light-touch and friendly, just to make sure there was no unpleasantness. There are trucks on the skyline, see?'

I did see: two going along the top of the Kame and one coming back. 'D'you know where they're taking all the earth they're taking out?'

'There's a pit near Lerwick being filled in. I'm sure I heard a theory that the peat was being saved to be put back in twenty-five years, but that sounds implausible. Peat's a living thing. It's a bit like chopping a branch of a tree off, keeping it for years, then laying it on the ground and expecting it to regenerate.' He made a face, then added, 'Jobs, of course. Most of this plant's come up from south, but that means accommodation's needed for the drivers, and catering. The trucks are a local firm, and they've expanded, taken on more drivers locally. There's money going into the community during the construction phase, through the community councils.' He glanced sideways at me, and fell silent.

There were great lumps of hacked-out peat breaking the smooth heather curve of the hill. The side of the road here was a horrid, black, slithery slester where the peat had been dug out, with oil-sheened water lying where the green curves of mesh had failed to contain the run-off from the hill. The sides of the track they were excavating were best-quality blue peat, with long claw marks where the digger had ripped two thousand years' worth of growth apart. Beneath the peat was grey shale, and a digger was loading that into another truck. The noise was horrid: the clank and clang of the digger, the rumbling scrape as it filled its shovel, then the clatter as the rocks fell into the truck. It felt like relentless destruction, man showing nature what his machines could do to it. Looking at it, I felt suddenly as if I couldn't breathe properly. I might have been away for half my life, but this was my home they were destroying. These were my hills. There was a pain behind my ribs and a tightness in my throat.

The work continued down the hill in a great gash leading past the Halfway House to the main road. We followed the road alongside it. Further down, heather fells were heaped up by the roadside, and a roll of the white mesh they were lining the road with flapped in the wind. A wire-fenced compound was plastered with KEEP OUT notices. There were protesters here too, obviously well warned to do nothing to hinder the work. I spotted Inga's red knitted hat among them. 'Can you pull in?'

'Not for long.'

He steered towards the side of the road, and I wound the window down. 'Inga!'

Inga turned and came over. She'd grown up at the end of the Muckle Roe road, in the house past ours, and we'd sat together on the school bus and side by side in the classroom all our school career. While I'd been running away to sea, she'd married Charlie, who'd fancied her since primary school, and moved into Brae. They had three children: Vaila, Dawn and four-year-old Peerie Charlie, who was my great pal, and a menace. Those three, along with Rainbow, were definitely in my frame for our trowie footprints.

'Aye, aye, Cass. You made it home for Christmas then.' She gestured at the wounded hill. 'See the present we're been given?'

'It's horrible.'

'And there's nothing green about it. If it wasn't subsidised to the hilt by the Government no business would touch it.' She gestured with her placard, which read *What's it costing electricity consumers?* This time I could see the figures. Allowing for the loss in transportation and including the huge cost of an interconnector to the mainland, Dad's wind electricity would cost its recipients in the north of England four times the going rate per megawatt. Beside her, Vaila was brandishing another placard with a mock-up photo of the view from Lerwick, a forest of white blades as far as the eye could see. She was almost as tall as Inga now, with the same dark eyes and hair. Her cheeks were flushed with cold or indignation. Her slogan read, *I'm the future. I don't want a lifetime of this.*

'There's someone coming up behind us,' Gavin warned.

'It's a truck,' Inga said. 'Delay it as long as you like.'

Gavin pulled a face. 'If I was a private citizen I'd love to.' He gave Inga a sudden grin. 'Like the rest of you. Sorry, Cass.'

'Hang on,' Inga said, as he slid the Land Rover into gear. 'Cass, I don't suppose you could babysit for me tomorrow? It's Charlie's works do. I had my usual teenager all lined up, but both o' her peerie brothers have just gone down with slapcheek, so she thinks she shouldn't. I said she could bring it to our three and welcome, get it over with, but I suppose it might spoil their Christmas.'

'Slapcheek?' Gavin said, interested.

'It's just one o' these winter viruses that goes round every couple of years. You get a temperature, the snuffles and a rash, and once you get the rash and ken you have it, you're no' infectious any more. Anyway, Cass, if you would, I can come and pick you up, and organise you a taxi home.'

'No problem,' I said, then belatedly, glancing at Gavin, 'That is, if you hadn't anything planned.'

He shook his head, looking amused. A beep came from behind us, and when we didn't move, the truck driver gave a sharp fanfare. Inga grinned. 'Go on, do him for impatient driving.'

Gavin pulled a face. 'Don't tempt me.'

'Phone me about times,' I said, and we pulled away just as the truck was about to ram us.

'It's one of the protesters' tactics,' Gavin said. 'Amazing the number of cars with trailers and caravans that have been using this road recently. It annoys the truck drivers very much, and when time is money, every delay is worthwhile. Especially now winter's setting in. Last month was pretty wet, and the hill was sodden, with water pouring everywhere, including into Sandwater Loch, so they had to stop work while they dug ditches to divert their dirty run-off. There's been a lot said about it not being properly contained, and going into the lochs.' His carefully neutral voice warmed. 'There are trout in those lochs that have evolved into a distinct subspecies, isolated up here since the Ice Age.'

'You're not in favour, then.'

'I'm officially neutral,' Gavin said. 'But off the record and only to you, I think it's vandalism. The power it'll germinate's going to Yorkshire, it seems. Well, let them dig their turbine roads and pits there.' He paused for a moment. I could see his Scot Nat strain coming out. 'It's like Faslane. Of course nuclear weapons are safe, but we won't moor our sub in the Thames, we'll put it up in the Highlands. It's only Scotland.'

Above us on the skyline, as we turned north to run between the hills, were more heaps of peat and the angular cranes of five diggers. The mess continued along the side of the road. There were digger tracks gouged in the mud by Petta Water, new planks and fence posts left in a heap, and long pieces of flat plastic binding curled through the grass. It was all so horrible that it silenced us both until it was well behind us.

It didn't surprise me that someone had resorted to sabotage.

skoit: a purposeful look, to look inquiringly, peer inquisitively (Old Norse skoda: to view)

'Shall we do some trowie footprints first?' Gavin asked as we approached the Voe turn-off back towards Aith. 'There's apparently a particularly good crop at Mulla.'

'Fine that,' I agreed.

We kept going towards Brae. As we came into Upper Voe, I looked across at Tirval's house and the hill behind. The Sneugie, he'd called it. It was moorland, and I'd a feeling I'd seen Rainbow's ponies grazing there, with a fence keeping them off the road. I craned my neck to see this end of the Kergord valley, with its little cluster of houses. Above them, on the far hill, the bulldozer lights flashed orange.

'Mulla,' Gavin said, and turned cautiously up into the access road.

The Mulla houses were detached wood-clad houses set in two rows going along the hill slope, with a garden around each one. They had been built for oil executives back in the seventies, but most of them were privately owned now, and repainted in the Norwegian style, dark red, blue, buff, cream. There seemed to be more cars than you'd expect parked along the road. Gavin drew in just after the turn-off and we got out.

We weren't the only people come to have a skoit. There were little groups of folk in rubber boots, scarves and hats all along the row, leaning over the wooden slat fences and peering into the gardens, and not a few householders leaning over from the opposite direction, both lots sheeksing as hard as they could go. There was a police car at the far end, and the two black-clad officers seemed to be alternately rubber-necking and sheeksing too.

The first thing to hit our eyes was a spectacularly visible banner made of a sheet tacked to the side of the first house's garage. NO WINDFARMS it said, in writing that looked like what you'd get if you asked a four-year-old to copy the words, then painted the result in scarlet letters a foot high.

Even from here I could see the footprints going over the top of the roof of the first house's garage, where the banner was pinned. Leaning over, I could make out a single meandering trail going through the garden. It ended in a pair of footprints, someone standing square on to the garage, as if they'd stopped then jumped up to the roof from a standing leap.

'Clever,' Gavin said. He began strolling up the side fence, avoiding the ditch that ran down beside it, and peered in. 'Cat footprints there, and one or two on top of this fence as well.' He followed them back down the hill a little. 'It jumped off here.' He crouched down to look in the ditch, kilt brushing the snow, then stood again. 'A convenient ditch.'

'If there was something going on, any cat would inspect it. Our trainees got up to far more high jinks this last six weeks without Cat waking me up as he slipped off to see what they were up to.'

Gavin made that 'Mmph' sound that indicated that he was listening. He put one hand out to finger the cat mark on the fence.

'Christmas coming too, of course,' I added. 'They were all high as kites.'

'They would be. Do you see anything odd about these cat prints?'

I looked closer, but had to shrug. 'I don't often look at cat prints in snow.'

'Around the print. I'm not sure if I'm imagining things.'

I looked harder. The fence had a broader top, maybe ten centimetres wide, and turning so that I saw a different slant of light, I thought I might be seeing what he saw: the suggestion that the snow immediately around the prints was slightly more compressed than away from them, the crystal stars less clear.

'It's not so clear as a print around the print, but I think I see what you're seeing. Are you thinking that the cat prints are attached to shoes or something like that?'

Gavin shook his head. 'The compacted area's too small.' He fished in his sporran for his phone. 'Can you put your hand by it, for reference? Thanks.'

'You couldn't walk on it either,' I said, looking at the fence top. 'It slopes down on each side. You'd mess the snow up.'

A little smile touched the corners of Gavin's mouth. He took several photos, then went up towards the garage and took several more. I followed him around to the front of the house. The line of prints came down the roof again and stopped there, immediately above the car parked in the drive.

'The people in this house were out for the evening,' Gavin said, 'and found the prints when they got home about half past twelve.'

I looked at the garage roof. It was only just above normal door height, above old-fashioned opening doors. I wouldn't care to jump straight down from it onto my feet, but I could easily drop to the ground from hanging from the guttering, and I'd land neatly in the snow-clear space where the car had stood – except there was no sign that anyone had done that.

The tracks simply came to the edge of the roof, the feet came together, and that was that.

We went back down the side of the house, looking along the row.

'Most of the houses have a patio in front,' Gavin pointed out, 'and then a grassed area with maybe a shrub or two. Perfect for leaving footprints, and enough people around for nobody to notice an extra car coming or going.'

We strolled gently towards the second house. There had been more trows in here, with three sets of footprints having apparently danced a figure of eight in the middle of the lawn, then spreading out. One set led to the garden we'd just visited, another set came down towards us and stopped a metre back from the fence.

'Will you look at that, now,' a wife next to me said to her friend. 'The tracks just disappear, like it had vanished into thin air.'

Her friend was made of sterner stuff. 'There's a bit of trampling this side of the fence, as if it had jumped over.'

'Lass, you'd need to have some springs in your legs to leap over a fence like this.' She patted the waist-high wood beside her. 'You can see yourself too that it didn't take a run at it, just stood and leapt. Naa, it's the trows been out and about this night.' She glanced sideways at us, registered Gavin's kilt and identified him as the new policeman. 'They're no' liking all this disturbance in the hill.'

I didn't think she actually believed any of it. She was just having fun thinking it might have been, and adding her mite to the gossip swirling around us. Gavin looked at the disturbed snow at our feet and shook his head. 'There've been a dozen pairs of feet along here at least,' he answered her. 'If it did jump over, the tracks are under all the others. Where did the third one go?'

'Up to the door o' the house,' the first wife said with

relish, 'and in through the catflap.' She lowered her voice, glancing around as if she was afraid someone might hear. 'And never came back out again. If you go up the side there you'll see.'

Gavin took a photo of the dance footprints. 'It looks like a reel of three.'

'That's just exactly what it was,' the wife assured him. 'They're danced a Shetland reel right there on the grass.'

We went up the side of the house, as she'd recommended. There was no point in looking for prints on the pavement, for it looked like half Shetland had been here. The patio was two metres by five, running along the house, and bordered by a wood fence. It had a smooth covering of snow, with a trail of little footprints leading to the door and ending there. 'Can you zoom in with your camera?' I asked. 'Are they the same as ours, with furry toes?'

Gavin took several shots and handed me his phone to look at. Yes, the enlarged big toe stood out clearly, and there was a suggestion of fuzz around it. It was hard to guess from here, but I thought they were roughly the same size feet as mine, definitely not as small as the littlest ones around our house, nor as big as the larger ones at Tirval's.

We strolled along slowly to the end of the row. Each garden had one or more sets of footprints crossing it. In one, two trows had started to make a snowman, then scattered suddenly, as if they'd heard someone coming. Both sets of feet ran to the fence, and vanished from there. In another garden there had been a snowball fight, and next door there was a big letter T in footprints in the middle of the lawn, with no prints around it. 'Imaginative,' I commented.

'No damage done,' Gavin said, 'nobody disturbed, nobody complaining, nothing to take notice of officially.' He paused to say hello to the officers. 'Nothing happening here?'

'Kids,' the female officer said, in the kind of voice that

suggested she had several of her own. 'It's given the place something to talk about. We've taken a few photos, sir, and chatted to the folk.'

'Anyone taking extra interest in it?'

The male officer shook his head. 'We kept an eye out for that, sir. Nobody that we've seen.'

'Ah, well, it was an outside chance. Feel free to head back to the station once you start getting cold.'

They nodded, and we began strolling back down the hill towards our car, Gavin scanning the faces as we went. Cars and people were coming and going all the time. Suddenly, Gavin stopped and turned towards the nearest house. It was the one with the snowman, and he'd already photographed it, but he took another couple of shots, and then turned as if he was getting one of the whole row, with the people looking in over the fences. He spoke softly. 'There's a young man down there, Cass, in a long black coat. Early twenties maybe.' He held the phone for me to see and zoomed in on a man in a black toorie.

Gavin had caught him looking up towards us. He had a pale, thin face alight with interest at what was going on around him. *He's joost a white-fissed skoam*, Magnie's mother would have said, or, more picturesquely, *a face like a skittercloot*. I thought the face rang a bell, that white, white skin and the cheekbones and chin jutting out.

'Don't let him see you looking at him. Know him?'

I risked a quick scoit down, head angled towards the houses to the right of him, and managed a sideways glimpse. He was tall and gangly in his *Matrix*-style black coat. 'He's not one of our sailors, I'm sure of that. But . . .' I frowned, trying to think, then shook my head. 'No.'

The police car at the end of the row slipped out and began to inch down the road. People moved aside to let it pass. The man in the black coat looked up, turned, and swiftly, smoothly,

42

began walking down towards the main road. He was around the corner and out of sight before the police car reached where he'd been.

I wondered what Tirval's great-grandson Robin, who spied on the trows for him, looked like.

Chapter Five

lichtsome: *uplifting, cheerful, goodnatured (Scots)*

We kept an eye out as we left, but there was no sign of the sjoamit man in the black coat on the pavement in either direction. 'He must have had a car,' Gavin said. 'I'll try showing the photo at the station. Okay – pet shop?'

'Harness,' I agreed.

It was odd to see Voe so deserted. The marina held only a few larger boats, with all the smaller ones migrated to their owners' driveways for the winter. The Pierhead car park was empty. We came past the green field where black sheep were grazing, then turned right to go along the road that would end, two miles on, at Tirval's house. A two-placard signpost at the turn-off read, in large capitals, *PET SHOP*, then, below, carved in rune-style writing on a varnished board, *World of Asgard*.

'World of Asgard?' I asked.

'He's a woodcarver,' Gavin said. 'You know – Asgard. It was the home of the Norse gods.'

'Oh, *Asgard*,' I said. I put on a Norwegian accent. 'I called in there just last week to have a cup of mead with Odin.'

'He does carved elves, and dwarves, and giants, and gods brandishing hammers or ravens, and willowy goddesses with plaits.' He drove slowly past the first two houses, and continued

44

along the track. 'I saw him at the Clickimin craft fair. Not as twee as it sounds. Doing a roaring trade too. I thought about getting you a line of them to go along the mantelpiece, but it would be too much dusting for you.'

Memory was stirring from way back. 'I think he might have come and talked to us about the Norse Christmas, back in primary school. The Yules. He looked like a Viking himself, big and red-headed.'

'He went the whole hog at the Craft Fair, Viking tunic and leggings, and a plait down each side of his beard. It's his wife who has the pet shop. She had a stall too, but she didn't have kitten harnesses with her, it was more pet Christmas stockings.'

Gavin turned the Land Rover into a cleared space in front of a cluster of buildings, just as I was opening my mouth to ask if people really hung Christmas stockings for their pets. I hadn't had a Christmas stocking myself since I was sixteen. The words were cut off by a sudden worry that Gavin might expect one.

We were among the houses that Magnie had indicated as being Tirval's grandson's, with wife number two. Below us, facing towards the voe, was the house, an eighties build with fawn harled walls and big picture windows. An older house and byre all in one line were the World of Asgard, with a pair of reindeer antlers nailed above the door. The pet shop was the newest building, white-harled with wooden trim and a ramp up to the entrance. An old brown van was parked beside it. There were a couple of plump black and pink pigs rootling round a very muddy field, and a clanking sound and mooing from the big byre beyond it: cows that wouldn't get back in their fields till spring. The smell of manure was warm on the air.

As the Land Rover backed into the space, we came around and halted nose on to a square of moss green turf with a low white fence around it. There were two young men fighting in it, whirling swords around their heads and whacking at each

45

other with dangerous nonchalance. The clanging ring of the swords made it clear they were real metal, but the only protection they seemed to have was Viking-style helmets, pointed skullcaps with a tongue coming down over the nose, and round wooden shields with a central metal boss. Otherwise they wore jeans, hoodies and trainers.

'Vikingr Hjaltlandi,' Gavin said, watching them with interest. 'It's the name of the Shetland branch of the Medieval Armoured Combat society.'

'It looks dangerous.'

Gavin nodded, eyes intent on the two men. 'They ought to be wearing armour. The swords are blunt, but heavy enough to do a fair bit of damage.'

We stayed in the Land Rover watching as the men circled each other, advancing and retreating as if they were following the steps of a dance. The taller of the two rushed forward, sword raised; the other's shield went up just in time for the blade to hit it with a resounding thwack. The smaller one spun around and came at the taller from behind, and for a moment the two swords blurred in the air, hacking at each other, then the men disengaged and began their circling again, intent on each other as lovers.

Suddenly a tall, fair woman came rushing out of the house door and down towards them. Her voice rung passionately into the silence. 'That's enough! Stop it, both of you!' The smaller one looked towards her and lowered his sword; the taller, taking his chance, swung his blade around in a fast sweep at the other's calves. I gasped and stretched my hand towards them in a 'stop' gesture, but at that split second the smaller man jumped up into the air, springing from both feet and bending his knees, so that the sword passed under him. Even as he landed, he was swinging his own sword towards the taller one's helmet. The other raised his shield, and the sword clanged off the metal boss.

The woman's face was scarlet with anger. The younger one took off his helmet, and I recognised Berwin. He flung his arm round his opponent's waist, and his opponent put a crooked arm on Berwin's shoulder, and they both laughed. The woman said something sharp and low that I didn't catch, and Berwin gave a cheerful apologetic wave, and headed into the shop. The woman turned on the taller man, who had turned square-on to her, angry defiance blazing from every line of him: the strong stance, the hand clenched on the sword-grip, the thrust-out chin. There was no love lost between him and Berwin's mother, that was for certain, and no wonder, if he encouraged Berwin in such dangerous games. Berwin's mother gestured towards the gate, and the man in the Viking helmet stood as if he was rooted to the ground. The very quietness of his reply made it ring towards us, as filled with venom as a cobra's hiss: 'Shall I tell my father you're ordering me out of my own home?'

For a long moment they stood glaring at each other, then Berwin's mother turned on her heel and slammed back into the house. The young man watched her go, then stabbed his sword into the ground, flung his shield after it, and strode off along the road between the house and the byre.

I glanced at Gavin. His face was thoughtful, hard to read; then he turned to me and smiled. 'Well, shall we go in and see what they have?'

A blast of intense cheeping hit us as we opened the pet shop door, dozens of canaries and finches all trying to outdo each other or drown out the Christmas music that was jangling softly in the background. There were several big aviary cages along one wall and opposite were sawdust-smelling hutches that housed the small animals: rabbits, guinea pigs, hamsters and a grey squirrel creature that I thought might be a chinchilla. A large snake was draped over a forked tree trunk behind a glass barrier, and there were other perspex tanks with rocks, bits of wood and hidden denizens.

The bits and pieces were at the far end, with the counter to the side of them: a riot of leads, muzzles, balls, shaped toys and the harnesses we were looking for, as well as a selection of fishing tackle which drew Gavin like a magnet. There was a shelf of cards and paintings beside the toys, little hand-sized pictures of animals in jewel colours: a mouse with a berry between its paws, a hedgehog, a fox with one paw raised. I realised, looking more closely, that they were framed photos of paintings, apart from one original, twice the size: the mouse. The reproductions were good, but the original was beautiful. I glanced quickly at Gavin to make sure he was occupied, then lifted the fox. There was a fox's earth near his grandmother's cottage in the Highlands, the one he hoped one day to return to living in, and he'd spent many hours there watching the foxes. There were none here in Shetland. If they had an original of this one, it might make the Christmas present I was beginning to worry about, since his mother knitted his jumpers, and he seemed to have every piece of fishing tackle known to humankind already.

Berwin was waiting patiently behind the counter. He was one of the most lichtsome bairns I'd had the good fortune to teach. He'd be in secondary three now, fourteen or fifteen. He was fair-haired and blue-eyed, with an open, sunny face and a ready smile. If you were explaining something, he listened till you'd finished; if you asked him to do something, he'd stick at it till it was done, no matter how tedious the task. He hosed down his lifejacket and overalls and hung them up himself, and his mast was always stacked so that it wouldn't fall down on the next person to put one up . . . in short, we instructors all loved him, and he was equally popular with his fellow sailors. We never had to persuade anyone to go out with him, and he never minded being given the newest of rookie crews, even in races. Pairs of girls who normally stuck together like mastic were willing to separate for the chance to sail with Berwin.

Inga's Vaila, I remembered, had been particularly smitten, though not to the extent of relinquishing her helm.

'Aye, aye, Cass!' he said. 'Are you home for Christmas? What can I get you?'

I put the painting back. 'We're after a harness for a kitten,' I said. 'She's getting on for six months old, but she's small.' I showed him with my hands.

'Oh, we have a good variety of those. Bide you there.' He went along to the end of the counter, and pulled half a dozen items from their hooks. 'How about these for size?'

I looked and wished we'd brought her with us to try harnesses on her, except that she'd have been far more likely to escape and get lost in Voe. Cat had grown quickly into the adult size he now wore, but I didn't see Kitten ever fitting into a cat-size harness. There was one made in webbing, which looked too big, even though it said it would adjust smaller, and I had no doubt she'd wriggle her feet out of it or into the straps somehow. The mesh one like a little jacket looked a better bet, though the cat on the box looked pop-eyed indignant at having to wear it.

'We have pet lifejackets too.' Berwin gave me his friendly grin. 'In case you were thinking of taking her on the boat, along with your Cat. I was expecting to see him coming in the door behind you.'

'Now he's got a girlfriend he likes staying at home,' Gavin said, turning from his examination of the fishing gear. He gave Berwin a quick look. 'Aren't you one of Cass's sailors? You were the one making the good starts at the regatta at the end of the summer.'

Berwin flushed, as if he was pleased at being remembered. I wasn't surprised; I'd discovered that Gavin, like my dad, had almost perfect recall of faces.

'Good finishes too,' I said. 'He won the Junior Interclub for us.'

49

Berwin said awkwardly, his face still scarlet, 'I hardly ever skive school, Mr Macrae. But you ken what it's like in the last week.' He was looking at me now. 'There's no real work, and I only had Maths and Geography the last two periods, all anyone would be doing would be online puzzles, and Mam has a Christmas bus, it's due any minute, so I thought I'd be far more use here. I was there this morning . . .'

Gavin gave him his most reassuring smile. 'Running you in for skiving is definitely below my pay grade.' He gave Berwin a moment to let the flush subside, then added, 'I ken all about birthday buses, but what's a Christmas bus?'

'Ah,' Berwin said. He thought for a moment. 'Well, the birthday buses you'd ken are the drinking ones. Some o' the older folk aren't so bothered about pubs, but they still want a spree wi' their pals, so their birthday buses are a tour o' the charity shops, with a stop for a lunch at the Mid Brae Inn, or the Pierhead here at Voe. The Christmas bus is kinda an extension o' that, except it's Christmas shopping. This one's coming down from Yell.' He made a face, but he was laughing too. 'It's total chaos, folk buying a handful of things, and you've just got them rung up when they spot something in the next person's basket that they want too, and you wait while they go and find it, and then you have to add that.'

I'd have betted that he bore it all patiently, and all the old ladies loved him.

'It's very profitable,' he added. 'They buy Dad's carvings too. He's done a special display, don't miss it.'

Gavin picked out a blue lifejacket with a shark fin on the back, then a green one with a scale-pattern back and crocodile tail. 'A lifejacket might be more use than a lead. Then she could walk around the boat, instead of having to be confined to the cabin. What d'you think, Cass?'

'If she was attached, though, she wouldn't be able to fall overboard. That would be better than having to rescue her.'

'Let me get Mam,' Berwin said. 'She'll know more about it.' He disappeared off through the door.

I picked up the shark one and pulled a face. 'It's a bit human-orientated. And a brighter colour would be better.'

'There's a Barbie-pink one over there.' He went over to look, and I followed him.

'The picture's of a dog. Would a dog harness be okay on a cat?' I unhooked the card support and turned it over in my hands. 'There's a D-ring for clipping her on. But it's miles too big.'

'You can use that one as a normal harness too,' a warm voice said from the doorway. We turned round.

She'd regained her poise to be exactly what you'd expect of Berwin's mother, a Norse goddess with hair as fair as his, and eyes as blue. Her hair was coiled in two plaits over the crown of her head. All she needed to complete the picture of a Norwegian woman was a white blouse and black embroidered bodice and skirt, except that her voice was unmistakably Whalsay, the island to the north-east of Lerwick, where that tall, fair Norse type still lingered. Inga and I had always had difficulty with netball games against the Whalsay school, because the girls seemed half-cousins to giraffes; we felt like Shetland ponies matched against racehorses. Not that I'd have played against this woman, of course; she was a good ten or even fifteen years older than me, which made Berwin a late baby – I caught myself up at that thought. She'd have been about thirty when she'd had him, and I was thirty-one now.

She smiled, and held out her hand. 'There are so many of us about when you're busy doing the sailing. I'm Frigg, Berwin's mother.'

I tried to suppress the startled look. Freya wasn't uncommon in Shetland – Gavin's ultra-efficient DS Peterson was Freya – but I hadn't come across a Frigg before. She gave a rueful smile. 'Frigg was Odin's wife, in Norse mythology.'

51

'I thought she was Freya,' Gavin said.

Frigg shook her head. 'Freya and her brother Freyr were lesser gods.' She looked at me. 'You should know about Freyr, the god of fine weather. Freya was the Norse equivalent of the Greek Aphrodite, known for sensuality and passion.'

I considered that as applied to Gavin's Freya, and felt an uneasy trickle down my spine. Maybe her aloof mermaid air covered intense feeling. If she was passionate about something, she wouldn't back off, I knew that.

Frigg abandoned the subject with a laugh. 'But you're not wanting to hear about Norse gods – though do have a look in my husband's workshop on your way out. Kitten lifejackets and harnesses, Berwin said.' She reached for another pink one, and laid it out flat on the counter. 'This is the XXS size, for dogs like Chihuahuas, up to 5kgs. An average female cat would be three and a half to five and a half kilos, so it'll fit your kitten up to full grown. It has a mesh underbelly, and clip fastenings, rather than velcro – a lot of animals hate that rip noise. It's light enough to use as a normal harness. It's a swim support rather than a life-jacket – we also have ones with a padded neck to keep the animal's head out of water.'

Gavin made a doubtful face.

'Maybe when she's bigger, and more used to wearing it,' I agreed. 'I think this would take in to fit her, and we could clip her on a safety line too.'

'You'd certainly see her if she went overboard in it,' Gavin said. 'Go for that one, then, Cass?'

I nodded.

'And I was wanting some pony feed too,' Gavin said. He added to me, 'I'm encouraging the pair in the field. I told Rainbow I'd feed them for her.'

From what I knew of Shetland ponies, any food offers would make them your best pal.

'That's in the byre,' Frigg said. 'I'll get Berwin back to ring this up while I get them. Anything in particular?'

Gavin hesitated. 'What do you have for ponies who're not in work?'

'Go and look,' I said. 'I'll get this.'

I let the door close behind him, and leaned forward to Berwin. 'I was wondering if you have the original of the fox picture, on the cards over there?' I tilted my head in the direction Gavin had gone. 'For a Christmas present.'

His face lit up. 'They're my brother's paintings. He's done quite a few of foxes. I'm not sure if he has that exact one, but he'll have one.' His eyes flicked to the door. 'His studio's in the old byre, down towards the shore. I'll give you his card, and maybe you could come back on your own.' He reached into a little cardholder by the display. 'There.'

Robin Callahan, it said in copperplate script. *Paintings and Prints*. 'Thanks,' I said.

His eyes were still dancing, but with mischief now, as if thinking of his brother had brought a pleasant memory to mind: a memory or something to come. There was a suppressed excitement about him.

'Berwin,' I said slowly, 'I don't suppose you know anything about trows?'

He couldn't quite suppress the grin, but he thought quickly and answered truthfully. 'Cass, you couldn't possibly live with my dad and not know about trows. Wait till you see his workshop.'

There was no need for me to ask any more. However they'd managed to spring-leap onto garage roofs and jump down unhurt, or disappear mid-garden, the local bairns were in the frame for the trowie visitation. 'I was over visiting Tirval this morning.'

He looked surprised enough for me to wonder whether he'd

been one of our visiting trows, expecting me to challenge him on that. 'Auld Daa?' Then enlightenment dawned. 'Oh, it was your boat there this morning.'

'Magnie mentioned he was your great-grandfather. He wanted to talk to me about trows and the windfarm.'

'Yea, yea, he's Dad's mother's father. He's a great one for the trows. Puts a glass of milk out for them every night, and if you believed all he says they do his house cleaning for him too, so long as he leaves the place tidy. I think Helge sneaks up while he's out, just to let him keep his illusions.'

'Helge?' I tried to remember Magnie's explanation of the family.

'She lives down in the second-last house, up from the shore a bit. She was Dad's first wife.' Modern children were well used to explaining the complications of their parents' marital life. 'After they split up she moved in with Dad's mother, and then when Granny died she left the house to Helge. My brother who does the paintings, he's her son. Robin.' The warmth in his voice made it clear his half-brother was his hero. 'The one I was fighting. You'd remember him if you saw him without the helmet. He picked me up from sailing from time to time. Red hair.'

'Oh!' I said, enlightened. 'Of course I know him.' Red hair was unusual in Shetland, and Robin's head was the brightest shade of flame-orange. An older brother with a car and an interest in trows . . . what was the phrase I'd teased Gavin about, *a complicit sibling*?

I looked back at the cards. 'So these are his work.' I tucked the card into my pocket. 'I'll phone him and try to come round tomorrow.'

Berwin's expressive eyes flared again at the mention of tomorrow. If he'd been Peerie Charlie's age he'd have been giggling with excitement.

There was a rattle outside the window: Frigg wheeling a

trolley with two bags of feed on it towards the Land Rover. She waved Gavin away with a gesture towards his kilt, and hefted each bag into the back, then trundled the trolley byrewards. Gavin came in to join me. 'A bag each of pony nuts and pony mix,' he said to Berwin, and fished his wallet out of his sporran. He added to me, 'It's just for the winter months. It saves Rainbow's dad from having to bring her out to the cottage all the time, if the weather's bad.'

'You may think it's for the winter months,' I said, 'but I bet the ponies'll think different.'

Gavin shook his head. 'They lose interest in dry feed once the new grass starts coming through. You'll see.'

We thanked Berwin and headed back out into farmyardsmelling air. It wasn't much after two, I reckoned, yet already the air was beginning to thicken at the sides of buildings, and the sky was darkening. I'd lost all track of time here, but we were almost on the winter solstice, so sunset would be midafternoon. I thought of Berwin and his flame-haired halfbrother, and wondered if there was anything particular the trows got up to on the night of the solstice.

'Well,' Gavin said, 'shall we inspect Asgard?'

Helya's E'en

Chapter Six

eident: *always busy, industrious [Old Norse,* idinn: *assiduous in work]*

The door to the byre was propped open, and had a sign on its inner side: *World Of Asgard – Leonard Callahan, Wood-carver.* The door space was filled by a heavy curtain made from moorit sheepskins sewn together. We came around it into a Norse long-house, bright with the warmth of a peat fire. The hearth was set bang in the middle of the floor and two black and white collies lay by it, heads up to watch us come in. There were tables and benches set out on each side of the door, ready for feasting.

My eyes were drawn straight to the candle-lit display at the other side of the fire: carved figures set out in tiers on a tree trunk with a serpent coiled around its roots, a gleaming white cloth draped for icy mountains not far above it, another of fire-orange further up, and a rainbow of semi-transparent cloth curving from a middle tier over the top one.

'Aye, aye, come you in.' It was Berwin's father who had spoken from one end of the long room. His table was set on a low platform, with a whitewashed wall behind him where his chisels and saws hung, and a power lathe to one side. 'Have a look around.'

Leonard's voice was deep and resonant. His face was strangely lit by the anglepoise lamp shining on his hands, with the lower half of his beard casting a shadow over his mouth, a sharp jut of nose, eyes in shadow under long, curved brows. His long hair was held back in a ponytail. He was in his early fifties, with the blue-tinted light picking out the first suggestion of grey in his red beard.

Something dark moved at his shoulder with a flutter of wings. A raven hopped down onto his desk and stood there, surveying us, bigger than I'd have expected, with glossy black feathers and a murderous beak. It eyed us with its head to one side, gave a derisive cark and returned to its perch.

'Quiet, now, boy.' Leonard smoothed its back with one hand. 'I hope neither of you mind birds?'

We both shook our heads. 'It's a privilege to see one so close,' Gavin said. He walked forward to a respectful distance. 'Is he Hugin or Munin?'

Leonard gave him a quick glance. 'So you know your Norse mythology? This is Munin.' The bird turned its head towards him at its name. His strong hand caressed its back once more, then opened in an 'off you go' gesture. 'Go on then, go out and bring me back the news.' The bird fluffed up its feathers, shook itself and then settled lower on its perch and closed its eyes.

Leonard turned to us and laughed. 'Intelligent enough to disobey orders.'

'Like cats,' I agreed. Now, closer, I could feel the magnetism of the man. He was strikingly handsome, with strong cheekbones, a straight nose and big, heavy-lidded eyes that looked straight at you as if you were the most interesting person in the world.

'Now I know you,' he said. 'Cass the Seafarer.' He smiled. 'Cass the Explorer, come home now to her own hearth.' He turned his gaze to Gavin. 'You were at the craft fair. I have you both here somewhere.'

He rose from behind his desk, and kept rising; he had to be well over six feet tall, and broad-shouldered with it. He gave me another of those intense glances. 'The people the Norsemen described in their sagas are still with us. I saw you at the sailing one day and recognised you straight off. Gudrun, or Aud the Deep Minded, one of the Norse women who sailed over the horizon to explore new lands. Here you are.'

He picked out a carving from the display and held it up on the palm of his hand. It was a woman in a long dress and wind-blown cloak. She had a plait falling over one shoulder. One hand was at her breast holding the cloak, the other reached forwards, as if she was touching the prow of a ship. Her head was up, her eyes on the horizon, and she was smiling.

'It is you,' Gavin said, delighted. 'Look at you, seeing noth-ing but the sea.' He looked at Leonard. 'How did I miss this at the fair?'

Leonard shook his head. 'I didn't take her there.' His heavy-lidded eyes slid across to me. 'She doesn't look right inside the Clickimin, with all that artificial lighting. Besides, I don't expect to sell her. I took her to last year's craft fares, and watched how people reacted to her.' His voice was made for spinning stories. 'Women love her. You see them picking her up, and for a moment their faces look like yours, and then they remember their children and their man, or their job, their house, whatever holds them down, and they sigh, and put her back on the table. Sometimes they look back as they walk away. And the men, well, the men are afraid of her – what an idea to put into a woman's head, that she can just leave every-thing behind and step out into the unknown.' He turned to Gavin, smiling. 'Will I sell her to you?'

Gavin's arm came up behind my back; his hand curved lightly over my shoulder. He shook his head. 'You'll be offer-ing to sell me the wind next, or the sea tides.'

'Ah,' Leonard said. He nodded. 'I had you right too. The King with judgement.' He put the seafaring woman back in her place and returned to his bench. 'The oil's barely dry on this one.'

61

He'd given Gavin a king's crown and long hair flowing down his back. This figure was seated, his Norse tunic draping over his bare knees just the way his kilt did. One hand was on the hilt of the sword lying in his lap, the other was resting lightly on its blade. You could tell that he was listening, in a court of justice maybe, or to his counsellors around his table. He'd decide nothing in a hurry, but whatever course of action he took in the end would be the right one.

Gavin gave his image a long look. His cheeks reddened, and he made a joke of it. 'I wish everyone had such a high view of the police.'

Leonard gave a booming laugh. 'Ah, if I'd put a police hat on him he'd never sell. Well, well, I'll leave you to have a look around.'

He returned to his seat and soon the gentle chink of his hammer striking the chisel echoed around the roof beams. I looked more closely at the display. The layer he'd put me back to was a Norse homestead. Many of the women here were Frigg, tall and slim with a baby in her arms or a toddler clutching at her skirt. There was another woman there too, shorter and stouter, her mop of curls held back by a headband: the farm servant, with a flat basket within her curved arm and a pair of hens at her feet, or carrying a heavy wooden bucket, body bent sideways and arm thrown out to balance it. Berwin was duplicated in a band of young warriors with shields and swords. A couple of trows peered round the corner of the longhouse, faces furtive with mischief. One had a bundle under its arm, with a wrinkled baby face within the folds of cloth: a trowie changeling they were hoping to foist on a human mother. The other had its hands stretched out to snatch a passing hen.

I crouched to start again at the bottom. The whole Norse cosmology was here. The soothsayers' land was draped in black and purple, with gold stars embossed on the cloth. The woman here was as tall as Frigg but you could see from the wood that she was dark-haired, long curls falling loose round her neck as she looked at the stars, or being pushed back by one hand as she held the other over a scrying dish of water. Next came the trows, dancing to a human fiddler, laughing together at a joke. The land of ice had flickering candles in blue glass holders. The dwarves lived in a mine, dark caverns lit by fairylights glittering like jewels against the black cloth, and above them blazed the land of fire. The humans next, with my little self back in her place at the edge of the croft, gazing hungrily out. The giants had big, blank faces, lit here and there by a kind of low cunning. The elves were straight from *Lord of the Rings*, elegant in embroidered tunics, but they had thin, malicious faces. Their laughter would be mocking. The top layer was the land of the gods. Frigg was here again, tall and gracious, one hand on Berwin's shoulder. Robin was there too – even in wood you could see the blaze of his hair. He'd been the model for the elves, I saw now; there was something unsettling about the mischief in his smile, the slight turn of his head towards his shoulder as if he was checking nobody was watching him.

'Loki,' Gavin said. He indicated another man. 'Blind Hod, carrying the mistletoe he killed Baldur with.' Hod's shoulders showed the same burdened slump as the woman who'd been the servant in the human land. 'Odin with his wolves and ravens, and Thor.' Thor might have been Tirval, young and strong, hammer in hand, and Odin was unmistakably Leonard himself. 'Hel, goddess of the underworld.' She was the dark soothsayer of the first layer. Gavin spoke up towards the dais. 'Have you all the gods here?'

'All of them,' Leonard agreed.

Seeing Robin's image had reminded me of Berwin's excitement. 'Leonard, is there any particular trowie custom associated with the solstice?'

He raised his head to look searchingly at me. 'A trowie

custom? No, unless they kidnap a fiddler to play for their big feast on the longest night. But you know, don't you, that it's Helya's E'en this night? Modersdnacht, they called it in the old days, and then when the Norse folk were Christianised they changed it to Mother's Night, and directed the old prayers to the Virgin.' He laid his chisel and hammer down and leaned forward. 'You need to learn the rhyme, for when you have bairns and grandbairns of your own. Once everyone's sleeping, you take a candle and go round the house. You start with the youngest child and say this over each bairn in turn, ending with the adults.'

His voice softened to the gentle note of a drummie bee drowsing round flowers in summer.

> 'Mary Midder had de haund
> Ower aboot for sleepin-baund
> Had da lass an' had da wife,
> Had da bairn a' its life.
> Mary Midder had de haund.
> Roond da infants o' wur land.'

'Now you say it after me. That way there'll be one more person to save it from being lost.'

He repeated it, with me saying each line, and then we said it together, with me stumbling, cheeks reddening, and finally, to make absolutely sure I'd got it, I said it on my own. 'I'll try it on the cats tonight,' I promised him. 'Thanks to you.'

There was a heavy step at the door, and the sheepskin was shoved aside. A man shouldered in, big and dark-headed, with a heavy, sullen face and broad shoulders straining his navy boiler suit. He gave us an incurious look and spoke directly to Leonard. 'That's all the equipment scrubbed now. For the pig.' His voice was abrupt, as if he didn't like talking in front of strangers. 'I'll start as soon as the Christmas bus has gone.'

Sow Day, the day the pig was killed for the mid-winter feast. I didn't want to be around for that.

Leonard nodded. 'Fine, Bruce. Wait till we close, in case of last-minute visitors. You ken the way they squeal. I'll be with you then.'

The man grunted and thrust his way out, and, oddly, it was the movement that made me recognise him from the still wooden figures. He was there, over and over, in the land of the giants: the bull-like strength combined with the impassive face. You wouldn't know what he was thinking.

Gavin gave me a quick look. He echoed my thanks, and we were just about to leave when the curtain swung back, and Frigg hurried in, one hand smoothing her crown of plaits, and spoke in a breathless rush. 'I was wondering,' she said to Leonard, 'if we really need to kill a pig for Christmas. I've just been speaking to Helge, and she wasn't sure of coming up, and of course Tirval will be having Christmas lunch with her, and likely Robin too, though she didn't mention him, and I'm sure Bruce doesn't want to eat with his employers, he likely just comes out of politeness, so it'll be just the four of us.'

Leonard's head went up. His shoulders broadened. He didn't stand, and his voice was soft where I'd expected it to suddenly thunder, but every word was bitingly clear, Odin giving his orders. 'Our house will welcome all the household for the Yule Feast.' The raven stirred from its perch and came to his shoulder; the two dogs lifted their heads. 'If you're not willing to act as hostess, I'll invite Helge up to preside, and you can go where you please for the day.' The glance he swept over her was icy in its contempt. 'Well?'

Frigg's cheeks burned in the firelight. She drew herself erect, and spoke with a desperate attempt at an ordinary tone. 'Helge must have misunderstood. I'll make sure she knows we're expecting her.' She turned away from him and walked steadily to the door, like a drunk trying to seem sober. I heard her foot stumble and pause as the sheepskins swung closed behind her, but there was no sign of her when we came out, less than a minute later, into the last of the winter light.

'I'd better run Christmas by you,' Gavin said, over tea. He went on slightly quicker, as if he was worried about it. 'There seems to be a lot going on.'

I put out my hand to his. 'I wasn't here to consult. Go on, hit me with it.'

'Well, your mother was keen we should go over to theirs for an evening meal on Christmas Eve. It sounded like a bit of an occasion.'

'Dress kilt. It's the *réveillon*. A big family meal, then we all head off to Midnight Mass. Remind me not to eat anything after breakfast on Christmas Eve.'

'Then I invited them over for Christmas dinner.' He gave me an apologetic look. 'I felt I should. How do you fancy roast duck?'

It was exactly as Gavin mentioned 'duck' that there was a kerfuffle at the catflap, as if someone was having difficulty getting through it. Kitten shot out of her box by the Rayburn and headed to the back door to see what was going on. We exchanged a startled glance and followed. It was Cat, backing his way through it, with something heavy in his jaws. As he continued backwards the first feathers appeared, and then the rest of it.

It was a duck; not someone's duck, I hoped, but a wild duck, the brown sort that puddled around the water's edge. It wasn't far off the size of Cat himself.

Having got it inside, Cat came over to wind himself around my ankles, gave his soundless mew and went off to investigate his food bowl. Kitten had a shot at pouncing at the corpse, but it was too big for her to play with it, and it wasn't playing back, so she went off to annoy Cat instead, leaving us looking at it.

'He can't have caught that by himself,' I said. 'It's far too big.'

'Maybe he found it dead somewhere.' Gavin picked it up by one wing. 'It's freshly dead.'

'Maybe it had a heart attack as he pounced on it.'

'A nice mallard.' Gavin sighed. 'A pity. I wouldn't like to risk eating it, in case it died of something else. A wild one would taste fishy anyway.'

'My welcome home present. It's a kind thought.'

'I'll put it in the outside bin.'

I went back to the table to find Kitten with her nose inches from my stew. 'Hey! No.' I lifted her down and she promptly jumped up again.

'The cats are invited too,' Gavin said, returning and heading for the sink to wash his hands. 'For the *réveillon*. And your dad's organised a taxi for Midnight Mass. He said it wouldn't do for me to countenance him driving after a dram or two, and when I offered not to drink he said sure, and it wouldn't do to see Christmas in without a glass of something.'

'An *apéro*,' I said, remembering Papy's last Christmas, when we'd gone to Poitiers instead of Dublin. 'Champagne with the oysters, red with the turkey and cheese, a sweet white with the pudding, finish off the champagne with the fruit, then some of cousin Thierry's *eau de vie* with the coffee.'

Gavin returned to his place. 'Doze through Midnight Mass and don't drive for three days afterwards. Next: Christmas decorations.'

'When I got *Khalida*, I put a piece of tinsel along the top of the bulkhead.'

'I got a tree, it's in the shed, but I wanted to do decorations together.' He glanced up at the clock. 'We could head over to the Aith charity shop and get some. It's open till nine.'

It was a ten-minute drive to Aith, over the dark moor first, with the headlights sparking glitter in the still-lying snow, then into the houses of East Burrafirth, dressed for Christmas with lights outlining roofs and fences and twining up into trees. 'Fairyland,' I said. 'Folk didn't do this when I was a child, you just had your Christmas tree.'

'I blame the *Home Alone* movies.' Gavin smiled. 'We must do a drive around Lerwick. There's one house that has everything you could possibly think of by way of lit-up snowmen, along with a Santa climbing the drainpipe, and reindeer with flashing legs.' He edged the Land Rover into a space in the line of cars. 'All set for a scrum?'

The Aith charity shop was one of my favourite haunts. It was in the former school, a handy five-minute walk from the marina, and sold books at five for a pound. If you timed it right there were half-price sale days, which made it even better value. Over the year and a half I'd been back in Shetland I'd acquired new bedding, a set of good-quality plastic plates, jeans and a pair of new trainers. Its official name was the Auld Skule Recycling Centre.

Light spilled gold from the tall windows onto the row of parked cars, and the hum of busy shoppers drifted out into the lobby. We paused at the door to let a young couple out, complete with child and toddler, all carrying bags, then went into the wide corridor. One wall was hidden behind shelves of shoes, with more in circular baskets. On the other side was the former school office, filled with tightly packed furniture.

We headed in the door on our left. Inside, the wall between two classrooms had been removed, and both rooms were packed as full as they could go with stuff and people. This one had folk browsing the bookshelves by the door or flipping through a dozen racks of clothing and boxes of smaller stuff: children's t-shirts, swimwear, hats and gloves. The other classroom had shelves of china, ornaments and bric-a-brac. There was a scrum of bairns collecting armfuls of toys while their parents lifted up humorous mugs, plates, photograph frames, cushions, jewellery and DVDs. Someone had put on a Christmas CD, barely audible under the hum of folk comparing bargains.

'We could do with bonny plates too,' Gavin said, 'for the Christmas meal.'

Naturally the women at the counter heard him, even though they were simultaneously wrapping china in newspaper, taking money and catching up on the customer's family and Christmas plans. 'Are you after a dinner service?' one of them asked. 'I think we might have just the thing. Someone brought one in on Tuesday, and we're no' put it out yet. Give me two minutes, and I'll fetch it out for you.'

She finished off the customer she was chatting to and came out from behind the counter. 'Come you wi' me. It's a right bonny old-fashioned dinner set, but it has gold upon it, so you'll no' be able to put it in the dishwasher.'

'The dishwasher is us,' Gavin said cheerfully.

She opened the staffroom door just enough to get through. The floor was completely covered in black bags with clothes lippering over the tops, carrier bags spiking bright plastic toys and boxes with paintings or bubble-wrapped ornaments. She saw me looking with my mouth open. 'Folk do a clear-out for Christmas, and we benefit from it.' She reached precariously for a cardboard box labelled CHINA, and Gavin leaned instinctively after her, one hand out. 'I'll pass it to you.' She handed it over. 'It came from an old wife at Nesting, God rest her soul. She'd a brought it out at Christmas, likely, just like you're planning to do.'

Once we'd excavated it from the bubble-wrap it turned out to be the prettiest sort of old-fashioned china, white bordered by a delicate flower pattern in jade green, and a scroll of gold around the edge. There were six plates, an ashet, two covered tureens and a gravy boat. It wouldn't last two seconds on a boat, but it would be good on a land table, and it was just Gavin's style of thing, old-fashioned and not too ornate. He glanced at me. 'Yes?'

69

'Definitely. We could decorate the table with greenery too.'
I looked at the woman. 'What are you wanting for it?'

She squeezed out from the room and managed to shut the door behind her. 'I think I would need to say £10.'

Gavin shook his head. 'I think we'd need to say £20 – an antique shop south would charge far more. Can we leave it behind the counter for the moment, while we look around?'

'That can you.'

We took a deep breath and headed into the scrum. 'Decent glasses too,' Gavin said. He stopped at the wine glasses section and began gently pinging each one. I carried on to where a waterfall of tinsel brightened a darker corner. I'd barely registered the variety of singing model Santas, plastic snowmen and deer among snowy fir trees when I felt a touch on my elbow.

I turned and found myself looking straight at Berwin's brother Robin. That blazing hair was unmistakable. Last time I'd seen him he'd worn it short and spiked on the top, longer beneath, like David Bowie album covers; now, it was longer on top, short below, and sleeked back in a plume above his brow, with fair strands softening its fire-orange. His eyes were dark-lashed and bright, dancing about so that it was hard to see the right colour of them; his face was dead white, that redhead skin without any freckles to colour it. He still had that angular teenage-boy look, nose and cheekbones jutting out above a thin-lipped mouth. He wore a shirt and green tailored jacket, the image of a successful young artist attending a gallery do.

He gave Gavin a quick glance and drew me further away from him. He spoke softly under the chatter. 'Berwin was saying you were interested in a fox painting for your man.'

I nodded.

'I'll be in tomorrow morning, if you want to call round. I have several of the originals.' He gave me a shrewd look. 'Prices from a hundred pounds to two hundred pounds, depending on size.'

I had my *Sørlandet* wages. If Gavin would like it, I could spend that much. 'I'll come round in the morning.'

'You know where my studio is?'

I nodded.

'You can put your boat in on my mother's beach.' He gave me the sideways, mischievous glance that his father had caught for Loki, and I was reminded of Berwin's excitement.

'We could maybe talk about trows too,' I said.

He gave me a quick, bright look and then a sudden charming smile that transformed his face from dodgy to likeable. 'Na, na, I ken nothing about them.' His dancing eyes dared me to challenge him. 'I'm just a painter. I'll see you in the morning.'

He swung around and threaded his way deftly through the crowd. It was only as he moved that I recognised that long, smooth stride. He was indeed the young man in black that we'd seen in Voe, blazing hair hidden under a black toorie, who'd disappeared so swiftly at the approach of the police cars.

Gavin had colonised the formal sitting room while I'd been at sea. One armchair had a scatter of books and fishing tackle around it, and there was a filled peat basket beside the fire.

'I've been researching the history of this croft,' Gavin said, gathering the books up. 'The Archives takes it right back to 1488. Busta was Bjarstadt, Bjorn's place, and this piece belonged to another Bjorn, Bjorn Refursson, Bjorn the Fox's Son.' He folded up a map and put it out of harm's way. 'There. Two minutes while I put the mince pies in the oven.'

'Voe mince pies?' I asked, hopefully. 'The puff pastry ones?'

'I'm addicted,' Gavin confessed. 'I got a bottle of port too.'

The kitchen emanated smells of best pastry and mincemeat while we manhandled the tree around the awkward corners, with Cat watching with interest from the stairs, and Kitten rushing madly around our feet, tail fluffed out. It was impressively

71

large, with its branches spreading out half the width of the wall, and the top almost touching the ceiling.

The balls and tinsel caused a lot of excitement. Kitten was straight in there, rolling on the tinsel and kicking it with her back feet first, then dribbling one of the balls around the room. 'Caley Thistle should be signing her up,' Gavin said, pausing to watch her. 'Look at that ball control.'

'Both front paws too,' I said. 'I bet most professionals can't do that.'

'They definitely can't do four paws.'

Cat forgot that he was a dignified older cat and came charging in to take it from her. She dodged neatly, leapt over him from a standing start and came back to grab the last piece of tinsel and trail it off round the room with Cat following until there was a scrum of grey and ginger fur in the middle of the carpet. Gavin laughed. 'Quick, let's get the lights on while they're occupied.' He opened the box and we contemplated the cat's cradle left by someone with no notion of the proper way to stow lines. I began untangling from what seemed to be a free end. 'Listen, we'd need to talk about money, and sorting out a bank account we can both pay into for rent and food and all that.'

'Yes, but this lot is on me. All this Christmas stuff.' His cheeks reddened. 'I know you earn less than I do, and I don't want to have you overspending. I've been thinking about how we can work it. How about we do the basics straight split, and if I want to add luxuries I will?'

I wasn't sure about that. 'It doesn't seem fair.'

Gavin stopped unwinding the lights for a moment. 'Yes, I understand you might feel like that. I know how broke you're used to being.' He gave me an apologetic smile. 'The Longship case, we went pretty thoroughly into your background. List of recent jobs.'

'Waitressing,' I remembered.

'It was a good record. Almost no periods of unemployment, no suggestion of anything illegal, and never any recourse to state aid.' He paused to disentangle the last coloured bulbs. 'There. I'll just get something to stand on. All the same – ' he disappeared through the doorway and came back with one of the kitchen chairs – 'we don't need to live a hand-to-mouth lifestyle, and being unfair cuts two ways. I've got used to my luxuries.'

It was hard to answer that. 'Okay,' I said reluctantly. 'But let's sit down sometime and talk figures.'

'I'll draw you up a spreadsheet,' he promised. 'Focus now, *mo chridhe.*'

I climbed on the chair and focused on getting the lights curving prettily round the branches, then, while I was there, Gavin passed me up a star for the top. 'Done. Shall I get us a glass of port for switching it all on?'

Laughing, we did a formal light-up, and solemnly toasted the Christmas tree, then I got plates for the mince pies, and we ate them sitting side by side on the couch, watching as Kitten systematically brought every bauble within paw reach down to ground level.

'I saw your young man in the charity shop,' I said, through a mouthful of flaky pastry and mincemeat. 'The one from Mulla, in the black coat, who disappeared so quickly. I did know him. He's Berwin's brother. Loki.'

'The Loki of his father's carvings? The tall Viking fighter?'

'The brightest red hair you ever saw, which is why I didn't recognise him with a toorie on. He's definitely one that would scheme things out. However he worked it, I'd put him down as your complicit sibling. The trowie mastermind.'

Friday 18th December

Tide times at Aith:
LW 05.00 (0.9m);
HW 11.16 (2.3m);
LW 17.37 (0.6m);
HW 00.05 (2.0m)

Sunrise 09.06, moonrise 12.16; sunset 14.56, moonset 19.23.

Waxing crescent moon

Chapter Seven

i da clay: in a low mood, brought on by misfortunes from outside

There had been an intense frost during the night. The orange-brown kelp on the shore was crinkled white with ice, and there was a glaze of ice in the curve by the point where the burn ran down. The lights of the houses on Muckle Roe twinkled in the still air.

'I need to do an errand in the boat,' I said, over breakfast. 'Christmas-related,' I added, as Gavin looked up. 'I won't be long.'

'I'll drive over to Aith and get the paper,' Gavin said.

'*The Shetland Times?*'

Gavin nodded. 'Nobody can do anything on a Friday until they've read the paper from cover to cover, sorted out their exact relationship to everyone in the Births, Marriages and Deaths column, commented on every letter on the letters page and disagreed again with the ref's decisions on the sports pages.'

'Have fun,' I said.

The cats bounded ahead of me as I headed for the boat, Kitten stopping every so often to try and scratch her harness off.

'You'll like being allowed out on deck,' I told her.

The sun shone on the boat, on the pale blue sea, but there was no warmth in it, and the ice glazing in the cockpit and on the sides of the cuddy stayed unmelted. I sloshed a bucket of seawater over it, then clambered aboard and started the engine. The birds were enjoying the still day: I glimpsed the herald deuks again and a scarf surfacing, tilting its yellow beak and diving again with a glimpse of webbed feet as it went over. Cat sat in his usual position on the cockpit seat, head up, ears alert, and Kitten sat beside him, radiating importance at being allowed on deck at sea.

It was a bonny run. The water gurgled under the boat's forefoot and swished along her sides, and I left a long wake of spreading ripples that shushed on the shore behind me. A creel boat was already out and working; this was their busy season, for the Christmas market. He'd be keen to get his lobsters and velvets off on the last boat before the holiday shutdown. I waved and turned east into Olna Firth. Tirval was up and doing, for there was a stream of blue smoke from his chimney. There was no sign of him outside, but I waved, in case he was looking out of the window, and headed the five hundred metres further, to where Robin's mother's house was.

It was an old house, with the stone walls unpainted, and the roof still covered in the black tarred felt that most folk had replaced with slates. The curtains of one window were drawn tightly shut, but light shone from the other window, and smoke rose from both chimneys. Robin's mother was out on the brig-gistanes scattering grain for the hens clustered around her feet. Most of them were black, but the sun picked out the orange manes and scarlet combs of the cockerels. She lifted her head and saw me coming slowly in. The tide almost covered the beach, but I could see a line of rocks marking the edge of where the beach had been cleared of larger stones to make a landing place, and her own boat sitting above it. I kept an eye on the bottom as I came in, and she gave the house behind her a quick glance, as if to check someone was still sleeping in the curtained room, then came down to meet me, striding down the stones with one hand held up in a 'stop there' gesture. I jumped overboard into ankle-deep water just as she caught the bow to hold me off.

I could see the likeness to Robin straight off. She was a tall woman, maybe getting on for six foot, but his gangling thinness was translated in her to willowy grace, his jutting cheekbones to a sculptured face with bones that would keep her beautiful though she lived to be a hundred. Her big eyes were set deep into their sockets, and fringed by long lashes as black as the curling hair that hung almost to her waist. Her skin was as pale as his, and there were tired dark circles under her eyes. She was wearing a canvas smock with pockets, like a fisherman's smock, faded navy, over working jeans and rubber boots.

I recognised her from the carvings too. She was the dark lady, the soothsayer. Even as I thought it, she pushed her hair back with one hand, just like one of her figures. The other hand tensed on my prow, ready to give the boat a shove backwards.

'This is a private beach,' she said. 'If you want to land, you can go over to the pier at Voe.' She indicated forwards, towards Lower Voe. 'It's just a mile further, if that.' Her voice was sharp, impatient, as if my intrusion was the last straw in a busy morning.

'Hang on,' I said. 'Are you Robin's mother?' Her head jerked up and round; now she looked at me properly. 'He said I could land here.'

Her eyes flared open, and I saw that they weren't dark, as I'd expected, but a light clear green, like seawashed glass. Her hands clenched on my boat prow, and a spasm of anger crossed her face. For a moment she looked as if she wasn't sure how to respond, eyes narrowing, teeth biting her lower lip, then she seemed to shake the thought off, and managed a smile. 'Are you a friend of Robin's?'

I shook my head. 'I wanted one of his paintings for a Christmas present, and he said to come round this morning. I won't be long.'

'Normally I don't let people land here.' She indicated the beach with a sweep of her hand. 'It's an attractive picnic spot, so in summer people do try, but of course they bring their radios and leave their litter, so now I just ask them to go elsewhere. There are plenty of other beaches.'

She didn't need to explain to me, and the radios and litter didn't sound like any boating folk from around here. Her breathing had quickened, as if she was nervous.

'Of course,' I said soothingly. 'I really won't be long.'

'Oh, no, it's fine.' She managed a shaky laugh. 'I'm sure you haven't brought a radio.' She looked past me into the boat. 'Just cats – oh, now I ken who you are, of course I do. You're Cass, who ran the sailing in the summer. Berwin told me all about you. He loved it. I'm Helge, Robin's mother, but you know that. Come ashore.' She began helping me pull the boat so that its prow was on land, and I reached in for the long rope to attach it further up.

Just that small effort seemed to have been too much for her. Her breathing was laboured now, and she bent over, one hand pressing against her breastbone. Her hands were skeleton-thin, and now I looked at her properly her white skin looked as much ill-health as natural pallor. 'Are you okay?'

Helge nodded, then straightened up. I could see she was making an effort to steady her breathing. 'You can tie – ' another pause for breath – 'up there – the strainer.' She moved to the line of boulders that defined the landing strip, and sat down. Cat, seeing we had arrived, jumped out onto the beach, and Kitten tried to follow, but was prevented by her leash. She mewed indignantly, and tried to bite through it.

'Is it okay if the cats land too?' I asked.

Helge nodded. 'They won't – chase the hens?'

I eyed Cat warily, after last night's duck, but he didn't seem interested in hens; he was investigating the tideline for a possible stray fish. 'I don't think so, but I'll keep an eye on them. Do you have a dog?'

She shook her head. 'A cat.'

I unclipped Kitten from her lead and she bounded off to see what Cat was up to. The neon-pink stood out brightly against the sandy pebble shore. I shouldn't have trouble finding her again.

I fished the longest rope out from the cockpit locker and attached it to the bow cleat, then headed up the beach with it. Helge's own boat was sitting at high-water mark, but not put away for the winter, as I'd half expected; there were fresh marks in the snow where it had been pulled out, and it was tied only to a strainer post at the bow, without additional ropes to the two shorter posts on each side. Maybe she'd used it to go over to the Voe shop yesterday, rather than taking the car on icy roads. I put a turn and half-hitches round the strainer and laid the rest of the rope on the ground.

Helge took a last breath and stood up again. 'Sorry about that. I was ill some years ago, and my chest's still not right. Side effects from the medication.'

It was a pretty serious side effect that didn't let a comparatively young woman help haul a light boat a metre up the beach; and what was she so nervous about, looking back at the cottage so often?

An idea dawned in my head as I looked at her standing there in her smock, jeans and rubber boots. Long dark curly hair, and a house by the shore on a track off the main Aith-Voe road, a track with other houses at the start of it, like ours. Even my French cheekbones were a faint echo of her First Nation ones.

'I think,' I said slowly, 'that I might have had visitors who were looking for you.'

She raised her head, surprise followed quickly by alarm. 'Looking for me?'

'They fetched up at our house, at the Ladie.' I gestured vaguely south-eastwards. 'They took it I was the person they wanted.' I glanced down at myself, then across at her. 'Boots, jersey, long dark curly hair. House by the shore.' I tried to find the words to explain without alarming her. 'Not pleasant visitors. Two men in dark suits.'

I'd thought she was pale before, but now all the blood drained out of her skin, leaving it a greenish colour. She opened her lips, paused, pressed them together to moisten them, then said, 'Did they say what they wanted?'

'They wanted me to retract my testimony, or just not appear as a witness. They suggested they'd make it worth my while.'

Her mouth hardened; her chin went up. Whatever she was involved in, she wasn't going to back down.

'They weren't safe people,' I said. I glanced up at the cottage, with a hundred metres of track to the road, then a mile further to Leonard and Frigg's cluster of buildings; beyond screaming distance. I hesitated, thinking of the closed curtains in a sitting room where the fire had been freshly made up, then asked, 'Do you live alone here?'

She nodded. I looked openly at her house, calculating whether she could run for help unseen from the front door, and make it to her car before they caught her. They were the sort to block her car in and stand one at each door.

'It's none of my business,' I said, diffidently, 'but I don't suppose you could get Robin, maybe, to come and stay while they're about?'

She flinched at the suggestion, then caught at the name. 'Robin! Here I am chatting and keeping you back when you're needing to get on.'

'Yes, you are, aren't you?' said a sardonic voice behind us.

We both gasped and jumped. Robin was standing there at

the corner of her house, dressed today as the working artist in jeans and a canvas smock like his mother's. The sleeves and neck of a thick jumper showed beneath it. He smiled mockingly at Helge and lounged forwards. Alarm crossed Helge's face, and she moved back to her door, one hand below her breast, other arm spread out as if to bar him passage. Robin came right up to her and spoke softly. 'You get back to your visitor, Mother.' He gave the closed curtains a contemptuous look. 'I'll look after mine.' He gave me that charming smile again and gestured to his studio with a flourish. 'After you, Cass.'

I looked Helge in the face. 'Thanks.'

Her eyes were huge in her pale face. I couldn't read her expression: distress, shock? She looked for a moment at Robin, and her eyes filled with tears, then she turned abruptly away from us, threw the last handful of grain at the hens and vanished back inside the house, shutting the door firmly behind her.

smeegin: *smirking, smiling mockingly, with a connotation of self-satisfaction (Norse and Danish dialect,* smkija: *to ingratiate yourself; Swedish,* smeeka: *to flatter or caress)*

I gave the cats a quick glance – both still busy on the beach – then turned and headed upwards towards Robin's studio. As I passed Helge's house I noticed the snow around it had people tracks, cat tracks and hen scratches, but no small footprints. The trows hadn't been here.

You get back to your visitor, Mother. I tried not to think about that all the way up to the studio. If Helge had a lover, all the better for her security with those two thugs about. I wondered why Robin disapproved so much; he didn't come across as the Hamlet type. Maybe he felt his mother was being exploited by some man who expected to have peat fires kindled for him in the sitting room instead of living by the always-on kitchen Rayburn in winter.

There had been some tramping out and in at Robin's door, one trail coming from Leonard and Frigg's, and a go-and-come heading roadwards, but there were no trowie footprints in the smooth spread of snow on each side of the doorway.

Robin came around me as I reached the door, and swung it open. 'Come in,' he said, and stood back to let me into the room.

I imagined it would be a good studio. The internal walls had been removed to give one big room, maybe six metres by four, and the new roof was half-glass, so there was a fair bit of light coming in, even in midwinter. It'd been plasterboarded inside, giving Robin plenty of white-painted wall to hang his paintings on. Good in summer, I amended to myself; the gas heater in one corner barely took the chill off the room. He slept here too, it seemed; above us, the last two metres of the hay loft had been kept to make a mezzanine floor, and there was a mattress with a pillow and tumbled sleeping bag on it.

He saw me glancing upwards and echoed my thought. 'It's fine in summer.'

'I slept aboard all last winter,' I said. 'Not again. And that was a space you could heat with a gas ring.'

'But with no space for hanging paintings.' His wicked smile danced out. 'Here I have a whole gallery. I'm on the gallery trail, you know, for tourists who go round Shetland via all the craft folk.'

'It's a good space for art,' I agreed.

'Not quite as good as in Edinburgh or the Borders. You need to be south to get the art world paying attention. If I had the money . . .' He shrugged. 'Ah, well. Coffee.'

I was glad to clasp my hands around the hot mug Robin handed me. There were a couple of chairs set by the gas fire, and today's paper was lying on the table. *TROWS PROTEST WINDFARM* it screamed, with a picture of the banner on the Mulla house. *More pictures and story on page 5.*

Robin saw me looking. 'The trows you were asking about got a good spread,' he said casually.

'You must have been interested too,' I retorted. 'You took the trouble to go over to Voe for the paper.'

He acknowledged the hit with a wave of his hand. 'I was up early.'

There was no car by the byre, but the track up to the road was well snowed over. Maybe he kept it up at his father's in this weather, or maybe he'd been the one who'd taken Helge's boat out. 'You're against the windfarm too, then?' I said.

I was surprised when he shook his head. 'I'm for it. Oh, I don't say I want the turbines here in Shetland, but we've got to act now to save the planet. The more green energy the better. Every unit we can generate is one less to be generated by coal or gas.' He gave me that sideways smile again. 'Don't tell Berwin,' he added.

Well, well. So he was encouraging his little brother to do a spectacular protest against something he himself was privately for. I wondered why. Perhaps he knew it would make Dad and the other developers more determined. Surely he wasn't hoping Berwin would get caught – or perhaps he was. I thought of that last, fast swipe of his iron blade at Berwin's unprotected legs. Maybe he got fed up of the world revolving round his golden little brother. Maybe he'd like to see him come a cropper . . . and that thought was followed by another. *Complicit sibling.* Berwin hadn't been one of our trows, I was sure, for his feet would be bigger than mine, but someone had driven ours out to the Ladie, well out of the way of all the other trowie activity, but, as all my sailors well knew, the house of the developer's daughter and her policeman. Where better to make sure notice was taken of the pranksters?

'Have a look round,' Robin said. 'Just ask if there's anything you want to know.'

He took his coffee over to his easel, and went back to work, leaving me to look, and wonder a little about the young man who'd masterminded a trowie anti-windfarm protest, yet said he was for the turbines, who preferred icy independence to begging a bed from either of his parents – not that I had a leg to stand on there, for, if I'd asked, Dad would have helped me with lodgings to save me sleeping aboard in the hert-hol o' winter. All the same, it was bitterly, bitterly cold.

If his paintings were a guide, I didn't think he'd be comfortable to live with. There were several of Up Helly A, over a metre square, with the feathered helmet of the Jarl silhouetted against the burning galley: so far, so conventional, but the flames swirled in burning orange and fiery red that shouted a defiant savagery from the walls. This Jarl was the Lord of Misrule; but I sensed that the anger covered bitter unhappiness. The gable wall had a table in the centre of it, a trestle of old boards. The first half of it had carving tools and a few palm-sized hedgehogs and mice in natural wood, oiled like his father's carvings. The other half was laid with animal bones: two sheep skulls with their curved horns, a smaller animal that might be a cat or an otter, a delicate gull skull with the long beak still yellow, and a scatter of bones. The paintings on this wall were still lifes using the bones from the table, and they would have been fine pictures had Robin not painted a white spark in the darkness of each eye socket, so that you had the illusion that the skull in the painting was watching you. I tried moving to one side and found the eye sockets watching me still. It was extraordinarily unsettling, and I wouldn't have given any of them houseroom.

The animal paintings were on the third wall, the colours glowing jewel-bright against the white plasterboard. Now I'd seen his other work I was looking for a hint of irony, a suggestion that these creatures were being anthropomorphised by humans into something cute and cuddly, but there was none. These were wild creatures caught going about their own lives without human interference or interpretation, and the very absence of commentary was itself a comment. Nature was itself, not a mirror of us. Robin's foxes would eat other creatures without pity or regret. I'd never seen a fox but I believed straight off that this was what they were like, beautiful in their wildness, cunning, ruthless; creatures who would kill every one of a cage of hens for the sheer fun of it.

I shot Robin a quick glance, and saw him intent on his painting, a smile on his lips. Smeegin, Magnie would have said. He was too pleased with himself altogether. I wondered if the trows had been out again in the night.

His sense of humour was none of my business. I was here to buy a painting. The whole family was here: the dog fox, poised against the hill, alert for danger, the vixen, grooming her cubs, the cubs themselves playing in the heather. Gavin would like any of these. My favourite was the dog fox, king of his world on the crest of one hill with another behind him. Robin had drawn them as low Shetland hills with heather growing from peat moor, so that an intrepid fox could roam to the height of his territory.

'That one's not for sale,' Robin said. I turned my head and found him watching me. 'But all the others are.'

There were no foxes in Shetland. I knew that. The only land mammals on Shetland had been introduced here: sheep, cows and ponies with the first settlers, five thousand years ago, pigs in the Iron Age, Arctic hares, hens and otters with the Vikings. Sailing ships had brought rats to Lerwick. The game-shoot brown hares of the south mainland, the snuffling hedgehogs to keep the laird's lady's garden free of slugs, had come in the nineteenth century. A few grouse lingered on the west side hills, brought in for the shooting, but I'd never heard of any attempt to chase foxes. You'd have to be mad to gallop slender-legged horses over wild Shetland hills.

'Why foxes, when there are none here in Shetland?' I asked.

Robin paused, brush in mid-air. He turned his head to give me a long look then gave that unsettling, untrustworthy smile again. 'For the tourist market,' he said. 'A fox reminds them equally of home and of their holiday here.' His brush began moving again. He spoke in bursts, over one shoulder. 'They don't know any better. Besides, folk have seen foxes here, so I'm only using a little bit of imagination. Okay, well, there's never been an authenticated sighting, just the occasional one found dead by the roadside. You ask your pal Magnie about the Gonfirth Fox. The thinking is that someone with a sense of humour brought that up from south.'

I could imagine Robin himself doing it.

'Crofters wouldn't want foxes up here. The shotguns would soon be out. And I like painting them, so I pretend.' He laid his brush down and turned properly. 'Well, can I sell you a painting, even if it's a fox from somewhere else?'

I put my hand up to the vixen with her cubs. 'This one.'

While I wrote a cheque, he parcelled the painting up with bubblewrap and put it in a plastic bag. 'There you are, and thanks to you. Safe journey back, and let me know how your man likes it.'

'I will.'

His face twisted into mockery. 'Give my mother my best wishes if you see her as you pass.'

I remembered the way her eyes had flared green when I'd mentioned him, and the antagonism in their brief dialogue. I wouldn't be passing on any messages. 'I see the trows didn't visit either of you.'

'Ah, my mother sains the house against them. Didn't you notice the straw cross above the door? As for me, well – ' His eyes were dancing; again I got that feeling of how very clever he thought he was. 'Maybe they were too busy with other mischief. The darkest nights are here, so they'd be looking to kidnap a fiddler to play at their feasts.' He gestured towards Voe. 'There's a field over there worth taking a look at. Good day.'

The door closed between us.

The cats had got bored of the shoreline and set out to meet me, with Kitten's pink harness bright against the snowy hill. She stopped every few steps to shake her paws disgustedly. Cat spotted me coming out and bounded over the hill towards me. I tickled the white fur behind his ears. 'A quick look at Voe, boy, and then home.'

It was coming up to eleven, with the sun climbed just enough above the hills to shine on the water. I wouldn't want to waste much time, with Gavin waiting for me, but Robin had got me curious.

Helge's door remained closed. I looked above it for the straw cross Robin had mentioned and saw it in the shadows below the eaves of the porch.

The cats jumped aboard as soon as I put my shoulder to the boat. I poled us out into deeper water with an oar, then set the motor chugging gently towards Voe while I gave the cats a sachet of food and fresh drinking water.

It was easy to spot the field Robin meant: the broad one between the road, the voe and the burn below Leonard and Frigg's house. As I watched, two cars slowed and stopped, and their owners got out, looking at something in the field. I saw a camera flash.

There were spyglasses in the cabin. I fetched them out and focused on the shore. Rocks and a shallow bank. The fence, with several sheep lying down beside it. Snow, pitted by sheep tracks. I kept scanning upwards. A pair of crofter-issue yellow rubber boots, standing upright bang in the middle of the field, with what looked like a bundle of cloth balanced on top of them.

I didn't have time to land. I putted two hundred metres further, then put the engine to idle and took another long look. A pair of rubber boots standing. The cloth resolved itself into a navy boiler suit. The lighter circle on top of it was a cap.

There was a line of footprints leading to the boots, stamped into the white snow. They ended where the boots stood upright under the boiler suit and cap, as if the crofter who wore them had vanished into thin air. *They'd be looking to kidnap a fiddler to play at their feasts*, Robin had said.

I had no doubt Robin was watching to see if I'd gone to look. I turned and saw him standing in his doorway, mug in hand, shoulder propped against the jamb. I raised one hand in acknowledgement of trowie cleverness, then upped the throttle and headed for home.

Chapter Eight

ammerswak: *state of unrest or agitation (Old Norse, * amask*: to trouble yourself)*

It was glass-still on the water as I went back past the house on the lake. A cold mist lay in the channel between Brae and Muckle Roe, and the sky to the south-east had a silvery brightness where the moon was about to rise. Up at the house the slanted light brought out the red in the flowering currant stems, and caught the sparrows' fawn breasts, making them glow rose. Cat swished his tail at them as he passed, and Kitten chittered; the sparrows cheeped insults back at them.

I stashed the painting in the shed, and had just got into the house when the phone rang. It was a woman's voice, tense and anxious. 'Cass? It's Frigg here. You were at the shop yesterday. I'm sorry to bother you, but I'm worried about Berwin. I didn't want to make an official fuss, but I thought maybe I could ask your man, if he's about . . .'

I lifted my head. My eyes met Gavin's; he made a face and nodded, stretched his hand out.

'He's just here,' I said. There was an agitated twittering from the phone, as if Frigg was giving a thousand apologies, it could be nothing, but she was anxious about it. The kidnapped fiddler trick, I had no doubt, the footprints, and the boots left standing in the field at Voe. I'd give no odds that they were

Berwin's boots and clothes, and that he played the fiddle, but letting his mother get in such a state didn't seem like him. I felt a twinge of uneasiness.

'When did you last see him?' Gavin said soothingly over the agitation. 'Yes . . . and his bed was slept in?' He listened for another half minute. I couldn't make out any of the other side of the conversation at all. 'He's not just gone off to school?' His face grew graver, listening to the answer. 'I see . . . how about his friends?' There was more twittering; I couldn't tell from Gavin's face whether she'd tried them with no result or didn't know because she hadn't wanted to try them. 'Right, well, given Berwin's age I think we should take this up officially.' The agitation at the other end went up a notch. Gavin listened patiently. 'I see. Well, how about I come over and have a chat with you both, and then we can get a search going if it looks like we need one.'

There was a flask standing ready by the draining board. I filled it with coffee and had a look in the fridge for roll-fillers. The jar of French pâté suggested Maman had been bringing him supplies in my absence. While Gavin made a last few soothing noises, I filled the rolls and put them in a bag. 'Do we eat en route?'

'I think we do. Berwin's gone missing after what sounds rather a good trick.'

'I saw it from out in the boat.' I added a couple of mugs. 'Rubber boots left standing in a field. Give me two minutes to take a few layers off.'

I changed quickly, and when I came back down Gavin had got the flask and rolls in one hand and our tentative town shopping list and bags in the other. 'If it's nothing we can still do our town trip, but if it's something I can drop you at the Co-op and either pick you up later or if you don't mind getting the bus to Aith or Voe, I've got cash, you can take a taxi the rest of the way.'

'No need,' I said. 'I'm babysitting, remember? I'll get the bus right to Brae.'

'So you are. And I'll fetch you from there. Be good, you two,' he added, to Cat and Kitten. 'No more dead birds.'

'Have there been many?'

'None as big as yesterday's duck. Cat showing off for the kitten's benefit. Oh, hang on.' He turned back into the doorway. I heard the rattling noise of a scoop in a bag, then he came out with a margerine tub of pony nuts. 'Let me just throw these at them.'

The ponies had heard the noise, and came over at a speed surprising in horses with such short legs. They skidded to a halt at the fence and stretched their necks over, whickering impatiently. 'No shoving,' Gavin said. He doled out the nuts in four piles, well spaced out, and I watched with interest as the smaller black and white pony chased the red and white one away from each pile in turn. She was wise to him, snatching a mouthful at the next pile before wheeling away and back to the end of the line, and in the end the nuts seemed to go down fairly evenly.

'She's much bigger than he is. It's odd she lets him bully her like that.'

'The smaller they are, the more determined.' He gave me a sideways grin. 'And he's the male, of course. Naturally she respects him.'

'Dream on,' I retorted.

We got into the Land Rover and headed out over the track and turned towards Voe. The hills around us were frosted white with snow lying over the heather, but the gritters had been and once we got off our track the main road was black, though the puddles at the sides were waxed with ice. The wire and posts of the fences beyond wore white frost-fur.

'What's my role here?' I asked. 'Do you want me to stay in the car while you talk to her?'

'Normally I'd say yes, but this time I'm unofficial, and I'd be glad of you to help me make soothing noises if Frigg starts getting upset.'

'Do we have an aim?'

'Find out if the boy is really missing as quickly as possible and get a search underway.' He spoke matter-of-factly, but he was frowning. 'We've only got another couple of hours of light, and it'll be a cold night.'

'The chopper has a heat tracking device.'

'He didn't look a parent-worrier, but then Cat doesn't look a bird-killer.'

'Meaning there's a girlfriend to impress?'

'Inga's oldest.'

'Vaila?' I was about to protest that she wasn't nearly old enough, but then remembered her set face beside her placard. When I'd been fourteen I'd thought I was grown up too, though my focus had been on winning races, not saving the planet.

'One of the things they tell you at police college: Juliet was thirteen,' Gavin said. He drove on up the hills, over the Camel's Back, around Gonfirth loch and down into Lower Voe.

Frigg was watching for us. She came stumbling out of the shop as we drew to a halt in front of it, hands held out before her. 'Thank you for coming! I'm so worried about him.'

She was in a right ammerswak. The goddess poise was gone. She was wearing the pinnie she'd worn yesterday, but the buttons were done up squint, and her fair hair was loosely caught up in a knot at the back of her head, with strands sticking out from it. She brushed one away impatiently. Her face was flushed, her eyes bright with tears. She was just about to speak when Leonard came out from between the buildings, followed by the giant-man, Bruce. Frigg sniffed, ran a hand across her eyes, and was silent.

Leonard said a couple of words to Bruce, who nodded, gave

Frigg the same blank, incurious glance he'd given us and slouched off into the byre. Leonard came forward to Gavin and spoke man-to-man. 'Gavin, I'm vexed Frigg's called you out with all this nonsense. The boy's up to a prank, and a clever one too, and I've no doubt he'll be home at the end of the day. He'll be at the school now, telling all his pals about it.'

'He's not at the school!' Frigg almost screamed at him. He put up a hand to silence her, without giving her a glance.

'It's a good trick, and I'm no' wanting to spoil it for him.'

'I understand that,' Gavin said, 'and I won't spoil it for him either, but all the same, since your wife's worried, I'd like to make absolutely sure there's no cause for concern.' He turned to Frigg, his voice soothing as honey on hot toast. 'Shall we go in and sit down? You can tell us all about it.'

'Come and look at the boy's trick first,' Leonard said. I saw Gavin wondering for a second whether he was going to let him take the initiative, then he nodded.

'Easiest to take the car,' Leonard said. 'It's the park in Lower Voe, by the road.' He gestured us towards his 4x4. He and Gavin got in the front, and Frigg and I squeezed in the back, and he bumped along the track, turned left into the village and parked by the old quarry. We got out into the cold air, breath smoking.

Berwin's trick was much more impressive from here. He'd obviously chosen the field for maximum visibility; it was right by the road through Lower Voe and in full view of Upper Voe and the main road. The trail of footprints stomped down from the house, across the little bridge, clearly printed in the clean snow, and then stopped dead in the centre of the field. The rubber boots shone duck-bill yellow in the sun, and the boiler suit was crumpled above them as if it had fallen from a suddenly disembodied owner, with the cap drifting down to lie on top of them. The black sheep grazed around, unheeding.

'I don't want to spoil his effect, but I need to get a closer look,' Gavin said. Leonard nodded. Frigg and I watched from the road as he and Gavin went down the edge of the park and approached the yellow boots from the side. Gavin was looking downwards; at one point, still several metres from the boots, he crouched down, kilt brushing the snow, and felt the sheep prints in the snow with one hand, then picked something up. It was small and brown; from here I'd have guessed a food pellet, like the nuts he'd just fed the ponies. He showed it to Leonard, who nodded. Gavin took another couple of paces forward, looking intently, then shook his head. His voice carried clearly on the still air. 'There's no sign of human prints under the sheep ones. I was thinking he might have arranged the boots and walked on, scattering sheepnuts behind them so that they'd cover his traces, but that's not how it was worked.' He looked at the prints again. 'Have you a ram among these sheep?'

Leonard shook his head. 'He's been and gone again. I put him in in November.'

'One of these prints is deeper, there.' He bent down to indicate it. 'And there.'

Leonard shrugged. 'Softer ground maybe. But there's no signs of other footprints, or a fight or a scuffle, or anything we need to be concerned about. However the boy did it, he managed on his own.'

'Certainly no signs of other footprints,' Gavin agreed, 'and the items are artistically placed.' He walked over to the nearest fence, running from the road to the shore. The sun had already melted the frost-fur from the top and bottom wires. Gavin leaned over it to look behind. 'No sign here either. He didn't walk up in the ditch.' He turned towards the rubber boots and stared without going any nearer. 'Are these all his?'

'The boots and the boiler suit are his, but normally he'd wear a black toorie. The cap's mine, for dog-showing days.'

I'd wondered about that. A cap was classic 'old man' wear,

but its lighter colour showed up against the navy boiler suit much better than a black knitted hat would have done.

'So,' Gavin said, 'he worked his trick and came back.' He began strolling slowly down the slope. 'There's no sign of anyone having climbed over the fence to walk back on the road.'

I gave the verge a glance. Behind it was a normal post-and-wire fence, with square mesh to keep the lambs in. The thin crust of snow that covered the metre-width of longer grass at the side of the road was unbroken, except by Gavin and Leonard's footprints along at the far side of the park, and the mesh sparkled silver. Beside me, Frigg shivered and wrapped her arms around her body. 'Let's follow them.'

'I don't think we should,' I said. 'In case of messing up the prints.' Surely she'd know that much about detective work. 'Besides, I don't suppose they'll find anything. The tide's as high as it'll go.'

Gavin and Leonard strolled down to the seawards corner of the park. Gavin leaned over the fence, looking intently in each direction, then shook his head. 'No obvious traces. The tide's almost to the fence. Do you have any idea when it might have been done?'

Leonard shook his head. 'I'm in bed by half past ten, and I sleep sound. I heard nothing in the night. He'd ken that, of course.'

Gavin nodded. 'High water last night was about midnight. If he'd done it before then, he could just have climbed over the lower fence and left the tide to wash away his tracks.' He looked towards the house. The shore ran smoothly in a curve to the burn mouth where the trows had taken ship. There was the little bridge across the burn, then the pebble shore turned to banks, low cliffs where the sea had eaten the sloping hill away. 'I'll just go along and have a look at the bridge for footprints. I won't be a moment.'

He left Leonard standing there and marched briskly along

the shore to the bridge. He went up to it keeping well to the side, looked intently, then shook his head. 'Boots coming down, nothing going back. Well, let's go and hear about this morning.'

Beside me, Frigg shuddered again.

'Come back in the car,' I said.

We drove to the house in silence. 'I'll watch the shop,' Leonard said when we arrived. 'You go in, go on, and get it out of your head.'

There was something very wrong with their marriage that he could speak so brusquely when she was so obviously frantic with worry. She showed Gavin and I into the kitchen and began picking up mugs, hands searching blindly as if she'd for gotten where everything was. 'I'll do that,' I said. 'You sit and talk to Gavin. Do you want tea or coffee yourself?'

She looked at me the way the sailing bairns did when I mentioned apparent wind without reminding them first what it was. 'I usually have herbal tea, but . . .' Her voice trailed off uncertainly.

'I'll find it,' I said. 'Go on, you sit down and relax, and tell Gavin why you're so worried.'

Gavin sat down at the table, and motioned her to sit at right angles to him. 'Just tell me all about it,' he said. 'I ken from what I've seen of him that Berwin's not one to go worrying you. Just start with when you last saw him. Last night, was it? What was he doing then?'

The straightforward question steadied her. 'Last night. I went in to give him a goodnight kiss at bedtime. He wasn't in bed yet then. He and Sheila, that's my daughter, they were playing cards in his room. I told them not to stay up much later, and they said they'd just finish that game then stop. Sheila had her work in the morning, you see, and Berwin had school. I heard them both moving about, in the bathroom and so on, and then I fell asleep.' She added quickly, as if he was about to blame her, 'I was that tired, the shop's been busy with the run-up to Christmas, people buying presents and stocking up on pet food, and there was the bus, it didn't arrive till nearly closing time. I just slept. Then this morning I heard him getting up and going out.'

'What time was that?'

'His usual time, I suppose – he's always up first. He showers and has some cereal, then unless it's really bad weather he bicycles to school.'

I could see Gavin calculating it out. Voe to Brae was six miles, add in another ten minutes to get Berwin to the main road, and allow a bit more for the snowy conditions. 'Would he leave about eight o'clock?'

Frigg nodded, then frowned. She gave the window an uncertain glance. 'I think it might have been earlier today. It's been a fine clear day, but I couldn't see the outline of the hill yet, so it must have been before seven. I wasn't properly awake. I was just aware of him moving about.'

'What about the other folk in the house? When do they get up?'

Having to think about routine questions she could answer was steadying her. I put the mug of chamomile tea into her hands, and her fingers clasped round it. 'Leonard's up and out first these days, checking on the cows and then feeding the sheep as soon as it's light enough. He's up and out by seven. Sheila has her breakfast with Berwin, then she leaves just before him.'

'How old's Sheila, and what's her work?'

'She's twenty. She works to the Council in Lerwick. She gets the bus into town. She doesn't like driving. She has a licence, but her eyesight's only just good enough and it gets her so nervous, especially in winter, that she prefers to get the bus. We're well served for buses here. The worker's one is seven minutes past eight, but it doesn't come down into Lower Voe, so she has to walk up to the stop. Once she's out he uses the bathroom, and then goes, and then I get up.' She added, apologetically, as if it was a fault, 'We only have one shower, you see, though there's a separate toilet, so we have it all worked out who gets the bathroom when.'

She paused for breath, and Gavin nodded. 'We'll need to ask Sheila if she saw him this morning. Could we contact her at her work?'

Frigg nodded. 'I would think so. She's at the White House.' Her hands waved in the air for a moment, uncertain. 'I don't know the number. It'll be in the book.' She stretched behind her and handed him the phone directory. He flipped through and found the pages for SIC.

'What department is she in?'

Frigg shook her head. 'She seems to go to different departments, wherever they're needing an extra pair of hands. She's not really qualified for anything, well, you know, she did all the usual things at school, accounts and computing and the like.'

I was beginning to feel sorry for Sheila. It was obvious that Berwin was Frigg's sole focus, the apple of her eye, with Sheila an also-ran.

'Is Sheila's name Callahan too?' Gavin asked. There was an apologetic note in his voice. Right enough, I thought, awarding him police brownie points, Berwin was their joint child, but Robin, just under ten years older, was his and Sheila could well be hers, the daughter of a first marriage. Twenty. Six years older than Berwin, only two or three younger than Robin.

Frigg nodded. 'Yes. She was only five when Leonard and I met, and her father wasn't around any more, so we thought – it seemed easiest, with Berwin on the way, and Robin already at the school.'

She trailed off as Gavin punched the number in. 'Hello? I'd like to talk to Sheila Callahan, if it's convenient . . . Thanks.'

He smiled encouragingly at Frigg, then focused on the phone again. 'Hello, Sheila. It's Gavin Macrae here, from the police. Now don't worry, there hasn't been an accident. It's just about Berwin – did you know about his vanishing trick?'

Her surprised 'No' floated clearly from the phone, but it didn't convince me for a minute, and she spoiled it by giggling.

'A clever trick,' Gavin said. 'Now all I need to know is when you saw him this morning.' He listened, nodding. 'So you didn't see him at all? . . . Yes, he could well have done that. And he's not phoned or texted you today?'

Another negative. Gavin shook his head. 'No, no, there's absolutely no reason to think anything's wrong. This isn't any kind of official enquiry. Your mother's a bit worried, that's all. He'd be wanting to tell his friends all about it. Thanks, Sheila.'

He laid the phone down and shook his head. 'She didn't see him this morning. He was gone by the time she got up. She thought he was dead keen to get to school and mystify his pals.' He drummed his fingers on the table for a moment. 'You've talked to the school, and he's not there. You're not aware of any falling-out with his friends?'

Frigg shook her head.

'And he's been as normal, not seeming down or anything like that?'

She took longer to think about that one. 'He's upset about the wind turbines. They all are, all his gang. But other as that he's been bright and cheerful this last while, you ken, looking forward to Christmas.'

'Is there anywhere else he might have gone? How about his brother's studio?'

I was shaking my head before I remembered that I wasn't supposed to have been there. Gavin gave me a sharp glance.

'I don't like him hanging around Robin,' Frigg said. Her tone was spiteful. 'He'll do him no good. Nor that mother of his. He knows I wouldn't want him going there.'

'So if he was wanting to make it look as if he'd really disappeared, he might hide out with either of them.'

I thought of the still-closed curtains in Helge's house, and the two smoking chimneys, and wondered for a moment if Robin's animosity to Helge had been a blind to stop me guessing Berwin was hiding out there. Then I remembered Helge's face, and the tears in her eyes, and didn't believe it.

'He wouldn't do that to me.' Frigg spoke with defiant certainty. 'Something's happened to him.'

Chapter Nine

ill vaandit: *disagreeable, having unattractive manners; bad or awkward behaviour; also said of job badly done (Icelandic, illa vandadur: carelessly carried out)*

Leonard must have been listening through the door that led to the shop, for he came in suddenly like a roaring bull. 'Wife, that's enough of this nonsense. I have plenty to be doing this morning, and there's a car coming along the road, so get you back to the shop. The boy's just playing a prank on us. He'll turn up. Go you and wash your face, and then think no more about it.'

She gave him a defiant look and blazed back at him. 'I'll no' think no more about it. He'd never worry us like this for nothing. That boy o' yours is at the back o' it. You ken fine Berwin would follow him anywhere.'

Leonard's face darkened. His big fist clenched angrily. 'Berwin thinks the world o' his brother, no thanks to you, and so he should. Robin's a son to be proud o', wi' his degree from the art college, and I'll no' have you belittling him in front o' strangers. Go and make less o' a spectacle o' yourself, and deal wi' your customers, for I won't.'

Frigg made an angry sound in her throat, and flounced out. We heard a door slam, and running water. Leonard drew a deep breath and sat down in the chair she'd left. He rubbed a hand over his brow, then looked straight at Gavin. 'My apologies to you. You're no' seeing our family at its best the day. My wife's aye been jealous o' me first family, especially wi' them biding here so close.'

'It's an awkward situation,' Gavin agreed. He turned his head to me and his eyes flickered towards the door. He'd get on better alone with Leonard.

'I'll go and give Frigg a hand,' I said, and headed shopwards.

There was a family in, the parents stocking up on dog food, and the children choosing Christmas presents for their pets. I hoped Cat and Kitten wouldn't feel too deprived if the best they got was playing with wrapping paper and a bit of duck skin from the dinner. Once the family had gone, in a wave of 'Merry Christmas!' wishes, I joined Frigg in wiping down the counters and polishing the glass tank fronts.

'I was in Robin's studio this morning,' I said, 'and Berwin wasn't hiding out there.'

'He could've nipped into one of the outhouses when he heard your car coming.'

I shook my head. 'I came by boat. I'm certain there was nobody moving about the place as I came in.'

The wiping hand stilled. 'You came in by boat? You'll have beached at her house, then.' The emphasis on the *her* made it clear who she meant. I nodded. Frigg stood for a moment, brooding. 'Did you see my boy there?' Then she shook her head. 'No, of course you'd have said already. How about her?'

'She came and helped me pull the boat up.'

Frigg's head jerked upwards. Her eyes snapped. 'Oh, she was able to do that, was she?'

I stared at her, and she waved the sharpness away with one hand. 'Sorry, Cass. It just gets me mad the way she phones Leonard for the least little thing – oh, not on this phone, I'd soon send her off with a flea in her ear. On his mobile. Sometimes it seems he spends more time there than he does here.' A tinge of red crept up her neck and blazed on her cheeks. 'She

104

was his first wife, you see, and they werena well suited, but when he met me, well, she didn't accept it. Wouldn't believe that they were over. She clung on in this house until Leonard had to put his foot down, and then instead of going right away, as any woman with any pride would, she moved in with his mother and stayed right on our doorstep. And Leonard had the gall to be pleased about it! Said it was fine that she was there to help his mother, and Robin was still here near his father – well, he was up here as much as he was down there, working mischief, until I put my foot down about that, when Berwin was old enough to need his own room. Still, at least she was down there and we were up here, and we didn't need to see much of her, barring her car going past, and Robin running in and out at all hours, whether it was convenient to me or not –' She ran out of breath, and spread her hands in a deprecating gesture. 'It's tough being a second wife. You have to tread so carefully. Right deep down, although he denied it, Leonard felt guilty about us, so he bent over backwards for her, and she was all sugar-sweet to him, naturally. Made it very clear she was trying to manage everything herself so that she wasn't bothering him, but if he could just give her a hand with sawing up this palette, or shifting furniture around.' Her voice was acid. 'Manipulative. I could see right through her. Then she told him she was ill.' The wiping cloth gave a last flourish round the glass front. Her voice softened slightly. 'Well, that's as may be. She had some sort of chest complaint that cold winter a few years ago, and the doctor put her on medication for it. A new medicine, it was, she had an awful lot of bother wi' it. Side effects. It helpit her breathing, but she had a rash, and headaches, and then came most awful tired, so she said. Went to the doctor again, and just got told that there was nothing wrong with her, and nothing like that on the list of possible side effects.' She glanced at me. 'You don't look as if you've ever needed a doctor in your life.'

105

'I've been lucky,' I agreed.

'The one we have up at Brae is just a waste of space. Oh, they get paid for chasing men up about blood pressure and this and that, so the surgery's always after Leonard, but any time I've needed to see him, well, I might as well not have bothered. Women's problems were ordained by God, it seems, so they don't need to do anything about them. The weaker sex. Everything is all perfectly normal, and if you just put up with it for a bit it'll improve by itself. If you push him he'll offer you anti-depressants. He had Helge on all sorts of things, until there was an outcry – someone who had a doctor who did listen properly, and discovered that the medicine was causing the problems. Now there's a court case coming up against the manufacturer.'

We think you should retract your testimony . . . My mouth went dry. 'And is Helge one of the witnesses against them?'

'Apparently. Hoping for compensation. Not much chance of that against a big multinational, I'd say, though I'd be glad if she got it. She'd buy that son of hers a house south, where he's got a better chance of making a name for himself, and we'd be clear of him.' Her face distorted to ugliness, and she took a deep breath and looked straight at me. 'Leonard's being all supportive, of course. She's been through a bad time, and I'm just being – ' She cut the last words off. 'How did she look to you?'

'Ill,' I said bluntly. 'She had no colour at all, and she had to sit down after just moving half the boat a metre up the beach.'

Frigg was silent for a moment. 'And there was really no sign at all of Berwin there?'

I thought of the smoke from a newly-kindled fire, and the window with the drawn curtains and didn't know what to say. Someone had been in that room, for certain. Maybe Berwin had gone there instead of school, and was sleeping the night's shenanigans off on the couch. This fire was smouldering and

106

ready to burst into flames at fresh fuel. If I said I thought he might be there, Frigg'd be storming along before I could say anything to stop her, and then the fat would be in the fire, whether it was Berwin or a perfectly legitimate lover. The word legitimate sparked off another idea. *He spends more time there than he does here*, Frigg had said. I wondered where Leonard had been this morning. He'd apparently just arrived from the direction of Helge's house when we turned up. Maybe Robin's angry contempt for his mother was because she was still sleeping with Leonard, in spite of his having left her for Frigg.

Frigg was staring at me, waiting for an answer. I shook my head. 'You've tried his mobile, of course?'

'He's not answering. It just goes straight to voicemail. I've tried texting too. Nothing.'

'And he never said a word to you about the trick, or that he was planning anything?'

'He, planning!' Her voice was scornful. 'I ken fine well who's at the bottom of this. His mother's son, as sly and deceitful as she is. I don't care what Leonard says. That boy's trouble, as you can see with just one look at that hair of his. Oh, he smarms around his father all right, and around Sheila and Berwin too, but he doesn't fool me.'

I remembered Robin's smirk, and the way he'd directed me to the field, and was inclined to agree.

'Berwin's not devious,' Frigg finished. 'He'd never think up something like that on his own.'

I thought about that for a moment, visualising Berwin's open face. He won races by sailing faster than the competition, by trimming his sails and his boat perfectly, by steering carefully. When I'd explained the idea of blanketing your opponents' mainsails to overtake them downwind, he'd looked at me as if he'd thought that was cheating. He wasn't tricksy, and he'd never want his mother to be in such a state.

107

Maybe Frigg's fears were catching, but I'd be relieved to set eyes on him.

We both jumped as the door moved. It was Gavin. 'Mrs Callahan, I'd like to make a few more enquiries before we either get the search parties out or, more likely, give your boy a telling-off for upsetting you like this. His trick's a clever one, and he's most likely getting the full effect out of it, but I'll go and talk to his pals at the school, in case he's contacted any of them. If you'll phone the school for me, and tell them I'm on my way, and I have your authority to make unofficial enquiries, that would be helpful. After that you try to relax, and get ready to give him a piece of your mind when he walks in as if nothing had happened. I'll phone after I've spoken to his friends.'

She stared after us, white-faced, as we went out into the yard.

We'd got only halfway to the Land Rover when the giant-man, Bruce, came out of the byre. He raised a hand to us, and Gavin stopped and turned towards him. He slouched over to us and grunted a greeting.

Close to, in the daylight, he was younger than I'd thought; my own age, or perhaps slightly younger, in his mid- to late-twenties. He was a black Shetlander, with black curly hair and dark eyes, and either he grew a beard quickly or he hadn't bothered to shave this morning, for there was already a blue shadow on his chin. He was dressed as he had been yesterday, in a navy boiler suit that smelt strongly of kye, and rubber boots. It was hard to tell, for his face wore the same sullen expression as before, but I thought he was upset about Berwin's disappearance. 'No sign of him?' he asked abruptly.

'No footprints back to the house,' Gavin said. 'Unless there are some in the yard here.'

Bruce was silent for a long moment. 'I think there might have been,' he said at last, then thought again, and shook his head.

108

'No. Maybe. I can't tell. There are too many folk coming and going, and the snow's lain since yesterday, and it froze last night.' He paused to look around the yard, criss-crossed with tyre tracks and feet going from house to byre and workshop. I could see Leonard's work boots heading to the workshop, Sheila's town boots stepping towards the drive. I tried to remember what Frigg was wearing on her feet, and thought it might have been some sort of fur-lined boots, mid-calf length. Bruce's wellingtons tramped in and out of the byre, with a barrow wheel between them. There was a pair of trainers weaving about. I nodded to them. 'Are those Berwin's?'

'Berwin's or Robin's. They both wear trainers. Robin was here earlier, taking Berwin's bike to go to the shop.'

Gavin's head went up. 'He took Berwin's bike? When exactly?'

Bruce paused to think about it. 'He was just coming back as I got to work. Half past eight. I kent it was the shop, because he had a carrier bag, and the paper was sticking out of the top of it.'

Gavin turned to look over at the shop. It was only a mile across the water from here, if that, but to get to it Robin would have had to cycle to the main road, down through Lower Voe, up to the really main Lerwick road where Sheila had got on the bus and back around to the shop. The road had been cleared, of course, but I'd have thought it'd take him at least ten minutes each way.

Gavin was thinking that too. 'So,' he said, 'Robin took the bike about the time he'd have expected Berwin to be wanting it to get to school?'

Bruce's voice hardened. 'Master Robin wouldn't have bothered about that. It was there, so he'd use it. Any tool to his hand was his. His brother could get the school bus, or get his mother to run him.' He cleared his throat and spat on the ground. 'Berwin wouldn't mind, not if it was for Robin.'

He didn't need to say he didn't like Robin. His voice rang with it. *Any tool to his hand . . .*

'Bruce,' I said. He turned to face me, moving his whole massive body around to look at me squarely. 'Who d'you think had the idea of the trick? Was it Berwin, or did someone else put him up to it?'

His mouth opened as if he was going to answer, then he paused and thought again. His face closed against me. 'I couldn't say who put him up to it,' he said at last. 'But where there's trouble you'll find Robin somewhere at the back of it.'

'How long have you known him?' Gavin asked.

'Robin?' Bruce frowned, working it out. 'Twelve years. I came here from school. I was sixteen, and Robin was just into secondary. Berwin, he was a toddler, and Sheila was still in primary.' His voice softened as he said her name, then hardened again. 'Even then, Robin was up to all sorts of tricks. Using them to cover up for him.' He glanced at the door of Leonard's workshop, and spoke with contempt. 'Loki suits him fine.'

I wondered what he meant for a moment, then remembered the carvings. Loki with Robin's blazing hair. The trickster. I wondered how badly a clever twelve-year-old had treated a big, slow-moving sixteen-year-old who'd come to his house as a servant.

There was a step at the door of the workshop. Leonard drew the curtain aside, and set the sign out. He glanced at us as he withdrew into the shed again.

'I'd better get back to my work,' Bruce said.

He turned and trudged away into the byre. The chains clanked and there was a low moo as he went in. The door closed behind him.

'I don't like it,' Gavin said abruptly, once we were safely in the car. 'Leonard sees the essence of people for his carvings, but he's blind to the reality of people around him. Bruce may be big enough for a giant, but he's not stupid. Loki's pranks were funny in the stories of the gods, but I bet he gave Bruce a hard time when he first came to work there. Frigg's his mother-goddess, and Helge's his mystic, but he can't see that they're ordinary women locked in a duel over the same man.' He looked at me and smiled. 'I'd likely better no' say any more.'

'It's okay,' I said. 'She was sounding off to me. Listen, though, I think I know what that visit yesterday morning was about. The muscle-men, I mean.' Quickly, as we drove along the main road towards Brae, I filled him in on Helge's fight with the doctor. 'That was the testimony they wanted withdrawn.'

'She must be a key witness if they've sent someone all the way up here.' He frowned. 'Or maybe they used local talent. I was too busy with trows to follow that car registration up yesterday.'

'Maybe Helge's digging her heels in. Maybe they already tried by phone, and she refused. Anyway, I think she might have had someone in her house this morning. Someone sleeping in her sitting room. The curtains were still drawn but the fire was smoking as if it was freshly lit.'

'Berwin?' He gave me a sideways look. 'Leonard? Or someone else entirely?'

I shrugged. 'I don't know.' I remembered Robin's venomous tone. *You get back to your visitor, Mother.* Would he have spoken like that about Berwin? And if he'd been part of the vanishing trick, he'd have known where Berwin was. 'But from the way Frigg was speaking, she'd be too proud to phone Helge and ask if Berwin was there. Might be worth a try, just so we can rule that out.'

There was a lay-by ahead. Gavin pulled into it, and took his phone out. A moment finding the number, then he dialled. Helge answered after only two rings, voice anxious. 'Yes?'

'Mrs Helge Callahan?'

I could tell from the silence that she'd recognised this was official. Her voice slowed. 'Speaking. Who is this?'

111

'Mrs Callahan, this is Inspector Macrae of the local police. I was wondering if you had Berwin with you.'

'Berwin?' She sounded startled. 'He's at school, surely, or has term ended already?'

'No,' Gavin said, 'he's not at school. You haven't heard the news, then?'

'No. What news?'

'He did a clever trowie vanishing trick in the night.'

'Ah. No, I've barely been across the doorstep this morning.' She paused, as if she was thinking what to say. There was a touch of amusement in her voice when she spoke again. 'So he's having fun mystifying everyone. Well, I'm sure he'll come home before it's dark.'

'Might he be hiding out at your son Robin's studio?'

I was about to shake my head when I remembered why I'd been there, and checked the movement.

'No. No, I'm sure he's not.' Her voice was firmer now. 'Sorry I can't help. I hope you find him soon.' There was a click as she put the phone down.

Gavin was silent for a moment, then he put the Land Rover into gear and drove on. 'Not totally convincing. I'll get the duty officer to call, maybe. I'm reluctant to interfere in a family feud. If he's safe and sound at Helge's, we'll leave them to fight it out between them all. I just want to know that he is safe and sound. Inga's daughter, Vaila, she's my best bet. What teenage boy could fail to boast to his girlfriend that his trick worked?'

112

Chapter Ten

perrnyimm: prim and proper (Scots, pernim: cheeky, saucy, pert)

The school was in party mode. As soon as we walked in we were hit by blaring Christmas music which sounded suspiciously like the same CD as in our day. The classrooms were empty; there were disco lights flashing in the canteen and children swarming in the corridors, wearing the brightest of Christmas jumpers and Santa hats, reindeer horns with flashing lights, or tinsel in their hair.

'Last day shenanigans,' I said. It was an odd feeling to be back inside the school again, with all these youngsters looking so much more sophisticated than we ever had. Good grief, they were wearing make-up, which even Inga never did, and giving us sideways glances as if we were old people who'd strayed in from another universe. 'The office is this way.'

The secretary was expecting us. 'I'll just take you along to the Depute Head.'

The Depute Head and I recognised each other straight off: he was Mr Morrison, my old maths teacher. 'Cass, good to see you again.' He shook hands with Gavin. 'Inspector Macrae. Dave Morrison. Nice to meet you. How're you finding Shetland?'

'I'll tell you once I've found my feet,' Gavin said.

'You're looking for news of Berwin Callahan, is that right?

Nothing serious, I hope.' You could see that he wasn't in the least bit worried about hearing a tale of vandalism or shoplifting; not Berwin.

'I hope not too, but his mother's anxious. Now, I've absolutely no official standing in this at all, it's not been called in as a case, but I'm hoping we can just make sure the boy's all right. Have you heard about the trick he played?'

Mr Morrison rolled his eyes. 'Heard about it at least twice from every pupil I've spoken to since registration. He vanished from the middle of a field and hasn't been seen since.'

Gavin's eyes grew intent. 'Oh? Is that the word going round the school, that he hasn't been seen since?'

'That's certainly the way it's being told, but I'd presumed he was lying low at home, for maximum effect.' He frowned. 'Actually, I was expecting him to saunter in at breaktime, to be the hero of the party.'

'You're sure, sir, that he hasn't?'

'I'll double-check.' He lifted the phone. 'Eileen, has Berwin turned up in school? . . . No, fine, thanks.' He redialled. 'Hi, Joanne, Dave here. I don't suppose Berwin turned up for the buffet? Yes, do ask them.' There was a pause as Joanne asked around. 'No? Grand, thank you.' He looked across at Gavin. 'He's not signed our late arrivals book, and the cooks are certain he wasn't at the buffet lunch. Now, what can we do to help?' He waved at the chairs. 'Have a seat.'

We perched on the school-issue armchairs. 'I'd like to talk to his particular group,' Gavin said. 'I'm with you that I think it's all part of his mystery disappearing act, and I rather suspect he's lying low somewhere.'

Mr Morrison nodded.

'Well, his mother's worried. If I can reassure her that one of his pals has heard from him today, we can leave him to go home in his own good time, and get the hot water he deserves.'

Mr Morrison frowned and shifted some papers on his desk, looking out of the window. Then he looked at me. 'Cass, you know him from your sailing. What do you think?'

'No,' I said. It came out louder than I'd meant. I repeated it, more quietly. 'No. I don't think it's like him.' I looked at Gavin. 'He's bright enough to have thought of the stunt but not tricksy enough. And missing the last day of school, no. I'd forgotten what day it was. There are no lessons and everyone just messes about until the afternoon disco, but it's all anyone's going to talk about until Christmas takes over – who danced with who, and who looked at who, all that. I don't like it.'

Mr Morrison nodded. 'Added to that, he's not one to give his mother a day's anxiety.'

'I believe there's a girlfriend to impress.'

'Vaila,' Mr Morrison said instantly. 'Now if he thought of the idea, she'd be the one to think of a practical way of doing it. You'll have heard about our trows?'

'Oh, yes,' Gavin said.

'She's leading my list for the organiser of that stunt. Well, let's see what Berwin's friends have to say. I'll need to be present, of course.'

Gavin nodded, and smiled at me. 'Cass is completely unofficial; we're on our way to Lerwick for Christmas shopping.'

Naturally he'd heard all about an ex-pupil taking up with Shetland's newest police officer, the one in the kilt. 'Cass was unofficially where she shouldn't have been most of her schooldays.'

'There's no question of third-degree,' Gavin said. 'I simply want to explain the situation, ask if any of them have heard from him, and if one has, ask them to text him and tell him to call his mother.'

Mr Morrison nodded. 'I can't see any of these parents objecting to that. You'll know his pals anyway, Cass, they're your sailors.' He got on the phone again, and a minute later a list of names was being boomed around the school: 'Rainbow, Vaila, Drew, John-Lowrie, go to Mr Morrison's office.'

By the time Mr Morrison had set four chairs out, there was shuffling at the door, then a tentative knock. Vaila and Rainbow were first in, looking suitably mortified and apprehensive at this public summons. They were followed by Drew, Berwin's closest rival for first place across any watery finish line, mad as a South Sea second mate, hair still in a topknot of blond curls, and with all the devious instinct that Berwin lacked. Last was John-Lowrie, who usually crewed for him, a big, quiet boy who acted as his backup. Pedigree . . . it escaped me for a moment, then I remembered. He was some kind of kin to the Callahans, though his hair was a paler shade of red than Robin's blazing orange. He lived next door to Rainbow, at the Voe end of the Kergord valley. His father owned the plant-hire firm here in Brae, and John-Lowrie and Drew usually spent their Saturdays oiled to the elbows underneath various trucks and cranes. They were Berwin's classmates, in S3, and the girls were the year below.

Seeing them in these unfamiliar surroundings made me realise how close to being adult they were. Maybe it was the clothes. Drew looked several inches taller in skinny black jeans and a grey-print t-shirt; John-Lowrie wasn't as tall, but he had an imposing width of shoulder, and just a hint of red down on his upper lip. Any First World War recruiting sergeant would have taken them. Vaila and Rainbow were obviously younger by comparison, but they were both 'dressed' for the disco, with glittery tops and make-up achieving wax-doll complexions. They could have been anything up to sixteen.

They sat themselves down, pernyimm as you please, both feet on the floor and hands in their laps. My instinct said that they all knew very well this would be about Berwin, and that though they were doing their best to look unconcerned, they weren't quite easy about him. Mr Morrison got them seated,

116

and made an 'over to you' gesture to Gavin, who leaned forward towards them, smiling reassuringly. 'This is good, that all of you ken me already. Drew, isn't it, that found the bicycle in the Longship case?'

Drew was naturally too old to look impressed, but his shoulders broadened at the reminder.

'And John-Lowrie, you're crew – I saw you at the regatta in September. Vaila and Rainbow, of course.' He sat back, relaxed. 'Now, this is absolutely not an official police matter. All it is, is this: I had a phone call from Berwin's mother, worrying that he wasn't in school where she thought he was. She's got the wind up good and proper, and all I want to do is reassure her before we have to embarrass him with a helicopter search.'

Four horrified faces turned towards him.

'Have any of you heard from him since last night?'

They gave each other uncertain looks.

'I'm no' trying to find out how his trick was done,' Gavin added. 'Very clever – have you seen it?'

Rainbow and John-Lowrie nodded. 'It looked really cool from the bus,' Rainbow volunteered. 'You could see the footprints just stopping, and then the empty boiler suit.'

'No texts, no calls?'

Vaila looked at Drew, then back at Gavin, and nodded. 'He messaged me to say he'd done it, and he'd see me today.' A flash of that uneasiness I was sensing crossed her face. 'I've been expecting him to walk in since breaktime.'

'What time did he message you?'

'A bit after eleven.' Vaila fished in her pocket and produced her phone. '23.07.'

'I heard too,' Drew conceded. 'He said he'd done it, same as to Vaila, and I was to set the rumour going that he hadn't been seen since. It was just for a fun,' he added defensively.

'And today? Any word?'

117

Drew shook his head. 'Like Vaila said, we were expecting to see him.'

'Okay,' Gavin said. 'Well, he's not answering his mother's calls, but have any of you tried to call him?'

Vaila nodded. 'I tried when he didn't turn up at break, but he didn't answer. Then Drew told me about the "never seen since" thing, so I thought he must have had an idea for an extra effect, maybe reappearing the same way or something.' She tossed her dark head, looking exactly like Inga. 'I was miffed he hadn't told me, so I left him to it.'

'I see,' Gavin said. He thought for a moment, then looked at Drew. 'How about you go out into the corridor and phone him? If he doesn't answer, leave the kind of message that would get him phoning back straight away.'

Drew nodded, and headed out. We sat and waited. Drew's voice echoed along the corridor. 'Boy, there's a right collieshang going on here. I need to speak wi' you, get back to me, right? Soon as you can.'

Mr Morrison fiddled with a pencil on his desk, pretending not to listen, but Vaila and Rainbow were giving each other uneasy looks, and John-Lowrie stared steadfastly at the toes of his trainers. My instincts said there was something they weren't telling us. 'Vaila,' I said, on a sudden impulse, 'since he's not turned up at school, what do you think now that Berwin meant when he said he'd see you today?'

It was a shot at a venture, and I'd hit gold. For a second her face showed acute alarm, then the shutters went down. Her face smoothed to innocence; her dark eyes opened wide and met mine with an air of telling all she knew. 'I still think he'll be coming to school. Maybe he's got some clever plan to reappear in the middle of the disco. Lights down in the last dance, set off those flashers on stage and then appear in the heart of us while we're all blinded.'

Drew had come in while she was in the middle of answering.

He gave her a warning glance, and she fell silent. Drew looked frankly round at us, gesturing with the phone in his hand. 'He's not picking up.'

'Okay,' Gavin said. He looked down a moment, then raised his eyes again, fixing them with his sea-grey stare. 'And there's been no kind of rows or falling out among you that might have made him want to give you all a fright?'

The relief on their faces was palpable. They could answer this. All four heads shook. 'Naa,' Drew said, for all of them. 'Berwin's not the falling-out kind.'

I looked at Vaila, and she shook her head again. 'Nothing.' Her voice had the ring of absolute confidence. Whatever had Berwin hiding, it wasn't a first-romance fall-out.

'And . . .' The faces went wary again. Gavin spread his hands. 'I'm sorry to ask you this, but has he mentioned any difficulties with his parents?'

Now they almost laughed. 'No,' Vaila said, straight off. 'He's not . . . Berwin's not . . .' She waved her hands for a moment, trying to sum up the sheer niceness of Berwin. 'Cass, you ken him! He gets on wi' aabody, even his folk. Really, there's nothing like that.'

'So why's he not contacting you?'

'I think,' John-Lowrie began. To his embarrassment, his voice came out in a bass rumble. A scarlet blush crept up under his white skin, but he took a gulp of air and tried again. 'I dinna ken what exactly he's up to, but I'm sure he's no' trying to gluff everyone.' He looked at Gavin. 'I dinna ken what it's like in the cities, but up here we're used to going off and doing things and nobody worrying about us. It'd never occur to him that there would be such a fuss.'

I found myself reassessing him as he spoke. I was so used to his playing second-fiddle to the mercurial Drew that I'd missed this sound intelligence. The others, I noticed, were listening too, and nodding.

'If he's adding to the mystery of his vanishing trick by bunking off school, he'll be up in the hills with faerdie meat and binoculars, watching birds, or gone along the shoreline to watch otters. He's interested in wildlife, well, we both are.' He blushed again. 'We're both keen on photography and he's just gotten a new phone with a good camera in it. He was dead keen to try it out on the otters.'

He flashed a glance round at the others, and Vaila came in to support him. 'Yea, he's been watching this holt along the shoreline from Helge's house. He saw the cubs on Saturday. He thought it was the first time they'd been out, and he couldn't wait for the holidays so he could watch properly. You ken what it's like ee noo, it's still half-dark when you arrive at school, and it's coming dusk when you leave again.'

It was exaggeration, but a fair point.

'If he was watching otters,' Mr Morrison said, 'he'd have his phone on silent or switched off altogether.'

'If there was a signal at all,' John-Lowrie said. He seemed to have taken over the leadership from Drew. 'He'll maybe no' even get Drew's message till he wins home again. Maybe if Frigg looked and found there was food missing, that would reassure her.'

'I'll suggest that,' Gavin said. He rose. 'Thanks to you all.' He brought a card out from his sporran, and handed it to John-Lowrie. 'If you hear anything, let me know at once.'

'Please,' Rainbow said. She got a barrage of warning looks from the others, and stopped.

'Go on,' Gavin said.

I saw her desperately trying to think of something different to say, and failing, under Gavin's steady look. 'I was just wondering if you were still going to do a helicopter search?'

'That depends on how worried his mother is,' Gavin said. 'And on what my superiors think. I'd have been happier if any of you had heard from him today, but it's reassured me that you're not particularly worried.' He looked over at Mr Morrison. 'That's me done.'

Mr Morrison gave a long, slow look around the group. I could tell that he wasn't quite satisfied either. 'Nothing else to add?'

The four heads shook.

'Off you go then.'

They went, with John-Lowrie turning at the last to look back at Gavin. 'I'll let you ken if I hear from him.'

'Well?' Gavin asked, once we were back in the Land Rover.

'There's something,' I said slowly. 'Not a falling-out; they were all fine with you asking about that. Something they've got planned for later.'

Gavin nodded. 'Yes. You were spot on with that question.'

'And Rainbow worrying about a chopper search, though that could be just wanting to spare Berwin the embarrassment.'

'Vaila was thinking along the lines of something spectacular by way of reappearance. Or do you think that was camouflage?'

'Not sure. No, I think she was expecting him at school. The dorts at being kept in the dark were genuine.'

Gavin sighed. 'All too inconclusive. Well, I'll report back to Frigg, but my feeling is we need to call this one in.' He plugged his phone in and dialled. 'Frigg? Hi, it's Gavin Macrae here. No word from Berwin?'

Her voice came out clearly, flustered. 'No, no, nothing.' Her breath jerked, as if we'd caught her in the middle of hauling feed sacks around.

'His friends had texts from him last night, after he'd done his vanishing trick. They were expecting him at school today, but he also told them to spread the rumour that he hadn't been seen since the vanishing, so he may have another plan to reappear.'

She gave a little stifled cry. 'Do you think so?'

'I think they're up to something. They're uneasy, but not seriously worried. One of them suggested that he might be off along the shore watching otter cubs. Did you notice if there was lunch-style food missing?'

'I don't know . . . let me go and look.' The phone gave off a faint hum as we waited, as if she'd left it by some machine. We heard the fridge door open and shut again, then the clang of something that might be the bread bin lid. 'Yes, maybe . . . I'm not sure. Sheila sometimes takes rolls for her lunch. I don't know . . . ' A tinge of embarrassment crept into her voice; she paused, then took a hold of herself and spoke firmly. 'Leonard thinks I'm just making a fuss. He's off to the town as if everything was normal. If Berwin's friends aren't worrying, well, I don't know what I should do. He was speaking about the otter cubs the other day, and looking forward to the holidays, to sit and watch them.' She took another breath. 'And he wouldn't have expected the school would phone me if he was absent. He's never off, and of course if there's a dentist appointment or something I let the school know beforehand.' She ground to a halt.

'How about clothes? Has he a special camouflage jacket for watching wildlife?'

'Oh, no . . . just his usual black one. Let me look.' She was quicker to come back this time. 'It's not there, but then he wouldn't have gone out without a jacket, in this cold. He'd be wearing it whatever he was up to.'

'I think,' Gavin said, 'that I want to pass this higher up the chain. It may well be that he's happily watching otters in a sheltered bay with no mobile signal, and I think that's far more likely than that any harm's come to him.'

Frigg gave a choked cry at that, but didn't speak.

'Tell you what,' Gavin said, 'we're going into town. I'll call in at the station and discuss it, and then get back to you. We won't start a major search without speaking to you again.'

'Yes. Thank you.' She rang off, leaving the air still jangling with tension. Gavin and I looked at each other and shrugged.

'I'd have liked to do our first Christmas shop together,' Gavin said. 'Ah well. I'll stop at the station first, and see what they think. We can work it from there.'

He started the car and we drove off towards Lerwick: back through Brae, and around the bends of the motorway to where we could look out over Swarback's Minn.

'Can you slow down?' I asked. 'Maybe even pull over? There's a passing place just before the last bend into Voe.'

'Awkward to get out of,' Gavin said, but he crossed the road and stopped the Land Rover. Now we were looking straight across at Tirval's house on the hill, and diagonally at Helge's, but the sun was already touching the hills, and blazing straight in our faces, so I couldn't see as well as I'd hoped.

'If he's watching otters,' I said, 'it's likely to be on one of these beaches across there, unless he's gone over the hill to Grobsness. I thought we might see him from here.'

I took the monocular and looked, but it was no good. The beaches were in shadow now, and the low sun flared in the lens. I still tried, along to the point from Tirval's, and then slowly back again, as far as Helge's beach. The light shone from both downstairs windows of her cottage. I went further back, as far as Robin's studio. I'd just steadied the monocular when a dark figure came into view, walking quickly along the side of the house and into the door. It was too far away to see who it was. The light went on. I waited for a moment, but the door remained closed.

I shook my head and handed the monocular to Gavin. 'It's too dark to see properly, but I don't think he's there.'

'If he had been, he'd be heading for home now.'

'Someone just went into Robin's studio, from the house direction. Lights on in Helge's.'

Gavin began at the point, scrutinising slowly, as I had, then

123

put the instrument back in its case. 'No. I don't think he's there either. Someone came out of the studio with a backpack.'

I could just make out the dark figure moving on the white hill, heading for Leonard and Frigg's house. Something was nagging at my memory. Something Frigg had said didn't make sense. She'd said there'd been no word . . . checking food . . . watching otters . . . 'That's it,' I said suddenly. 'Of course Berwin would have known.' I turned towards Gavin. 'Frigg said Berwin wouldn't have known about the school's system of phoning if you didn't turn up without warning beforehand, but of course he would. Just because he'd never used it, his pals would have. He'd have known that if they didn't hear from his mam first thing then they'd phone home.'

Gavin drove on in silence, thinking about it; through Upper Voe, with the Mulla lights twinkling in the dimming light, and onto the main road to Lerwick. Ahead of us, up on the Kames, the orange digger lights flashed. 'Their last day, before they go home for Christmas,' Gavin said. 'So . . . if Berwin knew the school would phone, either he's deliberately worrying his parents, or he meant to be at school, and something happened to prevent him getting there.'

He said no more, but there was a frown between his brows all the way to Lerwick.

Chapter Eleven

in an aet: uneasy, agitated (Old Norse, at: agitation)

The wind had died completely by the time we reached Lerwick. The wind turbines turned lazily above the golf course; the power station chimney smoke went straight up. Four of the big pelagic boats were in at their new pier by the ferry terminal on the outskirts of Lerwick, green, blue, black, red under the gleaming white superstructure, floating on mirror images of themselves. The sun was barely above the rooftops. Now was when it stood still, these days each side of the solstice. Only after Christmas would the light begin to creep back, a minute and a half more each morning and evening.

Gavin parked at the police station and went in. He'd be a while. I got out and stretched, then walked the twenty metres to the Hillhead and stood for a moment between the dolphin lamp posts of the Town Hall, looking out over the town. The War Memorial was capped with snow, but someone had shaken off the wreaths, and the poppies lay blood-red against the white. There were brightly waterproofed children chasing and laughing in the bairns' playpark beyond it, making joyful child-sized footprints in lines and circles. The houses in King Harald Street, three-storey houses built around the turn of the century for Lerwick's well-to-do, had Christmas trees in their windows and lights flashing from their gardens; the bonniest, for my money, was the one with a tree in each of its three main windows, lit simply with gold lights, a big one in the drawing-room bay window, a medium one exactly above it, and a little one in the attic dormer. Above me, the Town Hall clock bonged the first quarter.

I was standing there musing when a young woman in a dark-pink jacket and white scarf came walking briskly up the road that led back down to the waterfront. She slowed as she approached the police station, then stopped altogether, still on the other side of the road from it.

She was small and plump. Her hair was streaked fair over its natural brown, and cut in one of those tousled urchin bobs. Her face was familiar, but I don't think I'd have recognised who she was if I hadn't been thinking about Berwin. She was Sheila, Frigg's daughter, who worked down at the Ness. She'd picked him up from sailing more often than Robin had, or Frigg. Seeing her now, I realised she was Leonard's carved farm servant who carried buckets and fed the hens. She had the air of someone who got landed with tasks. 'I'm too busy, Sheila'll do it.'

She stood there for a moment, looking at the police station, round face worried. She glanced around her, took a step into the road, and another, then stepped back as a car came along. Her second attempt got her across and as far as the road leading up into the station car park, where she stopped again. She stood still, looking at the Police sign, then turned her head quickly. A burst of laughing chatter was moving towards us from the steep road that led down to the street, and a flock of young women laden with carrier bags came around the corner.

Sheila spun away from them and headed back down the road she'd come up with short, quick steps.

I was still staring after her when Gavin came out, looking around. I waved and went over to him.

'I'll need to stay in longer. Why don't you go and do the Co-op, then get a taxi back here with the shopping?' He made a rueful face. 'Sorry to land you with it.'

'Policeman's girlfriend,' I said. 'I know. You have the list.'

He produced it, along with a fistful of rather crumpled twenties. 'I'd meant to use my card, but I'll get more cash later. This should be enough.'

'I'll use my card,' I said, and handed the money back.

I'd said it more abruptly than I'd meant to. His face stilled. He shoved the cash back into his pocket. 'Of course you will.'

Suddenly it was a miserable day, and I couldn't see how to put it right.

'I won't kiss you in front of the station windows. See you later.' He turned away.

'Hang on,' I said. I needed to say something. *Make with the words, Cass.* 'Sorry,' I managed. 'Didn't mean to be so snippet.'

His hand closed around mine. 'Good luck with the babysitting. I'll join you as soon as I can.'

I nodded. My heart rose again. 'Gavin, just now . . . Berwin's sister came up here, hung around for a bit, then got cold feet and headed off.'

His head lifted. 'Sheila Callahan?'

I nodded. 'A minute before you came out.'

'Okay. I'll try and follow that up.' Station window or not, he leaned over to kiss me. 'See you later.'

I got the bags from the Land Rover and headed off Co-opwards.

The next hour was hellish. It helped that there was obviously some Co-op Order of Preference meaning that things were in roughly the same place as in the Brae Co-op, but I still had to do the occasional bit of backtracking, to the annoyance of people who wrote their lists according to where they'd find things. A radio boomed out, interrupting the Christmas

127

hits with announcements like 'Have you got the right stuffing for your turkey?' and 'Don't forget to claim your stamps on all Co-op brands.' I had a headache before I'd even left the fruit. And the lights were neon-bright, and the place was crowded, and they were out of Cat's tolerated brand of cat food, and when I finally made it to the end a family with two full trolleys nipped into the checkout queue in front of me. '*Never again,*' I swore to myself. If Christmas in a house was really going to be this much kerfuffle, next year I'd make up the list on the first Sunday of Advent, and buy a few things each week in Brae, to avoid this last-minute trauchle.

I finally got myself out of there, and into a taxi. There was no sign of Gavin at the police station. I dumped the shopping in the Land Rover and checked my watch. Half past three. A Peerie Shop drinking chocolate was calling me, and I'd taken several steps towards the street when I remembered we were in Advent, and drinking chocolate with cream on the top was out. *And it's still chocolate even without the cream,* my better self pointed out. My worser self, which had just suffered an hour of busy supermarket, wanted to kick a stone like a teenager, and had to make do with striding extra fast down the hill. I had an hour and a half to kill before the bus. I could do a cup of tea.

The Peerie Shop was stowed out with people and carrier bags, but I managed to squeeze into a corner downstairs. My tea had just arrived when Gavin phoned. 'I'll be here a while yet. We're not happy. But I'll get home to feed the cats – at least, I'll be home before you. They have a bowlful of biscuits, so they won't starve. Good luck with Peerie Charlie.'

'Thanks. See you later.'

I clasped my cold hands round the mug and swirled the tea, thinking. It sounded like there was going to be some kind of search; I wasn't sure what that would involve on land: cars, officers, door-to-door, the chopper, the lifeboat scanning the beaches? I sent Gavin a text: *Don't forget Tirval xxx*

His reply came straight back. *Phoned him already. Says he hasn't seen him. xxxx*

I sighed, finished my tea and headed back out into the cold. The Street was busy with shoppers, including a lot of men with beards, preparing to be Vikings at one of the fire festivals that kept Shetlanders occupied from the first Friday in January till the third Friday in March. There was a rather sparse, twiggy Christmas tree at the Market Cross, its lights not lit, with a notice proclaiming that it was a 'Talking Tree' and inviting children to text it. Good grief. Sometimes the supposedly rational modern world baffled me. When Gavin and I had children, they'd get the traditional religious myths and make up their own minds about believing them later, instead of this nonsense about talking trees at Christmas and Easter rabbits laying chocolate eggs.

The pause for tea had at least given me inspiration for possible stocking items for Gavin. I got some bits and pieces in the Shetland Times Bookshop, patronised the chocolate shop, got a good pair of gloves in LHD, then strolled gently along the Esplanade to the Viking bus station. Five to five. The bus would be leaving sometime soon.

I'd just settled myself on the plastic bum-park in the shelter when I saw Sheila Callahan coming up from the Ness towards the bus station. Of course this would be her bus too, stopping at Voe on the way to Brae and Hillswick. I did an unobtrusive walk along to the toilet, then came back into the queue behind her. If I could manage to sit beside her, perhaps she'd tell me what she'd chickened out of telling Gavin.

I was in luck. It was obviously a busy bus, for they'd laid on a proper coach-style one, not one of the modern sort where everything you did was visible to every other passenger, but with high-backed seats where you could talk in private. It was filling up by the time I got on, but she'd bagged a window seat, and the one beside her was still free. I paused, said 'Hi,' and swung myself in beside her.

She looked even more worried than she had earlier. Her hands fidgeted with the strap of her bag, and as we passed the Hillhead she looked along at the police station, biting her lip.

'You're Sheila, aren't you?' I said. 'Berwin's sister?'

She visibly jumped at his name.

'I'm Cass,' I said. 'You used to pick him up from the sailing sessions.'

She'd got a hold of herself now, but her breathing still came quickly, and the colour in her cheeks drained away and rose again. 'Oh, yea, I'm sorry. I didn't ken you for a moment.' She took a deep breath and began chattering, 'Yea, he fairly loved the sailing. I hope you're going to do it again next summer. He did right well at the regatta you held for them too. Are you biding on your boat for the winter? Surely no, in this cold.'

I shook my head. 'I'm at the Ladie.' I gave a pause, then began in a chatty tone, 'I was round at yours just this morning to look at your brother's studio. I bought one of his paintings.'

Her face relaxed instantly. She smiled, and her eyes lit up with family pride. 'Oh, for a Christmas present? Which one?'

'One of the fox ones – the vixen with the cubs tumbling about her. I liked the dog fox on his hill, but it wasn't for sale.'

Sheila nodded. 'That's a special one, but I like the ones with the cubs best, they're so cute. He's amazing, Robin. He's my stepbrother, you know, so we're not actually related, but we're really close.'

I looked at her glowing eyes and felt my heart sink. That clever, malicious young man and this kindly, homely girl? The benefits of their closeness would go one way, I betted. *Any tool to his hand was his*, Bruce had said. I wondered how often he borrowed money from her.

'He used to live with us, well, he kind of came and went

between us and Helge, but he and Berwin shared the big bedroom, and I had the little one.' She sighed. 'It was the fine, being all three of us together. But when he went off to university then Mam said it was time Berwin had the room to himself, and got rid of Robin's bed. There was a dreadful row about it, and Dad was mad, but Robin was even madder, and said if she was going to be like that he'd turn the old byre into a studio, and live there. Dad sided with him, and went to live at Helge's for a bit – ' She seemed suddenly to realise that she was talking to a relative stranger and waved the conversation away with a gesture of one hand. 'That was all ages ago, I don't know why I'm sheeksin on about it. And he's made the studio really fine.'

'It's great. He said he'd had a few visitors on the gallery trail.' I paused for a moment, then continued casually, 'He pointed out Berwin's stunt in the field, the disappearing act. I went along in the boat to look at it. How did Berwin do it?'

The cloud came over her brow again. 'I don't know how exactly.' Her face brightened again. 'But it was my idea – the idea of him disappearing like that and leaving only rubber boots and his boiler suit behind. We all thought it would be really cool, and we had a few ideas, but nothing that would work, until Berwin told me he'd cracked it. He was really pleased with himself, but he wouldn't tell me how he did it. And now . . .' She trailed to a halt and bit her lip. Then she turned and looked at me. 'Was it your man who phoned me, about Berwin?'

I nodded, and waited.

'I'm faered something's happened to him. He meant to go to the school, I ken he did. If he'd been going to skive off . . .' She reddened and broke off. 'Promise you won't tell Mam?'

Intrigued, I nodded again.

She lowered her voice. 'See, I've phoned for him a couple of times, just said he wasn't well, and he'd be back tomorrow.

There was one time he was watching a nest up in the hills, merlin chicks, and he wanted to see them hatch, and there was another time, I forget what that was, but you see, if he'd wanted to miss school he'd have got me to phone. He was going to go there.'

'That's what I thought.'

'And then, the other thing I wasn't sure about, well, I didn't stop and look for his bike, but there weren't any tracks in the snow.' I gave her a puzzled look, and she expanded. 'When I went out for the bus this morning. I was a bit annoyed that he'd gone off like that without telling me all about it, because we aye breakfast together, and it was my idea, so I thought he'd tell me how it had gone, but he wouldn't speak that night, even though I waited up for him coming back in. Well, I heard him come in, and expected him to come and tell me, but he just went to the bathroom and then to bed. So I went and keeked round his door, but he was in bed by then, and he just said sshhh, I'd wake Mam, and he'd tell me in the morning, and then in the morning he wasn't there.' She tossed her head, just as Vaila had done. 'Well, I thought, if he's going to be like that, hell mend him.' She frowned. 'Except that it wasn't like him. So I went off for me bus, and I kinda half noticed that the last tracks in the yard were Bruce going home. There was a fresh fall of snow, you ken, not much but enough to make it all covered again, though you could see the older footprints under it, but it was easy to see what ones were new. There was Bruce going to his van, and the van tracks out, and Dad heading out to the byre. Nothing other, and at the turning to the road there was no sign of bike tyres. I thought then he'd maybe slept in.' She gave me a shamefaced look. 'And I thought, serve him right, for no' letting me share what he'd done when it was my idea, I'm no' making myself late going back and waking him.' Her eyes filled with tears. 'Then the policeman phoned and said he wasn't at home or at school.'

132

'If he didn't go out the front, is there a back door? Facing down towards Robin's studio?'

Sheila nodded. 'But I didn't look at it. I wasn't needing to go out there. You think he might be hiding out with Robin, to give everyone a fright?' Her face brightened, then clouded again. 'But he didn't need to scare me. I haven't been able to think since that call.' She fumbled in her bag for a handkerchief. Her voice wavered. 'And I tried to phone him three times and only got the answerphone, and I tried Robin just after lunch, and he wasn't answering either.'

I was worried she was going to burst into tears on the bus, and gave the people across the aisle an uneasy look, but they were deep in discussion of the latest twist in some TV series. Sheila gave a couple of hiccups, then mopped her eyes and blew her nose, and lifted her head again. 'I'll try Robin again.'

She punched in the number and waited, then spoke in voicemail mode. 'Robin, is Berwin there with you? Get back to me when you get this.'

She put the phone away, and looked bleakly at me. 'What should I do?'

'Tell Gavin,' I said. 'I think they're busy organising a search right now.' I burrowed in my pocket for my phone, and found his number. 'Gavin, Cass here, I'm talking to Berwin's sister on the bus. I'll pass you over to her.'

I listened as she re-told him what she'd told me about phoning in for him, the footprints and lack of bike tracks. He made soothing noises, and she nodded, agreed, then passed the phone back.

'We're getting a search going now,' he said. 'I'll keep you posted.'

The bus was slowing down as it approached the Voe turn-off, but it didn't go down into Lower Voe; the stop was here, at the Vidlin junction. Sheila gathered her bags and began to rise. As she turned towards me, her eyes looked out of the window, at the junction car park, and her face brightened. Then she flushed, shuffled past me, and turned back once she was in the aisle.

'Good to have met up with you,' she said. 'And I'll try to stop worrying about Berwin. I'm sure he'll turn up soon.'

She stumbled along the aisle to the bus door, and got off. I looked across to the car park. There was a brown van there, with Bruce standing beside it. Sheila scurried across the road, and he took her carrier bag from her, and opened the car door. His hand rested on her back for a moment as she bent to get in.

I wondered if Sheila's family knew about them.

Chapter Twelve

ta'en the dorts: *taken offence at something, sulking (Scots,* dort*)*

Inga was in full organisation mode when I arrived. She was obviously combining dressing and feeding the troops, for she was simultaneously stirring a pan on the stove and laying plates on the table clad in a dressing gown over a silky slip, tights and bear-headed slippers.

'Thanks, Cass,' she said, as I took over the table-laying. 'It's great you got here earlier. I'll leave you to give the bairns their tea while I finish dressing. See if you can find out what's tripping their faces. Have you eaten?'

I shook my head.

'There's plenty. Stew and baked tatties in the oven.' She whisked off into the bathroom, popping her head back out to say, 'No Vaila, she's off at Rainbow's. A last sleepover before they're separated for the holidays. Not that they will be when they're only a five-mile bike ride apart.'

A sleepover at Rainbow's, huh? Maybe, I thought with a surge of relief, that was where Berwin was due to turn up again. I went off to find the children I did have, following the sound of the latest Disney must-watch. Peerie Charlie jumped up to greet me. 'Aye aye, Cass! Can we make toffee?'

'Toffee?' I said, startled. 'I don't know how.'

'She didn't say no!' he crowed triumphantly to Dawn. She

135

shrugged and contined to punch into her phone, adding 'Hi, Cass,' as an afterthought.

'Tea first,' I said firmly. 'Come on.' I held my hand out to Peerie Charlie and he switched off the cartoon and came over. I loved the feel of his little hand in mine. He was nearly four and naturally the more innocent he looked, the more you needed to watch what he was up to.

Dawn uncurled herself from the couch, tossed her phone down and followed. She was in the top year of primary now, and more like Charlie than Inga, with blue eyes and brown hair. She was the one I knew least, because Vaila tended to overshadow her at the sailing and Peerie Charlie grabbed all the attention in a domestic situation, but I didn't need to know her well to see that she was annoyed.

I doled out tatties, butter and stew, then sat down beside them. We ate to the accompaniment of Inga dipping in and out between bathroom and bedroom, and the occasional bass question from Big Charlie.

'All good?' Inga said, finally reappearing in full make-up, dark head tilted to one side, dangling silver earring in hand. She was wearing a dress of plum-coloured velvet which made the most of her curves. The strappy sandals made it clear she was walking no further than from door to car. Big Charlie was behind her. He looked surprisingly handsome in a suit, though his blond Viking looks went best with a velvet tunic and raven-winged helmet.

'Hey!' I said. 'Stunning. You don't look a day over thirty.'

'Mam isn't over thirty,' Dawn pointed out.

'Cass knows that,' Inga said. 'She was being cheeky.'

'And Dad's only thirty-one. Looking good, Mam.'

'If they give you those chocolate mints at the end, can you bring me one home?' Peerie Charlie asked.

'I'll save you mine. Now you two be good for Cass, okay? She promises not to read you sailing books or make you

136

watch sailing videos.' She gave me a pointed look. 'Don't you, Cass?'

'Behave yourselves,' Charlie said. 'Thanks, Cass.' He tousled Peerie Charlie's hair, gave Dawn a kiss, Inga kissed them both, and the pair of them headed out.

'More?' I asked. Both heads shook. 'Ice cream? Custard?'

Peerie Charlie's face brightened slightly; Dawn shook her head. I sat down again. 'Come on, you two. Out with it. What's got you so down in the dumps?'

Peerie Charlie kicked the leg of the chair opposite in a way that would have had him told off instantly if his father hadn't been halfway to the St Magnus Bay Hotel already. 'It's not fair.' His lower lip jutted. 'Vaila got to go off to Rainbow's and they're making toffee. And she said she'd share it, but I bet they eat it all and I won't get any.' His eyes filled with tears. 'I really like toffee.' He looked at me pleadingly. 'I don't think it's difficult to make. Mammy just boils it all up together, and drips it in water to see if it's ready and then I eat that bit.'

'They're having fun,' Dawn glumped. 'And I bet you anything they've got another trick planned, because Busta phoned to ask if Vaila would go in and be a waitress for the windfarm workers' Christmas do tonight, and she said no, even though she was complaining about being short of money just this morning.'

'Maybe she didn't think she could manage to be polite to them.'

Dawn ignored that. 'I wanted to go over to Rainbow's as well and she said I couldn't.'

'Well, listen,' I said. 'Let's find a recipe for toffee and make some. If you don't have the ingredients we'll go and raid the Co-op. And if we can't find the recipe for toffee we'll make something else. Biscuits or an ice cream sundae, how about that? It can't spoil your tea, because you've eaten it.'

They both brightened. Dawn got up from the table and began

to rifle through Inga's recipe books. 'Here it is! We need butter and sugar and tinned milk.'

Peerie Charlie bounced down from the table. 'Sugar.' He began opening all the cupboards he could reach, then slammed the last door, lip sticking out again. 'Vaila's taken it all.'

'We've got butter,' Dawn said. 'And the tin of milk.'

'It was in her rucksack.' Peerie Charlie wasn't going to be pacified that easily. 'I saw it and I asked her if she was making toffee and she said yes. She had bags and bags of it, and she didn't leave us even one . . .' His voice trailed downwards into a grizzle.

I picked him up off the chair and hugged him to me. 'Listen,' I said, 'you can have either a grievance or a good time. You can either keep dorting about Vaila or you can forget about her and enjoy yourself. Which is it going to be?'

'I can't forget about her,' Peerie Charlie protested. 'She took all the sugar.'

'We're going to buy more. C'mon now, take a deep breath and think all your crossness about Vaila being mean into your breath and then blow it all away.'

'Then it'll be in the kitchen,' Dawn said.

'Right,' I said, hanging on to my patience with an effort. I went over to the kitchen door and flung it wide open. 'Deep breath, and down the voe with all your grumping. Then we can have fun.'

Dawn was giving me that 'adults are mad' look but Peerie Charlie blew a huge breath, thought for a moment, then gave me a big smile. 'Like mindfulness,' Dawn conceded, and followed suit.

We raided the Co-op for sugar. We were on our way home when there was a thrumming noise in the air and a bright light in the sky down towards Aith. The helicopter was out searching for Berwin. If I hadn't thought asking about Vaila would have set them off again, I'd have probed a bit more about what she was up to, but the sound of what they'd said reassured me.

She and Rainbow wouldn't be having a toffee-fest night if she was worried sick about whether Berwin was okay. I hoped the helicopter crew would haul him over the coals when he turned up, and felt that spasm of concern again. It really wasn't like Berwin . . .

Toffee. When they said 'toffee' of course they meant what the Scots call tablet, sweet stuff with a creamy interior and crunchy crust which would have the pair of them bouncing all night if I didn't ration it. We got all the ingredients into the huge pan that Dawn insisted Mam always used for it, and began melting them.

'This bit takes ages,' Peerie Charlie said disconsolately, forgetting that he was having a good time. 'What can we do while we wait?' Then his eyes brightened. He said in that carefully neutral voice that he used for information like *There are chocolate biscuits in that tin*, 'Granny Beryl never had a visit from the trows.'

Oh, yes? I kept my voice casual. 'Didn't she?'

'She was mad about it,' Dawn said. 'She said she'd give them a flea in their ear if they came into her garden, but really she was mad that they'd left her out.'

'We could . . .' Charlie stopped and clapped his hand over his mouth, then beckoned Dawn over, and whispered into her ear. I focused on stirring the buttery sugary milky mess to make it clear I wasn't listening, but the ensuing discussion centred on whether someone who did sailing and lived on a boat (me, I presumed, as that description certainly didn't fit their Granny Beryl) counted as a proper grown-up. The shared wish to be doing something interesting seemed to get lifestyle winning over actual age; when Peerie Charlie came back to the table he was beaming. He scrambled back onto his seat and fixed me with his big blue eyes.

'You have to promise and swear,' he said. 'Crossyourheartandhopetodie, and then you have to do like this.' He made the sign of the cross on himself. 'Then you can't tell any big folk ever not *ever*. Not even by accident.'

'Swear on your boat,' Dawn said. 'Or on Cat's life. It needs to be a serious swear.'

I looked at the pair of them. 'Is it something that I ought to be telling your Mam? Something that's liable to get you hurt, like walking across frozen lochs or taking boats out by yourselves?'

They thought about that for a moment.

'We didn't get told not to do it,' Peerie Charlie said.

'It's not dangerous to us or anyone else, and it's not dishonest,' Dawn said. 'It's just a fun, but the fun would be spoiled if everyone knew.'

'And we're not going to do it again,' Peerie Charlie said. 'Well, not after tonight. Vaila said not.'

'Vaila's away doing something herself,' Dawn said, with an edge to her voice that suggested not all the grievances had made it down the voe. 'She needn't tell us what to do when she's not here.'

'Is it something to do with trows?'

Peerie Charlie shook his head so hard I thought he'd dislocate his neck. It was the most unconvincing denial I'd seen since the missing KitKats.

'If it's to do with trows I'll swear,' I said. 'On my *Khalida*, I won't tell any adults.'

'Okay,' Dawn said. She looked over her shoulder, as if she was afraid someone might hear her, and grinned impishly. 'Cass, can you walk on your hands?'

opstropolous: *rowdy, boisterous, the local version of English* obstreperous.

For some reason or other I hadn't tried to walk on my hands since I was twelve. There wasn't a lot of call for it on board a

140

tall ship. I spent the next fifteen minutes doing handstands and falling over in the living room under Dawn's instruction and Peerie Charlie's critical eye, while the toffee gradually got to what the book called a rolling boil. Once it began bubbling like lava in a volcano then every so often I put cold water in a saucer and dripped some of the mix into it. Gradually it went from splatted to honey consistency and finally stayed in a drop.

'Now you leave it on the worktop for five minutes while you grease the tray,' Dawn said. 'No, I'll do that while you have another go at walking on your hands. You're nearly there.'

I had another go and this time I managed to get right round the living room before my arms buckled. I collapsed onto the sofa. 'Are you going to tell me why I need to walk on my hands?'

'Beating first,' Dawn said. 'The toffee. Until it goes, like, thick way.'

I began beating, and discovered that cooking needed more muscles than you'd expect. At last granules appeared in the smoothness, and I poured it into the baking tray. It was setting even as I was scraping the last of it out.

'The scrapey bits go into a saucer for me,' Peerie Charlie said. 'But I have to let it cool.'

'Okay,' I said. I took the saucer through into the living room, and set it on the coffee table. 'Now, you two, tell me what we're going to do.'

'We need a plan,' Dawn said, taking on Vaila's mantle. She gestured at the window, where the lights of Granny Beryl's window shone through the darkness. 'We need to decide exactly what we're going to do and how, so that once we get there we're absolutely silent. Vaila and her pals spent weeks of break-times organising, to be ready for the first snow, and aabody kent exactly which houses they were going to do, and what they were going to do there.' She gave me a sharp look. 'You're minding it's to stay a mystery, like the Devon hoofprints?'

'Was that where Vaila got the idea?'

141

'They were doing a project on the supernatural in English. Vaila found it in an old book and thought it would be a fun, and then she got Berwin and his pals involved too, and word kinda spread and it grew. It was all really cool.' She giggled. 'We did your house, us and Rainbow, before going to join the others in Voe. We thought you were going to wake up and catch us.'

'Rainbow.' I remembered the trail of footprints leading to the mound, and then the muddle of hoofprints and trailing tails. 'The ponies . . . did you call them to the gate, ride them over to the mound the prints came out of, then ride them back from there?'

Dawn giggled, and Peerie Charlie nodded vigorously. 'I rided with Vaila on the little horse.' He made a snorting noise. 'He did like this. He wasn't pleased.'

'And then you got off at the gate and jumped onto the road, where it was clear.'

They nodded.

'We were a bit out of the way,' I said.

'I thought that,' Dawn said, 'but Rainbow had the idea of using the ponies, and Robin said it would be a fun. He drove us.'

Complicit sibling.

'And I writed the big banner,' Peerie Charlie said. 'Vaila wrote it, and I copied it, and then she did it big on the sheet, the exact same as I writed it, so it was me really.'

'It was a good banner,' I agreed.

'It was a good fun,' Dawn said. 'And it fairly got everyone talking – all the teachers were asking about it on Thursday morning. And did you see the paper? There was a whole page of "trowie antics" and wondering how we did them. So we absolutely mustn't get caught and spoil it.'

I nodded, and went over to the window. 'We need to get to the garden without leaving footprints, make the prints mysteriously, then leave again still without prints.'

'The approach is easy,' Dawn said. 'There's a burn just outside our dyke that runs down to hers, and it's not frozen in the middle.'

'Okay,' I agreed. 'Rubber boots and walk down the middle of the burn. Climb into the garden.' I remembered the Mulla houses. 'Dance a reel on her lawn?'

We all looked down towards the lit window that cast a white rectangle on Granny Beryl's icing-smooth lawn. 'She'll see us,' Peerie Charlie said. 'She'll look out of the kitchen window and see us and then she'll come out and catch us and she'll be mad and Vaila'll be mad and everyone'll be mad.'

'It's *Friday*,' Dawn said. 'From half eight to half nine she watches this programme about stupid people who buy a wrecked house somewhere abroad that they don't speak the language of, and get into a right muddle. She loves it.'

I could imagine Granny Beryl sitting and shaking her head at *the lack o' mother wit o' some folk*, and deploring the foreign food, foreign ways and fecklessness and unreliability of foreign builders.

'And you could lift the boy on the shed roof,' Dawn said. 'It's to the side of the house, so you can't see it from the windows. He could dance on that.'

'Okay,' I said. 'We go down the burn, we all dance a reel on this side of the house, watching like hawks for any sign of her coming into the kitchen, put Charlie up on the shed roof, he dances *carefully*, we get him down, and leave the way we came.'

Dawn nodded, eyes shining. 'Right. Let's do it.' She dived for the bedroom she shared with Vaila and came out with a carrier bag.

'Extra jumpers and snowsuits first.' Peerie Charlie scampered off for his all-in-one, and Dawn headed into the hall for an armful of jacket and waterproof trousers. I knew Inga wouldn't mind me borrowing one of her jerseys in the good cause of keeping her children amused. I shoved my feet into

143

her rubber boots. Only a couple of sizes too big. 'How about a pair of your dad's socks?'

'You need the trowie socks,' Peerie Charlie said. He dived into Dawn's carrier bag and pulled out a pair of socks, padded inside with wadding. On the outside there was a fake-fur foot with an extra large big toe. He pulled his on and did a monster walk round the hall, growling to himself.

'No trow noises,' Dawn reminded him. 'Gloves. Hat. Cass, these are yours.'

She handed me a pair of odd carvings. Each was an oval the size of my spread hand, with two pairs of velcro straps attached. On the other side were two projections, two to three centimetres deep, and carved like the end of a cat's leg, complete with pawprint. I remembered the cat prints at Mulla and grinned. 'Clever. They must have been very busy at breaktimes, making all this. How many were involved, in the end?'

'Most of Vaila's class, and some of Berwin's, and some of the peerie brothers and sisters.' She swelled with pride. 'The ones that could be trusted.'

'I didn't tell Mam,' Peerie Charlie agreed. 'Or Daddy or anyone.'

'And these.' The bottom of the carrier bag produced a painter boiler suit, the white paper sort, and another one cut around the waist to make a kind of Peerie Charlie-height cape. 'Snow camouflage.' She frowned. 'She's taken her own one. Never mind, Dad has one.'

I could have put two of me in Big Charlie's boiler suit. It gave us all a good laugh, and then once I'd rolled up the trousers and sleeves, sorted Peerie Charlie's cape and distributed toffee between us for encouragement, we set off.

It was a bonny, bonny night. The downward-angled streetlights lit the frost hanging in the air like spotlights in a theatre, the crescent moon shone white on the snowy hills, and over on the Ladies' Drive there were coloured lights along the

144

guttering which reflected in the still water. Every sound carried clearly: the chuckle of the burn, the crunching of the grass under our feet, and the distant thrumming of the helicopter, down towards Voe. A searchlight cone blazed in the night.

We scrunched to the burn, then clambered down into it. Dawn went ahead, feeling her way along the slippery stones in the bottom of it; I motioned Peerie Charlie to go next, and followed, keeping both hands on his white-papered shoulders, ready to grab him if he stumbled.

Inching along the hundred metres of burn must have taken us a good ten minutes. We arrived at last at the nearest point to Granny Beryl's house and crouched to recce the activity there. The big window showed the kitchen, with Granny Beryl herself busy boiling the kettle and buttering a couple of water biscuits for her TV snack. It felt like the world's slowest eight-o'clocks making, but at last she picked up the mug and plate, gave a final look out of the window and turned away. We watched as her square figure blacked out the doorway and disappeared into the bright TV reflections of her sitting room. A jaunty theme tune drifted in the air, followed by a manic-speed voice.

'Now,' Dawn breathed. 'Boots off and cat paws on. Once I'm over, hand the boy to me.'

She gave a careful look around then did a fluid gymnastic one-handed vault over the wooden fence and landed upright a good two metres away. The moon picked out the cat's-paw print on the fence, just like at Mulla. Peerie Charlie held up his arms for me to lift him over; I held him as far over the fence as I could, and Dawn managed some sort of one-footed balance that let her reach out for him. He stood on her feet while I did a one-handed jump over the fence, boy-style, and landed nearly as far over. The crunch of the snow as I landed sounded thunderous in the night, and we all froze guiltily, staring at the darkened kitchen window. At last Dawn nodded. She lifted

Peerie Charlie up towards me, and I settled him in a piggy-back. Dawn held out her arm, crooked, and Peerie Charlie hung on, nearly strangling me, while we did a couple of quick dance turns, then we headed towards the snow-covered shed roof. It was pretty nearly flat, and only just above my head, so once we'd got Peerie Charlie on my shoulders he was able to step up on it, and Dawn watched the kitchen darkness while I watched him anxiously, ready to catch him if he slipped. This was *mad*, I thought, my heart in my mouth, and I should never have agreed to it. He did a couple of jiggles in a very careful way, then edged back to the side to come down again. I caught him as he dropped, but he brought a gutter's worth of snow with him, which fell with a rush and a flump that echoed from the shed wall and re-echoed from the house. We all froze, staring at the darkened kitchen.

Suddenly the telly note changed. There was a moment's silence, then the frantic blare of adverts. Dawn did a fluid cartwheel to the corner of the shed, then stood upright again and reached out for Peerie Charlie. He launched himself from my arms and into hers with a rush that had the pair of them landing backwards in the snow, and I threw myself forward onto my hands and followed them. The oval pads with their cat tracks gave a surprisingly good grip on the snow.

The kitchen light went on. The bright rectangle on the grass was only a metre from the shed corner. I collapsed behind it with relief and found Dawn and Peerie Charlie snugly in a lee corner with only a dusting of snow blown into it. 'First adverts,' Dawn breathed in my ear. 'Second cup of tea.'

Granny Beryl couldn't see us behind here, but she could see the lit grass, with our reel footprints bang in the middle of it. If she glanced out while she was making her tea, and she was bound to, in case there was something happening in the houses up above that she wanted to know about, then she'd see them . . . she'd come out and look and we'd be caught. It would be all over Brae in seconds, and all over Shetland in minutes, that that daft sailing wife Cass had been encouraging Inga's bairns to play trows. It'd reach the police station, and embarrass Gavin in front of his new colleagues. I nudged Dawn, and jerked my head towards the wall behind this side of the shed, but she shook her head, and mouthed, 'Can't get out that way.'

A shadow moved in the rectangle: Granny Beryl coming towards the window. We all held our breath.

Suddenly the light in the sky dazzled. A thrumming, drumming noise echoed above the water. The chopper had finished searching the area around Voe, and was moving along the far side of the voe: Muckle Roe, the Burgastoo, Ladies' Mire. The shadow turned on its heel, shrank downwards; the light shut off again. We heard the snick of the front door being opened as Granny Beryl went out to see what was going on. The helicopter noise got louder until it was deafening above us, then it moved sideways towards the boating club and began flying in shorter sweeps. In the house there was that moment of silence again, followed by the jaunty theme tune and a recap voice. Granny Beryl's front door banged.

I closed my eyes in relief, counted to ten to let my heartbeat get back to normal, then stood up. Peerie Charlie tugged me down to crouch again and scrambled to stand on my knees, then launched himself into the air. He came down in the middle of a clear patch of snow and began a little jigging dance across the lawn to where we'd come in. Dawn flipped back on her hands and went around the outside of the garden, leaving a neat trail of cat pawprints. I went straight across. Between toffee-mixing and lugging Peerie Charlie my arms were beginning to feel like spaghetti. My pawprint trail looked like the cat had been at the whisky.

Peerie Charlie capered to the fence and stood waiting. Dawn did her neat vault over it from her handstand, and held out her arms to him. I managed to stagger all the way over, and was just standing on one foot contemplating the fence when the helicopter came swirling towards us. I swung over the fence and shoved my feet into my rubber boots. The other two were already halfway up the ditch, Dawn shoving Peerie Charlie on ahead of her. I half-ran after them and we slithered and slipped upwards and made it over their home fence just as the chopper swept towards Granny Beryl's house.

I grabbed Peerie Charlie's cape and hauled it off him, swept the fence free of snow with one hand, lifted him up and plonked him on it. 'Boiler suit down and stand on it,' I yelled at Dawn under the drumming that filled the air. 'We're watching the chopper.'

I wrenched the zip of my own suit down and dropped it between my legs. Dawn followed suit. The girl would make a good crew, obeying even when she didn't understand. We stood there looking up as the chopper drummed overhead, our ears ringing with the noise of it. It hovered dead above us.

Suddenly the night was split with merciless light, pinning us like butterflies to a card. The cold air swirled around us, strong as a gale at sea. 'Wave,' I said to Peerie Charlie.

He was a trained crew too. His not to reason why. He gave the chopper a big grin and waved. The light gave an answering dip on and off, then the helicopter rose and turned towards Weathersta. It began moving slowly over the houses.

Gradually the wind died, the noise receded. We could hear ourselves think again.

'Phew!' Dawn said. 'Why did you want them to see us, Cass?'

'They're looking for Berwin,' I said. I lifted Peerie Charlie down. 'Come on, boy, you need a hot shower.' I took his hand to encourage him up this last slope of garden. 'I thought if we disappeared they might think one of us was Berwin, hiding from them. I didn't want them to waste their time looking for us when they need to look for him.'

Dawn's face was pinched in the over-door light, as if she'd suddenly been reminded of something she'd managed to put aside. Her voice went back to being a ten-year-old's. 'But it is just that he's hiding to make the trick better, isn't it? That's what everyone was saying at school.'

'I'm pretty sure it is,' I said.

Dawn looked sideways at me, and fell silent.

The warmth of the house was bliss as we stumbled in. 'Showers or baths for you two, straight away, and then let's get you curled up under double downies in front of a film.'

'Can we make the couch into a bed and all sleep there?' Dawn asked.

'Sounds a great idea.' Peerie Charlie would be off in seconds that way, I knew, whereas if I tried to put him to bed he'd be up all night.

By the time I'd got Peerie Charlie showered, pyjama'd, teeth brushed and hair dried, I was shivering with cold. I got him under his downie in the warm sitting room and left him to watch *Ice Age* while I showered. I was re-dressed in jeans and t-shirt and towelling my hair when a car scrunched its way into the drive. A flashing blue light reflected in the glass pane each side of the front door, then was switched off. There were heavy footsteps on the steps, and the doorbell rang.

The police had come to call.

Chapter Thirteen

perskeet: prim, overly particular with an air of snobbishness (*Lowland Scots,* pershittie)

I didn't feel ready to face the police. My feet were bare, my face was pink from the heat, and my hair hung in tousled curls round my shoulders.

On the other hand, if they kept ringing the doorbell they'd wake Peerie Charlie, snuggled into his downie with his eyes closed. I turned the TV down a bit and went to the door.

There was a large officer I didn't recognise standing on the doorstep. He flashed a card at me and said, 'PC Farquhar of the Shetland Constabulary.' His voice suggested Glasgow. He glanced behind me, then looked down again from his great height. 'Is your mum about, hen?'

There was a stifled snort from behind him. I looked past him and saw the porch light shining on an immaculately sleek blonde head. It was my least favourite officer, Gavin's sidekick in the Shetland murder cases he'd done, DS Peterson.

She was looking perskeet as ever in boots and a black trouser suit. Her only concession to the weather was a black padded police jacket. Her green eyes were lit with amusement, but she cut in quickly to save her colleague's face. 'Hello, Cass. Babysitting?'

'Babysitting,' I agreed. 'Hello.' I stepped back and opened

the door wider. 'Come into the kitchen.' I put a finger to my lips and indicated Peerie Charlie, looking particularly angelic with his fair hair tousled into curls, and his thumb half in his mouth. 'Tea, coffee?'

They followed me into the kitchen and DS Peterson unwound her scarf and put it and her jacket over a chairback. 'Coffee for me, please. It's going to be a long night.' She sat down and turned to her colleague. 'Andy, I don't think you've met Cass Lynch yet. Her parents live on Muckle Roe. Dermot Lynch used to be Sullom Voe, but now he's one of the men behind the windfarm that's going up in the Kames. Cass is second officer on board the Norwegian tall ship *Sørlandet*.'

She didn't need to add that I was the new Inspector's partner. The mention of *Sørlandet* would do that.

'Currently on four weeks' leave,' I added. I shook hands with him. 'Their parents wanted our sixty trainees home for Christmas.'

He was still miffed that he'd taken me for a child. His expression said that he found it hard to believe I was promoted above a rowing boat, but under DS Peterson's eye he made an effort. 'Sounds an interesting job. Tea for me, if the DS is having.'

'Before we settle down, though,' DS Peterson said, 'we're checking out a report from the chopper. Three children out in the snow.'

I wondered uneasily how much the chopper had seen. It had forward-looking infra-red heat-searching equipment, so it could have spotted us playing trows from the outskirts of Brae. I was trying to think of something non-committal to say when DS Peterson's head turned to the kitchen door. 'Come in.'

Dawn sidled around the door. She was dressed in a onesie over her nightshirt, and had a towel wrapped around her head. 'That was us out in the snow,' she said. 'Peerie Charlie wanted to watch the helicopter.'

She was a much better liar than I'd have been. My voice gave me away, Gavin said.

'In that case we can relax till the next suspect call,' DS Peterson said.

I dished out their mugs, made a cup of tea for myself and sat down at the kitchen table with them. My feet nestled gratefully on Inga's underfloor-heated floorboards.

'Three children,' PC Farquhar said.

'The helicopter detects size, not age,' I pointed out, rather tartly. My lack of inches was a sore point, especially when I was with DS Peterson, who could look loftily over the top of my head. 'Peerie Charlie, Dawn here, and me.'

He gave me a sceptical look 'Isn't the big sister Berwin's girlfriend?'

I nodded.

'Where's she at, then, while you were messing about in the snow?'

'She's having a sleepover with her friend Rainbow. They live just outside Voe, one of the farmhouses at this end of the Kergord valley.'

'Not far from Berwin's house,' DS Peterson said. She exchanged a thoughtful look with PC Farquhar.

'Please, miss,' Dawn asked, as if she was talking to her teacher, 'is there any sign of Berwin?'

DS Peterson shook her head. 'Not so far.'

Dawn's shoulders slumped. She went over to the worktop and began pouring herself a bowl of cereal. DS Peterson turned back to me, but spoke to Dawn as well. 'You know the Coastguard has investigatory powers as well as the police?'

I nodded.

'Well, between us we put a request in for a land and sea search. We got his phone records, well, what we're allowed under data protection, which is basically details of the last activity.' She stopped there, to sip her coffee. I waited, hoping to be told without having to ask. When she'd dragged the silence out long enough she continued. 'His last two texts were sent at 23.07 and 23.09.'

'The ones to Vaila and Drew,' I said.

She nodded. 'We can get the place within metres from the nearest mast. Somewhere between where his boiler suit and boots were left and the shore. After he sent those texts he switched his phone off. It doesn't connect to the signal again.'

'He went into hiding,' I said. 'Voluntarily.'

'But he'd have told Vaila!' Dawn said. 'She didn't know where he was, she really didn't. I could see, in school today, she was pretending she didn't care, but she was mad as fire he hadn't told her what he was up to. She'd have expected him to tell her. They've been going out for ages and ages.'

'What do you think's happened to him, then?' DS Peterson asked.

Dawn's face crumpled suddenly. 'Something,' she said. 'I don't know what, but something. Something awful.'

I rose and put an arm around her. She gave a couple of gulps, then sniffed and moved away from me. 'Can I put on a different movie?'

'Can you do it without waking the boy?'

She nodded.

'Go for it, then.'

She took her bowl of cereal and padded off. The rapid-fire dialogue of *Ice Age* switched off and was replaced by the opening chords of a teen movie. I turned back to DS Peterson, who was looking thoughtful. 'Vaila. Why wasn't Berwin's girl-friend up to high doh?' she said.

'He messaged her,' PC Farquhar replied. 'She knew it was going to happen, him disappearing like that. And from Gavin's briefing, they all expected him in school, but they were only slightly uneasy about him not turning up.'

153

'I wonder,' DS Peterson said, 'if there's anyone else staying at Rainbow's house. Berwin's friend Drew, for example.'

'One spectacular stunt for his reappearance?'

DS Peterson nodded.

They've got another trick planned, Dawn had said, and Rainbow had risked asking about sending the helicopter out in spite of the warning looks of the others. It could be.

DS Peterson rose. 'Thanks for the coffee, Cass. I think we'll just pay a call along to Rainbow's house.'

They'd been gone maybe an hour when Gavin phoned. 'We've called off the search for tonight.' He sounded tired. 'There's no sign of anyone living outside between the Kergord valley and Brae. Nobody injured on the hill, nobody hiding out in a shed. Nothing.' His voice warmed into a smile. 'Only three children watching the helicopter search.'

My throat closed up. 'Did DS Peterson check out Rainbow?'

'Four teenagers innocently playing cards.'

'Oh? Drew and John-Lowrie as well?'

'Aye. But no sign of Berwin, and Rainbow's folk said they'd seen nothing of him. Freya and Andy Farquhar checked out their sheds. No sign. If he's hiding out somewhere, it's not there. They called along to Robin's studio too, no sign of life, and at Helge's. She insisted he wasn't there.' He paused. 'The curtains were still closed, but when Freya tried to question her about that, she bristled up and said her private life was her own, and if they wanted to come into her house they'd need to show her a warrant.'

'Strange,' I agreed. 'The teenagers . . . they weren't worried enough, earlier.'

'No. Freya said they were on edge now.' He gave a long sigh. 'We'll start searching the hills tomorrow, as soon as it's light.'

If there was nobody living out in the hills, they'd be

searching for a body, the casualty of a trowie trick that had somehow gone horribly wrong. 'Can I be any help with that?'

'Yes, if you will. We'll need to organise a search along the shoreline, and that's easier done from the water. The lifeboat'll be involved, of course, but every pair of eyes counts. Could you get Magnie and the other boat owners involved?'

'Sure. I'll phone around.'

'Thanks. Gather at half nine at the boating club, maybe? There's no point in going out before it's properly light.'

'I'll tell them.'

'I'm on my way home now. I'll talk to the cats for a bit and stoke up the Rayburn, then come and join you.'

'I don't want to keep you up. You've had a long day.'

'I'll doze on Inga's comfortable sofa till it's time to come home.'

'I could easy get a taxi. Really.'

'Shocking extravagance. No, no. I'll see you in about an hour and a half, two hours.'

He rang off. I checked the time: ten to ten. Late, but not too late to phone Magnie. Nobody would be sleeping till news of the search got round.

He had been sitting on his couch by the Rayburn, the phone at his hand, for he answered at the second ring. 'Now, then, Cass. What's the word from the search?'

'Called off for tonight, but nothing found.'

'Aye, aye.' He thought about that for a moment. 'Back out tomorrow?'

'Yea. Gavin was wondering if we peerie boat owners could go along the shore. Could you put the word out? Meet at half nine at the marina.'

'Yea, yea, I'll do that. I'll get phoning right now. Half nine. I'll see you there, then.'

Dawn's film had ended. I chased her off to bed, lifted Peerie Charlie, downie and all, and put him to bed too, then curled up on the couch and dozed off myself until I was roused by Gavin's knock at the door.

He was looking tired: there was a crease between his brows, and his mouth turned down at the corners.

'I should have insisted on that taxi,' I said, conscience-stricken.

'Och, I'm fine.' He ran a hand through his hair, making the curls spring up. 'I had a cup of coffee to wake me up.' He kissed me, then stood back, looking quizzically at me. 'So what exactly were you doing out in the snow with the bairns?'

I smiled at him. 'I can't tell you. Top secret, crossmyheartand-hopetodie. But d'you fancy a bit of home-made toffee?'

layin' on an aamos: *doing an action in the hope of good results; the ruined church at Cott was an* **aamos-kirk**, *where girls would leave a penny between the stones in the hope of a good husband (Old Norse, almusa: alms)*

Later, much later, when Gavin and I were home again, curled up in bed with Cat and Kitten squeezed onto my pillow, there was movement in the Kergord valley. A door opened in the dark, and four white-clad figures crept out. Each one had a full backpack, hanging as if the contents were heavy.

The helicopter had stopped its searching for the night. There had been no sign of Berwin anywhere, no sign of a warm body hiding out in a shed. Tomorrow the search would begin again, with all the manpower the police and coastguard could muster between them.

For now, the hills lay quiet in the moonlight. The higher slopes had reverted to the donkey brown of winter heather; below, on the more fertile land, the grazed grass lay under a

156

smooth covering of snow. The Burn of Kirkhouse ran between moulded curves of thin ice.

Two of the figures carried a tangle of lines in their gloved hands. They went softly up to the Shetland ponies standing in a corner of the field. There was the soft clink of bits, a snort, a stamp of hooves. The gate was opened and three of the walkers led four ponies out, while the fourth kept the others within the field. A last glance at the dark house, then the walkers mounted and set off southwards in single file along the valley floor, where the grass was smoothest. Once they were clear of the house, once their eyes had got accustomed to the starlight on the snow, its rider urged the lead horse upwards onto a track halfway up the hill, and the others followed. The walk quickened.

It took them forty minutes to get to the far end of the valley. They slowed the horses at the approach to the farm of Upper Kergord, and dismounted to walk them past, then mounted again to ride down the track to the yellow cube shed that was the site office for the windfarm diggings. All was quiet below them: no watchman, no searchlights. The bulldozers stood in ranks in their mesh compound by the smooth sweep of new road.

This operation had been planned. There was a fence just before the diggings began. They approached it along a sheep track through the heather, and stopped where there was no snow. Before the riders dismounted, one took off the rucksack on his back, and pairs of shoes were passed from hand to hand. The ponies stood patiently while rubber boots were exchanged for old trainers bought in the charity shop. They were well used to stranger antics than these. After that the smallest one went along the ponies, tying them to the fence, while the other three went straight to the ranks of motionless mechanical monsters that were ripping their hills apart. One climbed up and over the mesh, just as he did in the school multicourt

157

when a ball got kicked out. A breathed whisper ran from one to the other: *Locked . . . locked . . . all locked.*

They were ready for this too. The climber went to inspect the compound door while the other three gathered at the yellow cube. One backpack was opened. Light glinted on a hammer, scissor blades, a roll of sticky-back plastic. One figure stayed as lookout while the other two went around the back of the cube, where there was a small toilet window. The plastic glimmered in the moonlight, the scissor blades flashed, then two hands unpeeled the backing and smoothed the plastic over the window. The hammer struck once, with a neat clink, then tapped along the bottom of the glass by the frame. A hand reached up and slid under the plastic to open the window. The watcher came round to help lift the smallest figure in through; a moment's wait, a brief flash of a torch, then a fistful of keys was handed back out. Another trip, another fistful, then the smallest figure squirmed out, was caught by the waiting pair, and they returned to the compound, where the door was open for them.

It was dark between the diggers, and they felt safer there, but they risked only the briefest flash of the miniature torches they'd brought, to read the number plates on the keys. Gloved hands smoothed across the metal to find the filler cap openings, or opened the door carefully and fumbled inside the cab for the lever. One figure eased a folding bucket and a plant-watering jug from her rucksack, and went to the burn, glancing over her shoulder the while, then returned to the diggers. A paper bag rustled. The water carrier did another trip, and another; now, among the machines, you could hear water dripping underneath them.

They couldn't repair the window, but they reckoned the nightwatchman, when he came on duty tomorrow, would think someone else had organised a makeshift botch-job. Two went into the cube this time, one to hold the torch while the other rehung the keys back onto their labelled hooks with quick fingers, just as if nobody had interfered with them in the night. The others helped them out. They closed the window and scurried upwards to the fence where the ponies were waiting. They mounted and changed shoes for boots once more, then wheeled the ponies away and set off with fast-beating, triumphant hearts into the night.

Saturday 19th December:

HW 00.05 (2.0m);
LW 05.45 (1.0m);
HW 12.02 (2.2m);
LW 18.28 (0.7m)

Sunrise 09.07, moonrise 12.27; sunset 14.56, moonset 20.52.

Moon: first quarter

Chapter Fourteen

waandert: *not able to think straight (English,* wandered*)*

It was still dark when the alarm went off, and only just light enough to see when Gavin headed off in the Land Rover at eight. 'I'll probably see you sometime during the day. Wrap up warm, now.'

'Go teach your granny to suck eggs,' I retorted.

Outside, every bush was furred with silver; the sparrows in their tree were outlined against the milky blue of the first light over Linga. The half-moon still hung high in the sky, bright edge sharp as if it was a cut-out in silver paper.

The Rayburn had gone out, so I riddled it, put the ash in the bucket, then filled it with peats from the basket, a couple of twists of paper, a firelighter, kindling sticks and more peats. It all caught in a sudden lowe of bright flame. I left it to get going, and went to dress in clothes suitable for a winter's day on the water. By the time I'd got my full ocean gear on the sun had just made it above Linga, and melted the frost on the trees to glistening drops that caught the amber of the sun rising, but the grass was still crisply white, and the ivy leaves and moss along the wall were patterned with little spikes. Cat and the Kitten came as far as the gate, then Cat fluffed out his fur, shook himself, then turned and trotted back to the catflap. The box by the

Rayburn was a more attractive option. Kitten hesitated, then turned and charged after him.

It was a bonny morning, but bitter, bitter cold. The boat's ropes were frozen solid. I wrestled them free and dropped the ends in the sea to thaw them, then recoiled them on the jetty. The water was tinted gold, and an otter pottered along the shoreline, ducking under in that characteristic bottom-arched way, then coming up again on its back with a starfish to crunch.

There were several boats with their engines running when I arrived at the marina, and a cloud of blue smoke hanging in the air. Magnie was in the middle of a knot of skippers with a chart in his hands. There was a bit of nodding, then they separated off to their own boats, faces purposeful.

'I'm organised who's going where,' Magnie said. 'We're got from here down to Houbansetter covered. I've put you on the stretch from the point o' Grobsness to Voe pier. I'm on the opposite side, so if you see anything give me a shout on the VHF, and I'll come over.'

He'd given us the most likely stretch to find Berwin in, if he'd somehow gone into the sea after his vanishing trick and been washed away – except, no, he'd gone home and been in bed when Sheila had spoken to him. None of it made sense.

'Channel 8?'

Magnie nodded. 'Just pootle along right at the beaches, and give a look up the banks and all. The lifeboat's sweeping the middle. I'm spoken to the coxswain. He'll listen out on both channels.'

I went back to *Herald Deuk* and we headed out in a flotilla. Two boats peeled off at the end of Busta Voe, ready to head back marinawards along the sides. Four more continued south, to search Linga, Papa Little and Gonfirth, and Magnie and I chugged east towards Voe. We went right up to the pier and began working back at sauntering speed, ten metres from the shore. I hung my binoculars round my neck and alternated eye-searching with a spyglasses sweep. It was half-tide, coming in. There were white geometric shapes of ice over the kelp on the tideline, which made it more difficult: every slightly larger knobble of rock or lump of kelp had to be stared at until I was sure it wasn't a boy in a black jacket and dark jeans. The boots and boiler suit were still in the middle of the field, like an act of faith that he'd reappear the way he'd gone.

I'd only got as far as the bridge at the end of the field when I saw four figures running down and waving. My name came clearly across the water.

It was Vaila and Rainbow, Drew and John-Lowrie, all dressed up in rubber boots and six layers of jumper under fur-hooded parkas. I nosed the boat to shore, and Vaila waded in to catch her. 'Cass, can we come with you? We can look while you steer.'

'That'd be a help,' I agreed.

She hadn't been worried yesterday, but now it had hit her that Berwin really was missing. Her eyes were red, her skin blotched with crying, but her jaw was firmly set. 'We heard about the police search. Folk from every house in Voe are gathering at the hall, ready to help look on the hill. We were on our way there when we saw you and Magnie going along the shore. Is he on his own too?'

'He'd be glad o' the boys. I'll call him.' I cut the engine to idle and reached for the handheld. Magnie was all for extra eyes; he came over, collected the boys and set off again.

It was slow, meticulous work. Now I had the girls I could focus on going as close as possible. When I hesitated over letting them go ashore to double-check things we weren't sure of, Vaila insisted, sounding exactly like Inga. 'We can't keep the boat off rocks while you check.' Her voice was fierce. 'Rainbow, you hold the boat. I'll go up and look.' *Juliet was only thirteen*, Gavin had said. We stopped, checked, started again, and the shoreline went slowly past, red stony beaches, a stretch of low cliff, the marshy area where a burn ran into the sea. Above us a line of people was sweeping the hill. I was just coming along the banks below Robin's studio when I heard the growl of a vehicle coming along from the direction of Voe. I glanced behind me, thinking it might be Gavin, but it was a black 4x4 shoving its way through the snow. It had passed Leonard and Frigg's house, and was heading for Helge's. A black 4x4 – there were plenty of them, of course, but I was reminded of Wednesday's visitors, the muscle-men. The 4x4 slammed to a halt above the cottage. The passenger door opened and someone big in black got out. The driver's door next; his double.

I reached for the hand-held. 'Magnie, can you hear me?'

'Loud and clear, lass.'

'There's trouble at Helge's. Can you head straight there, top speed?'

'On my way.' His boat curved round and began heading towards us.

I fumbled in my pocket and shoved my phone at Vaila. 'Tell Gavin the two thugs have arrived at Helge's. Hang on, both of you.' I rammed the engine into top gear and focused on my steering while she relayed the message on. We reached the beach just as the men arrived at the cottage door. The girls leapt overboard, and I followed. I gave Vaila the painter. 'These are a nasty pair.' I put all the command I had in my voice. 'Stay put.'

I began running up the beach. One of the men hammered at the cottage door, the noise drowning out the crunch of my feet on the shingle. There was a pause. 'Hey!' I shouted.

They both turned to stare, looking at me, then turning to look at the cottage, then they visibly squared their shoulders. I stopped well short of them, outwith grabbing distance, and we glared at each other for a moment.

'There's another boat on its way over too,' I said. 'And I called the police.'

The one who'd been the driver sneered. 'Called them out from Lerwick?'

'That gives us plenty of time,' the other one chimed in.

I waved an arm at the figures on the hill. 'We're in the middle of a search for a missing boy. There are police everywhere.'

Helge's door opened then. She slipped through it and pulled it to behind her. Her face was set, her shoulders braced. 'What do you want?'

The driver's attention swivelled to her, gave her a long look, then turned to look back at me. 'Your friend here's probably told you already. We want the canary to stop singing. Be worth your while.'

I kept my eyes on the sidekick. Behind me, the roar of Magnie's motor was getting nearer, nearer. He throttled back; I heard his wash splash on the beach.

Helge's breathing was jerking in her throat, but she kept her gaze steady on them and her voice level. 'No.'

He used the same words he'd used to me. 'There's no need to stick your neck out. Just forget the testimony. Don't appear in court.'

His double chimed in, as though it was a routine they'd learned. 'You won't lose by it.' He looked at the closed door behind her. 'Get your door repainted, for a start.'

Her hand tightened on the handle, but she spoke calmly. 'I've made my statement, and I'll stand by it.'

Behind me there was a splosh as Magnie jumped ashore, followed by two more. The pebbles crunched under their boots as they came up to join me. Drew and John-Lowrie closed in one on each side of me, reassuringly adult-sized, and tougher than these muscle-men would expect. Magnie stood slightly apart. 'Are you having a bit of trouble, Helge?'

Helge looked from the men to us, then back to the men. 'I'd like you to leave, please.'

'No trouble,' the driver said. *We could take you all out*, his stare told Magnie, *but we can't be bothered.* His double had one hand in his pocket. 'Just giving the lady here a message from a friend who wants to see her keeping healthy.'

Helge's lip curled at the word 'healthy'. 'Well, you've delivered the message,' she said. 'I get it. The answer's no.'

The driver kept looking at her. 'You've got a son, haven't you, lady?'

Helge swayed and took a hold of the doorpost, but she didn't speak.

'A missing boy, huh?' his double mused. He turned and looked out over the water. 'It could be a bad place for accidents, this. Hills, water . . .'

'All you need to do is keep quiet,' the driver urged. 'Take a holiday, why don't you?'

'Tough on the family, losing a son,' the sidekick said. He took his hand out of his pocket. To my relief, it was empty. 'Well, lady, if you won't listen, you won't.'

Magnie took two steps forward. 'It sounds to me like you're threating this wife.'

'No threats,' the driver assured him. 'The lady here understands what we mean.'

'Tell them . . .' Helge moistened her lips.'Tell them I'll think about it.'

A blue light flashed in the distance. A police car came at speed along the road as far as Leonard and Frigg's, then slowed for the last bit of gravel track. The muscle-men set off in their car, only to meet the police nose to nose halfway. Both sets of people got out; not Gavin, I could see from here – two uniformed officers. There was a stand-off before one officer got his noteboook out.

Helge's door was pulled open from behind her. It took me a moment to recognise the tall, skinny figure in oversized blue and white striped pyjamas. It was Berwin.

★

He looked dreadful. His face was bone white, with purple shadows under his eyes, and he gripped the door jamb as if it was all that was keeping him upright. 'What's going on?' he said. His eyes came around the beach, clocking the two boats, the knot of people. He managed a smile for his friends. 'Aye, aye.'

'You get back to bed this minute,' Helge said. She grabbed him by the arm and half-hauled, half-supported him back indoors. Vaila dived after her, and the other teenagers followed. I looked at Magnie, and he jerked his chin after them. 'You go and find out what's going on. I'll call off the search.'

Above us, the police car was retreating into a gateway. It turned and began heading for Voe, with the muscle-men's 4x4 following. Off to be questioned, I hoped.

Berwin was in the room with the fire and drawn curtains. They were still closed, and the room was lit only by the glowing peats in the grate. The warmth was bliss after the cold water. There were pillows and a rumpled downie on the couch. Helge got Berwin under the downie, then remained at his head, watching him warily, as if she was worried what he'd do next. His friends gathered round the end of the sofa, looking at him accusingly.

'We thought you were dead!' Vaila snapped. Her voice rose. 'We've been that worried, and now here you are having a nice lie-in while I've been searching beaches for your body!' Tears sprang into her eyes. She stamped her foot and turned her back on him.

'You mighta let us ken, boy,' Drew said. I could see he was restraining himself in our presence, otherwise it'd have been put a lot more strongly. 'Are you been here all this time?'

Helge put out a hand as Berwin tried to struggle to a sitting position, and had to subside back onto the pillow. 'I dinna ken,' he said slowly. He closed his eyes for a moment. 'I dinna mind. We were at the school, planning . . . What day is it?'

Vaila turned and gave him a bitter glance. 'You ken fine what day it is.' She slid her arm into Rainbow's. 'Let's get out o' here.'

Berwin's eyes flew open again as she stormed out, and he half put a hand out towards her, then dropped it on the bedcover as if it was too heavy to hold up.

'You just rest,' Helge said.

'I dinna mind anything,' Berwin repeated. 'I was going to do the vanishing trick, in the park by the road.' He looked at Drew. 'Did I do it? I don't mind.' His voice was trailing away as he spoke.

'Off you go, now,' Helge said. 'He needs peace.' She smoothed his covers with one hand, then straightened and marched towards us, hands out as if she was shooing hens. 'Out. He needs to rest.'

'But what's he doing here?' Drew asked, moving reluctantly forward into the sunshine. 'How did he get here?'

'On his own two feet, I suppose,' Helge said. 'I found him. He was chilled to the bone, and talking nonsense. There's a bruised place on the back of his head, as if he slipped on ice and went down hard. Concussed, I thought, when I saw that, and I put him straight to bed.'

'Have you phoned the doctor?' I asked.

'I was just about to, when those visitors arrived.' She looked straight at me for the first time since she'd begun explaining, and managed a shaky smile. 'Thanks for the cavalry.'

Up on the hill above us, the news was spreading. There was a shout, the spread-out line of figures turned to a clump, and then began to walk briskly back the way they'd come.

The youngsters had been conferring in low, urgent voices. Now Drew came over. 'Can I bide wi' him? One of us would like to, and I think he'd rather it was me as Vaila, if he's no' at his best.'

Vaila's scowl said she didn't agree. I could see that Helge wasn't keen either.

'I'll just sit by him until he's feeling more himself,' Drew said. 'I won't excite him, or anything like that.' His voice was firm. 'We feel one of us should stay.'

I looked at Helge. 'Do you have medical training?'

She shook her head.

'If he's concussed, we should maybe call the ambulance straight away. May I take a look at him?'

Grudgingly, she moved out of the doorway, and switched on the light. Berwin gave a little moan, and brought his forearm up over his eyes. I went in and crouched by his bed. 'Berwin, it's Cass here. I'm a first aider. We'll put the light off as soon as we can. I just want to have a look at your head, is that okay?'

His murmured 'yes' sounded as if he was drifting in and out of consciousness.

'Can you turn your head so I can see where you hit it?'

He obeyed without opening his eyes. He'd certainly come a cropper. There was a nasty bash just below where his skull curved out from the neck, with the skin broken, and dried blood matting his hair. I touched delicately around it, but there was no feel of anything giving, and he didn't wince. There was no sign of fluid coming from either ear. 'Okay,' I said. 'Can you open your eyes, Berwin, and look at me?' His blue eyes opened. The pupils were pin-points in the sudden light, and he creased up his face as if it was hurting, but both pupils were the same size.

'Okay,' I said. 'Are you hurting anywhere else? Back? Belly?'

'No.'

'Can you press your belly for me? Does it feel soft?'

'I think so.'

Probably no abdominal bleeding. I nodded to Helge to

switch the light back off. 'You just lie there quietly now. We'll need to keep waking you to check you're still conscious.'

He gave a sleepy murmur, and I went back outside. 'He needs a doctor,' I said. 'There's no obvious skull fracture, but he's had a nasty shake-up, and I don't know what other injuries he may have.' He'd walked to the doorway; surely his spine was okay. 'He needs to be properly examined, and taken to hospital, if need be.'

'It's Saturday,' Vaila said. 'NHS 24.' I remembered that she was a veteran of Peerie Charlie crises. 'You get passed from pillar to post until they condescend to contact the duty doctor, and they could be anywhere from Eshaness to Sumburgh. It's quicker just to bundle him in the car and take him to A&E.' That was definitely Inga's voice speaking.

'Not without him being examined,' I said. 'He may have other injuries I can't see.' I looked at Helge. 'Let's go direct for calling the ambulance.' She nodded, though she still looked uncertain, and went into the house. I smiled reassuringly at Vaila. 'Don't worry. They'll probably send him straight home with a bandage that he'll take off the minute the house door's closed behind him.'

'I'll go with him to the hospital,' Drew said. 'I can liaise with his folk till they get there.'

'The ambulance'll pass his house,' I pointed out. I got my phone back from Vaila. 'Vaila, you go and sit with him. Just talk to him. I know it's mean when he wants to sleep, but he needs to be kept conscious.'

She nodded and hurried off, Rainbow following. 'What's the shop number?'

John-Lowrie dictated it as I dialled. Frigg pounced on it at the first ring. 'I have good news,' I said. 'Berwin's found, and living.'

I left a pause for her to take that in. She gave a little cry, then burst into tears. 'He's found! He's okay,' I heard her say. There was a click as another person took the phone. 'Leonard here. The boy's okay?'

'He's had a bash on the head but he doesn't seem to be seriously injured. He's here at Helge's. She's just calling the ambulance now.'

'We'll be over right away,' he said.

Chapter Fifteen

He/she widna tell da truth if a lee wid do instead: a phrase describing someone who's not to be trusted (English, He/she wouldn't tell the truth if a lie would do instead*)*

The next half hour was chaos. Leonard and Frigg were the first to arrive, anxiety struggling with enormous relief, and Sheila and Bruce behind them, in Bruce's van. The teenagers were kicked out of the sickroom and rounded up by Magnie for delivery home, though Vaila had a good try at getting Frigg's permission to go with him. 'I'd be no bother. I can get the bus home.'

Frigg shook her head distractedly, as if a fly was bothering her. 'Not now, Vaila. We'll phone you as soon as he's able for visitors.'

She and Leonard hurried into the house, followed by Sheila. Bruce leaned against one of the posts securing Helge's boat and reached down into the tideline for a piece of rope to make knots in. Vaila drooped at the shoulders, and kicked stones all the way down the beach to Magnie's boat. Drew and John-Lowrie exchanged anxious frowns before Drew followed her, and Rainbow looked back several times as she and John-Lowrie climbed up the track to walk home along the road. Magnie's boat had just headed off Braewards in a swirl of wash when a police car came trundling along the track and stopped in a gate space, to leave room for the ambulance coming down. It was Gavin, followed by DS Peterson, with her notebook at the ready for taking statements. Gavin smiled at me as he headed for the door of the house, and almost collided with Helge coming out. He took a quick look in, then came back out, and turned to Helge. 'I won't try to shove in there. Tell me about how he came to end up here.'

He gestured her forwards to the rock she'd sat on yesterday, and settled himself beside her, smoothing the green tartan of his kilt over his lap. I could see DS Peterson feeling that rocks were beneath her dignity; she compromised by leaning against Helge's boat.

'He just . . . turned up,' Helge began, uncertainly. She looked across at the sea, as if she was searching for inspiration. 'He says he doesn't remember anything. I got him into pyjamas and into bed.'

'When you say turned up . . .' Gavin said, and left the sentence trailing for her to finish. She remained silent for a moment, hands twisting together, then launched in.

'He turned up here. This morning, not long before those two men came . . . before Cass arrived. I'd got him into bed and I was just going to phone Leonard when I heard the knock at the door.'

'What was he wearing?'

I could feel her relief at something she could answer easily. 'Just normal clothes. Jeans, and his favourite hoodie, and a black jacket. Trainers. They were all wet, and he was so cold.' Panic crossed her face for a moment, as if she'd said something wrong, then smoothed out again. 'I hung them up above the Rayburn.'

'Tell me how you came to see him,' Gavin said. The patience in his voice would wear away stone. He wouldn't browbeat Helge or threaten her, he'd just keep asking.

Helge looked out at the sea again. Her gaze fell on me. 'I was

175

feeding the hens,' she said quickly. She was remembering how I'd arrived at the beach yesterday, I thought. 'I'd let them out, and I was out on the briggistanes here, giving them their meat, then I saw him coming along. He was staggering on the stones, unsteady on his feet, and I ran to him and put an arm round him, and helped him in. He didna seem aware o' where he was, and he wasna doing anything for himself. I got him undressed, and put a pair of pyjamas on him, and covered him up. I got a hot water bottle for him, and hung his clothes up, and then I was about to phone the doctor when I heard a car turning down. I looked, and it was those two men. I was worried they'd disturb Berwin, so I came out to meet them.' She looked at me. 'And Cass spotted them coming along, I suppose, and came in.'

She was looking at me, I thought, so as not to have to look at Gavin. Her shoulders were still tense. She jumped as DS Peterson spoke. 'Can you give a rough time for when he arrived, Ms Callahan?'

'A time? Oh, I don't know . . . what time is it now?' She glanced at the sea, three quarters of the way up the beach. 'Is it not long after eleven? It would have been about ten, I suppose, or a bit after. It took me a while to get him to the house.'

We'd left Brae at half past nine. I'd been within sight of the cottage by quarter to ten, and after that we'd been concentrating on the shoreline. It wasn't possible that Berwin had staggered out of wherever he'd spent the day and night and wandered down towards Helge's cottage and been helped in the door without our seeing him. Gavin flicked a glance at me, and gave a tiny headshake, which I took to mean that scepticism was radiating off me. I turned and fiddled about with the boat's prow, shoving her back into the water and resetting her, but keeping one eye on the trio on the beach.

'What direction did he come from?' Gavin asked. I glanced over my shoulder and caught the panic in Helge's face. She hesitated, glancing over her shoulder at the snow lying thick and unbroken eastwards except for my tracks and Robin's up to Robin's studio and his to and from his father's house, then waved one hand westwards, towards Linga and the wide Atlantic.

'From that way. He was just on the grass at the end of the beach.'

She didn't seem to hear that she'd changed stones to grass, but I saw Gavin clocking it. DS Peterson's pencil scribbled.

'So he came from the direction of Tirvil's house? Your father's? Might he have been hiding in there all the time he's been missing?'

He asked it as simply as if he hadn't known already that Tirval had said he hadn't seen Berwin.

'He might,' she said uncertainly, then shook her head. 'No. Well, maybe during the day, but Tirval would have sent him home before it got dark.' She finished more quickly, as if with a sudden inspiration, 'Maybe he was on his way back home after his prank, and he slipped on the ice. It's a treacherous path.' Her shoulders relaxed. 'Yes, that could easily be what happened.'

Gavin stood up and gave a long look towards Tirvil's house, visible above the low headland that separated Helge's beach from his. There was a meandering footpath with several sets of prints in the snow, and above us the car track that led from Leonard and Frigg's house to Helge's continued on to Tirval's. There was no reason whatsoever why a boy hiding out with Tirval and returning to his home a mile back along the road would have come down to the shoreline to pick his way along the banks. Unless, I conceded, he'd fallen, woken up dazed and made his way to the house he woke up facing; except that, one, the chopper's heat-seeking sensor would have found him last night, and two, if he'd lain there from dusk to this morning in last night's frost, he'd never have woken more.

Finally, my thoughts concluded, Berwin was a good height, with feet to match. The prints on Tirval's path all looked Helge-sized to me. QED.

'Well,' Gavin said comfortably, 'we'll soon see if that's what happened, even if Berwin's not able to tell us. You've got his shoes in the house, did you say?'

Hoist with her own petard. She hesitated, biting her lip, then nodded.

'By the Rayburn?' Gavin persisted.

She nodded again.

'Just go in and get one, will you, Freya?' Gavin rose. 'We can easily track his prints in the snow, especially if he was the last person down the track, which he must have been. Wasn't he?'

Now she was fairly caught. She sat silent, looking miserably down at the stones by her feet. Gavin sat down again beside her, and waited. She twisted her fingers in her lap again, then turned to him, mouth opening.

It was at that precise moment that there was a distant siren, growing louder, and blue flashing lights coming along the road. Helge leapt to her feet, the relief on her face almost comical. 'That's the ambulance.' She snatched the shoe from DS Peterson's hand. 'I'll go and put all his clothes in a bag, ready for him.'

'They're completely dry now,' DS Peterson said, 'and clean. He could take them to the hospital, to come home in.'

Helge froze, then turned on her heel and scuttled away. Gavin nodded to DS Peterson in acknowledgement of a point scored, then strolled over to me. 'Don't you have a home to go to, Ms Lynch?'

'Ah,' I said, 'it's empty. No man wanting his tea . . .'

'There are two perfectly good cats, waiting for you to return.'

'Well spotted,' I conceded. 'Cat decided he preferred his box by the Rayburn. He'll be a land cat before he knows it.'

'You're putting me off. I can't use third–degree with a civilian present.'

'You used it on me,' I pointed out. 'I know all about your methods, DI Macrae. Confess, or you start tying flies.'

He laughed, and took a hold of the boat. 'Want a shove off?'

I made a face at him and climbed aboard, shoving myself off as I went. 'No need to get your feet wet.'

I poled slowly backwards, taking my time about it. Gavin and DS Peterson waited by the door. The ambulance men went in; Helge and Leonard came out. There was a stiffness between them, like conspirators caught in the act. I wondered again who the pyjamas belonged to. Going by the way they'd draped round Berwin, they could easily have fitted Leonard. Helge said something short and urgent in Leonard's ear, with quick glances around at Gavin and DS Peterson. Leonard nodded. 'Yea, yea, lass, we'll be sitting by him till he wakes.' He put an arm round her. 'Now don't you fret, he'll be fine. All we Callahans have hard heads. He's just shaken up the wits o' him, that's all.'

It didn't quite allay her worry, but she tried to smile. Then the ambulance crew appeared, supporting Berwin on a stretcher between them, and heading for the ambulance. Frigg came straight after them, and Leonard said something reassuring to Helge, and followed, leaving Sheila and Bruce. Sheila tried to follow Leonard and Bruce caught her arm. She shook him off and ran after Leonard, calling urgently, 'I'll come with you.'

Leonard raised one hand in a dismissive gesture, without turning, and continued upwards to his car. Sheila's shoulders slumped. Bruce came up to her and urged her towards the van. They got in and drove off after Leonard.

I was at the point where I'd have to turn the boat and start the engine. I'd reversed the oar and begun to scull round when there was a shout from above me. It was Tirval standing in his doorway. That was all the excuse I needed to let the boat drift round again. He began making his way down the footpath between the two houses, placing his stick carefully. His voice floated clearly through the still air: 'What's going on? Who's that on the stretcher?'

Helge looked up towards him and gave the only possible response, in the best tradition of Victorian heroines. She fainted.

I impressed myself by the speed I got the boat back on the beach. Gavin and DS Peterson had barely got Helge laid down on the beachstones when I was back beside them. 'Can I help?'

'I'm a qualified First Responder,' DS Peterson said. Her fingers were at Helge's neck, checking her pulse. 'She's just fainted. She'll come round now her head's down.'

I suspected she'd come round already and was giving herself a break. I turned and went over towards Tirval, who was making his way down the path on the hill at a good speed. A crunch on the stones beside me was Gavin catching me up. 'Cass, I need to go into Lerwick with Berwin. There was a good deal of money and time used searching for him, so I need to get to the bottom of where he was and what he was doing. I'll be back to pick you up for the party.' He glanced at the path Tirval was coming down, the only place along the whole beach where there were prints on the grass. 'Put your foot beside that print.'

I set my sea-booted foot beside the print he'd indicated. My sea-boots were a generous size 4, to allow for socks; the only prints going up and down this track were rubber boots at most two sizes bigger, nothing like a teenage boy's feet. Nor, as even I could see, was this walker staggering, or supporting an injured person. They were simply Helge's prints, going briskly up to Tirval's with an ice-cream tub of freshly baked scones, or his dinner in a basket over her arm. Berwin hadn't come from here.

But nor had he come from Robin's. Then he must have come along the road from his own house. That made sense; Sheila had said he'd come home at night, and then not gone out of the gate in the morning. He must have come along this way, along the road.

My curiosity was definitely pricked now. The head injury was genuine, there was no question about that, and Helge had been telling the truth when she'd said he was wearing ordinary clothes, and wet. But as DS Peterson had spotted, they were clean now, and dry, which meant Helge had had time to wash them. The trainers too; trainers took ages to dry, even on a Rayburn.

Gavin had reached Tirval now. I heard his voice reassuring: 'Helge's just fainted, sir. It was Berwin in the stretcher. He turned up at Helge's. He's given his head a crack, so they've taken him for a check-up. He'll be fine. He's just shaken his wits a bit.'

'Berwin? What was he doing along here?'

'He wasn't visiting you, sir?'

Tirval shook his head. 'I wasn't lippening a visit from him this day. His mother needs him in the shop on a Saturday.'

'When did you last see him, sir?'

Tirval shot Gavin a sharp look. 'You're still thinking he was maybe hiding out with me while the helicopter was searching all over?' He shook his head again, and was silent while he negotiated the last step between grass and beach. 'No, no. I wouldn't let him do that. When I last saw him, well, he was down here last Sunday, watching the otters, and then when it came dark he went off to meet up with some of his pals at Hamargrind.'

Rainbow's house.

'He came along one of the weekday nights for a yarn and a game of cards. Tuesday, that would have been. I'm no' seen him since. Well, thank the good Lorad he's turned up safe and sound.'

'Amen to that. Now all I need to do is find out where he was and what he was doing while we were turning the place upside down looking for him.'

'He'll likely tell you himself once his wits have settled.' He turned his attention to me. 'You're maybe not had a chance to have a word with your father yet.'

'Tomorrow,' I said. 'We'll be having Sunday lunch with them.' I shrugged. 'But I don't think it'll do any good. They're well stuck in now. I'm not sure Dad would have the power to stop it even if he wanted to.'

Tirval shook his head. 'He can expect trouble, then.' His eyes went to Helge. 'She's coming round.' He strode over to her and supported her to a sitting position. 'Don't try to get up yet, lass. You're been overdoing it. Na, na, dinna try to talk. Bide you still.'

'Right,' Gavin said. 'I'll get off to the hospital and see what they say about Berwin, and what he says himself. Freya, I'll leave you to take Helge's statement. See you later, Cass. It's two thirty, isn't it, that this party starts? I won't manage to be home early enough to eat beforehand.'

'You won't need to,' I assured him.

Gavin raised his hand and headed briskly for the police car, kilt swinging. DS Peterson rose. 'Well, Mrs Callahan, let's get you into the house. Shall I go into the kitchen and make a cup of tea while Cass and Mr Smith get you settled on the sofa?'

Helge nodded. Her skin couldn't go any whiter, and her lips were bloodless.

'I think bed would be the place for you,' I said to her. 'It'll give you a rest from the police for a bit too.'

She shook her head wearily at that. 'I might as well get it over with.' A tinge of colour spread along her cheekbones. 'Give my statement.'

'I can leave you alone with DS Peterson for that, if you'd rather.'

Her eyes flared wide. 'No. Stay.' Her hand clutched my arm. 'I think you'll understand. You feel things. That police-woman, she looks as if she has ice in her veins.'

I rather liked that as a description of DS Peterson, whose green eyes and aloof demeanour always made me think she'd changed a mermaid tail for legs.

'Are you started the broth off yet, lass?' Tirval asked her.

Helge looked startled. 'I'd forgotten all about it, with all that was going on this morning.'

'I'll do that then, while Cass gets you to bed.' Tirval followed DS Peterson into the other main room, and I tried to steer Helge towards the stairs, but she was having none of it. 'I'm not going to bed. I'll lie on the couch.' She was shivering, but her hands didn't feel cold, and the arm under mine was tense. It was strange how anxious everyone was, when they should be giddy-headed with relief that Berwin was safe. His friends too, so concerned to stay with him; surely it didn't matter now if, in his dazed state, he gave away trowie secrets?

Helge lay down with Berwin's pillow under her head, and his downie spread over her. She looked tired to death, as if she'd not slept for two nights. Once I'd got her settled I checked what she took in her tea and went through to the kitchen to get it.

The back extension to the house had to be the bathroom, for the other main room downstairs remained the kitchen. It had been refurbished recently, with units and a work surface all along two walls, and cupboards above, and a rather beautiful Aga, gleaming green enamel with two little lids covering the hotplates. There was a scrubbed wood table in the middle, with a beachball-sized parcel on it, which Tirval was starting to unwrap. I looked at it curiously. Those brown smears on the sacking wrap looked like blood.

'It's half a cow's head,' DS Peterson said.

I recoiled. 'What, an actual head?'

'Cow's head broth,' DS Peterson said cryptically. 'Tomorrow's Byaena's Day.'

I wasn't going to gratify her by asking. A cow's head. It would have come from Leonard's herd, I supposed. They'd maybe killed one for a special roast for Christmas Day – no, because Frigg had mentioned killing a pig. Maybe they'd just killed one for the freezer. I wasn't sure I fancied cow's head broth. Fish in all stages of dismemberment I could take, but my stomach jolted as Tirval unfolded the sacking and revealed a cow's head, fur and all, sliced in half down the middle, remaining eye open under impossibly long lashes. There was a tongue in the bag beside it, far too big, you'd think, to fit in its mouth.

The kettle boiled. Tirval washed the head in cold water then put it in a cauldron and poured the boiling water over it. 'Five minutes boiling,' he said, 'to scald the hair off. Then you wash it in cold water again, and then simmer it for hours for the broo. Tomorrow Helge'll scrape the flesh off for supper on Byaena's Day, that's the Sunday before Yule, and I'll clean it properly for the candle on Yule Day.'

That rang a distant bell. 'You put the candle in the eye socket, and carry it through the house to wake everyone up on Christmas morning.'

Tirval nodded approvingly. 'Yea. Leonard's new wife, she was wanting to give it up this year as an old superstition, but Leonard put his foot down. Helge and Robin and I, we'll go up and wake them, same as always.'

I took Helge's tea through to her, and a plate of digestive biscuits, and DS Peterson followed with the other mugs. 'Mr Smith's getting stuck into sorting out your cow's head,' she said. 'Now, just you relax and have your tea, and then after it you can tell me all about how you came to find Berwin.'

The red came into Helge's cheeks again. Her white hands cradled the mug. 'I'd rather get it over with,' she said. 'It was a bit like I said. He did fall and hit his head, and I brought him back here. But it was on Thursday. Thursday night.' She took a deep breath, and began again, looking at me. 'I don't sleep well. I used to go for a walk at night, if it was moonlight enough to see, but I'm not really able to do that just now. I can row though. And on Thursday, well, there'd been a bit of an argument, and I was upset.' She paused for a moment, thinking about that. 'Yes. I'd better explain that. See, we've always gone over to Leonard's for Yule. Robin's his son, he wants to be with his father at Christmas, but he wouldn't leave me on my own, and Leonard wouldn't have that even if he would, so we've always gone over. But this year Frigg decided she wouldn't have us.' Her voice burned. 'Wouldn't have Leonard's own son at the table. She phoned and talked away about Robin and I'd prefer to be alone, but that's what she was saying. Well, she must have told Leonard, for I hadn't yet, I was waiting till I cooled down, and he was raging angry. He came round to tell me it was none of his doing, and we were to come as usual, and then she phoned too, sweet as sugar, and so sorry I'd misunderstood what she was saying, of course they'd expect us on Yule Day.'

I remembered that little scene in Leonard's workshop. Frigg must have been nervous about his reaction, that she'd brought it up casually before strangers. I tried to remember her words. She'd tried to make it sound as if Helge was calling off, but Leonard hadn't been fooled. *Our house will welcome all the household for the Yule Feast.*

'So I was all churned up about it, and I couldn't sleep. It was such a bonny still night, and the moon shining on the water so that it was clear as day. I rowed in under the shadow of the banks, so that nobody would see me – ' She paused, and shrugged. Her eyes met mine. 'You know how sometimes you want to just be out, and looking, without everyone seeing you? Not that there was anybody about at that time of night, but if I'd been out in the middle, sure as eggs are eggs then somebody would be up and watching, and the next thing I'd know it would be all round Voe that I'd been out rowing at midnight.'

'Was it midnight?' DS Peterson asked.

Helge shook her head. 'Not quite as late as that. Half past ten, maybe. Anyway, I rowed gently along the banks, enjoying the moonlight, and I was just getting near Voe when I realised I wasn't alone after all. I saw someone climbing over the fence from the park with the black sheep in it.' The park with Berwin's disappearing act. Her eyes were wary, darting from DS Peterson to me and back again, and she spoke slowly, as if she was picking her words. 'He was climbing over the fence towards the beach, and I saw it was Berwin – I couldn't see his face, of course, but you know someone by the way they move. I kent about all the trowie footprints, and I thought it might be some new prank, so I didn't call him. He set off along the beach, and then the feet went from under him and he fell his length, and gave his head a right crack. I heard it even on the water. I rowed straight over. He was out cold. I looked up at the house, and there were no lights on, and he was right by the water, wet already, and I didn't like to leave him there while I went up for help. Then he began to come around, but he didn't seem to know where he was or who I was, and when he tried to stand he couldn't do it, his head was spinning too much, he said. Well, I didn't know what to do. I couldn't get him up to the house. I could get him into the boat, so I did that, though it was more a tumble than a clamber, and he lay in the bottom of her while I rowed us back.' She was talking more easily now. 'By that time the tide was full, so the house was only twenty yards from the boat. It must have taken half an hour to get him that short distance. I couldn't get him up the stairs, so I put him on the couch, and got his wet clothes off, and a pair of pyjamas on him. He was barely conscious by then, I had to do everything. I got a hot water bottle to his feet, and a downie over him, made him as comfortable as I could, and put his clothes in the washing machine so he'd have them for the morning.' She paused again. 'Well, I kent I should have phoned Leonard straight away, but they were all asleep, and the boy was safe with me. What was the point of waking them all up in the middle of the night when they didn't even know he was missing? He'd had his wits shaken a bit, and he'd be fine in the morning.'

Now the scarlet was rising up her throat, colouring her jaw and cheeks. Her voice was rough with embarrassment. 'And then in the morning, well, I woke up still mad at Frigg. What right had she to say his son couldn't go to his father at Yule? And then I was tired, from the rowing, and getting Berwin into the house, and getting him undressed, then sitting by him worrying all night, and it blazed over me how much I hated her. She met Leonard at the trade fairs when I was at home with Robin, and set her cap at him straight away.' Her face hardened. 'She chatted him up till he fell for her, and she nagged him until he moved in with her.' She lifted one hand from the mug in a *don't say it* gesture. 'I know. He had a choice. Of course he did. But I know Leonard. He loved me. Yea, sure, the glossiness had worn off, we'd been married seven years then, Robin was at the school. All the same, he wouldn't have gone falling for another woman without a lot of work on her part. And we'd built the house together, he and I, when we married, so he let Robin and I stay there, and he and Frigg had lodgings in Lerwick.' Her mouth turned down. 'It salved his conscience. But she wanted it, so once Berwin was on the way she made a fight for that too. A lodging in town was no place for a bairn to grow up, she insisted to Leonard, and she was there on his back the whole time, and I wasn't. I had no money to buy them out, so it was me had to move.' Her eyes sparked. 'I had to leave the house I'd helped build. I came to Leonard's mam, in this house,

187

she was getting elderly then, not able to manage on her own, and Robin ran between the two houses. It's his home too, he grew up there just the same as Berwin did, but now he's having to sleep in that ice-cold studio so that Berwin can have a room to himself. I offered him a room here but he was too angry to take it. He'd sleep in the studio and be damned to her.' She sighed. 'And the rage just swept over me. I'm sorry for it now. When Berwin woke up still not sure where he was, and not remembering what had happened, I thought, well, he was staging a disappearance. Let her worry! She doesn't even get up to make his breakfast in the morning. The first she'd ken he was gone would be the school phoning to ask why he wasn't there.'

Her whole face was scarlet now, her chest heaving. There were tears in her eyes. She lifted the mug and sipped the tea feverishly. 'So I let him stay and sleep. Even when the helicopter was searching. I'm sorry about that. This morning, though, I was starting to get worried. He still wasn't properly conscious, and I thought I'd have to call the doctor, in case there really was something serious wrong with his head.'

'What was your exit strategy?' DS Peterson asked.

Helge gave her a blank look.

'How were you planning to bring Berwin back to life?'

Helge shook her head. 'I didn't really have a plan. I thought maybe Berwin might go along with the disappearance theory – pretend that he didn't know where he'd been. Or maybe I'd just have admitted I let him bide here and didn't tell Frigg. She kens fine why!'

'Didn't you worry about Leonard worrying?' I asked.

She looked at me, and nodded. 'Yea. But I didn't think he'd worry too much. He's no' a worrier, Leonard. He'd say the bairn was up to some ploy, and he'd turn up soon enough, safe and sound.'

'Well,' DS Peterson said, 'I'll just get you to read this through and sign it to say it's a fair representation of what you said, then I'll pass it on upwards. I believe you told the police you hadn't seen him, when an officer called. I don't know if the Coastguard'll want to charge you for wasting their time.'

Helge made a *can't be helped* face, and put out a hand for the notebook. I rose and gathered in the mugs, to take through to the kitchen.

It was a good story, a plausible story, the simmering hatred of the wife who'd taken her man and her house, Frigg's attempt to cut her out of the Yule feast, and then the boat trip in the moonlight that had given her the chance to strike a blow back at her.

I just didn't believe it.

Chapter Sixteen

haeing a spree: *having a party or celebration*

Gavin and I caught up during the drive to the Brae Bairns' Christmas Party. We were both smartly dressed, Gavin in his green kilt with his good green jacket, the one without baggy pockets, and me in my dress, black with sprigged flowers and a dancing skirt. I'd washed my hair and left it in a black cloud of curls, and I'd done my best to apply some make-up.

'Berwin said he remembered us coming into the shop, but nothing after that,' Gavin said, 'until he woke up at Helge's in a pair of his dad's pyjamas.'

'His dad's?'

'That's what he said.'

I was silent for a moment, considering that. *Dad went to bide at Helge's for a bit,* Sheila had said, about the row over Robin moving out.

Gavin was following my thoughts. 'Local gossip has him living in both houses. If one wife annoys him he goes to the other one for a few days.'

'Emotional blackmail to keep them both doing what he wants.'

Gavin sighed. 'But not illegal. He'd probably say he was doing nothing wrong. They're both his wife – well, barring a little matter of a divorce. It's not actually harming anyone.'

'Except themselves. Helge can't move on and find another man, Frigg can't fight their differences out properly.'

'It's certainly liable to brew the kind of poisonous situation that made Helge hide Berwin like that.'

'Yes,' I said. 'Did DS Peterson believe her story?'

'With reservations. The boy had certainly ended up there with a crack on the head, and she thought he'd come there by boat.'

'Yes,' I agreed. 'That rang true.' I was about to add that I'd seen the next morning that she'd had the boat out, when I remembered that Gavin didn't know that I'd been to Robin's. 'Once she got him into the boat she relaxed, and she was quite easy telling us about getting him into the house.'

'When, though? Because his sister told us he'd come home after the disappearing trick.'

I nodded. 'I'm sure Sheila was telling the truth. It all made sense, the way she told it.'

'I agree. So, Berwin came home, he slipped out the next morning and headed along towards Helge's and Tirval's, instead of to school as he should have.'

'John-Lowrie thought he might have been watching otters at the beach past Tirval's.'

'Maybe. That would bring the boat in, which him falling on the road wouldn't. Maybe he slipped there, and knocked himself cold.'

'Can Tirval see that beach from his house? Because if he can, there's not much would get past him.'

'Maybe he did see, and phoned Helge to bring a boat to come and get him. But then, he'd have phoned Leonard . . . unless he's on Helge's side against Frigg.'

Leonard's new wife, he'd called her, after fifteen years.

'Maybe the boy was on the other side of the headland, the Grobsness side, and Helge rowed round there for the exercise, and found him. But why should she say it was in the night if it

191

wasn't?' He shook his head. 'It doesn't hang together. Anyway, the boy's safe and relatively sound. A nasty crack, the doctor said, but no damage done according to the X-ray and scan. They sent him home. Nothing too active for a couple of days. The Fiscal's thinking about charging Helge with wasting police time.'

We were coming into the outskirts of Brae now. The hall was strung with coloured lights, and the car park was filling up. Gavin swung the Land Rover neatly into a space and switched the engine off. 'Ready?' He reddened and added, 'You look very bonny.'

'You look smart too.' I reached into the back for my ice-cream tub of cake, and we headed for the door. We were greeted by two men I vaguely recognised from the Boating Club, Gavin put a donation into the box and I bought a page of raffle tickets, then we were offered a dram and a piece of Christmas cake, and waved onwards into the hall.

The noise was indescribable. It looked like a good half of Brae's primary department was here, along with their brothers and sisters, their parents, grandparents and anyone else who had the faintest claim to them. The adults were seated all round the outside of the hall, chatting away and retrieving toddlers that ventured too far into the middle. The youngest children were racing round and screaming with excitement, with Peerie Charlie well to the fore; the middle primary, our youngest sailors, were going in a gang from the front hall to the main hall to the kitchen hatch and back. The oldest ones, Dawn among them, were in a dignified huddle by the stage. The younger girls were dressed to the nines in pretty party frocks, the older girls had bright tops, and many of the boys were in their best gansey. Most of the men were wearing a gansey too, and the women were in their party best. I was glad of my pretty frock.

The secondary bairns had colonised the comfortable seats

on the balcony. Berwin was with Vaila, still white-faced, but not wearing any kind of bandage. I hoped his folk would retrieve him early. The chaos below didn't seem quite what an invalid needed. Rainbow wasn't there, nor John-Lowrie; they'd be at the Voe party. The band on the stage were older pupils too, playing Christmas tunes.

Inga was over on the far side, with Granny Beryl on one side of her, and Charlie on the other. There were a couple of spare seats beside Granny Beryl. I greeted them, and sat down beside her.

'Now then,' she said, straight off, 'you'll have heard that I'm had those trows aside me, last night, as ever was.'

'Trows?' I echoed.

She nodded vigorously, making all the freshly permed curls of her fringe shake. 'They danced on my lawn, and one o' them climbed up apo my shed. Lippers! If I catch them I'll give them what for, you mark my words.'

On the far side of her, Gavin's hand slid into mine. Rumbled. 'Did they visit anyone else?' I managed.

'Not that I heard. Of course the chopper maybe frighted them off.'

'It can't have been our three,' Inga said, from the other side of her. 'Vaila wasn't home last night.' She gave me an expressive look behind Granny Beryl's back. 'Cass was babysitting.' I could see her thinking how to phrase it so that I could agree, just as she used to when we were suspected of trouble at school. 'I'm sure she wouldn't have encouraged them to play trows.'

'Definitely not.' Inspiration made me add, 'We were busy making toffee for the party.'

Granny Beryl sniffed, and looked as if she was about to keep probing. Gavin leaned forward past me. 'Young Charlie's a livewire,' he said admiringly to Beryl. 'He's leading all his pals.'

That diverted her. Peerie Charlie, though of course a trooker and a lipper, was the apple of her eye, and if she'd been forced on oath to say what she really thought of him, she'd have to admit that there wasn't his equal for brains and daring from Skaw to Sumburgh, and she expected him to become Prime Minister at the very least, or maybe Lord Advocate, if he stayed in Scotland, or a sea-captain, like her late father. By the time she'd told Gavin of his latest misanter the trows were forgotten. I squeezed his hand gratefully as she was diverted by one of the hall committee coming forward to welcome everyone and get the bairns' games going. The first one was pass the parcel, and the noise mercifully abated as the children were organised into class-age circles. The band launched into 'Rudolph', the brightly wrapped parcels began revolving, and I relaxed and looked around.

I knew a lot of the folk from the sailing. Magnie was over at the far side with Jeemie, whose Starlight we both crewed in come regatta time. He didn't have any bairns to lay claim to, but it was a party for the whole village. He'd have slipped a generous donation into the box, and bought a sheaf of raffle tickets. Immediately above him, on the balcony, Vaila and Berwin were conferring about something. Vaila was urging caution, I thought, but Berwin was determined on something and arguing his case, a hectic flush staining his cheeks. Vaila made an *if you must* face, and looked across at Gavin and me. Berwin nodded emphatically, then winced.

Vaila saw that I was watching. She looked hard at me, moved her gaze to Gavin, then beckoned us over. 'Shall we?' Gavin said in my ear.

I rose, feeling as if everyone was watching me, and he followed me around the circles of parcel-intent children and up the stairs. Vaila shifted a couple of her friends so that we could sit down.

'How're you doing?' I asked Berwin.

'A bit woozy,' he admitted.

'I told him he shouldn't come,' Vaila said.

'Once I start letting you boss me about, I'll have had it,' Berwin said frankly, which surprised her into silence. He looked at Gavin. 'Thanks for coming over. I was wanting to speak to you.' He paused, then went straight to the point. 'I'm faered something's happened to me brother Robin.'

There was a sudden silence below us as the music cut out. Berwin closed his eyes for a moment, as if he was gathering his strength. Vaila's hand crept into his. 'I'm been trying to get hold of him. I'm left him several messages, and told him to get back to me, but he's no' answering.'

'When was the last time you heard from him?' Gavin asked.

'I don't ken. Me phone's gone missing, I musta dropped it on the beach.' He made a regretful face, then brushed that away. 'But I thought . . . see, I dinna ken who those two men were, that fetched up at Mam-Helge's this morning. But they were threatening her. I heard that. And they threatened Robin. Well, suppose it was them knocked me out? I can't remember what happened. They mighta thought I was her son. And then they realised they'd got the wrong man, and went after Robin.'

I looked at Gavin. He was thinking that over. 'They're local men,' he said, at last. 'Lerwick. Well, when I say local, they're from south, but living here now.' He paused, and lifted his head to look at them. 'Have you heard stories about drug users being threatened?'

Vaila and Berwin shook their heads, though two of the boys behind them exchanged looks, as if they'd heard.

'Nasty,' Gavin said. 'If someone's owing them money, what they do is grab them, drive off with them in the car to somewhere isolated, and then phone the parents, threatening to harm the person if the parents don't pay up for them. Naturally, the person begs the parents to pay up – well, wouldn't you, if you were alone in a car with that pair?'

Vaila and Berwin envisaged it. 'Yes,' Berwin said, and Vaila nodded agreement. 'I'd be terrified,' she added frankly.

'And if you were the parent?'

'Pay,' they said together.

'And of course,' Gavin finished, 'the person's not going to involve us. They're breaking the law in buying the drugs in the first place. The parents aren't going to say anything, because they know these enforcers know where their child lives. So we hear these rumours, but if we try to ask anything there's a wall of silence.'

'But now you ken who they are,' Berwin said.

Gavin nodded. 'We had suspicions of this pair being involved as enforcers. We're deciding whether we keep an obvious eye on them, and risk them being swapped for ones we don't know, or keep a covert eye and hope to catch them doing something we can prosecute. Okay.' He delved into his sporran for a notepad, and handed them and me a piece of paper and pen. 'Can you each write down what the pair of them said that referred to Robin?'

I tried to focus, in spite of the beat of the band, and the shrieks from below as the parcels got to what had to be the final layer. They'd definitely said something to Helge about her son. I tried to visualise her, standing there with one hand on the doorpost. It was before Berwin had come to the door. They'd asked if she had a son, that was it. I scribbled it down. *Got a son, have you, lady?*

'Magnie was there too,' I said. 'And Drew, and John-Lowrie, and Rainbow.'

Gavin made a shhhh movement of his lips, and I went back to thinking. It had been the driver who'd said that. His friend had gone back to Berwin. *A missing boy, huh?* Then something about it being a bad place for accidents. Then the driver had said all she had to do was keep quiet and take a holiday. And the other one had said, *Tough on the family, losing a son.* Helge had replied, *Tell him I'll think about it.*

I scribbled it down like a play, and handed it to Gavin. He

read it and nodded, then, as they finished, compared Vaila and Berwin's versions. 'I couldn't hear very well from in the house,' Berwin added. 'And my head was buzzing. But he said, "*Hard on the family, losing a son*." I'm sure of that. I thought they meant me, and then I thought of Robin, that he'd been killed, maybe that we'd been in an accident together, and that's what got me up.'

Gavin looked at Vaila. '*It could be a bad place for accidents*. You and Cass both say they said that.'

'If Cass said it, it'll be right,' Vaila said cheekily.

'Future, though. Conditional. *Could be*. Did you both take it as a threat, rather than something that had happened?'

We both nodded. 'I'm sure it was a threat,' I said. 'And that's how Helge took it. She said to tell him – whoever sent them – that she'd think about it. Before that she was saying she'd stick by her statement.'

'So,' Gavin said, looking at Berwin, 'they hadn't harmed Robin before this morning.'

But he's not answering his phone,' Berwin insisted.

'Okay,' Gavin said. He sat back in his seat and spread his hands towards them. 'Now I understand that you're worried. But your brother's an adult who's got a perfect right to head off on his own for a few days without telling anyone, and we can't go nosing into his private business without a really good reason.'

They thought that over, and nodded.

'What you could do,' Gavin finished, to Berwin, 'if you're absolutely positive your brother wouldn't mind, would be to go to his studio and check it out. I absolutely don't mean snoop among his private papers, or anything like that. Don't go in or touch anything, just look. You ken him. You'll see straight off if he's just gone out for a walk or if he's left for a few days.'

I remembered the person with the backpack that we'd seen leaving the studio. That had been yesterday. Friday. Just after lunchtime.

Berwin thought it over and nodded.

'The *Mary Celeste*,' Vaila said. 'A still-hot cup of coffee left on the table, and sheet music on the piano.'

'I'm not sure your English teacher's being a good influence on you,' I said. 'What's wrong with reading a nice cheerful play like *Romeo and Juliet*?'

Vaila grinned. 'You did a good job last night,' she retorted. 'Granny Beryl's right turned about it.'

'We were letting Peerie Charlie watch the helicopter,' I said virtuously.

'Robin wouldn't mind that,' Berwin said to Gavin.

Gavin scribbled his number on a piece of paper and handed it to him. 'Phone me if there's anything you're uneasy about. Otherwise, you leave your brother his privacy.'

Berwin nodded, and Gavin rose. Below us, the pass the parcel ended, and there were squeals of excitement as a couple of adults came out with packets of crisps and cartons of juice.

We made our way back towards the stairs down to the hall. At the top of them, I caught Gavin's hand. 'Gavin, I might be the last person to have been in the studio.'

He turned to look at me. His face didn't change, but his eyes were suddenly remote. There was a long pause, and I felt myself going scarlet as if I'd been carrying on a clandestine affair with a boy ten years younger.

'Christmas present-related,' I said.

His hand tightened on mine, and he smiled. 'Your expedition on Friday morning?'

'He was fine then, busy painting, and showing no signs of doing a moonlight flit. He sent me up to Voe to have a look at Berwin's disappearance.' Sheila's voice came back into my head. *We all thought it would be really cool.* All. Not just her and Berwin. Had Robin been there too, and somehow led Sheila into suggesting it, so that she'd think it was her idea? Pulling the strings behind the curtain. Then I remembered what else she'd said. I turned to Gavin. 'Sheila tried to get hold of him

198

too, sometime on Friday, when she was worrying about Berwin. After you phoned her, it must have been, because before then she was just annoyed at Berwin for not telling her all about it.'

'She told you on the bus?' I nodded. 'Between one thirty and five.' He was just noting it when his phone rang. He hauled it out. 'Inspector Macrae?'

I thought I recognised DS Peterson's voice at the other end, speaking quickly. Gavin's face went very still. He turned his back to the people in the hall, and took a couple of steps towards the entrance. I saw him nod. He spoke briefly, then put the phone away and turned back to me. One look at his face made the breath catch in my throat.

'I'm sorry, Cass, I'm going to have to go. I'll run you home first, if you like.'

I shook my head. Whatever it was, it was serious. He didn't have time to mess about putting me out to the Ladie. Besides, I'd always been perfectly capable of getting myself home, though not, I conceded, in a dress and strappy sandals. 'No, you get straight to work. I'll get myself home.' I did a quick mental survey of the contents of my purse and suspected it was about £5, not enough for a taxi. I wasn't going to ask for money. I could borrow from Inga if nobody was going my way. 'Someone'll give me a lift, or I'll get a taxi.' I hesitated, then asked, 'Can you tell me . . .?'

He leaned forward to kiss my cheek. 'Thanks, Cass. I'll see you when I see you.' He made a face. 'Policeman's girlfriend. Almost as bad as being a sailor's partner.'

Then he turned and strode through the doors. I watched as the Land Rover lights pulled forwards, shone into the hall, swung away. The engine noise roared briefly over the band and child noises, then was swallowed by them.

I gave myself a shake, and went back down to our seats.

★

Naturally everyone had seen him go. The faces were carefully turned away from me, but there was a lot of reaching for devices, and not just among the younger ones. Granny Beryl had embraced the new technology as soon as she'd realised it kept her in direct touch with friends in all areas of Shetland simultaneously. She was scrolling through Facebook as I sat down, then she hunched her shoulder to me and got on the phone to one of her cronies. 'Aye, aye, Agnes. What's this I'm hearing about goings on at Lunna?'

Lunna! I visualised my map of Shetland. Lunna was on the east side, to the north of us. Lunna House had been the first HQ of the Shetland Bus, the Norwegian operation running guns into occupied Norway and bringing people in danger in and out. Our history class had been taken to see it, way back when I was in third year. There was the house and the kirk below it, with what was thought to be a leper's squint in one side, though our history teacher didn't agree, and a scattering of crofts further along the headland. It wasn't the kind of place to create a riot that needed Shetland's full police force turning out.

Granny Beryl was enjoying keeping Inga and I in suspense, muttering into her phone in a way that would have done credit to an undercover reporter. The noise levels in the hall rose again as the bairns finished their crisps and juice and began to rush around. Peerie Charlie waved to me as he thundered past.

'Well,' Granny Beryl said at last, putting her phone away, 'what d'you think of that now?'

Inga visibly gritted her teeth. 'Beryl, you ken fine well you're no' told us yet.'

Beryl gave the dramatic pause its full length. I felt the blood pulsing in my throat. 'They're found a body.' My throat froze. For a moment I couldn't breathe. She gave us a quick inspection with her little eyes, then, satisfied we were suitably shocked, launched into her tale. 'That was Agnes o' Mooradale – you ken Mooradale, it's the croft after Lunna House, halfway along to the antiques man at Outrabister. She was at the school wi' me, and then she was in the bedroom next door to me at the hostel. So the minute I saw Lunna on Facebook, I thought, well, Agnes'll ken all about it. I'll gie her a ring. The place is flashing wi' blue lights right now.' She gave me a sideways glance. 'That'll be where your man went, then.'

'Beryl,' Inga said, on a warning note.

Beryl sighed, but resisted the speech about the young ones of today being that impatient they couldn't let a body tell a story in peace. 'The south wife that bought Lunna House, she has a dog that she takes out for a run on the beach after lunch. Well, the dog ran along a peerie way, and then stopped dead, sniffing, and then set off as if the devil was chasing it, towards the kirk end o' the beach, and made its way atween the big rocks at that end. Once it got to the end it stopped and howled.'

She gave another dramatic pause. Inga rolled her eyes, but didn't speak.

'The wife called the dog, but it was growling now, and she could see the movement of its head as if it was worrying something. A dead sheep, maybe, and she didn't want it eating that, so she picked through the rocks to where the dog was. It was pulling at something, and she told it to leave it alone. Then she got closer yet, thinking she could maybe see if there was an eartag on it, so she could get in touch with the owner to come and bury it. She thought it was a black sheep, and then she got closer and realised it wasna a sheep at all. It was a body.'

The word jolted even though I was expecting it. 'Did she know who it was?' I managed.

Beryl shook her head. 'What the dog was tugging at was one of the shoes, it was feet end towards her. She didn't look at the head end.' There was a slight tinge of contempt in her voice for this sooth body who didn't have the gumption to get all the information she could. 'She kent right off he was dead. She just saw trainers and dark jeans, though dark's how they'd look soaked wi' water, and she grabbed the dog's collar and hauled it away from the body, and the pair of them stumbled home to Lunna House. She phoned Agnes, as being the nearest house, and went into hysterics on the phone. Agnes, she went along, and her man, Donnie, and Agnes soothed the wife down and made her a cup o' tay while Donnie went along the beach to look, and phoned the police. A young man, he said.'

My heart sank. I looked across at Berwin and Vaila, busy on their young person equivalent of Facebook.

'Did he ken him?' Inga asked.

Beryl shook her head. 'No' he. But he wasn't sure he wid a kent him in any case. A body that's been in the water, you ken, and he thought this one had been maybe een or twa days, going wi' the tide, until the sea had shoved him up over the rocks and he'd stuck there as it went back out.'

I wanted to ask about hair colour, but the words stuck in my throat.

'So Agnes sat with the wife until the police arrived, then that blonde woman took over, and started asking her all about it. The sooth wife had calmed down by then, so Agnes left them to it and came home.'

To get straight onto Facebook, I thought cynically. I looked at Inga behind Beryl's back and made a tiny movement of my head towards Berwin and Vaila. 'Robin,' I mouthed silently.

She understood straight away. It was barely a second before she rose. 'I'd better make sure that boy's not forgetting to go and pee.' She swooped down on Peerie Charlie and bore him off, protesting that he didn't need to, up to the toilet, just along the corridor opposite where Vaila and Berwin were sitting. She shooed him off towards the men's, and waited casually just beside them, chatting. It was so beautifully done that I felt like giving her a round of applause.

They'd obviously heard. Berwin's face was even whiter than

202

it had been, and Vaila was speaking urgently to her mother, hands moving. Inga nodded at the first long speech, shook her head firmly at the second, retrieved Peerie Charlie and let him charge down the steps ahead of her. 'Charlie,' she said, when she reached us, 'Berwin's beginning to feel he's overdone it. Could you give him a run home?'

Charlie rose with a speed that suggested the noise of children's parties did his head in. 'No bother.'

'Leave Vaila here,' Inga added. 'I told her she was to stay.' She gave Charlie a warning look that let him know there was more to it. His eyes widened. He looked down at Beryl, busy on her phone again spreading Agnes's account, then back at Inga. His face stilled a moment as he thought it through, then he nodded.

'I'll maybe sit and have a yarn wi' Leonard.'

'I'll expect you when I see you,' Inga agreed. She sat down again. There was a blare of music from the band, and an announcement that the bairns were all to sit down, and supper would be served. Across on the balcony, Charlie gave Berwin an arm to lean on through the doors, and Vaila went out with them then returned, trailing her feet.

Helge, Leonard, Berwin, Sheila. If it was Robin, they'd know soon. Gavin would be at Lunna by now, and he knew a young man who might be missing. Someone in the team would be bound to know if the body was Robin.

The door to the kitchen opened, and the workers began circulating with trays piled high with hot food: slices of pizza, sausage rolls, meat pies cut into quarters. One of the men preceded them with a container of cups and a sheaf of paper napkins. I wasn't hungry, but I could do with a cup of tea. Beryl helped herself generously and tucked in. 'No word from your man about who it is?' she asked me, between mouthfuls.

I shook my head. 'I'll hear when everyone else does.'

I realised that Charlie going rather left me stranded. Inga

would have run me home no bother, except that now she had the children on her hands. If she'd lend me proper clothes, I could take *Khalida* home. I thought of the dark water reflecting the stars, and the stillness, and longed for it. To be out there, on my own, in my *Khalida* . . . and the run would do her engine good. It would be a clear night, so there'd be light for me to moor up at the end of the pier. Magnie had a survival suit that would fit me aboard his boat, and he could drop me off at the marina as he passed. I looked across the hall to where he'd been and realised he'd gone. I grinned. Of course, he had neither bairns nor grandbairns to recognise him. He'd reappear under a ton of false whiskers.

The tray came round again. I took a slice of pizza and two sausage rolls for later, but shook my head at the fancies.

There was another set of games, which the children played with sugar-fuelled energy, then a stir at the main door. The organiser on the stage exchanged a nod with the men there, and laid her finger on her lips. 'Listen! I think I hear something.'

About half of them stilled enough to hear a bell ringing, just outside the hall.

'I think we have a visitor.'

Peerie Charlie led the excited shriek of 'Santie!'

The organiser managed to get them all to sit down in a big circle, and they sang *Jingle Bells* a couple of times before finally Santie himself appeared, hauling a large and obviously heavy sack stuffed with colourful parcels. He was wearing what looked like a new Santie outfit with breeks and jacket and an impressive false beard made of nylon hair, and yes, he had Magnie's walk.

Dishing the presents out took ages. The sack was packed so that the smallest children's parcels were on the top, and the oldest right at the bottom, and as each child's name was called it came forward, nodded to the question 'Have you been good?', grabbed its parcel, muttered or shouted 'Thank you, Santie' and ran off with it. Peerie Charlie assured him, in a loud voice, 'I've been really good, Santie,' which gave the hall a laugh.

Finally the last present was dished out. The children managed a chorused 'thank you, Santie' and a last singing of *Jingle Bells* as Santie headed out of the door, waving and ringing his bell (the old school bell from the case in the canteen, now I looked at it properly). The organisers rushed round with black bags collecting wrapping paper, and the band struck up a Grand Old Duke of York. I was touched that Peerie Charlie came straight for me. 'You're too big for a present,' he said, 'but you can dance with me.'

It was a very long Grand Old Duke of York, but a parent in the middle began a second set of up-and-downers, so it took only half the time it might have. Peerie Charlie and I had fun spinning and charging up and down when it was our turn, though our arch was a bit uneven. The band ended it with a chord and a 'Thank you, folk, and merry Christmas!'

Around us, parents were gathering up bags, jackets, presents and children. The children were beginning to droop with tiredness; the parents exchanged grave looks over their heads. Word was spreading. Inga picked Peerie Charlie up and slung him on her hip. 'Come on, boy, bed for you. Cass, are you stranded? D'you want to wait till Charlie comes home, or just bed down on the couch?'

I shook my head. 'I'll take the boat home. Can you lend me warm clothes?'

Chapter Seventeen

veesitors: *Shetland pronunciation of English* visitors

Khalida's engine was reluctant to start, but once I'd coaxed it into life I cast off and we backed out of the berth. I set *Khalida*'s nose for the middle of the rocky entrance and chugged through the darkness, my eyes slowly adjusting, into the starlit evening.

Ah, it was bonny out here. The hills each side of me glimmered white in the moonlight, and the bright stars were reflected in the dark water edges. The lights of Ladies' Mire and Muckle Roe, Sparl and Weathersta shone out golden on each side, and the streetlights of Aith were just visible above the point of Queiensetter.

Charlie hadn't returned by the time I left Inga's, nor phoned, which Inga and I silently took as confirmation that the body had indeed been Robin. Otherwise, he'd have returned, or, if he was staying for a dram and a yarn anyway, he'd have phoned to allay our anxiety. Inga dug me out socks, jeans, layers of tops, a jumper and Charlie's survival suit. It was a lesson to me, I reflected, winding the leftover belt around itself, not to wear clothes I couldn't go on a boat in. Vaila's rubber boots smelled strongly of horse, but they were the best fit, and I promised I'd get them straight back to her.

Before casting off, I'd made myself a mug of tea and set it to cool in the mug-holder while I sent Gavin a text: *Going home by boat xxx*. He hadn't replied yet.

I was glad of the warmth of Charlie's suit. The air was cold and crisp; my breath smoked, and the stars were steel points above my head. They were my own familiar stars, the Plough, the Twins, the Bull with his red eye, Orion the hunter with his dagger in his belt, his hare and dog at his feet, defending the seven sisters. The Milky Way ran across the sky like a spangled ribbon, and above the hills to starboard there was the green glow of the Mirrie Dancers. *Khalida*'s engine put-putted gently in the silence, with the exhaust splurtling behind me every few strokes; the water rippled under her forefoot and trickled along her sides, tinted green to starboard, red to port by her sidelights. Her slatted bench was comfortable under me and her tiller fitted snugly in my hand. Slowly, I felt the tension ease from me. It was good to be on the water again; it cleared my head. I was competent and in charge here, not floundering among joint finance and the intriciate world of two joined people; not thinking of Robin. I didn't try to speculate, just let myself be at home in this starlit night.

I glanced to port as I passed the point of Weathersta. There were lights on in Helge's cottage and in Tirval's, shining out into the night and reflected in the clear water, visible as I crossed the end of Olna Firth, then blotted out by the white bulk of Linga. I edged further into the middle of the voe, in case of lobster pots, and reached for my spyglasses to inspect the yellow mussel raft lights flashing between us and the Ladie. However well you knew your own territory, it was a different place in the dark, with distances altered and well-known steering points become invisible. The hill above the Ladie rose well back from the shore, so I was confident that the water's edge wouldn't be too black for me to see my way in to the pier.

I negotiated the mussel rafts and chugged gently into the Sound of Houbansetter. It had been a long day, I reflected: up and searching, then the muscle-men at Helge's and the discovery of Berwin, alive and only slightly bashed, then the party – and now Robin. I had a sudden vivid image of him at his easel, surrounded by his unsettling paintings, turning to give me that smile that both charmed and mocked, and in the regret for a life cut short felt a sharper pang for this life, the little boy who'd seen his mother usurped, his home taken over by a stranger; the young man whose talent had taken him to college and whose lack of money had brought him back, who played dangerous games with his brother, then stood laughing beside him, one arm crooked on his shoulder; the young man whose rebellious unhappiness made him antagonise the two women who should have loved him, Helge and Frigg. And Helge, her son, her only son – how would she bear it, especially as his last words to her had been so contemptuous?

We came past Doig's Point and into the sound. To port, our cottage lay in darkness, and I felt a pang of disappointment even though I'd expected nothing other. Goodness alone knew when Gavin would make it home. The Blade opposite lay dark on the water with only a narrow point of snow where the tide hadn't reached. I put the engine into neutral to let *Khalida* slow down for the approach to the pier, and nipped forward to hang the fenders and fender board.

It was while I was on the foredeck that I saw the vehicle at the cottage turning space. My first thought was that Gavin had come home after all, and gone out for a walk; my second, that he'd have texted to say he was home.

I reached for my spyglasses and focused them on the vehicle. It was too dark to see detail, but I could make out the shape of a long vehicle outlined against the snow. Not Gavin's Land Rover; that was a squarer shape, with a light top. This was more like a black 4x4, with a smudge in the front that might be people waiting inside. Even as I looked, a light flared briefly; someone lighting a cigarette.

I changed my mind about mooring up. Whoever was waiting in the car wouldn't know this was me. All they'd see was a small white motorboat heading through the sound, with one neon-suited person aboard. If I just kept going there'd be nothing suspicious about that.

There was a movement on shore: a grey shadow slipping forward to the end of the pier. Cat knew his own boat. I could just see a smaller smudge at his heels, camouflaged against the sandy gravel. Whatever was going on with the strange car, it had unsettled him enough to lurk outside in safety. I wondered for a moment if I should try to pause at the pier and let him leap aboard, before I remembered the way the pier stuck out below the surface. I couldn't get close enough for Kitten to jump. 'Back soon, boy,' I called softly.

I put the engine into gear again and headed forward. A glance behind me showed that Cat and Kitten had returned to the shadows. I tried to visualise exactly where the various lobster buoys that littered the sound were, or had been, back in October. If I'd known I'd be going through Houbansetter in the dark I'd have been tempted to spend the night at Brae. There'd been a newish buoy, just this side of the Blade. I should be well clear of that one. There was one just on the far side of the mussel lines past the pier. I set *Khalida*'s nose further west of their flashing orange light. Somewhere, hard to see even in daylight, was a growler, a buoy that had been left unlifted for so long that it had grown long seaweed hair which pulled it almost underwater. If I ran straight into that one I'd be scuppered, left floating with its rope wrapped firmly round my propellor – though, on the other hand, I'd be anchored nicely offshore till daylight, and while I was at it I could cut the rope off well below water and get rid of that hazard. If need be, I still had the rubber dinghy aboard. I could tow *Khalida* to the pier. Better not to tangle with it, though. I turned *Khalida* further west, well clear of the Quiensetter point's dark beach and snowy back, and hoped to miss it.

I made my way out through the sound unsnagged, cut the engine and texted Gavin again. *Visitors waiting at cottage. Think black 4x4. xxx*

I'd barely put the phone back below when it rang, the noise startlingly loud in the silence of the night. I grabbed it. 'Aye aye.'

'*Halo leat.* I'm just about to set off home. Is it a welcoming committee for you, d'you think?'

'I think it might be the muscle-men again, unless you have them under lock and key.'

'We let them off with a warning, but every incident helps. It's an ill wind . . . Where are you now?'

'Just into Aith voe. I didn't want to obviously stop or turn back with them watching, in case that alerted them that the boat passing was me.'

'Hmmm. By now they'd have found out more about us, I'd have thought. Unless someone told them you don't drive, they'd expect you to come back alone while I was busy over in Lunna – have you heard?'

'A body washed up on Lunna beach.' I hesitated. 'Robin?'

'Yes. I've been with his folk this last hour.'

The lights I'd seen as I passed; Helge, Tirval, Leonard.

'Which means we're only ten minutes away. I'll bring a squad car with me, in case they're intending trouble. At the very least we want to talk to them about whether they knew Robin. Don't land before I arrive, okay?'

'That's exactly what I'm not doing,' I pointed out. He laughed and rung off.

Ten minutes. I made myself another mug of tea and sat peaceably in my cockpit, sipping it, eating my pizza and sausage rolls and waiting for things to start happening. I could still see our cottage above the headland, and just make out the dark bulk of the vehicle by the line of road.

It seemed no time at all before there was the first flash of car lights in the sky above the cottage, as an unseen vehicle made

210

its way up the far side of the hill, then the lights themselves breasting the hill, two sets of lights. The second set began revolving blue, the colour flashing over the white snow. Gavin's Land Rover went past the parking place, and stopped; the police car behind stopped too, short of the strange 4x4, blocking it in. Time I joined in the fun.

I set the engine going again and retraced my careful path to the stone pier. It had a lip sticking out underwater, maybe a metre below the surface at this state of tide, which meant I had to be sure to keep her well off. I dug out my kedge anchor and dropped it as I approached, then glided cautiously in. Cat slid out from under a salmon bin as I edged towards the pier and lassooed the forrard bollard, then the aft one. Above me, there was a murmur of efficient-sounding voices, with the occasional louder protest from one of the muscle-men. I kept an eye on it as I secured *Khalida*'s lines. Gavin backed his Land Rover beside the 4x4, the police car came to the end of the road and turned, there was a pause while the muscle-men and police officers rearranged themselves – I thought I heard the snick of handcuffs – then the 4x4 came out and followed the police car over the hill. Gavin came walking down towards me. 'Anything needing tied?' He looked at Charlie's neon-yellow suit and smiled, shaking his head. 'Anyone else would have got a lift home by road.'

'Roads are over-rated.' I added a mid-spring and threw the end of the rope ashore. 'Just this one. Thanks.' I measured the distance with my eye and leapt after it. He caught and hugged me. 'It's good to have you to come home to,' he murmured into my cheek.

Cat came straight over to me with his plumed tail fluffed out, and greeted me with a silent mew. I bent down to stroke him. 'I'm sorry, boy. I couldn't stop.'

Gavin put an arm round my waist and we walked companionably up the drive and into the cottage, the cats bounding before us. The kitchen light was dazzling to my night-accustomed eyes. He poured us each out a shot of Scapa Flow, and I fed the cats, then made us scrambled egg on toast while Gavin sat with Cat on his lap and gave bits of information. 'The last call out from Robin's phone was on Thursday evening, to Berwin.'

'Before the vanishing trick.'

Gavin nodded. 'There was a stream of unanswered calls on Friday: three from Helge, two from Sheila. We're waiting for permission to listen to his voicemail. The phone was still logging into a signal until yesterday afternoon. The last time was just before three, not far from the turn-off along the road leading to Lunna, which makes it likely that that was when and where he went into the water.'

'He went?'

'I'm trying not to pre-judge. He fell, or he was pushed, or put.'

'You don't know anything to decide which?'

Gavin shook his head. 'We're past the highest tide now, so we put a tent around him and left him as he was. The Forensics team'll arrive first thing tomorrow.' He paused for a moment, then went back to what he had been saying. 'There's a place just after Lunna, a mile before the ferry terminal, where the road runs right above the water, with a steep bank down. We'll look tomorrow for traces of someone having fallen down there. You never know. The Coastguard's computer programme that predicts where a body might float to makes it about there too.'

'Three was not far off high water,' I said.

'Yes. The tide would have taken the body out of Dury Voe and into the main tide race between Whalsay and the mainland, and that runs for two more hours northwards than it does southwards. He had a whole day in the water, four hours' worth of north, and then the incoming tide washed him round into Lunna Voe and onto the shore.'

'But surely – ' I began. 'I mean, I thought bodies sank.'

212

Gavin nodded. 'Yes. But he had a backpack on, one of those waterproof ones with a waistbelt and chest strap, and it seems to have acted as a float.'

'We saw someone with a backpack leaving the studio.'

'It's logged. Could you recognise them as Robin?'

I shook my head. 'Too far away. The time's right, though, isn't it?'

'Yes. If his lungs were full of air, rather than water, that might make a difference to him floating too. If it was murder, perhaps the person expected the extra weight of the backpack to sink him, but didn't want to make sure by putting a stone in, in case the body didn't go out with the tide, but was left on the shore somewhere. A stone would be a dead giveaway.'

I put the scrambled egg on the toast, and set the plates on the table. 'Will you need to be working all day tomorrow too?'

'Police work isn't what it used to be, the lone inspector and his sidekick sergeant who work all hours till the case is solved.'

I sat down at the table, and Cat changed laps.

'You do a mean scrambled egg. Freya'll be in charge tomorrow, and she'll brief us all when I go in on Monday. Tomorrow we have Mass, and lunch with the family, in traditional fashion. You've no idea the habits we've acquired while you've been on the high seas.' He glanced at Cat, purring in my lap, and patted his own for Kitten. 'Your parents are expecting us all. A real French lunch, with about fifteen courses, and ending with coffee with liqueur in the bottom of the cup, which I've never been able to try, due to driving. It smells fantastic.' He glanced at the combination of Inga's jeans and Charlie's jumper; the corners of his eyes crinkled. 'You might want to make it a dress occasion.'

I realised that I'd left my only pretty dress in a carrier bag in Inga's hall.

Byaena's Day

Sunday 20th December

HW 00.53 (1.9m);
LW 06.33 (1.1m);
HW 12.49 (2.1m);
LW 19.23 (0.8m)

Sunrise 09.07, moonrise 12.35; sunset 14.57, moonset 22.17.

Moon: first quarter

Chapter Eighteen

the Yules: the old Shetland word for the Christmas period (Norse, Jul)

The temperature dipped to well below freezing in the night; I awoke cold, and turned over to curl into Gavin's warm back. I expected to get straight back to sleep, and I was starting to drift off when Robin's death hit me again. I didn't believe it was an accident any more than Gavin did. Someone had killed him.

The muscle-men should have been the prime suspects, but I couldn't convince myself. For a start, as Gavin had teased out of us, Vaila, Berwin and I were agreed that their comments yesterday had been a future threat, but by then Robin had already been dead for nearly a day; sometime between lunch-time, when we'd seen the person with the backpack, and three, when his body had been put into the water.

Motive: love, lucre, loathing. There'd been no sign of a girl-friend in his studio, but that didn't mean he didn't have one, or hadn't recently fallen out with one. Lucre didn't sound likely; artists living in ice-cold studios didn't have money. Loathing seemed a better bet. Frigg loathed him; she'd got him out of the house, but he still strolled in and out, borrowed her car, influenced her daughter. Why kill him now, though? Being forced to have him over for Yule dinner wasn't enough of a motive. Jealousy over Leonard's love for him, a way of hitting back at Helge?

Helge. There was something wrong there. I remembered the mockery in the way he'd said she wouldn't mind me putting my boat on the beach, when she obviously had minded. Her eyes had flashed with anger as I'd mentioned his permission. He must have had a bedroom in her house too, probably still filled with his teenage books and posters, just as mine was at my parents' house, but he was sleeping at the studio. I remembered Berwin standing in the doorway with Leonard's pyjamas hanging round him, and wondered if it was anything to do with that: anger at his father for going between his two wives, anger at his mother for letting him; the contempt I'd heard in his voice. If some sort of row had broken out between him and Leonard, maybe Leonard had lashed out, Robin had struck his head in falling . . . Leonard had a van, and he would easily be strong enough to carry Robin to it. But however afraid for his own safety he was, could a father really throw his son down a cliff to let the sea take him?

Or maybe, when Robin wouldn't answer the phone, Helge had gone along to the studio and they'd argued – but I didn't believe in Helge striking out with a weapon hard enough to kill her own son, and I was certain that she couldn't have moved Robin's body. Not on land . . . she'd been able to move a semi-conscious Berwin using the boat, but a dead weight was different. I tried to think of a way they could have argued that would have him near enough the sea to fall into the boat, but that was no good either, because Laxo, where Robin's body had been put into the water, was on the other side of Shetland, so she'd have to get him into land transport at some point, and there was nowhere she could do it. The only place the road ran down to the sea was at the pier, and she'd have been seen there, messing about with a body mid-afternoon.

He'd had a secretive air about him, Robin, sleekit, as if he'd enjoyed finding out people's secrets. I'd have betted he knew about Sheila and Bruce. He'd have teased Sheila nicely about it, to keep in with her, but he'd have enjoyed firing pin-pricks at Bruce. Maybe he'd gone one joke too far, or maybe he'd threatened to tell Frigg about them. I remembered her comment to Leonard: *I'm sure Bruce doesn't want to eat with his employers*. That didn't suggest that she wanted her daughter to take up with the hired help. I envisaged that: Robin lounging in the doorway of the byre and laughing, Bruce lashing out at him. Robin going down hard on the stone floor. Bruce's van was right there; he could easily have lifted Robin into the back, taken him to Laxo and thrown him over the banks. His revenge on the boy who'd taunted him; a secret revenge on Leonard, who'd carved him as a foolish giant.

Then the snow began, landing softly as cats' footfalls on the skylight, and the sound lulled me to sleep. When I woke again the hills were smoothly white against the still-dim sky. The garden had turned to Narnia, with every branch carrying its own double in snow, and the trowie footprints covered over by powdery whiteness. Cat came to the doorstep with me, hesitated, then slunk over it, leaving a snail trail leading to his underbushes hideout; Kitten tried it with one paw, sneezed, and followed him in a series of leaps. The ponies were already down at this end of their field, heads hanging hopefully over the fence. The larger one greeted me with a whicker, and the smaller one gave a loud snort, just like Peerie Charlie's imitation.

Getting ready for Mass was a bit of a scramble, between showering, feeding the cats and going down to check on *Khalida*'s ropes before brushing my hair and finding my missal. Failing my pretty dress, I put on the uniform I'd worn to come home in, navy cargo breeks and my navy jumper with the bars on the shoulder. Gavin fed the ponies, so that when we finally made it outside, there was contented crunching from the field. It was twenty to ten, and the sun was rising in a glory of misty-red sky that coloured the snowy hills around us blush pink and made Aith's white houses glow rose. The sea was mirror-calm, the palest of blues. Two otters surfaced, dived and surfaced again in front of the Blade. It was so still that I heard the crunch as one of them bit into his catch. Across to the west there was a bank of dark cloud; there'd be more snow soon.

We clambered into the Land Rover. 'We must get you used to driving this beast,' Gavin said. 'I got a set of those magnetic L-plates – you're supposed to take them off, you know, when it's not a provisional driver at the wheel. I know nobody does it, but one of the downsides of being in the police is that you have to be squeaky clean.' He gave me a sideways look. 'You do have a provisional licence?'

I put on a virtuous expression. 'A policeman friend gave me the form a year and a half ago.' It had been Gavin's parting shot in the Longship case.

He smiled, and took his hand from the wheel to touch mine. 'Is it really only a year and a half? I feel like I've always known you.'

I smiled back, and managed a stiff, 'Me too. Anyway,' I added, after a pause, 'I filled it in, and got the offical permit.'

'Good.'

It was beautiful out among the hills. The smooth sweep of white was broken only by the occasional long line of peat bank, dark against the snow and capped by a three-inch layer, like icing on a Christmas cake. Even the verges joined in the winter wonderland: the freeze in the night had stiffened the long grass, and each separate blade had its layer of snow.

'I was thinking I'd maybe try for a couple of driving lessons during this leave, just to see where I've got to,' I said. 'I expect it's like dinghy sailing. There's an official RYA way of doing even the simplest thing.'

'Don't copy me,' Gavin said. 'We're not even at Voe, and I've failed it six times already. I turned the key before putting my seat belt on, for a start.'

'Then depending on what the instructor says, maybe I can book a course of lessons in my next leave, finishing with the test. I could even do one of those intensive week courses, though I think they're all south, so maybe not.'

It came on a serious shower of snow as we hit the main road. The windscreen wipers quickened to double speed, *flack, flack*, and still there was snow running down the window, as if we'd caught a foaming wave going over us. The tyres hissed through pools of water on the salted road, but the ditches at each side were white with snow lying on frozen water. The Kame was empty now of bulldozers, the ugly scarring magicked away by the smooth blanket of snow.

'I was listening to the radio the other day, an environmental programme,' Gavin said, 'and they spoke about a windfarm that had been going to be built in the Thames Estuary being stopped because it was an over-wintering ground for the rare red-throated diver.'

'Ah,' I said. 'That'll be the same rare red-throated diver that nests in these hills, then.'

'Possibly even the same individual birds. As for the peat they're digging up, well, the original plans said it was degraded peat, but opponents are posting pictures showing the diggers in the middle of peat higher than the cabin roof.' He brooded over that for a moment, then conceded, 'Yes, there's good wind up here.'

'Plenty of it,' I agreed. 'Maybe even too much. Don't they have to switch them off if it's too windy?'

'They do. But, this is the good bit, if they're switched off the developers get paid the full sum they might have earned in subsidy, when normally they get at best fifty or sixty per cent of the potential megawattage.'

I thought about that. 'So it's actually to their financial advantage to be somewhere so windy that the turbines have to be switched off regularly.'

Gavin sighed. 'And don't tell me it's only here for twenty-five years. Shetland folk will be living with it for fifty. Two generations of something that'll spoil their views, affect their health, hit their tourist industry hard and bring them a handful of jobs and a remarkably small amount of money. Oh, and double the price of their electricity, to pay for the undersea cable.'

We'd come to Sandwater. Even the snow couldn't make this any better. We looked in gloomy silence at the scars on the hill above the isolated house. The loch where otters played was frozen over completely, but you could see the thicker lines of white where the burns ran from the workings.

'You personally may benefit quite a bit,' Gavin said. His voice was diffident. 'Had you considered how you'll feel about that?'

I hadn't thought about it. I knew, of course, that as a director, Dad would have shares in the company, but I hadn't considered it in making-us-rich terms. I thought about it now. 'Dad will benefit,' I said at last. 'But I'm not taking it.' I looked at the disfigured hills. 'I don't want it. But I won't tell him so until I'm pushed to it. He'd be hurt. He believes he's doing it for the good of the community, but he'd want to share what he makes with us too.' I sat up in my seat, and said more cheerfully, 'He can build Maman the country's smallest state-of-the-art opera house. That should use it up quite nicely.'

'Yes.' His voice modulated to carefully casual. 'If it gets sticky, with him wanting to share it with you, how about suggesting a trust fund for the grandchildren's education?'

I gave him a sideways look. His face was fixed on the road ahead. We'd come around the hill past Sandwater, and now I could see the sea again, that lovely clear winter blue beckoning me. I felt it wrench at me as I turned my face away from it. 'Good idea,' I said equally casual. 'With the proviso that he doesn't insist on calling the first boy some unpronounceable Irish saint name.'

'Oh, he has that settled. He was telling me a couple of Sundays ago that his father was Patrick, and sure, we'd need to think of being traditional and calling the first boy after the grandfather.' His voice had warmed into teasing now. 'I didn't dare say that the Scottish tradition was father's father first, which would make him Kenneth.'

I thought about it all the rest of the way to Lerwick, with the hills swan white around us, and the sea dancing on my left hand and dazzling ahead of us in the distance as we came down the hill into Tingwall. Above us, the five Burradale windmills stood motionless, white against the blue sky. I tried to imagine them three times the height; impossibly huge.

'You'll see a forest of the things from all over Shetland,' I said, looking up as we went below them.

'It's only now that people are realising that. I get the impression that they all shrugged when it was first mooted, and said 'It'll never happen', and now suddenly it is. The protest crowd's growing every day. Shetland Eco-Energy released pictures too, you know, mock-ups of how wonderful it would all look, how unobtrusive, pretty white windmills against a blue sky, and it rather backfired. Folk in Lerwick, even at the south end, suddenly realised they weren't just stuck away in a boring piece of road.' He half-smiled. 'You'll get an excellent view of them all from the Hillhead. From anywhere in Shetland. Fair Isle, even.'

'I said I'd talk to dad for Tirval,' I said. 'About the trows.'

'Good luck with that one.'

'I'll allow him a couple of whiskies first.'

We met Maman and Dad at the door of the church, and went in together. They were a handsome couple, my parents. Dad was into his sixties now, but his hair was still dark, with only a distinguished-looking touch of grey at the ears. You'd never have taken him for anything but Irish; he had those slightly rugged Pierce Brosnan-style looks. He wore his dark suit for Mass, as smart as if he was about to make a business presentation.

Maman oozed French elegance, her dark hair swept up in a chignon, her skin immaculately powdered, her expressive eyes made darker by a sweep of liner, her lips scarlet. She moved as if she was somebody, and so she was: Eugénie Delafauve, international interpreter of roles by Rameau, whose voice persuaded purple prose out of cynical critics. Put together, they were a lot to live up to. I was glad of the gold bars on my shoulder.

It was the last Sunday of Advent, and the church was still bare, but the music group was busy tuning up, and Father David came down the aisle preceded by altar children in white robes to the sound of *The Angel Gabriel*, with Maman's glorious soprano soaring up to the roof. The small children were invited to the front to take turns in lighting the candles of the Advent wreath, white, white, pink for last Sunday and the final white, leaving only the central one with its wick still unblackened; then they stomped off for their own liturgy, leaving the adults to enjoy the familiar reading from Luke: *In the sixth month the angel Gabriel was sent by God to a virgin in the town of Nazareth . . .* I sat in my *Sørlandet* navy, with my knee against Gavin's, and my hand tucked into his. Maman was on my other side, elegant in her white wool coat. She turned her head to smile at me. We all recited the creed together, and went up for communion, and my heart was warm with the joy of it, Gavin and I, and Dad and Maman, all of us being a family together, after so long apart. After all those years at sea, I'd come home at last. There was a baby behind us, snuffling irritably through the post-communion hymn (the *Magnificat* to the tune of 'Wild Mountain Thyme'). I caught at my thoughts – the child I'd lost when I'd barely learned he, she, was there would have been born now. My eyes filled suddenly with tears, and I bowed my face on my hands to hide them.

The hymn ended, and Father David rose. I flicked the sadness away and stood, slipping my hand into Gavin's again. He gave me a quick look; his hand tightened on mine. If I wanted it, if we wanted it, if God willed it, we could have a baby in our pew next Christmas, warm in my arms. Suddenly, fiercely, I did want it.

The main announcement was today's after-Mass activity, decorating the church. The children were in charge of the Christmas tree, once their adults had carried it through from the Parish Room. There were strings of lights for inside the church and in the Parish Room as well, since it was a conservatory at the back of the presbytery looking out over the children's playpark. Lots of adults would be needed to bring the crib items through from the garage, and please could we remember to put the oilcloth underneath the straw, otherwise the church cleaners would be after Father David's blood come Epiphany. He said the blessing and dismissal and exited with dignity to 'O Come, O Come, Emmanuel'.

Maman kissed us both, and she and Dad headed home to supervise the lunch. Gavin and I got busy pinning a long string of lights at windowsill height on each side of the church while a procession of people with awkwardly wrapped bundles dodged each other up and down the aisle. I recognised the camel's nose sticking out from one blanket.

I was surprised at how many people Gavin'd got to know already in the parish, and not just to nod at; he was linking them to their offspring, shrieking excitedly around the Christmas tree, and asking after something they'd been doing at work, or commenting on a hobby they'd obviously told him about. Naturally there was no talk of the young man found dead at Lunna, who'd been included in the bidding prayers. When there was a pause, he turned and gave me an apologetic look. 'It's so good to be a member of the community again, instead of one anonymous person in the Police Scotland troubleshooting squad.'

We got to the last pew and doubled what was left of the string along it, then switched it on to admire the effect: a line of

225

little stars leading to the altar, where already the men had set the stable up. The camel had taken his place up at the altar foot, waiting for his kings to join him. They'd move forward a little each day between Christmas and Epiphany.

'Duty done,' Gavin said. 'We'd better not be late for lunch.'

We headed back at speed along the west road, over the top of the Westings hill, where the landscape was spread below us, the snow-girt houses, the cliffs of Westerskeld dark between the blue water and white hill-backs, the three shelves of Foula just visible above them, distant but incredibly clear, like a landscape seen through the wrong end of a telescope. These ditches were filled with snow too, and topped by the freeze-dried grasses, like an untidy fringe. There were six seals lying on the rocks in Weisdale, and a hump-backed heron intent on the water at its feet.

The cats, when we arrived at the house, were obviously used to this Sunday routine. Cat got his harness on and jumped into the Land Rover front seat; Kitten gave only a protesting squeak as Gavin put her into a little wickerwork basket with an open front. 'Shall we stop at Inga's for your dress?'

I made a face. 'It'll take ages to change into.' But it was our first meal all together. I sighed. 'Okay. I can change at the boating club.'

Going by the smell of roasting mutton and the clattering noises, Inga was busy dishing up lunch as I came through the door. I called and went in, and sure enough Dawn and Peerie Charlie were laying the table, Charlie was sharpening the carving knife and Inga was scurrying round the kitchen, pinny on and face flushed. 'I just called for my dress,' I said. 'Dinner with Maman and Dad.'

'By the door,' Inga said. She put her oven glove down and came into the hall with me, closing the door behind her. 'Any more news?'

I shook my head. 'DS Peterson's in charge today. How's the family, how's Berwin?'

The corners of her mouth turned down. 'Stricken. He and Sheila thought the world o' Robin. Vaila's gone over. I didn't want her to, but she said he wanted her.' She handed me the carrier bag. 'Have a good dinner.'

I nodded my thanks and we drove round the curve to the boating club. Cat instantly expected to get out, and Kitten put her small paws on the wicker mesh and tried to see where we were. I managed to squeeze out without letting Cat escape, and changed as quickly as I could, thankful that whatever the dress was made of could spend the night in a carrier bag and emerge uncreased. Stockings. Petticoat. Cardigan. I shook my hair out of its plait and teased a comb through it. Powder, eyeshadow. It made my eyes implausibly blue, Dad's Irish eyes. Mascara, lipstick. I grimaced at myself in the mirror, and headed out. Gavin whistled as I got into the car.

'Just so long as nobody saw me,' I said. 'That would be my street cred gone.'

'You'll get it back as soon as the points races start.'

The house I'd grown up in was three miles further along the road leading across the bridge to Muckle Roe and round the curve of the island to the Røna, the channel from the end of the voe out to the wide Atlantic. Inga's parents still lived in the last house, at the very end of the road. My dad had built his eighties harled bungalow above a red sand beach, where I'd launched my own Mirror dinghy, *Osprey*. We'd have been able to semaphore him from the Ladie if Papa Little hadn't been in the way. The ploughs had made it this far over the week, and there was snow piled on the verges, but the road between them was white again, pressed down by a few tyre tracks.

I paused by the car door, looking across at the familiar view. Brae up to the left, Weathersta, Linga hiding the passage down to Voe, then, behind it, the hills where the diggers were working. Nobody could accuse Dad of spoiling someone else's view while keeping his own intact. There'd be turbines all along that ridge: Gruti Field, Scallafield which had been my weather prophet every summer evening, the Mid Kame behind. Something stirred in my memory as I looked, then slipped away before I could catch it.

Cat and Kitten knew exactly where they were. Cat stood for his harness to come off, then bounded into the house through the catflap Dad had made for him. Kitten squeaked indignantly to be released. By the time we got in, they were already tucking into a plate of scraps, with Kitten making sure her head was in the way of Cat getting anything like his fair share. It was like going back to my childhood, the house warm and smelling deliciously of casserole, and Maman bustling round the kitchen in her green-striped apron. The casserole turned out to be chicken in cider, preceded by little strips of cured meat and bottled asparagus from Cousin Thierry's farm, and followed by apple tart with soured cream. Naturally there was an aperitif, Pinot, also Cousin Thierry's – 'We visited with the car,' Dad said, 'and came back laden.' There was proper Breton cider with the casserole, and after the dessert, just as Gavin had said, Dad produced a bottle of eau de vie, a clear alcohol which went down like firewater and gave back a pleasant aftertaste of raspberry.

'The French government tries to stop it,' Maman said. 'They will not give more licences. It is pity. But Thierry will continue to make.'

'What proof is it?' Gavin said. He nudged me. 'This, Cass, is why I want you to get your driving licence.'

'Sure, I'll be giving you a bottle home with you,' Dad said, 'now you've got company to drink in. It's not stuff for a man to be drinking by himself. I couldn't tell you the proof, but it'd give whisky a run for its money.'

We took our coffee through to the big square sitting room with Maman's piano in one corner, and the green Chinese rug, where Cat and Kitten were already enjoying the fire. All that drink made me feel pleasantly reckless. I let Dad get settled with his whisky, then said lazily, 'I was speaking to an old man the other day, Dad, who wants to talk to you. He reckons it's the trows who are causing your sabotage.'

Dad choked into his whisky, then set his glass down with a slam. His dark brows drew together. 'Who's been talking about sabotage?'

Chapter Nineteen

halligaet: (behaving in a) preposterous, wild or unrestrained way (metaphorical, from Faroese, høllur: *unevenness, a lump in a worsted yarn, and from Old Norse,* hllr: *sloping)*

'How did your old man hear about sabotage?' Dad looked at Gavin, suddenly formidable. 'Have the police heard?'

Gavin shook his head. His eyes sharpened to alertness. 'Are you saying, Dermot, that there has been sabotage, and that you've kept it under wraps?'

The anger died out of Dad's face. He shot a glance at me, then back at Gavin, then nodded. 'There's been trouble. We had a meeting about it with the contractors and decided there'd been enough adverse publicity. Best to keep quiet about it, and not encourage copycats.'

'What sort of trouble?'

Once he started, Dad told us about it readily enough. 'Though you'll be keeping this between ourselves, please. Now, we'd had more than the usual share of accidents, even given the terrain. There was the bridge, that had been passed as fit for trucks to go over, but in the event it wasn't up to the job, and we had to re-build it. There was a truck that went off the road, the side of the road just collapsed under it. Nobody was hurt, and by the time they got it upright then you couldn't see if anyone'd been digging into the side of the road to weaken it. There was a truck overturned on the hill, too. Same thing. The press had a field day with pictures of capsized trucks, and there was a lot of gloating in the anti-windfarm groups on social media.'

'But all those could have been accidents? Probably were accidents?'

'Probably.' Dad sighed. 'But there were the other things. The first time, it was nuisance value. The plant – the bulldozers and the like – was left up on the hill at night. Well, sure, this is Shetland, you wouldn't be expecting any trouble. Shetlanders aren't like that. Inga and her mob of protesters can shout all they like. The work's going ahead. But damage, no, we didn't expect that. So, the first time. Well, now, that was – ' He glanced at Maman. 'It was while you were singing at that chateau on the Loire. The last week of November. The three machines up on Scallafield had all four tyres let down in the night, and the valve caps thrown away.'

Gavin nodded.

'Like I said,' Dad repeated, 'we don't want the publicity. We thought it was worthwhile to get a man in to keep an eye open during the night, but of course that didn't completely cure the problem. He'd be seen patrolling, because he'd need to take a car between the two sites, Scallafield and then up on the Kame.' He glanced at Gavin. 'You've seen it, of course? Scallafield's on the west of the valley, and the Kame's on the east, with the site offices in the valley between them, and to get from one to the other you have to go back to the site office and around the curve of the hill. The next bit of vandalism was a week later. The watchman was up on the Kame and out of his car, looking and listening, when he thought he saw a blink of a light on Scallafield, and then there was a rap as if someone was using a hammer. He jumped straight back into his car and came around, but by the time he got to the top of Scallafield they were gone. This time the two back tyres on each of the machines up there were punctured. It must have taken a sharp tool with a bit of force behind it to do that. A chisel, maybe. That cost us two days' work, waiting for the spares to come up from south. That was . . .' He paused, calculating. 'The last Saturday of November.' His face darkened. 'Deliberate criminal damage. These tyres cost a packet.'

'Your man didn't see any cars around?' Gavin asked.

Dad shook his head. 'But they could have been parked among the trees in Kergord, or even just along the road a bit, or the person could have walked over the hill, or along the valley.'

'No mechanical knowledge required,' I said slowly. I should have kept quiet; Dad's eyes turned to me. 'Cassie, what's this nonsense about trows?'

'The digging's upsetting them,' I said, catching at the diversion from my thoughts. I'd promised Tirval I'd put his case, and I'd do my best. I leaned forward towards Dad. 'According to this old man – ' Dad snorted into his whisky. I raised my voice slightly. 'He's a sensibly dressed, perfectly compos mentis ex-seaman. He says there are two separate tribes that live in those hills, one just above the south of Voe, on the Sneugie, that's the hill this side of Grobsness, and the other lot up on Gruti Field, that's the hill after Scallafield. Your diggings are disturbing the Gruti Field ones, and they're moving northwards, and getting into the territory of the Sneugie ones.'

Dad humphed disbelief.

'He says he sees them. He watches them. He has an idea of numbers and families, and he reckons the windfarm's what had them going down round the houses. You're disturbing their rabbit-catching grounds and causing a famine, and they're not happy.' I took a deep breath. 'I know it sounds mad. Don't forget, though, in Iceland they check with the elves before building any new roads.'

Dad's face reddened. He started to speak, then stopped and visibly counted to five.

'I don't suppose,' I finished diffidently, 'that you might consider going around trowie hadds, instead of straight through them? After all, the trows could move back once the digging's finished, if their dens are still there.'

Dad gave me a disbelieving look. 'Cassie, my girl, you don't suppose right. The roads have been carefully calculated, and they're not shifting for trows, elves or any other mythical creatures. You're not going to start telling me, now, that you've taken to believing in trows?'

I'd seen odd things at sea, including a beauty of a seaserpent, but I wasn't so sure that there was likely to be anything unknown living in the hills of central Shetland; though of course faked prints didn't disprove real trows. I shrugged in my best teenage fashion. 'I told him I'd ask.'

'Well, you can take back the answer no. The windfarm's coming, and the trows will have to learn to live with it, like everyone else who doesn't like it. They'll take the money fast enough.'

'You want them to live with the wind turbines and not take the benefits either?' I retorted. Gavin's hand came out to grasp mine.

'Sunday, Cass,' he murmured. He looked at Dad. 'The young man found dead at Lunna, that Father David mentioned in the bidding prayers, well, the old man who spoke to Cass is the dead man's great-grandfather. Was that the last of the vandalism?'

'It was not,' Dad said. He took a sip of his whisky and kept the glass in his hands, turning it around. 'After that we told all the boys to bring the plant off the hill at night, and park down by the office. It lost us near an hour's work at each side of the day, but it meant all the machines could be watched at night by one man, and pacified the insurance people. There was no more of it for a couple of weeks, and we thought that had put paid to it.'

'A couple of weeks,' Gavin said. 'Mid-December.'

Dad nodded. 'The night of the eleventh. The Friday before last, and this time it was serious damage.'

I remembered the trowie banner, and felt a sudden sinking of my heart. Even serious damage was being kept under wraps, so the next week they went for serious publicity. Oh, Vaila, Berwin, bairns, what had you got yourselves mixed up in? A chisel, Dad had said, to slash the tyres. Had Robin been using their trowie antics as cover to let him do serious damage?

Dad shot me a sharp look. 'The drivers went to their vehicles and everything looked just as usual, but when they got into the cabs and tried to move off, they found that every single bucket or digging claw was loose.' He looked around us, hands moving as he explained. 'The diggers, see, you want them to be versatile. The hydraulic arm has a shaft on it, like a wheel axle, that holds the bucket or grab on. You line up the holes in the arm with the holes in the bucket and put the shaft through, then there's a nut with a bolt on each end of the shaft to hold it there.' He paused, checking we'd understood. We all nodded. 'Someone had gone through the fleet in the dark undoing every nut and taking out the shafts. When the plant's parked, you rest the arm on the ground, so there was no weight on them, and no noise as the bucket came loose. Their watchman swore he was awake and doing regular patrols all night, and he could well have been. All the vandal or vandals had to do was move behind the vehicle they were working on. Easy enough to hide from a man with a torch in the dark. We've erected a mesh compound now, and the watchman brings his dog with him. That little prank lost us several days' work, by the time the firm had tracked down the shaft and nuts for each individual vehicle – naturally, they were all different – and it cost a good deal for the replacement shafts and nuts, and even more for the couple of ram-shafts that were put out of true as the bucket came off. There are still a few vehicles sitting idle.' He looked at Gavin. 'You can see why we didn't want the publicity. There are too many people who'd make heroes out of the vandals.' He returned abruptly to where we'd begun. 'The drivers were warned not to talk, on pain of dismissal, and they're all employed from down south anyway, because there was no Shetland firm had the plant to do a job this big, and staying in the same hotel, so they would only have each other to talk to. The watchman's local. He's raging mad at being tricked in the night like that.'

'Mad enough to get even if he found out who tricked him?'

Dad's face froze. 'Are you saying there's something wrong about your man's death?'

Gavin answered like a policeman. 'We don't know that yet. We need to ask Cass's old man who told him about the sabotage, in case that's relevant. I'd taken it that it was common knowledge and minor damage, since there'd been nothing reported officially. I'll need to get you to give me your watchman's name.'

Dad hesitated a moment, then answered. 'He's a Voe man. Bruce. Bruce Herculson. He works during the day to the Callahan man that does the carvings.'

'We'll call on your Tirval on the way home,' Gavin said. 'I said to your dad I'd keep it quiet, and I'll respect that if I can, but I think we need to know how he knew about the sabotage. Maybe Bruce Herculson told Robin or Berwin, who passed it on.'

I was about to say that Berwin and Vaila were definitely involved in the trows when I remembered my promise. I left the thought unspoken, and kept on thinking. I knew Robin had been part of the trowie antics. He'd driven them to our house. Vaila had come up with the idea, after her school project had thrown up the 'Devil's Hoofprints', and maybe she and the others had had all the ideas of how to carry it out, using the skills they had, lightness, agility, gymnastics, the ponies, but someone had carved the cat paw 'snowshoes', and

Robin had had sculpting tools. I wondered if Berwin had shared their casual 'Wouldn't it be fun if . . . ?' with him, and he'd convinced them to turn it into reality, a bit of anti-windfarm propaganda. Except that he was for the windfarm. *Don't tell Berwin that.* Maybe the banners were Vaila's flourish. Or maybe he was just saying that to throw Dermot Lynch's daughter off the scent. No, I thought he'd meant it; in which case he wasn't the saboteur . . . I remembered, with a sick feeling, that Drew and John-Lowrie had the mechanical knowledge to take bulldozer arms apart without even needing to think about it. Yet, as Dad had said, vandalism wasn't the Shetland way, and it was a far cry from trowie pranks to wrecking bulldozers. Did they feel any action was justified to save their home? I remembered the scarred hills and wasn't sure I disagreed. Maybe it had been Berwin who'd told Tirval about the sabotage. I wished I could talk to Gavin about it.

And Bruce, as the nightwatchman. Strong enough to lift a body, with a handy van to drive it to where it was thrown in the water. Suppose he'd found out that Robin was the saboteur, the one who was making a fool of him and playing hide-and-seek in the dark hills, among the bulldozers. I thought of his smouldering sullen face and could see him striking out in anger over that.

There was a police car parked outside Leonard and Frigg's door. The curtains of the long kitchen window were drawn against prying eyes. Gavin drove smoothly past and bumped along the road to Helge's and the track to Tirval's. When he stopped, Cat looked up, noted that this wasn't home and snuggled his nose under his tail with a *close that door, there's a draught* air as we got out.

Tirval came to the door to meet us.

Robin's death had hit him hard. His beard was still neat, his tie knotted exactly over the top button of his shirt, but his hand shook on the wooden staff, and his blue eyes were less

236

sharp, his movements less sure. It took him a moment to recognise me; then he held out his hand. 'Cass. Inspector. Come in, come in.'

He showed us into his immaculate living room. Gavin's head went up, and his eyes widened. 'Quad speakers?' he asked. 'And that's surely a Nagra.'

The pair of them went unintelligible for a moment. I looked at the new item on the coffee table, the halved cow's skull, bleached white against the dark wood. It lay on its side, the walls of the skull and jaw curving upward, like an oval bowl. A thick, short candle like the ones we had on the altar at church was stuck upright in the socket, wick unburnt. He must have finished it yesterday, before the bad news came, or perhaps when I'd seen the light on my way home he was doggedly working away at it still, armouring himself against Robin's death with the knowledge that even after the darkest days, the sun would return.

'Sit down. Will you take a cup of tea?'

I glanced at Gavin, wondering if he wanted to be this relaxed, and nodded when he did, even though I wasn't sure my stomach could hold much more. We sat down on the couch together. I gestured at the coffee table. 'Is that the cow-head light for Christmas Day, that you were making yesterday?'

'Today's Byaena's Day. We'll be having brose for our supper, made with oatmeal and the fat from boiling the skull.'

It was probably very good, but I wasn't sure I fancied it. 'It's come very clean.'

'I bleached it,' Tirval said, from the doorway. 'There's nothing like half a bottle of Domestos for cleaning a skull, though you have to boil it up outdoors, or the house'll smell of it till summer. Do you take sugar, Inspector?'

'Just milk, thanks,' Gavin said. He put a hand out to the skull. 'May I?'

'Yes, yes, inspect away.' Tirval disappeared kitchenwards

237

again, and Gavin lifted the skull. 'One of Leonard's cows, did Thorvald say? The size looks about right.'

'I suppose so.' There was a macabre feel about it, the gleaming bone, the white candle in its heart. Gavin set it down again and settled comfortably on the couch until Tirval came in with his tray. I let him serve up tea, then said, 'I tried talking to Dad about your trows. It didn't do any good.'

Tirval shook his head. 'No, I didn't think it would, but you have to try peaceful methods first. They're not happy, not happy at all. I wouldn't like a driver to get hurt.'

'You mean with an accident to a truck?' Gavin asked. He didn't have his notebook out, but I knew that he'd be able to write down every word of the conversation accurately afterwards.

Tirval nodded. 'There've been more trucks than usual with the side of the road going under them. Easy enough for a trow to burrow into the side of the road in the night.'

'But it didn't stop the developers,' I said. 'So they tried other things.' Out of the corner of my eye I saw Gavin frown at me: leading a witness. I sat back and took a few sips of my tea, but I needn't have bothered dissembling. Tirval nodded vigorously.

'They're not a mechanical society, the trows, but they can understand the basics. They can see, for example, that a flat tyre won't work. They've had plenty of chance to examine old cars left up on the hill – folk don't do that nowadays, of course, with the Amenity Trust ready to take them away, but there used aye to be old cars put up into the hill, out of the way, and if you kept an eye on them you'd see how bits would be scranned, over time, and never enough at one time to be noticeable, a seat here, a wheel there. It makes sense they'd do that first.'

'Letting the air out of tyres?' Gavin said.

'The machines were sitting there, up in the middle of their territory.' Tirval leaned forward to him. 'You have to imagine what it's like for them. Centuries of peace up there, with the occasional daytime walker, while they're sleeping, and the hills to themselves all night. Now, suddenly, these monsters are churning up the hills all through your night, and crouching there like dragons during your day. The rabbits and wild birds you eat are scared away. Wouldn't you do something to stop them?'

'What did they do?' Gavin asked.

'There were the truck accidents. That didn't stop the bulldozers, though, they were up there already, and they just kept working away. So they let the tyres down, but they wouldn't understand, of course, that they could just be re-inflated. After that they slashed them.'

Gavin nodded, his sea-grey eyes fixed steadily on the old man's face.

'But that still didn't stop the monsters, though it at least got rid of them at night. So they crept down and disabled them. Detached the bit they dug with, and threw the bits away so that they couldn't dig any more.' He sighed. 'They don't understand about modern money and supply chains. They thought that once the machine had lost those bits it just wouldn't work any more. They had a week of peace, and then the machines came roaring back. That's when they started to move.' He shot Gavin a fierce glance. 'You saw the tracks.'

'How do you know, sir, that they did all this?'

'Ah,' Tirval said. He was silent for a long moment, then he reached forward and picked up the cow-skull light and turned it in his gnarled hands. 'It'll be a sad Yule for us this year. Him that's gone – '

He paused. I remembered that older folk never named someone who'd recently died.

'Well, I'm no able to go up and about the hill the way I once could.' He set the half-skull down again, and reached to pat Floss on the head. 'You and me both, lass, we're no' able for

239

that now. We've had our day.' His voice wasn't melancholy, just matter-of-fact, and there was pride in it as he added, 'And a good day it was too. You've brought a few trophies home from the shows in your time.' He looked back at us. 'I couldn't be up on the hill at night, but him that's away, well, he loved roaming the hills when the rest of the world was asleep. I told him all about the trows when he was peerie.' His face twisted. 'Such a fine boy, he was, with his head of blazing hair. My Loki, I'd call him.' He paused for a moment, hands clenching. 'Then when he grew up, well, this last while, when I've been over old to go and see for myself, he's been telling me. Up in the hill, watching them. He told me about what they'd done to try and protect themselves.' His voice grew heavy. 'But it never works. Humans and their machines. We're too greedy. You see it all the time on the TV. The forests mown down in the Amazon, and the rivers run dry, and the sea filled with plastic.'

He turned his head as if he could see through the walls to where his hills would soon be topped by gigantic turbines, and made a gesture as if he was pushing them away. 'But the earth'll take its revenge in the end.'

Gavin waited, but Tirval remained silent, staring at nothing. Then he shook himself. 'Well, you're no' wanting to listen to an old man yarning all afternoon.' He rose. 'Thank you for coming to call on me.' His eyes came back into focus; he smiled at me. 'Thanks to you, Cass, for doing your best.' He jerked his chin hillward. 'They'll sort it out for themselves, I've no doubt.'

'I'm sure they will,' I agreed. I called the cats and we went back out into the dim light.

'It was Robin,' I said, once we were all safely into the Land Rover. I hoped he couldn't see the relief that was filling me. Not the bairns; Robin, who was beyond being brought to book for it. 'He told Tirval about the sabotage. In the kind of detail only someone involved would know.'

'Yes,' Gavin agreed. He glanced ahead at Robin's studio. A police car was parked in front of it, and there were lights shining into the darkness. 'I'd better stop and update Freya.'

Chapter Twenty

unken craitur: Shetland version of unknown creature, *also used of an unknown person*

We drew smoothly into the lay-by above the studio. Gavin took out his mobile and tapped in a number. 'Dermot? It's Gavin. We've talked to Cass's old man, and it was our dead man who told him about the sabotage.'

Dad's voice said a few words I couldn't catch. He didn't sound happy.

'Yes,' Gavin said. 'I'll keep it as private to the investigation as I can, but I'm afraid we do have to follow it up. Sorry about that.' Dad was still speaking. 'Speak to you later, Dermot,' Gavin said firmly, and cut him off. He put the phone away and opened the car door. 'You're welcome to come too, but we'll have to stay outside the door until Forensics has been. We'll need your fingerprints too.'

I glanced at my dress and pulled my jacket closer around me. 'I'll stay put, with the heater on.'

'Won't be a minute.'

He slipped out of the car and down the path to the door, leaving me thinking. Robin had been the saboteur. I sank down into the seat, contemplating that. A campaign of damage, starting with undercutting fragile road edges and weakening a bridge. A teenage memory surfaced. When we'd read *Shadowed Valley* in school, about the Weisdale clearances, the reason why that very area they were digging up now was grazed by sheep instead of having a dozen houses on it, well, the teacher had told us about damage to a bridge. It had been three young men of the place. Black, that was the name of the landlord, Black by name and black by nature, who'd turned the tenants out of their houses. Some of the young men had sawn through the supports of the bridge he'd be driving his gig across in the hope it would collapse under him. Robin would have read *Shadowed Valley* at school too, probably with the same teacher. Then there was the damage to the bulldozers on the hill: tyres let down, tyres slashed with something like a chisel, and the last episode, before they'd locked their diggers up behind a mesh fence. I wondered how much knowledge you needed to take a bulldozer arm apart. Dad had made it sound very simple, just a matter of unscrewing a couple of nuts. An adjustable wrench would do it. Expensive delays . . . but that's all it would do, delay. It would annoy Dad and his partners, but it'd certainly make Dad all the more determined to continue.

I'd thought that far when a shadow crossed the Land Rover windscreen and darkened my window. 'Cass?' DS Peterson asked.

I opened the door. The cold air filled the space. Cat flicked his tail in annoyance and put his paw over his nose. 'Hi.'

'Gavin told us yesterday that you'd visited Mr Callahan on Thursday, is that right?'

I nodded.

'Can I get you to come down and just give me a brief account of what you did here, from the doorway? That way we'll know where to look for your prints.'

'I'll get my boots on,' I said, bowing to the inevitable. I came out onto the road with my red sailing jacket huddled round me above my blowing skirt, stockinged legs and strappy sandals

243

and felt her eyes on me. 'Sunday lunch with my parents,' I explained. I grabbed my boots from the footwell below Cat. 'Home soon, boy,' I promised as I shut the door.

'You can tell us if you see anything different or missing.'

It seemed I was on the side of the angels this time, or at least not yet Chief Suspect. I exchanged the sandals for boots and we headed towards the studio through the creaking snow, DS Peterson leading me at the side of the path. There were no footprints on it now, but I supposed Forensics might be able to brush off the new snow to find compacted prints underneath. The only cars in the lay-by were the police car and Gavin's Land Rover. I wondered if Robin had a car, and if so, where it was. At Leonard's, probably.

Gavin was chatting to the officer waiting by the door. He gave me an encouraging nod and headed back to the Land Rover. I propped myself against the lee doorframe and looked in.

'Start with why you were visiting,' DS Peterson said.

'I wanted to buy one of his paintings, for a Christmas present.' The dog fox poised against his heather hills glowed on the white wall. 'I arranged with him to come over on Friday morning.'

'You didn't mention to anyone that you were going there?'

'The painting was for Gavin.'

She glanced across at the sinister Up Helly Aa scenes, brows rising.

'One of the fox paintings,' I said.

She turned to look, and nodded. 'So take me through your visit.'

'I beached the boat at Helge's and Robin met me there.' I wasn't going to tell her how he'd spoken to Helge. 'We walked up the park to here.'

'We saw your footprints,' DS Peterson agreed. 'Yours, his,

244

and nobody else's. You came once from the direction of Helge's cottage, and he went up and down from his father's house.'

'We saw him,' I said. 'We were looking from the Brae road to see if Berwin was on the shore watching otters. A dark figure coming into the studio, and coming back out with a backpack.'

'So Gavin said. Around 13.45. Are you certain of that identification?'

I shook my head. 'It was just too far to see. I assumed it was Robin because this was his studio.'

'Male walk, female?'

'It really was too far to see.'

She nodded. 'So, you walked over. Then what?'

'Robin gave me coffee.' I looked across at the table in the corner. 'In a white mug.'

'There are two rinsed mugs in the sink. Did you sit down at the table?'

'No. I drank it while I was walking round, and he went back to painting.'

'Did you touch anything?'

I shook my head. 'Just the mug. I went round the room, then I stood and looked at the fox paintings. I chose the one I wanted, and wrote a cheque on the table while Robin parcelled it up. I put the mug back on the table.'

'You didn't talk?'

I shook my head. 'Hardly at all. I was glad he wasn't bombarding me with information, you know, doing a hard sell. We spoke about the trowie headline in the *Shetland Times*. He'd been interested enough to go and get it. He said he was pro-windfarm.'

Her head went up. 'Oh? Did he give reasons?'

'The planet can't wait, and any non-fossil energy is good. Then, when he was showing me out, he suggested I take a look at the field Berwin had disappeared from.'

Her head went up. 'Can you try to remember the exact conversation?'

I had a go. 'Oh, it was the snow. Neither he nor his mother had trowie footprints, though Tirval had had them. I said something about them not having been visited, and he said – ' I screwed my eyes up, concentrating. *Maybe I went out to them. Maybe they were too busy with other mischief. The darkest nights are here, so they'd be looking to kidnap a fiddler to play at their feasts.* I repeated it. 'Then he said something like, "*There's a field over there would be worth taking a look at*" and closed the door.'

'And did you go and look?'

'Just from the water. I could see the boots and boiler suit.' I remembered Robin in his doorway. 'Robin watched me go. I raised a hand to him on my way past.'

'Time?'

'It was coming up to eleven as I pushed off. I hesitated over whether I should take the extra time to go and look. So the last time I saw him . . . five minutes up to the head of the voe, five minutes back . . . Say five past eleven.'

'And did you talk to Helge again on your way out?'

Checking the time; a witness to see Robin alive after I'd left. I shook my head. 'She was back inside, with the door closed. I suppose she might've seen me passing, and she would have heard me shoving the boat off.'

DS Peterson noted that, then turned to face the room. 'Have a look round and see if anything's changed in here.'

I turned my head in a slow circle, but it all looked as it had done. 'I can't say. There's no obvious change in the position of the chairs or anything like that.'

'Bed area?'

I looked up to the half-loft and tried to focus. I hoped she'd let me go soon. My teeth were chattering in the intense cold. 'I think the sleeping bag was left open, as if it was airing. It had a paler inside. It's been smoothed out.'

DS Peterson scribbled that down in her notebook. I set my jaw and fixed my eyes on the painting of the dog fox in front of his hill. There was something niggling at me.

'Well, thank you. Are you going home now?'

I nodded.

'I'll follow you as soon as we're done here. I'll get a look at the painting you bought, and go through your visit to Callahan properly.'

Oh joy. 'Okay. See you.' I headed up for the car before she could think of any more questions and dived into its warmth, shuddering. 'Full heater, please. I wasn't dressed for that.'

'All fine though?'

'Yeah, yeah.' We bumped out of the lay-by and headed homewards: past the drawn curtains of Leonard and Frigg's house, which had been Leonard and Helge's first home. Gavin's headlamps flashed momentarily into the long darkness of the Kergord valley, caught the roof of Vaila's friend Rainbow's house, then homed in on the road.

The valley. It had the Kame on one side, and Scallafield on the other. *Scallafield*. I knew its shape like my own hand, the smooth back and sudden cliff-brow. I'd seen it from my bedroom window morning after morning, from the school run each weekday. I'd looked at the snow gathering on it and hoped for school to be closed; I'd watched the mist tendrils creep over it on summer evenings and known it would be another fine day tomorrow.

The dog fox in Robin's painting was posed in front of Scallafield.

I wanted to talk it through with Gavin, but a shyness about his Christmas painting held me. Presents were supposed to be a surprise. I hoped it wouldn't be tainted for him by Robin's death. I considered that for a moment, and thought not. The observation, the glowing colours, were the best of Robin, the laughing young man leaning on his brother, the person he could have been.

247

I shoved that thought away and went back to Scallafield. *For the tourist market.*

'Gonfirth,' Gavin said. 'Nearly home.'

Ask your friend Magnie about the Gonfirth Fox.

I glanced over my shoulder at the hill on my left. I didn't tend to connect Gonfirth with Kergord because you saw them from such different places. Gonfirth was here, on the B road north from the west side, and Kergord was down a winding road off the main road eastwards to Lerwick, but actually, due to Shetland's jigsaw-piece shape, the Kergord valley was just the other side of this hill. If Robin had roamed the hills at night, that would have been where he'd gone.

'Sit still,' Gavin said, bumping to a halt at our gate. 'I'll get it.'

I was out of my side before he could unbuckle himself, and then it was only a mile further to our house, and in the kerfuffle of letting the cats out, feeding the ponies and getting myself decently dressed again, I had to stop speculating, but the back of my brain kept working away at it, and once we settled down in the sitting room with a fire in the hearth, and the Christmas tree lights on in the corner, and Cat on my knee, Kitten on Gavin's, the thoughts came back.

Suppose there were foxes on Shetland. They could easily breed in the Kergord valley and not be seen. People didn't look for wild animals in Shetland's interior, they looked seawards: otters, seals, whales. There'd be plenty of rabbits for them to eat, wild birds, maybe the occasional lamb, which wouldn't be popular with the crofters. Someone who knew about them would keep quiet, for fear of a cull in the run-up to lambing. Someone who knew . . . but would anyone know, if they lived somewhere like the Kergord valley? There were houses at each end of it, but only moorland in the middle. Nobody would be up there at night to see them, and they'd be in their dens – no, what did foxes have, earths – during the day when walkers

248

might be up there. There would be tumbled piles of chambered cairn up there, trowie hadds. A trowie hadd would make a good place for a family of foxes to live. Pawprints, well, presumably a fox's footprint would be exactly like a dog's. Crofters would be up there with dogs, doing the yearly sheep round-up, or just checking their flock. Nobody would think 'fox' if they saw a dog footprint.

I thought of Tirval. He used to go up watching, he said. I remembered his words. *Now the Sneugie here, there's a tribe of them live there . . . then in the valley, there's a larger group. That area there's never had houses, too far from the sea, so they colonised it.* He'd said he was talking about trows, but suppose that was some private code for the foxes? *Robin, my great-grandson, he reckons to have seen as many as a dozen.* Blame the sabotage on the trows – but why had the damage been done?

All I knew about foxes would go on a postage stamp. I reached for my laptop and found a bombardment of images of urban foxes – long-legged, bright-orange rangy animals out and about in broad daylight. If they were that easy to see, everyone would know about them here in Shetland.

The Gonfirth fox . . . I tried googling fox shetland and got the activities of a councillor whose surname was Fox. I tried again. Gonfirth fox shetland threw up a Shetland chat site with pictures of a police officer holding a dead fox dangling by its tail. Most of the comments assumed it was one that someone had found dead on a road south, and slung into their boot to liven things up here, just as Robin had said. 'It'd better no' be a live een,' one person said. 'Think o' lambs and henhooses. We dinna want foxes up here.' I reckoned that would be the reaction of most crofters. However, one contributor said he'd seen a live fox three times in Shetland, including a white one.

An Arctic fox? I knew we had Arctic hares, but we so rarely had snow on the hills that they stood out like a sore thumb. An

Arctic fox would be even more visible. Surely everyone would know about that, just as they'd known about the pair of snowy owls that had bred on Fetlar back when I was a child.

I thought about the windfarm sabotage. Foxes could shift territory as the diggers came closer. They'd have to; slashed tyres and broken ram-shafts wouldn't stop a multi-million pound commercial project. They'd just delay the inevitable. Delay it . . . until?

'When do foxes breed?' I asked, abruptly.

Gavin looked up from a book on trout fishing. 'South of England or the north of Scotland?' he asked.

'Is there a difference?'

'The Scottish ones breed up to a month earlier.' He showed no surprise about me asking. 'The female coming into heat is triggered by darkness. You'd expect cubs in March down south, but as early as February in the Highlands. Not that you'd see them then, of course. They don't leave the nest for six weeks.' He kept his head raised, waiting, but when I didn't ask any more questions, he went back to his book.

Shetland foxes might breed earlier yet. We were in December now. The females could be pregnant already. If the windfarm diggers had been on time, they'd be at the top of Scallafield just when the females were about to give birth, and trundling along Gruti Field while they had dependent cubs. If there really were breeding foxes up there, delay would give them time to move.

'I need to phone Magnie,' I said, and headed into the kitchen.

He was at the boating club; I could hear the chatter of voices and soothing country music in the background. 'Magnie,' I said, 'can you tell me about the Gonfirth fox?'

He gave it a moment's thought. 'Now, lass, that's going back twa-tree years. Let me get out o' here.'

I waited and heard footsteps, a door shutting out the noise.

'That's better,' Magnie said. 'There's some kind o' a darts tournament, and I couldna hear myself think. Now. Foxes. There's been a few over the years, but the Gonfirth one, that was, what, five or six years ago, maybe even more. That was a strange one. See, every so often they find a dead fox in Shetland, killed on the road. Now there aren't any breeding here, so whether it's someone bringing up a live een wi' no road sense for fast cars, or whether they just found one dead on the road south and slung it in the boot o' their car to baffle people . . . though sooner them than me, foxes are smelly things, nobody kens.'

He paused to think again. 'The Gonfirth fox. Yea. There were two or three folk in Gonfirth caught a glimpse o' something like a small brownish dog sniffing around. Nobody said muckle about it because you ken how folk would make a fool o' you, ask what you'd been drinking, but there were rumours going round. Now, one o' the folk, I kent her. She and her man had come up to Shetland from Surrey, where foxes to them are like rabbits to us, and she was determined that what she'd seen was a fox. Smaller, she said, and a bit darker than the ones she was used to, but she had no doubt about it. Then a dead one turned up, just past Gonfirth, at your turn-off. The Natural Heritage folk took it away for examination, but I doubt I never heard what they found. It was a mangy-looking thing.'

'I saw the photos,' I said. I thought about that for a moment. The police officer holding it had its tail up at his shoulder, and the nose was still not far from the ground. In dog terms it would be sheepdog-size, I reckoned. 'Did your wife from Surrey have a dog?'

'A black Labrador.'

'A fox would be small in comparison to that, I s'pose.'

Magnie chuckled. 'You're fairly right there. It was getting toward the table stage, that dog, you ken how they go as they get older.'

251

'Yea, a fox would be slimmer.' All the same, a dog person would have a mental idea of a small-dog size. 'Did she reckon it was the same animal, the one she'd seen and the one they found?'

Magnie hesitated. 'Are you thinking this has to do with Tirval's boy's death, over at Lunna?'

'I think it might.'

'Well, then, she reckoned it wasn't. Hers was smaller, she said, and not so red. See, the idea of it being a fox caused a bit of talk, and it was coming to lambing season, so the crofters were reaching for their shotguns. She reckoned that some-one else who kent about it had brought up a dead one from south to take the heat off the one she saw, calm things down. She didn't say that in public, just to me, because she kent I believed her.'

'Can you manage to pin down when this was?' I asked. 'Or might your wife remember?'

There was a long silence. 'She and her man left Shetland a year ago last summer. It was well before that, in the hairst, and no' the hairst before that either. No, here, it was the year that Jeemie's niece married. I mind them speaking about the fox at the wedding. She married in October, in the school holidays, and their boy was the page boy, all riggit like a Scottie in a peerie kilt. Geordie, you ken him. He'd a been four, maybe, and he came eligible for the sailing last summer, so that makes it five years past.'

'Okay,' I said. 'Thanks.' Five years ago. Robin would have just started art college then. I wondered if he'd had a car to drive to and from Glasgow to Shetland; if he'd planted the dead fox to protect a living one.

I'd just put the phone down and gone back into the sitting room when there was a flash in the darkness outside, then the shafts of headlights bumping down our track. Gavin lifted his head. 'Freya said she'd be over.' He smiled at me. 'Now you're dressed to deal with the police, and on your own territory.'

'Makes it easier,' I agreed. 'I suppose I'll need to get a double grilling to prove the Inspector's girlfriend doesn't get off lightly?'

'Every i dotted, every t crossed,' Gavin agreed. He lifted Kitten to his shoulder and rose. 'Shall we bring them in here, or would you prefer the kitchen?'

'The kitchen,' I said immediately. I did a mental double-take, surprised at my instant reaction to the idea of DS Peterson invading this comfortable, homely room, with the Christmas tree bright in the corner, and my laptop on one chair, Gavin's book lying by the other. She had Gavin all day. This was our space. 'But we can offer a cup of tea.'

'A big concession,' Gavin said gravely, and went out to meet them.

DS Peterson came in blowing on her fingers. 'It's well below freezing out there. This is great.' She stretched her hands out to the Rayburn. 'Yes, please, coffee.' The young police officer, Shona, followed her.

'Hi,' I said, and went to put the kettle on. Once we'd got settled round the table, with Gavin banished to the sitting room, DS Peterson looked at me. 'Unless the person with the rucksack was Robin, it does seem that your visit on Friday morning meant you were the last person to see him.'

I felt a cold feeling in the pit of my stomach. 'Not Leonard or Frigg?'

She shook her head.

'But – ' I said. I paused to think about it. The obvious way to the main road from the studio was to go up the track which went between Leonard and Frigg's house and their byre, and out through their customer parking space, in plain view from the pet-shop window; the way the walker I'd seen had been going. 'Didn't Leonard or Frigg see him pass?'

'Leonard went into town straight after lunch. There are various shops that sell his carvings, and he was stocking up for the days-before-Christmas panic. His stuff's popular – the right price to show you've made a bit of an effort, but not prohibitively dear, and a character to suit every taste. He gave us the list of the ones he visited, and I've got an officer going through them, but I've no doubt it will check out.' She gave me a dry look. 'If you're wondering if he already had Robin's body in his boot, best detective-style, there's no sign of a trip to Lerwick in Robin's phone, you know how you can trace it checking for a signal? After that Leonard came straight back to the house, arriving there just after three thirty. He knew the time because of the radio programme changing just as he parked the car. There were customers there, so he couldn't ask Frigg outright if there was news of Berwin, but he looked into the shop and saw from her face that there wasn't. After that he stayed in his workshop, carving. The door wasn't closed, because it was his busy season, with Christmas coming, but there was the curtain hung across it, so he couldn't see anyone, though he heard various cars come and go, and several people came in to look and yarn.'

She paused, and I nodded.

'Frigg said she was kept busy all afternoon. She was a bit flustered, but she said she was so worried about Berwin that the afternoon was a bit of a blank, and she was annoyed at Leonard for going off just as normal when she was worried sick. Once she concentrated properly she managed to give a list of customers, with rough times, and we verified that on her till. Almost all of them were regulars, not strangers. They began arriving just after Gavin's phone call, 13.45, and were steady for over an hour, when she went to make herself a cup of tea, and realised she had no milk, so she stuck up a 'Back in a minute' sign and drove over to the Voe shop.'

'Round about three o'clock?' I asked.

'Slightly later. The shop till had no customers between 14.51 and 15.19, but you have to allow five minutes before 15.19 for them to find what they wanted and bring it to the till.'

'How long would it take to drive from Voe to Lunna?'

'It's four miles,' DS Peterson said. 'Six or seven minutes. Ten at most. We'll have a better idea of whether it was possible when we've spoken to all her customers.' She gave a wry smile. 'She's the one who could have had the body in the boot. Forensics'll be taking her car to pieces. Unfortunately he used it too, when he needed a car. She wasn't very happy about that, but Leonard insisted.'

'She didn't like him,' I said. I hesitated, not wanting to spoil her sudden chattiness by asking too much. 'What about the windfarm's nightwatchman? Was he about?'

'Bruce Herculson. Yes, he was there, in the byre, mucking out. He was in and out, nobody keeping an eye on him. He could have been there all the time, as he said, or not. Forensics'll check out his van too, and he's adamant that Robin didn't use it. He was disarmingly frank about how much he disliked him.'

'And Sheila would still have been at her work, and she didn't drive.'

'Didn't, not couldn't. Preferred not to. She was at her work in theory, but there's a gap where none of her workmates saw her about, they don't think. She's the sort of person who gets taken for granted. Naturally she didn't have a car there, but all her workmates did, parked out of sight of the office window, with their keys to hand in a coat pocket or handbag. She could have arranged a meeting with Robin when she last saw him, and "borrowed" a colleague's car. You saw her at the police station, didn't you? When?'

'Just after quarter past two. I was standing under the Town Hall clock.'

'Ten minutes to go and get the car, twenty to Voe. She could have been at Lunna at the time Robin's phone made its last search.'

'But she thought the world of him. Her face lit up when she mentioned him.'

DS Peterson suddenly straightened, and I realised all this forthcomingness was just softening me up. 'Yes, she liked him. Did you? How well did you know him?'

'I didn't know him,' I said. 'I knew who he was, because he'd picked Berwin up from the sailing. His red hair was unmistakable. That's how I knew him in the charity shop.'

She took me through it all several times, in different words, with Shona typing away furiously. The meeting in the charity shop; the chat with Helge; the visit to the studio; going further towards Voe to see Berwin's disappearing act. Once she stopped I brought the painting out from behind the sit-ootery sofa, where I'd re-stashed it, and undid the bubble wrap.

It was even bonnier than I remembered. The colours glowed in this dim light: the dark red vixen with the playing cubs grouped around her. DS Peterson nodded appreciatively. 'Nice.'

'Gosh,' Shona said, leaning forwards. 'I've never seen wild foxes before. They're completely different from the urban ones that raided our garden at Uni. We used to put down dog food for them. I think our cubs all had lighter bits under the chin, and they were brighter orange.'

The creature Magnie's friend had seen had been smaller and darker, and someone had said they'd seen a white fox, and Bjorn Refursson, the Fox's son, had once owned this land. If the Vikings had brought otters to Shetland for their pelts, well, why not foxes too?

'I want to get Gavin in on this,' I said abruptly. 'I think it could be important.'

He was tying a fly now, book propped on his knee and

Kitten watching his fingers from the chair arm. His fingers stilled, and he looked up as I came in. 'Discharged without a stain on your character?'

'Snow white,' I agreed, making a crossed fingers gesture. 'But I'd like you to take an early look at your Christmas present.'

He set his fly down carefully on the mantelpiece, out of the reach of paws, and came through. The painting was flat on the table. His face didn't change, but his hand came up to caress my shoulder. 'Am I just to look and comment?'

I nodded. DS Peterson's eyes flicked from my face to Gavin's, watching.

'It's an Arctic fox with four cubs,' Gavin said. 'Iceland?'

I let out my breath in a long rush. 'No,' I said. I looked across at DS Peterson. 'The painting of the dog fox on the hill, the one that wasn't for sale. That was Scallafield behind it. It was the only one that had a hill you could identify. All the others had just heather and sky, like this one.' I paused for effect. 'I don't think it's Iceland. I think Robin painted them here.'

There was a long silence. Gavin began re-wrapping the painting in its bubble wrap and gave it back to me. He smiled. 'Hide it again till Christmas.' Then he pulled a chair over and sat down, facing DS Peterson. 'Well. Does this throw our case open? Where do we go from here?'

I put the painting back behind the sofa and stood leaning against the door jamb. I was shut out now, just as Gavin would be shut out if my friend Anders and I were sailing *Khalida*. DS Peterson was his crew. Cat came to rub round my ankles, and I picked him up.

'The possibility of Arctic foxes breeding in Shetland, in the valley where the windfarm's being built,' Gavin continued. 'Our dead man knowing about it, and keeping quiet.' He glanced at me. 'Were you thinking delaying tactics, Cass, when you asked about cubs?'

I nodded.

'A reason for Robin Callahan to sabotage.' He looked across at DS Peterson. 'A motive for someone else to silence him.'

'We need to take another look at the paintings,' DS Peterson said. 'Get a wildlife expert in.' She made a deprecating gesture. 'Sorry, Gavin, but even if you've seen more foxes than I've had breakfasts, it needs to be official.'

'Of course,' Gavin said. 'Scottish Natural Heritage. They're bound to have someone.' He turned his head. 'What's the forecast, Cass?'

'Light snow this evening, clear tomorrow.'

'Perfect.' He looked back at DS Peterson. 'How about we get an SNH expert and a couple of others out along the hill? If there's fresh snow they can look for footprints. Maybe set up one of their movement-sensitive night cameras.'

DS Peterson made a dubious gesture. 'We have to follow it up, of course, but foxes, well, you see them in the city all the time. These ones, I can see they'd be better camouflaged against the heather, but if they were breeding here, wouldn't everyone know?'

Gavin shook his head. 'Red foxes, yes, but these are Arctic foxes. They live in long, long underground burrows, maybe a couple of miles of tunnels, and come out to hunt at night. Even if you're looking for them you're lucky to see one. Look, I'll get on to SNH right now. I know the man to talk to.'

He went back into the sitting room, and we waited as he spoke, voice persuasive. Cat wriggled from my arms, gave DS Peterson his grumpy look (could a cat not be allowed his evening rest?), allowed Shona to admire his plumed tail and headed out of the catflap with a click. Kitten came charging through and whizzed after him without pausing to look at us.

Gavin came back, nodding. 'He's not sure he believes it, but he's keen to take a look if there's even a possibility of a breeding group of Arctic foxes in Shetland. He'll swear a couple of his colleagues to secrecy and bring them along. Cass, since it was your idea, d'you fancy being an extra pair of eyes? Neil'll brief you on what you're looking for.'

I nodded. I could easily spend the morning looking for a creature that shouldn't be here.

Tammasmas

Monday 21st December

HW 01.43 (1.8m);
LW 07.27 (1.1m);
HW 13.39 (1.9m);
LW 20.23 (0.9m)

Sunrise 09.08, moonrise 12.41; sunset 14.57, moonset 23.38.

Waxing gibbous moon

Chapter Twenty-one

hugger-smugger: secretive, hugging secrets to yourself (possibly Faroese, smog: secretly)

It was a beautiful day out in the hills. The sky was a clear, clear
blue, with only a fret of cloud around the western horizon; the
snow lay powdery smooth on the grass in the valley floor, and
in crumpled lumps on the heather. The burns had been frozen
to white streaks meandering down the hill, but the broad river
ran chuckling between its ice-sheeted banks. The air was
stingingly cold, but clear and sharp as fresh white wine.

Gavin had dropped me off at Voe on his way into town.
'Have fun,' he said. 'See you when I get home.'

His SNH expert turned out to be a very tall, very skinny
man in his mid-thirties who introduced himself simply as
Neil, and went straight into instructions. 'Shout straight away
if you see anything that might be a dog or cat print.' He looked
at me. 'Let me decide for certain. Do you know the rough
difference?'

I shook my head, and he bent down to the snow. 'Okay. A
cat print has the pad and four toes spaced equally.' He drew it.
'A dog also has four toes, but the middle two are closer together,
so you get a cross-shape in the middle of the print, and there
may be claw marks. A cat retracts its claws, a dog can't.' He
looked up to see if I'd got it, and when I nodded he stood up

again. 'We're looking for a possible entrance and exit to an earth. It's more likely to be lower in the valley, close to the water.' He turned to the two students he'd brought with him. 'Susie, Phil, you go one each side of the river. I'll take the valley edge, and Cass, you go along as the outlier, just up above.'

We all nodded, and set off, walking slowly along the lines he'd indicated. The heather was deep enough to be hard to walk in, and the ground under it twisted with roots and rabbit holes. I'd be lucky not to break an ankle. I paused and looked upwards, and saw what looked like a sheep track, just another twenty metres up the hill. It would be easier going, and I could look downwards from it.

It felt like a needle in a haystack job. I'd had experience of being part of a Coastguard search and realised then how very small a human body became in a stretch of hill, humped by peat banks and heathery knowes and burn brows, an inch of map expanded into a huge expanse of terrain. We were looking for a small trail of footprints in this wilderness of white.

My track turned out to be a good one, used by Rainbow's ponies to go southwards towards the windfarm and come back again for their evening hay and pony nuts. The round hoof-prints stood out plainly; there was a good bit of weight in a Shetland pony. To the side of it I spotted rabbits going along, first front paw, second front paw, back legs coming together. There were sheep, neat cloven hooves that trailed in the snow to their next position. There was a bird with three toes, like three cigarettes laid in a fan shape, which I wondered about until an indubitable grouse, exactly like his portrait on the whisky bottle, flew up from almost under my feet with an indignant *chack, chack, chack.*

Below me, there was a bit of excitement: Susie was bending down by the water, and Neil came over to see what she'd found. I stopped to watch, glad of the breather. Her hand went out; Neil bent over, then knelt to look properly. His shaken head and shrug said no, or at least inconclusive.

My path went up over a craggy bump in the ground, half-buried upright rock like a small cliff face topped by heather. I glanced down from the height of it and froze. There, below me, at the start of a line leading down towards the water, was a neat trail of footprints. They were bigger than Kitten's tiny ones, slightly smaller than Cat's, and so clear that even from here, four metres above, I could see the central cross and pinpricks of claws. They went out, but didn't return. An underground warren with several entrances, Gavin had said.

I looked down at the others. Neil had stood up again, and they were moving slowly on, heads bent, eyes intent on the snow.

'Hey!' I called 'Up here!'

The heads jerked upwards. I retraced my steps on the track and stopped where it began to go up around the rocky face. Now I knew to look for it, I could see where the heather masked a darker hole, precisely as big as it needed to be, maybe fifteen centimetres in diameter. I called again, and Neil came bounding upwards with long strides that left a ploughed trail in the snow.

'Prints,' I said, 'coming out from below that upright slice of rock.'

I could tell he wasn't expecting anything. He looked forwards at the snow on the narrow ledge, and shook his head.

'Try looking from above,' I suggested.

He went up to the top, where I'd been, and leaned forward, looking intently. Below us, the others waited. Then he whistled and shook his head, still staring downwards. 'I wasn't sure I believed it,' he said. He turned and gave me a broad grin. 'You've found something. You really have found something. Canine, no question.' He took out his phone and began flashing. 'Right, let's get away from here.' Given the pony tracks, half a dozen horses stomping over their heads twice a day, I wasn't convinced we'd worry the possible foxes, but I went downwards obediently as Neil shooed me away and down to the others.

'Canine prints,' he said jubilantly. His bony chin jerked upwards. 'One track, coming out of the base of the cliff there.' He nodded to his satellites. 'Go and look, but keep it quiet, and don't approach the earth.'

We watched from below as they climbed the heathery slope, and stopped halfway up, crouched to peer, then ploughed down again, their faces alight with excitement.

'Not a word to anyone,' Neil warned them. 'I know it's a lot to ask, but not *anyone*. Not even in the office. We don't want even a whisper to get out before we've found out if it really is a fox, and a breeding population.' His eyes went along the valley to where the bulldozers stood in their yellow ranks. 'If it is, then we need to get protection slapped on them, quick.'

'Would it stop the windfarm if there really were Arctic foxes breeding here?' I asked.

'Too right it would,' Neil said. 'A species previously unknown in Shetland, obviously not widespread. A delay at the very least until we found out more.'

'Gavin said that this area used to belong to someone called "the Fox's son". Bjorn Refursson. Is it possible they've been here since Viking times?'

'Brought in as a fur resource? Why not? Some domesticised as Shetland collies, and some gone wild.'

'Could they even be a subspecies by now?' Susie asked.

'Possible . . . possible. Generations of in-breeding.' His eyes were alight with the possibilities. 'That's why we have to keep it quiet. Even the suspicion of it could inspire some wind turbine fanatic to want to remove the problem.'

'Then why,' I said, '*why* didn't the man who was painting

them say anything about them? Surely he wouldn't want the windfarm disturbing them.'

Neil shrugged. 'Not sure what to do for the best?'

I remembered Robin's self-contained confidence, and didn't buy that explanation.

'The windfarm wouldn't really bother them once it's up,' Phil said. 'It's all at the top of the hills. It might even help them, though not for a reason I like.' We all looked at him, and he made a face, mouth pulled down. 'Dead birds,' he explained. 'Foxes are scavengers.'

'That's true,' Susie said thoughtfully. 'Maybe he believed they were better existing unknown, even if they were disturbed by the diggers for, what, three years? They might not even be that disturbed by the digging. It's up there and they're down here. Urban foxes aren't in the least worried by traffic.'

Maybe. I wasn't sure about that either. And where did the trowie antics come in?

'What do we do now?' Susie asked. 'Shall we try and find where the prints go to?'

'Cameras.' Neil's voice was decisive. 'No more disturbance. We've left enough scent around.' He scanned the hillside above us. 'There, up above where the prints are. Just below the path Cass was walking on. There's a cleft in the top of the rock that you could wedge a camera in, pointing downwards.' He glanced at me. 'Movement-sensitive night camera. We can leave it for a week. That'll tell us more. Who's the crofter, d'you know?'

'Rainbow's dad,' I said. I gestured towards the farm at the end of the valley. 'These pony tracks, the sheep up there, they belong to him. He'd be the one to get on your side.'

Neil made a face. 'Crofters get edgy about foxes. I've seen it in the Highlands. That's maybe why your artist kept quiet about them.'

I made a wry face and stood up for my own folk. 'Crofters

in general, maybe. But Shetland folk are really interested in their wildlife. This isn't just a fox that might kill his chickens. This could be a population of something really rare that obviously hasn't been killing his chickens. He's far more likely to join you in protecting it.'

Neil paused, thinking. 'Do you know him?'

'Vaguely. His daughter sails. I know him from him picking her up afterwards.'

'Won't you need his permission to set up a camera?' Phil asked.

'Yes,' Neil conceded. His shoulders squared. 'Right, let's go and talk to him.'

The talking took a while: ten minutes on the weather before the valley was even mentioned, and another ten before the word 'unusual' was used. Rainbow's dad kept an impassive face and waited for Neil to explain what he was on about, and finally the possibility of a camera was mentioned, with a vague explanation of finding out more about the fauna of the valley. Rainbow's dad nodded and gave permission without further questions. I wondered if he'd been one of the people who'd seen a small brown dog and thought better of mentioning it. Neil gave me a lift home to the Ladie and headed off to Lerwick to fetch the camera, simmering with suppressed excitement.

My legs felt like spaghetti from all that tramping round uneven ground. I put the kettle on and had just collapsed into a chair when I remembered it would get dark soon enough, and I still had my *Khalida* to move back to Brae.

It would be cold. I added an extra jersey to my normal sailing gear, doubled up on socks and made a couple of rolls and cheese. Breakfast felt a long time ago.

The cats followed me down to *Khalida*. 'She's not her usual self,' I warned them, 'no cushions.' It seemed they didn't mind;

she was their own boat, and I was going out in her. I started the engine, and they leapt aboard and made themselves at home while I untied the *Herald Deuk* and put a long line on her, ready to tow behind. It was Tammasmas, the shortest day, and the sky was dimming already, even though it was still clear, and not much past one. I found a long-ago jingle running through my head:

> *The very babe unborn cries, 'Oh dül, dül',*
> *For the brakkin o' Tammasmas Nicht*
> *Five nichts afore Yule.*

Dül was sorrow. It was something to do with doing no work after dusk on Tammasmas Night. I approved the principle. Doing nothing for the evening sounded good to me. A restful night in front of the fire . . .

It took me a while to get myself organised. I scooped the snow from the cockpit seats so that Cat and Kitten could sit comfortably, got lifejackets on the pair of them and clipped the Kitten in. They acted as Clerks o' Works thereafter, watching with interest as I sorted out everything else. I rigged up a bridle for *Herald Deuk* from the two aft cleats and tied her close on a shorter rope while I released *Khalida* from the pier, pulled us out into the sound on the kedge rope and got that anchor hauled up and stowed away. I turned *Khalida* 'round so that her nose pointed Brae-wards, and let our little satellite slip backward on the full length of the lines I'd rigged. A last check that there was nothing new trailing, and we were good to go.

Ah, it was grand to be in my own boat, instead of tramping the hills. The ice-blue water had darkened to grey and stilled to mirror calm with the top of the tide. The beaches and banks were shadowed, but the last rays of the sun were bright on the snowy eastern hilltops, and the half moon glimmered above them. The sky was clear, so I'd have moonlight on the water after the sun set. I'd have no difficulty in seeing my way home. I made myself a mug of drinking chocolate, my own familiar mug that fitted as snugly as the tiller in my hand, and munched my rolls, sharing the cheese with the cats. Cat was pleased to be aboard his own boat again too, I could see that. He sat upright in his usual corner, neck craning to see above the cockpit sides, whiskers alert, head turning to watch. Kitten copied him, stretching up on her hind legs to look over at the water creaming past us. The engine gurgled like a friendly seal snuffling, and *Herald Deuk* shooshed behind us.

It was a slow passage, towing, but it wasn't long after two when we made it into the marina, and I knew we'd make better time on the way home, so I let the cats explore their home territory while I tied *Khalida* up and got the *Deuk* ready to take us back. While I was at it I nipped up to the toilet and sent Gavin a text: *Putting Khalida back heading home in Deuk now see you later xxx*

I'd just come out of there when Magnie's car came scrunching down the marina drive. I raised a hand and waited. He stopped by me and opened the passenger door. 'Hop in, I'll give you a lift along to the gate.'

'I need to go back to the Ladie before it gets too dark,' I said.

He nodded. 'I saw you'd gone home by boat after your man was called away. I'd have offered you a lift back to the Ladie, but by the time I'd got all the Santie gear off you'd gone, so I thought Inga must have run you, until I came past the marina and saw your boat gone.'

We got out of the car and strolled along the pontoon. Cat came charging over to join us, Kitten racing behind him with her tail fluffed out. I offered a cup of tea, but Magnie shook his head. 'I just came down to hear what you found in the Kergord valley.'

'*Nothing*,' I said urgently. I looked him straight in the face. 'There's no talk about it, is there?'

'No' that I'm heard yet. I just happened to be heading for Lerwick first thing and glanced across as I was going through Voe, and saw your man's car stopping, and you getting out, and the wildlife man's, wi' several folk in it. I'm no' mentioned it to anybody, but I'll no' have been the only person to have seen you.'

If I couldn't trust Magnie, there was nobody I could trust. 'I'm not allowed to say anything,' I said. 'But we followed up on your Gonfirth fox.' I looked him straight in the face, and he nodded comprehension. 'If anyone should ask, please, you never heard any word of that. Squash any rumours as hard as you can.'

His brows drew together. 'This windfarm's got folk awful riled, and there's a lock o' money involved in it too.' His voice went casual. 'If it should happen that, say, a kinda rare animal was found in that area, the sooner you can get it protected the better. If it was something that might stop the windfarm going ahead, well, it might just happen that someone would shoot it or gas it to prevent it becoming a problem.'

I nodded. 'It might.' I looked at him. 'Magnie, did you know much about – ' I remembered the Shetland way of putting it – 'him that's away?'

'A piece. What were you wanting to ken?'

'Why he wouldn't have told anybody. That sabotage Tirval talked about, you haven't mentioned it to anyone?'

Magnie shook his head. 'Nor heard about it from anyone else.'

'Yes, that's the thing. The windfarm's been keeping it quiet. Dad told us. But Tirval said it had been Robin who told him . . . which has you asking how he knew.'

Magnie nodded. I could see he was thinking it through.

'So,' I concluded, 'if he wanted to sabotage the windfarm, well, why didn't he use this?'

'Your answer would be, I reckon,' Magnie said, 'that he didn't want to.' He thought about it a bit more and came up with the same answer as Phil of the SNH. 'The turbines wouldn't harm them once they were up, and it's remarkable how tolerant creatures can get of disturbance, if it's gradual.' He gave me a sideways look. 'Foxes particularly. You see them in the towns trotting along the pavements, just like a dog. Then there'd be bird carcases for them to eat, and fewer visitors, since nobody's going to be walking along there any more, if they ever were much.' He thought a bit more. 'No houses either. You ken how folk build along in a ribbon. Once one's got the Hydro and the water to them, well, it's cheaper for the next one to build just along a bit, far enough for privacy, close enough to be neighbourly. It would have been just a matter of time before they were spreading inwards into the Kergord valley. Not now, of course, with the turbines. Nobody'd want to build under those.'

'So the sabotage was just delaying, until after the cubs were born.'

'Maybe, maybe. He was an odd one,' Magnie said. 'He had a bit of a difficult upbringing. Safe and secure until he was five, and then suddenly his dad took off with Frigg, and he had a new sister, then they moved into his house and he had to share his room with a baby brother, when he wasn't down with his mam, and then his dad began moving about too, depending on which wife was in favour.'

I thought about that, and about Robin as I'd seen him in the studio. Charming but aloof, absorbed in his work; wanting to set me puzzles. Hugging his cleverness, the painting that wasn't for sale of the dog fox in front of Scallafield; brandishing his secret in plain sight. Scoring off the world because he knew something that they didn't; hugging the secret that was truly his own. 'A hugger-smugger,' I said.

Magnie grunted agreement. 'There's a fair few o' the

anti-windfarm folk keen on wildlife. You could maybe enlist them in to do a patrol, keep an eye going.'

'Tell you what,' I said. 'How about you have a word with Rainbow's dad? I canna say anything, but if you were to call round, casual-like, and tell him I sent you, maybe you could get your heads together and think about who you trust and what can be done.'

'I'll do that,' he said. He gave the sky a glance. 'Yes, yea, you'll still be home in daylight if you get going now.' He put a hand on the bow. 'Are you ready?'

'Thanks,' I said. I refastened Kitten, and backed out.

The water glinted silver out in the open voe. The western hills were outlined by the last of the sun's light, the eastern ones glowed white in the moonlight. I set *Herald Deuk*'s nose for the Sound o' Houbansetter, between the two yellow mussel lights, checked the cats were securely settled in their box below and pushed her up to full speed. After *Khalida*'s rattle and thump, it felt even stranger to be gliding along with only the sound of the waves curling under the bow, and the rattle of water along her fibreglass sides. I wondered if they were making them in yacht-size yet, not that I could afford it.

I glanced down into Olna Firth as I passed. A light shone out in Tirval's house, but Helge's was darkened. I wondered if she was up with Tirval, or maybe with Leonard, grieving together, or if she was alone in her own house, mourning her son.

Thinking of Helge reminded me of the discrepancy in her story about finding Berwin compared to Sheila's. Sheila had said that Berwin had come in on Thursday night, after his 'disappearing act', that she'd spoken to him in his bedroom, but Helge said she'd found him on the beach.

I turned my head forwards, came out from the shore a bit in case of lurking lobster buoys, and thought about that: the line of footprints leading out into the middle of the field and ending there. How had Berwin done that?

I'd seen the trowie footprint methods now. I visualised the children at our house. Robin had driven them to the top of the road. They'd walked in the verge ditch to the top of the field, then called Rainbow's ponies (I'd seen how well that pair responded to a suggestion of food), mounted them there and ridden them to the 'trowie mound' heap of rocks. They'd all dismounted, taken their boots off and walked down to our back door, leaving a trail of trowie prints. Peerie Charlie had come as far as the catflap, then one of the others had lifted him up, carried him around the house and stood him on the windowsill. I remembered the prints that had seemed to be lagging a bit; someone lugging a heavy small boy. Gavin had spotted that. Peerie Charlie had jumped down from the windowsill, as if he'd come through the house, then they'd all made their way back up to the rocks and called the ponies over, making sure their dismounting and mounting prints were covered with hoofmarks. They'd put their wellie boots on again, ridden back to the top of the field and returned to the car – the car I'd heard departing.

More of Rainbow's ponies were in the field next to Tirval's trowie prints, but there were no ponies in the field Berwin had disappeared from, just sheep, and even a solidly-built ram couldn't have carried a strapping teenage boy. A memory came back. Gavin had asked about a ram in the park. He'd been looking at the sheep prints when he'd asked that. Something in the prints had made him think there was a ram: prints that were larger or heavier than the lighter prints of the ewes.

The dark bulk of Linga slid past me. I kept my eyes on the shining water, the blinking yellow lights ahead, and willed my brain to think. Berwin had gone out in his rubber boots, and walked through the deepest snow into the centre of the field, with his trainers slung around his neck by the laces, or stuffed

274

in the pockets of his boiler suit. I tried to visualise him. A backpack would be easiest, leaving his hands free, but nobody had mentioned a backpack at Helge's, when they'd talked about his clothes.

I thought of Berwin. Strapping was unfair; he was muscular and tall, but skinny with it, a lightweight compared to John-Lowrie. He could probably walk on his hands, as Dawn had, but with 'snowgloves' with sheep prints on them. Or maybe they'd been snowshoes. I kept trying to visualise it. If he'd had snowshoes with prints, he'd have had his hands free. He could have scattered sheep nuts behind him, so that the sheep would follow him and cover his tracks. Then he'd vaulted over the fence onto the beach, swapped the snowshoes for trainers and headed homewards. Adding sheep nuts to things he needed to carry definitely suggested a bag.

But how had he headed homewards? *Boots coming down, nothing going back*, Gavin had said. *No sign of him having gone over the fence onto the verge.* He'd got to the beach and then . . . I visualised the field. The sheep tracks, the frosted grass verge, the wire of the fence glinting in the sun. Glinting. The fence down to the beach had glinted grey metal, where all the others were furred with frost. The snow had been shaken off that one, and it was one of the anti-sheep-escape fences with the long wires linked every ten centimetres by upright wires. I remembered Inga and I using those to walk along as a child. You held on to the top wire and placed your feet between the upright wires on the bottom horizontal. No footprints. At the road corner he'd have jumped clear onto the black tarmac, which led all the way to his house.

He'd gone home. He'd spoken to Sheila, told her to be quiet . . . and then he'd gone out again, back down to the beach, and slipped and fallen. Maybe he'd dropped something, or left something behind. One of the snowshoes? It didn't matter that it was a dead giveaway, now the prank had been done, but he might want to repeat the trick. That could be it. He'd sneaked into the house and hurried into bed in case he woke anyone, then, when there was no sound from his parents, he'd got up again to stow his bag of props away safely, and realised he'd dropped something. He'd have to go back for it . . . he was in too much of a hurry, and it was dark, and he slipped and cracked his head.

That made the two stories fit together. Helge had seen him fall, and been unable to get him back home. She'd got him to her own house and made a bed for him on the sofa. While she'd been keeping watch on him and worrying, she'd washed his clothes and hung them up to dry, so they'd be ready for the morning – except that come the morning he still wasn't well enough to get up and out. Maybe she'd expected Frigg to phone her, first thing, to see if she'd seen him, and when she hadn't, jealous rage had made her keep quiet. A fine mother Frigg was, not even to know her son hadn't spent the night in his own bed! Let her think he'd gone off to school. Helge wouldn't have known about the changed system, or maybe she just didn't care. The boy was safe – she wouldn't have wanted harm to come to Berwin – but it would serve his mother right if she had a day of anxiety.

I remembered Helge's face, scarlet with mortification as she came out with the true version of her story. She wouldn't have admitted to that unless she'd had to – so what was giving me this instinctive disbelief?

I was almost at the Sound of Houbansetter now. I steered carefully between the mussel rafts, gave Doig's Point a good clearance and glided gently into the berth. It was just light enough to see what I was doing with her mooring warps and the engine. I released Kitten from her lifejacket, took Cat's off too and slung them both over my arm to carry them up to the house. About four o'clock. Gavin would be home in a couple of hours. I should have nipped up to the Co-op while I was in Brae. I'd need to look in the freezer for tea.

I had absolutely no warning. The cats were still behind me, doing a dusk foray on the shore. The vehicle must have been parked behind the brow of the hill. Someone'd been watching the voe, and known I was coming home.

I came through the gate and into the dark shadow of the house. Something moved in the blackness, and suddenly a blanket was flung over my head, smelling of wool and dust. An arm was around my chest, pinioning my arms. I kicked out forwards as hard as I could, and felt my boot connect with someone's shin; at the same time I tried to drop downwards, but the arm held me. I tried to elbow backwards but the stifling blanket blocked that move. Then someone pressed a hand over my mouth. There was a sweet, chemical smell through the wool, and I felt myself going giddy. Then blackness.

Chapter Twenty-two

yasp: *lively, agile (Norse, jabba: to run)*

I awoke in a moving vehicle. It took me a moment or two to realise where I was. My head was spinning, and I felt as if I might be sick. My mouth was smothered with cloth. Whoever had grabbed me had gagged me too. If I spewed then I'd choke. I forced the vomit back with an effort, tasting it sour in my throat, and tried to assess what was going on. A moving vehicle, and I was in the boot of it, because I was lying on a floor, not across a seat or in a footwell. The blanket was still over my head, tightly secured with what felt like rope. The gag was something like a hankie in my mouth. I worked it forward with my tongue, but the muffling folds of blanket stopped me from getting it right out of my mouth. My wrists were secured with something thin and hard, like a cable tie. I managed to wriggle a finger up to touch it. Guess confirmed. Damn. There was no chance of working my hands free. My legs were free. I stretched them out, and touched the side of the car – no, it felt noisier than a car, a different style of engine note. A 4x4 was my suspicion, or a van of some kind. Bruce Herculson had a van, and probably Leonard too, but I didn't see that either of them would have it in for me. I didn't know anything about Robin's death.

On the plus side, I was alive. I wriggled fingers and toes,

flexed what I could move and added unhurt to the positive total. The blanket smothered what I could feel, but there was a hard knobble at my jacket hem that I hoped was my penknife. I began moving my hip on the floor, trying to work it upwards and out of my pocket, but the vehicle was moving too much. When it stopped, I'd try again. In the meantime, I'd let Gavin know I'd been here, in case it came to that. I lay still again and began easing the blanket upwards with my fingertips, an inch at a time, until I could feel the edge of it, arched my back and reached out behind me, stretching my fingers as far as they would go until they touched cold metal. Fingerprints. I pressed all five fingers everywhere I could reach. Fingerprints, Gavin had said once, was their easiest, cheapest, quickest ID, far better than DNA, which wasn't used nearly as often as the TV crime dramas would have it. I could give them DNA too. I was nearly there with the gag. I lifted my head so that the folds of blanket hung looser and managed to wriggle the last of it out of my mouth with my tongue. I worked up a good ball of saliva, then with a grimace, pressed my face onto the floor, spat into the blanket and did my best to rub the damp place on the floor covering. The blanket stopped me giving them a hair, but I could do footprints. I wriggled onto my back and pressed both feet firmly on the floor. My best sailing boots would be a good identifier; there weren't many Shetland sailors who took a size 4.

The vehicle was going up a hill now, round a very slight curve then down. It slowed for a tighter curve then began climbing. The Brig o' Fitch, the Scalloway turn-off. We were almost in Lerwick.

Lerwick meant people. If they took me out of the car here I might be able to shout for help. We came down the hill and swung around. We'd be passing the power station. A pause for the mini-roundabout. Past the ferry terminal; past the Co-op in a rumble of trucks; round that roundabout and heading for the town centre. I listened and felt the movement with all my senses. Straight along, heading for the Esplanade, round that roundabout and over the speed bumps. If they stopped in the car park that might give me time to get my knife. A halt: the traffic lights at Ian's Fish and Chips. On again, and then, where I'd expected the swing round up Church Road, the speed slowed to a crawl. The vehicle went off to the left. I felt the unevenness of flagstones under the wheels. We'd turned along the road that led to the Boating Club. The vehicle squeezed through the narrowest piece, turned into a parking space and stopped.

I knew exactly where we were now: in the heart of the oldest part of Lerwick, leading east from the Esplanade. If you stood by the lifeboat and looked along it, you saw the way all of Lerwick had looked before they'd built the new pier in the days of the herring fisheries boom: grey, stone-built houses with the sea washing at their feet, and loading gates in their sides. One or two still had pulleys above their windows, and one had slatted windows on each side where the fish had been hung to dry in the circulating air. Between the houses were little crescents of yellow sand, or passageways leading down to sea steps, where a boat had once been parked. They still had the names of the merchants who'd traded there: Bain's Beach, Stout's Close. I reckoned that the vehicle I was in had parked in front of the Old Manse, Lerwick's oldest-still-inhabited, just past the Boating Club and opposite the former Sea Scouts' hut at Copland's Pier.

Knowing where I was heartened me. There was a long pause. I heard footsteps and teenage girls chatting and laughing. The sound diminished into the distance. Another wait, then I felt the vehicle shake and rise as the driver got out. A heavy person, by the feel of it. A hand on the door of where I was held. My brain raced, calculating the odds. There wouldn't be anyone around to see me being bundled out; the wait had been to make sure of that. I couldn't run, not muffled up like this. I might be better to stay dopey, and wait for a proper chance to get away.

On the other hand, here in the street was my best hope of rescue. There were houses here, flats, people at windows. Now might be my only chance.

Rough hands hauled me out of the tailgate. I still wasn't sure whether it was one person or two. I played half-doped until I was on my feet, then, suddenly, I wrenched away and began running, blinded by the smothering blanket and gasping for breath. 'Help!' I yelled, and kept shouting it. 'Help, help, help!'

He grabbed me before I'd gone twenty metres. I kicked and wriggled as I felt the hands close round me, then went limp as he hustled me along the street, still shouting. I got a slap across the head with a force that made my jaw rattle, then I was swung over someone's shoulder. A doorhandle snicked, and I felt the light change as we went into a building. He began climbing stairs. One landing, two. Another door opened, and I was dropped on the floor, hitting my funnybone with a thud that sent a jab of pain up my arm. A heavy boot landed a kick on my thigh, then I felt my ankles being grabbed and heard the faint zip sound of a cable tie being tightened.

'That,' a man's voice said, in an angry mutter, and with an American accent, 'should fix you.'

Footsteps vibrated through the floor, and the door closed. There was the sound of two substantial bolts being shot home. I let the steps recede down the stairs before I relieved my feelings by swearing heartily into my blanket, then levered myself into a sitting position. Whoever was responsible for dumping me like this was going to be very sorry.

The next hour was frustrating and so bitterly cold that I was grateful I'd been grabbed in full sailing gear. I wriggled and squirmed as hard as I could, but the pocket with my knife in was firmly zipped, and though I could reach the zip tag, I couldn't get enough purchase to pull it down. The rope was too tight around me to ease the blanket off, and when I got to my feet I could only shuffle half an inch at a time.

While I was fighting, I was thinking. The muscle-men I'd met had been taken off into custody last night, and anyway they'd put on American accents. The man who'd spoken earlier had sounded like the real thing. Hired muscle, with an efficient line in tying someone up. A rich pharmaceutical company with a fortune to lose, if Helge and the others won their case, could easily afford several pairs of thugs. The muscle-men at Helge's hadn't believed her when she said she'd think about it, and they'd been dubious about who I was, and they'd reported back. Maybe they'd put me here to keep me out of the way while they silenced Helge. I needed to get free.

I was desperately trying to force my hips through the circle of my tied arms when I heard a noise below, heavy steps and a stumbling noise. I dropped back on the floor and lay still. The bolts grated back and the door opened. Heavy boots vibrated on the floorboards. Someone came right up to me. 'Do we let her go now?' His voice sneered. 'The cop's nosy girlfriend who likes playing detective.'

Yes, the other muscle-men had been asking around, and passed the information on.

'The morning'll do,' the man who'd brought me here replied. 'We need to deal with the other one first.'

I felt the floor jump as something heavy fell on it, then the two sets of boots stomped off. The bolts slammed, the feet retreated down the stairs. There was a long silence, then there was a gasp, and a scraping noise, from the other side of the room.

I wasn't alone in here.

'Who's there?' I said sharply.

I was answered with a muffled noise. The person was gagged, as I had been.

'I'm Cass,' I said. 'Cass Lynch. Keep speaking and I'll work my way over to you.'

The person kept grunting and I stretched out and rolled in that direction until I felt myself bump against another person. I wriggled until my back was to them and felt with my fingers. They were blanketed, just as I was, and I touched the rope round their middle.

'I need to be able to touch your hands,' I said. 'Can you roll so that your back's towards me?'

The person managed to hump themselves over. I began pulling their blanket upwards and at last felt their fingers under mine. They were ice cold; a woman's hands, long, as if it was a tall person, and so thin that the skin was loose over the bones.

'Helge?' I said.

The muffled response sounded like a yes.

'I'll wriggle upwards until your hands are at my pocket. There's a penknife in there. If you can get it out, I'll cut your hands free, and then you can cut mine. Then we'll think about getting out of here.'

I edged upwards on the floor, and then shuffled until her hands were at my pocket level. 'If you feel with your fingers now you'll feel where the lump of it is, and the edge of the pocket.'

It was strange and embarrassing to feel her fingers moving on me, fumblingly locating the knife, the edge of the pocket, unzipping it, working their way inside. The way her hands were tied meant she was having to work with the backs of her fingers, and it took ages before the knife began to move upwards against my hip, slowly, slowly, and then fell with a clatter on the floor. Helge lay backwards with a sigh, and I reached with my bound hands for my knife. It came sweetly into my hand. I found the indentation for the saw blade, and eased it open.

'Hold very still,' I said. 'I'll take it slowly.'

It took several minutes to get my hands into position, with the knife cutting upwards between her wrists, and I sawed with little strokes, in case the knife slipped. My own hands were aching by the time the cable tie snapped and her hands fell free.

'I'll get this rope off too,' I said. 'Then you'll be able to see what you're doing. Hold still.'

I wriggled again till I could reach the rope around her waist, then relieved my feelings by slashing it savagely from inside. It gave at last. There was the noise of the blanket being shoved off, and a damp thud as Helge's gag hit the floor. I heard her take several deep breaths, then she sat up and felt for the knife. There was a sawing sound, and the rope round my waist gave. I flexed my upper arms, then her hands felt round my wrists. The cold blade touched me as she positioned it between them. Now, I thought wildly, if she was our murderer I'd had it – but why would she kill her own son?

My wrists fell free. I hauled the blanket off and gulped in the cold air.

We were in what looked like the attic of an empty house, lit only by the orange glow of a nearby streetlight falling in through the skylight. The floor was boards, the walls plaster-boarded under a wooden beamed roof. There was a row of coathooks and various other hooks on the plasterboard, as if the room had been used for storage, and in the middle of one wall was a whiteboard with a list of instructions below a slightly sloping title: Gybing your Spinnaker.

I knew straight off where we were: in the former Sea Scouts' HQ, the building on the corner of the last beach as you went through old Lerwick towards the white building with the upside-down former Foula mailboat as a shed. I'd taken an RYA Level 3 class in this very loft, among a litter of spare buoys and lifejackets. This lodberry had been used by the Lerwick sea scouts for fifty years, until some apparatchnik in the council had decided it was a disposable asset which could be sold for conversion into flats. It had its own slip, the big room below, an open-plan room above, with a balcony over the sea and this attic space. It had been ideal for the scouts, and they'd run a campaign to buy it themselves, but hadn't managed to raise the council's asking price, so the sale had gone ahead – except that the planning department, when applied to for permission for conversion, had ruled that it couldn't be used for housing because of the flooding risks, given that it was built right over the sea, with the lower floor liable to be awash in the January flood tides. The purchasers had called off, the sea scouts hadn't been allowed back in, and there the matter had rested.

I slashed through the cable ties on my ankles and headed for the door. An experimental shove with one shoulder demonstrated that the bolts were indeed substantial, and that anyway the door opened inwards. I gave it a tug. No movement, and the hinges were inaccessibly between the door and the jamb.

Helge had got herself to her feet too and was beginning to stamp about and flap her arms to warm herself. She must have been grabbed from her house, for she was wearing only normal indoor clothes. It was hard to see her colour in this light, but she was shivering, and her teeth were beginning to chatter. I took off my lifejacket and gave her the outer jacket from under it. 'No, take it. I'm in full boating gear.'

She hugged it to her. 'Thanks. We've got to get out of here, before they come back.'

That suited me. 'Keep moving to warm yourself. I'll look.'

The skylight was one of those old ones with a projecting iron bar, a bit rusty, but it opened with a shove and a squeak. I stood on tiptoe to look out. The seaward wall of the Old Manse glimmered with white paint against the black of the flagstones. Below me, the sea hushed gently halfway down the slip. I turned my head sideways. The roof slates would be treacherous under their layer of snow, but if I went carefully I should be able to make it across them to somewhere I could get down. There should be a drainpipe, or there was the courtyard on the other side, with the door onto the slip. It wasn't really what the prudent climber would recommend, if it was possible to get help from outside to unbolt the door.

I thought about that for a moment. Where was my phone? If my captor hadn't taken it I could call Gavin and see if he could send a couple of stout officers to let us out. That would be embarrassing for us both. I could call the Boating Club, just two doors along, and get a couple of stout sailors to come to the rescue. That would be a better bet. 'Is my phone still in my jacket pocket?'

Helge dug a hand into each pocket, then shook her head. 'We'd be heard if we shouted from the window.'

'We would,' I agreed. 'The next time someone passes on foot.' I glanced at my watch. It felt like hours had gone by, but it was only five past four. If we could get out of here quickly then we could find Gavin before he left at 5 o'clock and ask him to give us a lift home.

'My gloves should be in my pockets,' I said. Helge fished them out, and handed them to me. 'Can you give me a leg up? I'll see if there's a way out over the roof.'

She stretched over me, looked out and shuddered. 'Not me. I don't do heights.'

I wasn't sure I did snow-covered roofs, but I sprang up to the window from her linked hands and wriggled my front half through.

The tide below me was only half in, so there wouldn't be enough depth to dive into from here, though that might be a possible if I got as far as the front of the house and swung down onto the balcony; but then, the sea temperature would be dangerously low. I wondered how strong the windows giving onto the balcony were; but it would be no good getting back into the house if the main door was locked. I needed to get right out. I wriggled slightly further and looked to the right, towards the street. The house had a drainpipe from guttering to ground at that corner. If I could manage to work my way along the roof, I could climb down that.

It was my captor's bad luck that he'd grabbed me from my boat. I had my lifejacket with its clip-on safety harness, my seaboots with soles designed to grip like glue on a slanted wet deck, my sailing gloves. I couldn't have tried it otherwise. My first, careful step, with gloved hands still clutching the window frame, showed me that my boots would grip equally well on wet slate. I brushed the snow off before I moved out, then made my bent-low way, inch by cautious inch, along the lower edge of the roof. It was only six or seven metres, less than the length of my *Khalida*, but it felt like a thousand miles. I tested each slate as I brushed the snow from it, searching for the most solid before I risked shuffling a foot onto it. The roof had the slightest of lips before it ended, and that helped. The gutter was good old-fashioned iron, and felt solid enough for me to put my left hand on as I inched my way along to the corner. Two stories below me, not as far as *Sørlandet*'s first mast platform, the water washed up the slip.

Getting onto the drainpipe would be the riskiest bit. I'd have to hold the pipe with my hands and roll my body over the gutter. I lay down on the join between roof and gutter, clipped my harness around the drainpipe, reached out and downwards and took a firm grip of the topmost kink of the downpipe, angling my hands so that I wouldn't have to move them for a more secure grip for those seconds they were taking the weight of my body.

'Be careful,' Helge said anxiously from the window.

I took a deep breath, said a prayer, and gripped my hands like glue, then forced my body to slide outwards into the air. It swung against the corner with a thud that knocked the breath from me, but my legs had been trained aboard tall ships,

287

and they were gripping the pipe. My feet were firm against the wall without me needing to direct them. I unclipped my safety line and reclipped it below the wall-fastening. Slowly, carefully, I went downwards, hand over hand, knees gripping, part-sliding, part-abseiling, and dropped the last metre onto the cobbled slant of the pier.

Now to get Helge out. The blue outer door had a stout-looking mortice lock keyhole, but to my surprise, when I tried it, it was unlocked. I wondered if my captor had picked the lock and left it like that for ease of access. The door into the storeroom had a Yale lock, but that didn't matter; I didn't need to be in there. I charged up the stairs and unbolted the door to let Helge out. 'How are you doing?'

'Just watching you do that was terrifying,' she said. 'Let's get out of here.'

She explained as we walked swiftly along the crooked street, 'I had the radio on, waiting for the lunchtime news, and I didn't hear their car arrive. The back door just opened, and they walked in, flung a blanket over me before I could even scream, and marched me off. Then they just dumped me on the floor and left me.'

'They?' I asked.

'Two men. Two thugs. Not the ones who were threatening me on Saturday, a different two. Americans.' She echoed my thought. 'Big companies play rough.'

'You saw them?'

She nodded.

'But why me? I'm not involved.'

She stopped walking for a moment and thought about it. 'I think . . . I thought, the other day, that they still weren't convinced which of us was which. Something about the way they looked from me to you, and back again. As if they thought I was a set-up to let you get away, and you were the one they were really after.'

'I don't think they're very bright,' I agreed. 'But one said I was "the cop's girlfriend" and they grabbed me first – to stop me warning you, maybe, or to stop me calling Gavin?'

Helge shuddered. 'I was so scared, because they flung me into their van as if it didn't matter – I wouldn't live to complain. But I was angry with it. I wasn't going to be silenced on their say-so.' She paused for a moment. When she spoke again, her voice was filled with pain. 'I was thinking too that it must have been them who killed Robin. Killed my boy, just like that.' She brought her hand up to squeeze my arm. 'Thank goodness they did grab you.'

We came at last into the brighter lights of the Esplanade. A group of youngsters came towards us. One of the girls was staring at me. She nudged her pal beside her, and the pal stared too, then they both looked carefully away as they passed us, and burst out into giggles as soon as we were clear behind them. I turned to look at Helge, and her lips twitched. 'We maybe need to visit the lavatory,' she said.

We went in. The mirror showed me that a fair bit of the slime on that drainpipe had worked its way onto my front and inside legs, with a smear or two on my face for good measure. I dealt with my face, enjoying the hot water on my cold skin, and, in default of paper towels, used toilet paper to rub the worst of it off my black sailing suit. Only a proper wash would get rid of it all. I looked the result over in the mirror and decided that there was *no way* I was going anywhere near the police station like this. Nearly five to five now. The bus would be at the Esplanade by ten past. I could start walking from Voe. My legs were in good practice today. The only snag to that of course was that for all the thugs had talked about morning, they'd also spoken of dealing with Helge first. If they came back and found us gone, the first place they'd look would be our homes. Theirs might be the car that offered me a lift. I made a face at my dishevelled reflection. 'What d'you want to do now? Thing is, we don't know when they'll go to look at us again. We don't want to be sitting ducks a second time.'

'I won't be,' Helge said. Her face was set. 'It's only a week till the court case. I'll get everything organised and go south early. I can be on a flight tomorrow. I'll tell our lawyers this bit of the story. Intimidation of a witness should add a bit to their penalty.'

'You don't want to go and tell the police?'

She shook her head defiantly. 'For this night, I'll get Leonard to come with me to the house, while I get my things, then ask him to run me to a hotel. They'd not take me from there.' Her voice hardened. 'And they killed my boy. I want them caught for that. I don't want the police distracted with a story of kidnapping that only has our word for it.'

I had a shot at persuading her, but she was adamant. If she went south in the morning, she'd be away from them, and safe under the protection of her group's lawyers. I'd tell Gavin all about it as soon as I could, and let him set the law in motion. Hearing Helge talk of going home made a sudden longing for our cottage wash over me, with the fire in the hearth, the Christmas tree, the cats on our knees. The bus to Voe, then. I'd ask Frigg if I could phone Gavin, and wait there till he came for me.

A gush of vinegar-warm air gushed out from Ian's as we passed. The bus driver wouldn't allow chips on the bus, but we could eat quickly in the shelter. I dug in my inner pocket for my purse, and found I was wealthier than I thought: £7.50, and odd coins.

'Hungry?' I asked. We got a poke of chips each, fresh from the fat, and a cup of tea, and took them to the bus shelter. Helge's face was white in the silvery streetlighting, but the colour was starting to creep back into it, and I hoped the journey in a warm bus would restore her body temperature.

I'd finished off most of my chips by the time the bus arrived, jam-packed with people and bags. I stuffed the wrapped packet in my pocket to pick at quietly behind the shelter of the seat in front. Helge and I slumped into the first double seat and Helge let out her breath in a long fwhoo sound. 'Safe now.'

'I hope so.'

We lapsed into silence. The bus grumbled its way up the golf course hill, then hummed happily to itself as it reached the wide, smooth main road. The hills passed us in the darkness, the ugly scarring hidden.

We got off at the Voe stop, walked down the hill to the marina, then trudged up the hill towards Leonard and Frigg's house. At least, I consoled my legs, they could rest now. Gavin would come for me.

'Come in and get a cup of tea, at least,' Helge urged as we reached the gate. She took off my jacket and handed it back. 'Thanks. Leonard'll run me home and stay as bodyguard while I get organised.'

'If it'd be okay, I'd like to phone Gavin, get him to come and fetch me.'

The farmyard was in darkness, lit by the light from the shop window, making sharp shadows of the loading trolley, the bags of feed by the byre door. One of the dogs came bounding up to us, barking, followed by an older one that moved stiffly, tail wagging. It stopped in front of Helge, who bent down to pat it, then followed her to the door and waited at the step, watching, as she went inside.

My foot was on the threshold as Frigg began shouting. I froze, not sure if I'd been seen behind Helge or not. The kitchen was filled with warm light, and Leonard, Sheila and Berwin were sitting at the table, plates in front of them. Frigg had risen, her chair pushed back from her place. She was facing the door,

291

and so angry that I expected her plaits to fly from her head and weave around her head like snakes. Her voice was vicious. 'Don't you come in here, my lady! You're not welcome, no, you won't take a step over my briggistane ever again, not if you were dying.'

'Frigg,' Leonard protested.

She whirled around and turned on him, one arm flung out dramatically at Helge. 'She let us worry about Berwin. All that day and that night, I was worried sick, and she didn't even lift the phone to tell us he was safe. The helicopter was combing the voe for him all evening, and we were sitting here waiting, and she didn't tell us.' She spun round to face Helge again. 'Did you enjoy thinking about us here? Was that your revenge on us both for loving each other?' Her face twisted with spite. 'Well, you've got what you deserve. Your boy's dead, *dead*, and serve you both right.'

Leonard rose and gripped Frigg's shoulder. 'That's enough.' Her mouth opened, and he shook her. 'Enough, I said!' His voice roared.

Helge screamed out over him. 'Robin tried to kill Berwin!'

All the sounds in the kitchen seemed to stop: the brrr of the fridge, the chink of cutlery on plate. We all held our breaths for that instant: Leonard with his hand hard on Frigg's shoulder, Frigg blazing defiance, Sheila's mouth open, Berwin's eyes wide with shocked disbelief. Helge took a step forward and collapsed onto Frigg's chair, as if all the strength had gone from her. 'Robin tried to kill Berwin,' she repeated. 'On Thursday night. I saw him.'

Chapter Twenty-three

be me feth: *a phrase asserting the truth of what the speaker is saying (English,* by my faith*)*

Leonard's hand fell from Frigg's shoulder. He backed to his chair and sat down, not looking behind him, eyes fixed on Helge's face. Frigg remained standing, eyes defiant. Sheila turned towards Berwin, who shook his head and stopped abruptly. I waited in the doorway, frozen. The words rang in the air: *Robin tried to kill Berwin.*

'He hit him,' Helge said. She was speaking to Leonard now, as if the rest of us weren't there. 'I was coming along in the boat, in the shadows, and I saw Berwin coming down through the park. It was after he'd left his boots and boiler suit there. He came down through the park with the sheep following him, he was throwing them nuts, and then he climbed over the fence. He stopped on the beach to take some kind of shoes off and put his trainers on, and while he was there this shadow just rose up from the beach bank.' Her thin hands made an upward movement. 'It was so quick. I saw the arm go up and come down, behind Berwin, and I heard the crack echoing. Berwin fell in a heap. The person began pulling him down to the edge of the sea, and laid him there on his back, with his feet towards the house, as if he had been walking home and had slipped and hit his head. I didn't know who it was, or what to do, it was all so quick. Then he, the other person, came out into the moonlight and started going along on the fence, then jumped off into the road and headed up towards this house – '

Sheila gasped. I could see that she was remembering. An uncertain look settled on her face. Her lips parted.

'Then I recognised Robin,' Helge said. She held out her hand to Leonard. Her voice was anguished with disbelief. 'Robin, our Robin. He'd hit Berwin on the head and left him to drown in the sea.' Her voice cracked. 'And I didn't know what to do. By the time I really realised, he'd come into the house here. He'd never known I was there, never looked.' She closed her eyes for a moment. 'I went to Berwin. He was semi-conscious and struggling to keep his head above the water. I hauled him out of there, and got him into the boat, and took him home.' She spread her hands, repeating, 'I didn't know what to do. I didn't know whether Berwin knew who'd hit him, or if he'd remember . . . I thought he could get a good night's sleep, and I'd see how he was in the morning, maybe persuade him he'd fallen, that I'd seen him fall. But he wasn't better in the morning, he was out cold, and I didn't know if I should be getting a doctor, but then if they took him to hospital and asked him what had happened, and he said Robin had tried to kill him . . .' Tears were spilling from her eyes, and her voice reflected the agony she'd felt. 'I tried to phone Robin, but I only got voicemail. I watched out for him coming back to the studio the next morning, but I must have missed him, sitting with Berwin. Then Cass arrived, saying he was there, so I knew I'd get him then.' One thin hand came up to shade her eyes. 'I didn't want to see him. I just wanted to protect him. I left him a voicemail saying I'd booked him on the boat for that night, he knew why. I wanted him safely off the island, at least. Abroad even, if need be. I wanted to protect him. If Berwin died . . .' She lowered the hand and looked at Leonard again. 'I wanted to talk to you,

294

see what you thought we should do for Robin, but Berwin was your son too.'

'He only spoke in a whisper,' Sheila said, slowly, like someone in a dream. 'I put my head round the door, but I didn't put the light on, and I saw him hunched down in the bed. He whispered, "Ssssh, you'll wake them. I'll tell you all about it in the morning." And I closed the door and went back to bed.' Her face was blank with shock. 'It was Robin, all the time.'

My eyes moved to Frigg and suddenly I knew, as clearly as if she'd spoken the thought in my head, that she'd known. She'd known that it was Robin who'd slept in Berwin's bed, in the room he'd had to share with his baby brother, child of the woman who hated him; in the room he'd been turned out of when he went off to college, the house that had been his until Frigg had shouldered her way into his parents' marriage. He'd hated Frigg just as fiercely as she'd hated him. He'd killed her son and gone to his room to gloat.

It was time I was out of here. I backed smoothly into the shadows and set off at a half-jog towards the road.

in a skrit: in a rather disorganised hurry (Norse, strita seg: to exert or brace oneself)

She came after me. I'd kept my speed up till the turn-off down to Rainbow's house, where I developed a stitch and had to stop altogether, bending over until it eased. I set off again at my fastest walk, up towards Gonfirth Loch, past the loch itself, and was heading alongside the next small loch where the divers nested when I heard a car coming up behind me.

My first thought was relief. A car, not the muscle-men's van. The cavalry had arrived, some kind soul who'd stop and save me two of the four miles between me and home. They might well even go out of their way to take me right into the Ladie. I imagined a kindly voice saying, 'It's a cold night, lass, and no bother to me, I'm in no rush. I can easy put you right home.'

I stopped walking and stood facing the road, one hand extended. The car slowed, its headlights blinding me, and stopped. I leaned forward to open the door, and as it came towards me the inside light went on.

I was looking straight into Frigg's face.

'Hiya, Cass,' she said, in an ordinary voice. 'Helge told us you'd set off to walk home. Hop in, I'll drive you there.'

Her voice belonged to a friendly neighbour. Her eyes blazed, tormented, in her calm face.

I slammed the door, turned and ran upwards, stumbling over the uneven ground. I'd leave prints in the snow here, but if I could get up to the hill ridge then I'd be among the brown heather. There'd be ditches I could hide in, and mounds of stones, Tirval's trowie mounds up on the height of the hill. My breathing rasped in the darkness, and my boots scraped on the crunching heather stems. I felt like I was making enough noise for an army.

The car started up below me, drew forward to the next passing place and stopped again. The headlights snicked off, and for a moment it was utterly black, then I began to see the ground under my feet, the black of rock sticking through the white snow. I stumbled on. Below me, a door snicked, then slammed. A beam of light wavered upwards, went past the line I'd come up and returned. I saw my prints, a line of black shadows in the glare. The circle of light came up towards me and suddenly all the reflective strips on my sailing jacket glowed, outlining me in the dark: wrists, shoulders, hood. I turned my back on it and ran on. She would be quicker up the hill, because she was following me rather than leading, but if she kept her torch on me she wouldn't be able to watch her feet, and if she used it to light her way she wouldn't be able to watch where I was going.

The circle stayed with me for a moment, its brightness blinding my eyes to the ground in front of me. I kept climbing, and at last it flicked away from me and focused ahead of her. That was better! Now I'd be able to see again, as soon as my eyes adjusted to the moonlight, and I had only another twenty metres of snowy hill to go before I reached the bare heather. My breath burned in my throat, and my thigh muscles were beginning to tremble. Twenty metres – fifteen – ten – five –

She would have been able to see my dark figure moving against the snow. Now I'd reached darkness the torch circle moved from her feet and up the hill, following my tracks. I turned quickly and took several steps back towards Voe, as if I was making for the nearest houses. The torch found me; the figure on the white below turned to that angle and began moving upwards again. As soon as the light had left me I made a half-turn and hurried in the opposite direction, going level with the hill to keep below the skyline. There were rocks at the summit. I could see the lumps of them outlined against the sky. Cover, except that if she saw them too I'd be a sitting duck, especially with such a powerful torch. I hoped it used batteries like water, and would run out soon.

She knew she'd lost me now. The circle of light stopped and began casting around, and I flung myself down and began wriggling forwards on my elbows, like a bizarre game of spying. The ground was bitterly cold. My right hand suddenly jolted down into space, and tumbled into soft moull, an arm's length below. It was a place where the peat had crumbled, leaving a heathery bank long enough and high enough to hide me. I rolled down into it and lay there, heart racing. The light shone above my head for a moment, then moved on.

Two minutes. I'd allow myself a count of a hundred, then I'd go again. Instinct had had me casting towards home, but that wouldn't help me. If she kept hunting me it would make more sense to go over the top and down to the pony track that

I'd walked only this morning. It'd be easier going, and it would take me straight to Rainbow's house, where I'd find shelter and safety.

I took deep, steady breaths, listening all the time for the sound of her coming closer, cheek pressed against the cold moull to feel the first vibration of footsteps. Nothing. I risked easing my head up above the bank and saw the torch circle casting slow, deliberate circles across the hillside, sweeping gradually my way. She was still too close to me. I rose and hauled my betraying jacket off, turned it outside in so that the navy lining was outermost. That was better. I rolled my life-jacket together so that the harness clips wouldn't chink, tucked it under my arm and hurried upwards again, watching that moving torch. There was a boulder ahead; I dropped into its shadow, tucking my legs in and hunching over them. The light approached, paused, circled around me, as if it was prying into my darkness, and stayed, unmoving. *Ms Lynch, that's your spot-light. Mr Tarantino is ready for you*, I thought wildly.

While the light wasn't moving, she wasn't either. Unless, I thought with a sudden panic, unless she'd wedged it, and was creeping up on me. I wriggled backwards out of the circle of light, and sideways, so that I could see past it. I couldn't see her. My heart began to beat irregularly. She could be anywhere in this dark, with her torch left to blind me. I began moving, crouched down, along the line of the hill, and spotted her at last, below me still, a dark figure against the last of the snow, coming upwards at the edge of her torch beam. Hide-and-seek in the dark.

I could see better in my dark than she could, walking beside her thin cone of light. I gave a quick look round. There was rougher ground ahead, gouged burn ditches and tumbles of heather. She'd see she could search there for ever, and still not find me. I dropped down behind a heathery knowe and felt among the wiry roots for a stone. The old tricks were the best. I found one that fitted comfortably in the palm of my hand and chucked it as far in that direction as I could. It landed with a satisfying click, just like someone stumbling on rocky ground, and gave a couple more snaps as it bounced. The noise echoed beautifully in the silence.

Below me, Frigg froze, then spun around and went back for her torch. The searchlight went across my hiding place without stopping, heading for where the sound had come from. I waited until I was sure she was really going that way, then began creeping cautiously in the other direction, back towards Voe, but still on the road side of the hill. I was almost at the summit now. I paused for a moment, then slipped quickly over the hilltop and far enough onto the other side that I could only just see over.

The torch stopped moving. I ducked quickly as it went round in a slow circle. It dazzled over the top of the hill, and slid on. Suddenly, it switched off, leaving us in darkness. There was a long silence. I waited, heart racing, listening with all my strength. At last I heard her coming up the hill, frighteningly close. The torch snicked on again; I didn't dare to look over the brow of the hill, but I saw its bright glow. There was a heathery bulge on the hill just metres from me, but I didn't dare to move to it. If I could hear her, she'd hear me. I closed my eyes and prayed, and listened as the sound of her brushing through the heather grew fainter. She was going; please God, let her be going.

It felt like an hour that I waited there, though it probably took only fifteen minutes for her to walk back down to the road. I heard the car door snick, and the engine start. I gave a long breath of relief. Suddenly I was trembling all over. I clambered up the hill again and sat in the shade of a rock to watch her go.

She was going south. The car cast twin lights forwards: the Grobsness turn-off, Gonfirth, the schoolhouse corner. I waited for them to appear past the spur of hill, going on to the South Voxter turn-off, the East Burrafirth road. Nothing; blackness. I leaned forward, straining my eyes. I should have seen them, a flash or a glimpse at least, even if the road was invisible from here.

Then I heard the engine, faint in the distance, coming closer. She was coming back, but there was no sign of her lights. I kept watching the schoolhouse corner, and thought I saw a darker shadow moving against the snow. I shifted my gaze to the rise after the Gonfirth houses, and saw it again: a car without lights creeping along the road. I wouldn't have seen it if I hadn't been looking for it. It came around the curve and stopped just past the Grobsness turn-off, then backed in so that its nose was facing forwards. Now only the angle of its roof was visible against the snow: the rest of it was grey car on grey road, with no sun to spark a bright twinkle from hubcaps or windscreen. From there the driver could watch all this sweep of hill: the way I'd come back to the road to head for Voe, the way I'd go if I was going home.

I settled my back more comfortably against my rock and tried to think what she was planning. She wouldn't expect me to stay up here for any longer than I had to. I'd come down as soon as I thought she was gone, and then she'd . . . what? Let me get onto the road and then come out suddenly behind me, mow me down? She hadn't expected me to run from her; she'd planned to get me into her car.

I remembered her blazing eyes. I wasn't sure she was planning at all, just reacting. Now she had time to stop and think. She might have left home with an excuse of going to give me a lift, but she'd easily had enough time to do that, have a cup of tea and head home again. Leonard would be wondering where she was. Give it a bit longer and he might well bring his van this way in case she'd slid off the road. Furthermore, she hadn't caught me. She'd need to think up a story: *I offered her a lift, and suddenly she jumped back and ran off into the hills . . . I was worried about her, I spent a bit of time searching.*

Okay. Well, she might be expecting me to come out, but I didn't have to. I was dressed for a cold sail and warmed by all this land work. So long as I kept dry I'd be fine. There was water on the hill, and I'd had those chips. I angled my sleeve to shade my watch and pushed the 'glow' button. Twenty to seven. I'd give her till seven. I sucked a few mouthfuls of snow, wriggled my hands into my fleece-lined pockets, stretched my legs out comfortably, and set myself to wait.

It was a bonny, bonny night. The air was cold in my lungs, but the stars were bright above me, and the hills were pin-pricked with points of gold light; you never realised how many houses there were in Shetland until you saw them spread out in the dark. I picked out Dad and Maman, on Muckle Roe, and Inga's parents, past them. The sea lay like scrinkled silver paper between the dark headlands.

It had been a long day, with far too much walking involved. I could feel my eyelids heavy. Out of the corner of my eye, it looked like the boulders on the top of the hill were moving. Trows . . . Robin had used the trows, used Berwin and Vaila and their friends. The trowie tracks around the houses had been cover, but not for sabotage, for murder. Berwin had told them what they were planning, and he'd gone along with it, so that when Berwin's body was found on the shore it would look like another trowie prank gone wrong . . . I forced my eyes open, but it was a struggle to keep them that way . . . my head was drooping forwards . . . then something warm touched my hand. I felt a sharp bite. My eyes jerked wide.

For a long moment, the Arctic fox and I stared at each other. He was smaller than Cat, with rounded, furred ears and slanted dark eyes above a long-nosed muzzle like a wolf's. His coat shone silver in the moonlight. His teeth were bared, ready to come in and scavenge if I was weak enough. My hand throbbed where he'd bitten it. I sat up and flapped both arms at him and growled, as if I was Cat seeing another cat off. He took a step backwards, then turned in one fluid movement and ran, graceful as a swan in flight, paper-white on the dark hill, his brush tail streaming behind him.

Below me, the car engine started; the lights went on. It curved out of the turn-off and headed towards Voe. Frigg was heading home. It was time to make my best speed out of here.

I'd just reached the road when I saw headlights, coming from south. A heavier car . . . I tensed, ready to run, then saw the square shape and roof bars of a Land Rover outlined against the snow. My heart gave a hopeful thump. I stopped walking and waited.

It was Gavin. He flung the door open, jumped down and hugged me to him. I could feel him shaking. 'Helge phoned me,' he said, into my hair. His arms tightened as if they'd never let me go, then relaxed. He stepped back and spoke lightly.

'Can I give you a lift?'

'You're going in the wrong direction,' I said.

'I'll turn at the next passing place.'

'Oh, in that case,' I said, and clambered in. Even though I hadn't felt particularly cold, the warmth felt wonderful on my face. 'Can I put the light on?'

'There's a torch in the glove compartment.' He curved into the next passing place, reversed a bit and turned the Land Rover, then set off homewards.

I found the torch and shone it on my hand. There were two neat punctures in the flesh between forefinger and thumb, reddening nicely and slightly swollen. 'You don't have any antiseptic? Your wretched fox bit me.'

'Dettol in the glove compartment too, and cotton wool.' I could hear he was smiling. 'How about you save the whole story to tell me in one piece, once we're home? I lit the Rayburn, so there'll be water, if you want to collapse into a bath.'

'Bliss,' I said.

'I'll tell you my side first. I think it'll be quicker.'

'You arrived home, no Cass?'

'That wouldn't have surprised me. No, it starts before then. At one fifteen we had a phone call from Aberdeen about two unpleasant characters heading this way. One of the officers at the airport had recognised them. A pair of Americans with a record of intimidation followed by action. They'd hired a van at our airport, and set off into the blue. The two we'd taken into custody had American numbers in their phones. I didn't like it. An officer spotted the van half an hour ago, outside the Thule, with them inside having a pint, meek as mice. I sent an officer to Helge's house, to make sure she was safe, but there was no sign of her. Then I came home and found no Cass, but also no *Khalida*, a returned *Herald Deuk*, two rather annoyed cats who hadn't been fed their tea yet, two cat lifejackets on the doorstep along with your phone and the *Deuk*'s battery, and no sign of you, your sailing clothes or your lifejacket.' He was trying to keep his voice light but I could hear the worry behind the casual tone.

'Unusual,' I conceded.

'Cass investigating was a possibility, but not in your sailing gear. *And*,' he said, 'as a clincher, not in your sailing boots. Your best, expensive sailing boots in which you'll only reluctantly walk on land.'

I glanced down at my feet in the dark of the footwell. 'I hope they're not too scratched by that heather.'

'Ergo,' Gavin finished, 'you'd come home, and got as far as the doorstep before . . . someone interrupted you.'

'You should join the police,' I said, impressed. 'You'd make a great detective.'

His voice lightened. 'And that linked up with an odd report we'd had at 16.35, from a woman in Stout's Court. A bairn in dark clothes climbing out of the skylight of the old Scout

303

building. Wearing some sort of climbing harness, she said, though it lookit more like one of these inflatable life-jackets, with a rope dangling from it. By the time the officers got there, there was no sign of anyone, but the woman said she'd kept watching, and the person who climbed out went back in, and then came out with a wife in a red jacket, like one of these sailing jackets, and they set off down the street.'

'Can't do anything unobserved in Lerwick.'

'My officers had a look, and found cut ropes and cable ties, so when I came home to find you gone, well, after the initial shock, I thought, that climber in the black suit sounded like you. You'd escaped just before bus time. I threw some food at the cats and came to look for you.'

'They were after Helge,' I said. 'DS Peterson would need to talk to her again. She saw who grabbed her. I only heard them. They ambushed me with a blanket. More importantly though, Helge's come out with the truth about finding Berwin. That crack over the head, she saw Robin hit him with a stone and lay his body in the ebb. Then he headed up to the house. It was Robin who spent the night there, not Berwin. After that, her story was true. She picked him up with the boat, and took him home, but she didn't know what to do, because of not admitting that Robin had tried to kill him. Then when he woke up not remembering, she thought she could keep him safe until she'd got Robin off the island.'

'Did she tell you all this?'

I shook my head. 'She told Frigg and Leonard and Sheila and Berwin, at their house. There was a massive row. I'll tell you inside.' We drew up at the gate. I hopped out to get it, and then back in. I was pretty sure my hand was swelling now; it was throbbing like the bass of a dance band, and it felt hot. 'You don't suppose the wretched beast had rabies or anything like that?'

304

He turned his head to smile at me. 'Stop tantalising me. I want the full story once you're home.'

Gavin phoned DS Peterson while I got the bath run. I was just taking off my sailing gear in the bedroom when he appeared with one of those round fizz-balls, and gave it to me. 'I had this in among your Christmas things, but I thought you might like it now.'

'You're a star,' I said. I got into the bath and dropped it in, where it hissed round in the water, creating film-star amounts of froth. 'You can come in,' I called.

He peered around the door, saw that I was decently concealed under an inch of sweet-smelling foam and reappeared with two cups of tea. 'Now,' he said, closing the toilet seat and sitting on it, 'tell all.'

I did my best: the muscle-men, the escape, the row in the kitchen, and Frigg coming after me, the chase on the hillside. 'But she'll say, of course, that I took a sudden panic, and she was worried and was looking for me.'

'You'll need to tell it all to Freya.'

I made a face. 'And then she drove off, cut her lights round about our turn-off and came back without them, and stopped again, and waited at the Grobsness turn-off with everything dark. Why would she do that if she wasn't planning to harm me? So I waited too, up on top of the hill, among the stones, and I must have dozed off, because the next I knew, something had bitten my hand, and I woke up and there it was.' I conjured up that startled moment. 'The Arctic fox. It wasn't as pretty as I expected from the photos. I'd thought it would be like a Shetland collie, but it was more a mini-wolf. It ran when I chased it.' I inspected the bite again. All of me was scarlet now from the heat of the bath, so I couldn't tell if it was red, but I did think, comparing it to my other hand, that it was swelling up. I sighed. 'It's a good thing my tetanus jab's up to date.'

'So,' Gavin said, thinking it through, 'Frigg didn't know that it had been Robin in Berwin's bed when she phoned me. She was worried about him being missing, but she didn't behave like someone who thought someone else had attacked him. If she'd thought Robin was responsible, she'd have accused him to us.'

'More likely she'd have been at his door, threatening him until he told her where Berwin was.'

'But sometime through the day, you think, she found out it had been Robin who'd slept in his bed.' He was silent a minute, thinking. 'Sometime before I phoned back, after we'd spoken to his pals at the school. Remember she was backtracking about her anxiety, saying she'd made too much of it. What might she have done between us leaving her at one and me phoning at one forty-five?'

The beautiful hot water was lulling my brain to sleep. I waited for him to come up with the answers.

'She'd have looked in Berwin's room again,' he said. 'Leonard wouldn't listen, he'd gone off to town, just like it was a normal day. She might have lain down on his bed, just to feel close to him.' His eyes sharpened. 'A hair on the pillow, the wrong smell. The wrong noises in the morning. All the odd things in her subconscious that drove her to phone me in the first place.'

'Prints,' I said. 'Sheila remembered there were no prints going out of the front door. Maybe she opened the back door and found the prints of Robin leaving, and knew his trainers.'

'Washing,' Gavin said. 'There was washing out, to the back of the house. I noticed it fluttering as we went past, after we'd been at the school. Sheets, duvet covers.'

'She'd gone out to hang it up, and seen his prints. She'd

have realised it hadn't been Berwin there overnight, but Robin. His prints heading back to the studio.'

'And she thought he'd killed Berwin. She didn't know Helge had saved him, and nor did he. He thought he'd got rid of the body. Maybe he denied it all, or maybe he laughed at her. So she killed him. Then what?' He frowned, thinking it through. 'She has a body on her hands, and she's got to get rid of it, fast, in between customers. She gets the warning of them turning in and coming up the road, so she could make sure she wouldn't be caught in an awkward situation. She has the trolley, and she's used to shifting heavy feed sacks. She gets him into the boot of her car. She does a hurried clear of the studio, as if he's gone away for the weekend; she was the person with the backpack. She drives quickly to Laxo, parks the car right by the barrier over the bank, and tumbles him over. She hurries back to the Voe shop, buys her milk. I'll get Freya to check if she really was out of milk. Back within fifteen minutes, ready for the next customer. She could have done it.'

I nodded. I was afraid that she had. Poor Leonard; poor Berwin; poor Sheila. Poor Helge, mourning her son.

Yule E'en

Tuesday 22nd December

HW 02.40 (1.7m);
LW 08.30 (1.2m);
HW 14.36 (1.9m);
LW 21.29 (0.9m)

Sunrise 09.08, moonrise 12.46; sunset 14.58, moonset 00.57.

Waxing gibbous moon

Chapter Twenty-four

hoop: *Shetland pronunciation of English* hope

We needed all the lights on in the kitchen to have breakfast, even with the glimmering white of the snow outside. It was nearly eight before the outline of the hill opposite was visible against the sky, and nine before you could actually call it light, though a grey, murky light with the clouds like cobwebs, and only the occasional chink of pearl grey promising proper light later. I sat for a moment on the bench in front of the house, watching the otters diving for fish as the hills gradually lightened in front of me. My spirits were dragged down by tiredness and the thought of that family at Voe. I wondered if DS Peterson had gone round last night to talk to Frigg. She'd phoned, late yesterday evening, but Gavin hadn't said what had happened, so I didn't ask. He'd breakfasted in silence, a crease between his brows, and headed to the Land Rover with his shoulders squared, like a man who knew it was going to be a tough day.

It was Yule E'en. In Norse times, the Yules had centred on the 23rd December. There were all sorts of things I should be doing today, like making sure there were clean clothes ready for tomorrow, and the house scoured, and washing my hands and feet in water with three burning peats placed in it, to keep off ill-luck.

I decided to bake sun cakes, if I could find a recipe. I went back indoors and fired up my laptop; 'sun cakes' got me a page of Taiwanese recipes. I tried Norwegian sun biscuits and got *sandbakkelse*, which looked good, but the recipe called for special tins. Sun biscuits without Norway gave me an Indian manufacturer. I sighed, and tried 'sun biscuit shetland'. According to the site, shortbread was made for Yule cakes in Shetland. I'd never tried shortbread, but it looked easy, worth a go if I had the ingredients. Rather to my surprise, a search through the cupboards showed that I had; maybe Gavin was a shortbread maker, because I couldn't think of any other reason for having rice flour in the house.

The cats watched with interest as I kneaded the mixture and flattened it into a round dish. I pinched the edges, made a hole in the middle and put it in the oven. The mixture tasted good, anyway. I washed the bowl up and considered the day. The boats were fine. I'd done enough walking yesterday to last me till well past Christmas, and the house looked perfectly clean. I could wrap Gavin's presents properly while he was out.

I'd only just got paper, scissors and sellotape all spread over the floor when it was time for me to take the sun cake out. I was pleased with it; it smelled good, the points round the edge stood out sharply, and the hole was still open enough to thread a ribbon through.

I was kneeling down surrounded by paper and trying to smooth out a piece without Kitten diving under it from the other side when I heard the snick of the gate. My first thought was that it might be the muscle-men come back. I leapt for the back door and turned the key, then hurried up the stairs to look out from the skylight.

There were two bicycles standing against the fence at the top corner, just before the steep downhill, as if somebody didn't want to have to cycle back up there, and two heads below me, one dark, one gold. Vaila and Berwin. I opened the skylight, and they looked up. 'Two seconds,' I said.

It took only one look at their faces to see how very wrong everything had gone. I hurried down the stairs and brought them straight into the vanilla-smelling kitchen. 'Have a seat. Tea?'

Both heads nodded. I made three mugs and broke up the sun cake to go with it, then settled down beside them.

'They've taken Mam away,' Berwin said. His face was white. 'The police. The blonde officer came last night, after tea, and talked to Mam, and then they took her away, just like that. Dad's in Lerwick now, organising lawyers, and Sheila went with him to keep him calm, but I couldn't just stay there, waiting, and Vaila thought you might know – might be able to tell us – ' He trailed off, hands trying to express what he couldn't articulate.

'What to do,' Vaila said. She took a bit of sun cake. 'What to do to help Frigg, I mean.'

This was an awkward one. 'Do you have any idea of what was said last night? I mean, do you know if your mum's admitted . . . what she's saying?'

Berwin reddened. 'I listened,' he admitted. He gave me a defiant look. 'I needed to know.'

'I'd have listened too, if I'd been you,' I assured him. 'And?'

'It was because it hadn't been me in my bed that night.' His voice was bleak. 'It had been Robin. Helge said – well, you know, you were there. She said he'd tried to kill me. Robin!' The pain in his voice wrung at my heart. Robin, his big brother. He'd adored him and looked up to him all his life, and Robin had used his trust to try to kill him. He looked straight out of the window, not meeting my eyes; Vaila's hand reached for his. 'He carved the snowshoes for me, like the cat ones, you ken about that, but with sheep prints. He was going to wait with my trainers at the banks. I don't remember . . . but Helge said she saw him hit me. She thought he'd killed me. He dragged me down to the water, and left me there. I think I might remember that, the water cold on my face.' He repeated, fiercely, 'But I don't remember anything else. Would it help Mam if I pretended I did, or make it worse?'

'Telling lies wouldn't help anything,' I said. I was sure of that. 'So DS Peterson asked your mam about Robin having spent the night at the house.'

He nodded. 'But she didn't ask like that, she asked when Mam realised he'd spent the night there, and Mam said she only knew when Helge said, and then the police officer began taking her through the lunchtime of Friday, asking what she did, and what customers there were, and what she did in between them, and she began to get all flustered, and contradicted herself, and it was obvious that she was hiding something. Then they started asking her about you. About why she'd gone after you last night, and she said she wanted to give you a lift home, but you ran off into the hills. She said she was worried about you.'

He stopped. Two pairs of eyes were fixed on my face, brown and blue.

'That could easily be true,' I said. Berwin gave a long, relieved sigh. I tried to think what Frigg's lawyer might say in court. 'It's absolutely true that your mum didn't try to lay a hand on me. I'd just got away from a pair of nasty thugs, you know, that pair that came to Helge's house, and I was jumpy. I got nervous when she stopped and ran off into the hill. She tried to find me, and I hid from her, and she went away.'

'But you thought she'd done it,' Berwin said. 'Killed Robin.'

I wanted to say that what I thought wasn't evidence, but that was weaselling out of it. I nodded and tried to explain. 'It was her face. I was looking straight at her when Helge said about Robin spending the night in your room. I saw that she knew.' I spread my hands. 'But it was like telepathy. I looked at

314

her face and saw it. That's not evidence either.' I looked straight at him. 'What do you think?'

He flushed, and looked away. There was a long silence.

'DS Peterson talked about evidence,' Vaila said. 'She said the boot of the car would be checked, and the house. Then she started to take Frigg through it all again, and she was just getting more and more muddled, and in the end she began crying. That was when DS Peterson said they'd take her in for questioning, and she could have a lawyer if she wanted. Then they got her into the police car, just like the cop shows on TV, one holding on to her and the other one pushing her head down, and drove off.'

Berwin looked up again, and said roughly, 'Will she go to prison? Now, I mean? If they arrest her, what's going to happen?'

'That depends on her lawyer,' I said. 'And on the circumstances. There's a big difference between planning to kill someone and suddenly losing your temper and striking out at them. She'd had a bad day, your mother, worrying herself sick about you. Well, suppose something made her realise that Robin had spent the night in your bed.' I had a sudden flash of thought about that. It hadn't just been confusing the time Berwin had come home, making it seem he'd disappeared later. Robin had been claiming back the room he'd been turned out of. I wondered how long it would have been before he'd persuaded Leonard that he wanted to be there to support them all, and moved back in.

'He planned to kill me,' Berwin said. 'He meant to do it. He was the one who came up with how I could do the disappearing trick, the sheep prints, and climbing along the mesh of the fence. He knew Sheila knew I was going to do it that night. That was why he went to my room. She'd have worried if I hadn't come back, and come to look for me. He planned not to have anyone look for me before morning. By then I'd have been dead of hypothermia if I hadn't drowned.'

That was better, for him to think about Robin's actions. I moved cautiously on. 'And Robin liked winding people up. Suppose your mam had challenged him about what he was up to, and he gave her a cheeky answer? She was worried about you, and he was just laughing at her. Maybe she just totally lost her temper and went for him.'

Some of the bleakness left Berwin's face. I refilled his mug and broke him another piece of sun cake. 'It could have happened like that,' he said. 'She has a temper, Mam. She can get awful mad about things. Will that be manslaughter, then? Will they let her come back home until the sheriff sees her?'

I wished Gavin was here. 'I don't know. I don't think you get bail on a murder charge, but if that's how it was, her lawyer will tell her to plead guilty, and in that case I don't think there'd be a big trial, stuff in the papers, all that.'

'But she might still go to prison.'

'But not for as long,' Vaila said. 'And prisons aren't as bad as they used to be.'

Berwin pulled his hand away from hers. 'It's still prison!' He stood up, pushing his chair back with a scrape, and turned away from us.

'Listen,' I said.

Reluctantly, his head came around.

I moistened my lips. 'I killed someone once,' I said. My fingers came up to touch the bullet scar on my cheek. 'My boyfriend. Alain. It was in the middle of the Atlantic. He shot at me, and I tacked the boat and the jib knocked him overboard.' They could see how much I hated remembering. Vaila began drawing patterns on the table, cheeks flushed; Berwin looked away from me. 'I threw out a horseshoe buoy, and I searched, but I didn't find him. The sea carried him away.' I gave a pause, then leaned forward. 'That's all a long time ago, but what matters is this. I explained it all to the police when I got back to Scotland, and they agreed it was an accident. I hadn't meant to kill him, and what I'd done couldn't reasonably have been expected to kill him. I didn't get punished, but, you know, it would have been easier for me if I had gone to jail. I'd have had a chance to atone. I'd have felt I'd paid for killing him, instead of him being dead, and me walking away scot free.'

Berwin thought about it. 'You think we shouldn't try and keep Mam from going to prison?'

I shook my head. 'You find her the best lawyer you can get. Make her case the best you can. I think I'm just trying to say that maybe even prison is better than dragging guilt around with you.'

'But in the end you didn't kill him,' Vaila said. 'Mam spoke about it. Another boat picked him up. Didn't that take the guilt away?'

I answered her honestly. 'It took away that he was dead. It didn't take away that I'd done it in the first place.' I looked at Berwin. 'Don't you think that right now your mam would give everything she has to have Robin alive again?'

He nodded. The bleak look was still in his eyes, but he sat down again, and lifted his mug. Overnight, I realised, his face had lost the last curves of childhood.

I remembered the way I'd hidden myself away from everyone after Alain's death, pushed away any attempts to help me.

'And tell her that you love her,' I said. 'That she's still your mum, whatever went wrong with Robin.'

He thought about that, and nodded. 'I'll be strong for her,' he said.

And for your dad, and for Helge, I wanted to say. *You're their only son now.* I kept quiet. Helge and Leonard would work things out between them. I wasn't sure Frigg would still have a husband and a home to return to, after prison.

'What have you done to your hand?' Vaila suddenly demanded. It was a moment before I realised she was speaking to me. I glanced down at it. The skin was still puffy and red around the punctures, and I'd noticed I wasn't using it. I could give them this, at least, to bring hope into their day.

'Cross your hearts and hope to die,' I said.

They both nodded. Vaila's right hand went up in the sign of the cross, just like Peerie Charlie.

'You won't have to keep it a secret for very long.' I extended the hand for them to see. 'I fell asleep up on the hill, last night, and got bitten by someone who thought I was a handy carcase.' I looked at Berwin. 'One of Robin's foxes. You know, his paintings.' I reached behind me to Gavin's painting. Berwin looked at it, and nodded.

'I had to show it to Gavin early, when the police came to question me about having been in Robin's studio.' I looked at Berwin. 'He was really pleased. I could see how much he liked it. But the reason I wanted him to see it was because Shona, the young policewoman, said it didn't look like the foxes she saw in the city. Gavin watches foxes, so I knew he'd know, and he did. He said it was an Arctic fox.'

'Robin liked them,' Berwin said. 'He had photographs he painted them from, that he took in Iceland.'

'Yes,' I said. 'But you know the painting of a dog fox on its own, the one that's not for sale?'

They both nodded, slightly puzzled.

'The hill behind the fox, that's Scallafield, painted the way you'd see it from Muckle Roe. That's why I recognised it. He might have said it was Iceland, to keep the secret of them, but Robin was painting foxes he'd watched here.'

Both mouths dropped open. '*Here?*' Berwin said.

'We don't have foxes in Shetland,' Vaila said.

'People see them from time to time, and keep quiet about it. So, with the painting as a clue, we took a walk in the Kergord valley yesterday, with a man from the nature lot. We found a track in the snow.'

Vaila stared at me. 'A fox track?'

318

I nodded. 'The nature man planted motion-sensitive cameras there yesterday. He said he'd leave them for a week before he looked.'

'An Arctic fox!' Vaila said. Her eyes were round with disbelief.

'The trowie dogs,' Berwin said suddenly. His face was still, his eyes clouded, as if he was struggling with a memory from long ago. 'When I was peerie, I wanted to see Grandpa's trows. I pestered Robin about them, because he said he'd seen them too, and he took me up into the hill at night, to watch for them. He said if I was very, very quiet, we might see them, and if we were extra lucky we might see their dogs. We watched the boulders on the hill, and I thought I saw one move, and then another one.'

'An illusion caused by staring at it,' Vaila said. 'Like seeing the morning star as a UFO.'

'But I was certain I'd seen something like a small dog, moving between them. Then when we went back in, I tripped over the doorstep, and Mam came and caught us. She was most awful mad about it. She was always snarky at Robin after that. I think that's why I shoved it back in my memory.' His face went bleak. 'I felt it was my fault they didn't get on, because I'd pestered him to take me.' He was silent for a moment.

'It wasn't your fault,' Vaila said. 'Your mam never liked Robin because your dad loved him, and it gave Helge a foothold in your house.'

Berwin made a face, and waved that away. 'But now I'm thinking about it, I'm remembering I saw it. It was summer twilight. A small brown dog, slipping between the boulders on the height o' the hill.'

'They could live here,' Vaila said. 'There're plenty of rabbits. Hill lambs too.'

I glanced down at my hand. 'Trust me,' I said. 'That one was definitely making itself at home.' I reflected a moment, and added, 'It was beautiful. So white, and it slipped away like water.'

Vaila was starting to calculate. 'Is it . . . would it be a protected species?'

'It might be. It would depend if it's a breeding population, or just an individual that someone released here, trying to be clever. But Gavin's been having fun in the archives and one thing he found was that once this land belonged to a Bjorn Refursson – Bjorn the Fox's son. If the Vikings brought otters here for their fur, well, why not foxes too?'

'If it came with the Vikings,' Vaila said, 'might that be long enough ago for it to be different from the Scandinavian ones?'

'A Shetland Arctic fox,' Berwin said. His eyes met Vaila's, in wild hope. 'They'd have to stop some of the windfarm then. It'd get special protection, surely. The whole valley might become a designated area. They'd have to stop working for now, at least, until they found out more about it.'

'And foxes are cute,' Vaila said. 'People care about cute animals. We could use Robin's paintings as posters. Mega publicity.'

Her mother's daughter. Berwin frowned, and I cut in quickly.

'I think he'd like that. He kept quiet to protect them – ' and because he liked secrets, I added to myself, liked thinking he was one up on everyone else – 'but wouldn't it be good to use the paintings he did of them?' I glanced down at Gavin's present. 'They're beautiful paintings.'

'We've got two weeks,' Vaila said. 'The machines won't start moving again till after New Year.' Her eyes met Berwin's in a look I couldn't quite read. 'A week for your nature man to see if he gets any footage. Then he'd need to talk to, oh, I don't know, Scottish government conservancy people.' She turned to me. 'I won't tell anyone, I promised, but we could start planning a campaign, couldn't we?'

'Thing is,' I said, 'if word gets out, well, someone who's for the windfarm might decide the best way out of the problem is to go and shoot it. Them.'

They understood that straight away.

'But,' I said, 'it's on Rainbow's dad's land. Magnie kens too. I think they're doing something.'

'I'll speak to Rainbow's dad,' Vaila said. 'We could help with that.'

They rose, and stood awkwardly for a moment. 'Thanks, Cass,' Berwin said at last. 'I'll do my best to help Mam.'

'Good luck,' I said. 'I hope it all goes well. Keep me posted, won't you?'

'And you'll keep us posted about the fox?' Vaila asked.

I nodded. 'Cross my heart and hope to die.'

Christmas Eve

Thursday 24th December

HW 04.50 (1.7m);
LW 10.56 (1.1m);
HW 16.57 (1.8m);
LW 23.30 (0.9m)

Sunrise 09.09, moonrise 12.55; sunset 14.59, moonset 03.33.

Waxing gibbous moon

Chapter Twenty-five

redding up: *tidying up, disentangling (Old Scots,* redd up, *Norwegian and Swedish,* rada: *to place in rows, to arrange, to put in order)*

For me, murders had always ended with an arrest. Now I saw the aftermath. Gavin was busy all that day and the next, and Christmas Eve, liaising, organising, coming home late and not inclined to talk about it, glad to focus on planning our Christmas dinner with Maman and Dad.

Inga, through Vaila, kept me up to speed. Frigg was flown to Aberdeen the next day, and kept in custody there. She was pleading guilty to culpable homicide, accepting that she'd killed Robin, but saying that she'd struck out at him in anger without intending to kill him. It was as Gavin had thought; after we'd left she'd gone up to Berwin's room, and lain on his bed, clutching his pillow to feel close to him – and then she'd realised it smelt of Robin. It had been Robin who'd slept in Berwin's bed last night. She'd gone downstairs, not sure what to do, and had begun, 'sort of on auto-pilot,' Vaila had said, to make lunch. The frying pan was in her hand when Robin had come in the door, smeegin to himself. She'd confronted him, asked him where Berwin was, and he'd just laughed at her, and said he didn't know, with that annoying smug smile on his face. Maybe the trows had taken him, he'd added, and she'd seen red and struck out at him. She'd hit him again when he was on the floor, she thought; she said she couldn't remember. Then she'd come to and found him dead at her feet. She'd got the trolley she moved bags of feed with, and hauled him onto it. She'd just done that when the phone rang: Gavin, saying his friends didn't know where he was, but had suggested otter watching. I remembered how breathless and flustered she'd sounded, and no wonder: a phone call from the police while you were dealing with your murder victim would fluster anyone.

She'd kept busy between customers. She'd gone down to the studio and quickly packed a few items into his backpack, as if he'd just headed off. Down south to join his friends for Christmas, why not? Leonard was used to him coming and going. Helge would worry; well, let her. She'd backed her car to the door, got his body into it, closed the boot, reparked the car. While she was serving and smiling, she was thinking, thinking. She would throw him into the sea. The road to Laxo, there was a place there where she could haul the body directly from the car to the water, and if she chose a time between ferries the road would be deserted. A quick look at the timetable showed a ferry at 14.45 and another at 15.30. High water was at three.

She scribbled the 'Back in a minute' notice and slipped out just before three. She met the cars coming off the newly arrived ferry just past the Laxo turn-off. It was at that point, she said, that what she'd done really hit her, and for a moment she was tempted to give herself up right there and then, phone the police and tell them everything. Her heart was racing and she felt sick as she parked the car right on the verge above the cliff. But she thought of Berwin, gone, and gritted her teeth.

He was heavy, so heavy, but the barrier was at the same height as the car boot. All she had to do was haul him out and over it, and let him fall. It was only when it was too late, when he'd tumbled and rolled down the cliff and splashed into the sea, that she wished she could undo it all.

There would be a court hearing after the Christmas break, and then her trial, in maybe a year's time. I'd thought her pleading guilty would mean the trial would be simpler, but it seemed the court would still need proof of her version of what happened. Forensics had taken the kitchen apart for blood-stains, so assuming they'd get that evidence, apparently it all turned on whether her conduct was 'culpable and reckless', that is, whether what she'd done in striking out at him with the frying pan in her hand could be assumed by any reasonable person to cause harm. Given that Shetland folk tended to buy a frying pan by weight, it didn't look good. Her disposal of the body would count against her too.

In Scotland, the sentence for murder was automatically life.

When Gavin came home at five on Christmas Eve I saw him shoving it all behind him, switching it off before he came across the kitchen to hug me. 'I just need a shower before I feel human. What time's the taxi coming?'

'Six. It's going to be awful complicated driving for the poor taxi driver. Us and the cats to Muckle Roe, then back via here to drop them off, then into Lerwick, and back out via here again.'

'On the plus side,' Gavin said, with the first hint of a smile, 'two long country journeys with two cats and us is probably a treat compared to a evening's worth of carloads of drunks.'

He reappeared from the shower in all his dress finery: his scarlet kilt with the goatbeard sporran and polished silver fas-tenings, and his black dress jacket with the Bonny Prince's button sewn below the collar, given to his several-greats-grandfather who'd guided the prince to a hide-out cave. He looked magnificent, and I felt suddenly shy.

'You look bonny,' he said, smiling at me. 'All set then?'

Cat was already waiting at my feet, knowing something

interesting was going on, and the Kitten was squeaking complaints from her basket. 'Ready,' I agreed. For the first time I wished I had a proper dress coat, rather than have my pretty dress hanging below my incongruous scarlet sailing jacket.

The taxi driver taking us to my parents' house turned out to be a cheery soul who had cats himself, and was very interested in the way Cat wore his harness just like a dog. 'I have a young one, and I'll maybe try that on him.'

The house smelled wonderful, and the meal was spectacular. Dad opened the champagne, real champagne, as soon as I'd hung my jacket up, and we had a glass of bubbly and little chunks of dried sausage in the living room while the cats scrounged turkey from Maman's last-minute preparations in the kitchen. There were sprigs of holly on the table between Maman's great-aunt's best china plates. We had another glass of champagne with the oysters, then a puree of potatoes with celery, washed down by a heavy red wine, followed by roast turkey with chestnut stuffing. There was a cheese board and a chocolate Yule log, made by *Les Délices de St Michel*, Maman's local patissier, and finally we went back through to the sitting room for best cognac and a plate of chocolates. I told stories about our trainees and the voyage, Gavin added an anecdote or two of his youthful stalking days and Dad countered with horror stories from building sites, then Maman capped those with tales from the world of opera. It was all relaxed and family. My heart was warm with the joy of it; for a moment the candle flames blurred in my eyes.

We had an extra cup of coffee to keep us going through Midnight Mass, and then got our coats on for the drive. The cheery taxi driver was bang on time, and I squeezed into the back with Maman and Gavin, putting Dad's long legs in the front. We dropped the cats off at home, then drove on through the darkness. All the houses were in Christmas Eve mode, with every light twinkling, nearly every window lit.

Peerie Charlie would be asleep by now, along with all the other excited children tucked into their beds all over Shetland; parents would be doing last-minute wrapping, eating Santa's mince pie, drinking his glass of whisky, putting the reindeer's carrot into the kitchen for inclusion in the Christmas lunch, tiptoeing up into bedrooms to leave the stockingful, or more likely pillowful, of presents.

The church looked beautiful. The Christmas tree branches were bowed down with ornaments; the familiar figures were in their places in the stable, Mary in her rose dress and blue mantle kneeling over the empty manger, Joseph standing behind her, the ox and donkey lying in the straw, the shepherds with their crooks. The women of the choir wore bright silk dresses, and were grouped around the organ, music sheets in their hands. Father David opened proceedings with a prayer, and then we had half an hour of carols and readings of peace, reconciliation, hope: *The lion shall lie down with the lamb . . . they shall do no hurt, no harm, on my holy mountain.* We had all the old favourites whose words I still half-knew: 'On Christmas Night All Christians Sing', 'Once in Royal David's City', 'O Little Town of Bethlehem', 'It Came Upon the Midnight Clear'. The Christmas tree was blessed, and then, as the Town Hall clock chimed out midnight, a solemn little girl led the procession of Father David and his altar servers down the aisle. She was carrying the plaster baby on a white cloth. I'd done that once; I remembered the feeling of awe mingled with terror in case I dropped him. The choir sang the Gaudete, and then we all launched into 'O Come, All Ye Faithful', and the Christmas Mass had begun.

It was the loveliest Christmas Mass I'd ever been at. I was older now, my faith deepened by sixteen years of knocking around the world. I was no longer responsible for Alain's death. I had Gavin, and I'd come home at last. Peace, hope, a new beginning. We turned to kiss each other at the sign of peace, and went up together to receive communion. My heart was filled with joyful contentment as I slipped my hand into Gavin's for the final blessing.

I'd expected to doze all the way home, but I found I was still wide awake as the driver turned off the main road to bump over the hill to the Ladie.

'See you at one tomorrow,' I said, as we clambered out. 'Merry Christmas!'

Kitten came out of her basket to greet us, but there was no sign of Cat. 'Out hunting, I suppose,' Gavin said.

'No more dead ducks, I hope.'

I'd just said the words when there was a kerfuffle at the catflap. Kitten shot towards the door to see what was happening and hurtled back in, looking alarmed. The catflap snicked, then there was a flapping, quacking noise.

Gavin and I dived into the little hallway. Cat was coming backwards through the catflap, nose buried in the back feathers of something that was determined it wasn't coming in. Its wings were free and flapping on the other side of the door. Gavin leapt for the door and opened it enough to get through, and I grabbed Cat by the scruff of the neck, hoping that would open his jaws enough for it to escape.

'A fine mallard,' Gavin said, catching it in both hands. It pecked at him, and he threw it upwards into the dark sky. Its wings opened, and it flew off with a final indignant quack. Cat made a bound after it, and Kitten went charging after him, and the pair of them disappeared into the darkness, leaving Gavin and I breathless and staring at each other in disbelief.

'He couldn't really have understood that we didn't believe he'd caught it,' I said.

'Of course not,' Gavin agreed. 'All the same, let's not disparage his hunting abilities in his hearing again. We don't want him bringing us a sea eagle.'

Auld Yule

Wednesday 6th January

*(Auld Yule, or Christmas on the 6th of January,
continued to be celebrated in remote parts of
Shetland within living memory, and is still
celebrated on the island of Foula.)*

Chapter Twenty-six

We were down at Gavin's family farm in the Highlands for New Year when Neil of the SNH phoned. Gavin put him on speakerphone so that I could hear too. He was trying to sound calm, but his voice throbbed with excitement. 'I retrieved the camera today. We got some great footage. There are definitely three pairs, possibly four, and one of the females is heavy with cubs. Arctic foxes, no question, and of course we'd need to trap one to examine it properly, but I think, I really do think, they could be a subspecies. I'm starting to talk higher up the chain. I'll talk to the Cabinet Secretary for Rural Affairs and the Minister for the Environment as soon as Parliament opens after the recess. I'm hoping to get a protection order on them until we can find out more, but I've a feeling that might take a special Bill in Parliament. I'll send you a few clips to watch.'

I leaned in over Gavin's shoulder on one side and his brother Kenny leaned in over the other. The film was grainy, in shades of grey, with the fox's coat glowing white in the darkness. His eyes flashed eerily as he turned his head up towards the camera. 'That's him,' I agreed. I lifted my hand to examine the puncture marks; still just visible.

'But your dad will still get a good half of his windfarm,' Gavin said. 'He'll get all the turbines on the Nesting side of the main road, and probably the ones on the Weisdale Hill.

Just not each side of the valley. Not Scallafield and Gruti Field, or along the Mid Kame.'

'He's not going to be pleased,' I said.

He was even less pleased on Wednesday 6th January, the day we came home; the day the diggers should have gone back to work.

Gavin wasn't due back on duty until Thursday, but he called in at the station for a catch-up on our way from the airport. I waited quietly in a corner, drinking a vending-machine coffee and taking advantage of the better wi-fi to check that *Sørlandet* was where I expected to find her, while officers bustled around me.

'Forensics,' Shona said, brandishing a sheaf of papers at DS Peterson. They glanced at me. I made it clear I was thinking my own thoughts, and listened with both ears.

'Good,' DS Peterson said, scanning it. 'Very good. One of Robin's hairs in the car boot, and one caught in the trolley, down low where his head would have been if he'd been lying on it.' She scanned down further. 'Blood down the edge of the kitchen lino and in the U-bend. Robin's blood group. Frigg's fingerprints on his trainers.' She gave me a sideways look. 'Add that to the two cartons of within-date milk hastily shoved into the freezer. All confirmation of her story.'

Shona scanned down further. 'This doesn't fit. She hit him three times. Once while he was standing and twice on the floor. The marks were clear, in spite of the water damage.'

There was a long silence. Culpable homicide. Behaviour liable to cause someone's death.

DS Peterson turned to look at me. 'Other news: Sheila's taken time off work to run the pet shop, she and Bruce between them. Two sets of muscle-men appeared in court yesterday on charges that included breach of the peace and intimidation, and were remanded in custody. Helge's court case is on-going but I'd say myself that it's looking good for her group.'

The phone rang. DS Peterson went for it, and listened to the indignant male voice on the end of the phone, then said, 'One moment, sir.' She looked up at me. 'Cass, d'you mind?'

I shrugged and went out to sit on the wall outside. It was a bonny day, clear and still. A blackbird was singing in a nearby tree. *Sørlandet* had left Bermuda yesterday, and was heading back towards Florida, to collect our trainees and us before we took her through the Panama Canal and set out across the Pacific. In four days I'd be back on board, becoming absorbed in the life of the ship. My heart leapt at the thought of standing on deck again, with her masts towering above me, and the curves of white sail, and the deck rising and falling with the ocean swell. I'd have the sea wind in my face, cold and salt, and the albatrosses soaring over my head. I felt the thought of it all clutch around my heart and pull me away from this land life, away from Gavin.

A door banged in the police station. DS Peterson came out, with PC Farquhar at her heels. They got into a police car and drove off. Shona and another officer I didn't know followed them in another car. Two more followed in the third car. Either they were bored, or there was a major incident going on. I watched the station door for Gavin coming out and waited to be told.

He came out in less than five minutes. His brows were drawn together, his smile preoccupied. 'Sorry, Cass, I'm going to be here a bit longer. D'you want to go and do some shopping, something for tea?' He paused, made a face, and told me what was wrong. 'Sabotage at the windfarm.'

My mouth fell open. 'Serious?'

'Expensive. Bulldozers, diggers, everything that was parked in the compound. Someone seems to have put something in the tanks. When the drivers tried to start them this morning nothing would start. Worse still, it seems likely that it was done the first night of the holidays, so it's had a full fortnight to cause damage. The engine of every one will have to be dismantled, and a lot of parts replaced. The head man's raging.'

'Why do they think it happened then?' I asked.

'The compound was guarded every other night, after the bother they'd had. That was the only night. There was a big party on up at Busta for all the workers, including Bruce Herculson. They reckoned it would surely be fine for one night, with the machines all locked up in the compound.'

'Everyone would have known about the party at Busta.' It was ringing a bell in my own brain. Someone had mentioned it.

'No prints, of course, the snow's long gone. There might have been something on the floor of the office, where they took the vehicle keys from, but that was well trampled by drivers collecting their keys before they realised anything was wrong.'

'How did they get into the office?'

'They broke a window at the back. Very neatly, covered it with sticky-back plastic, then tapped it with a hammer. We might get prints from that, but I doubt it. Everyone knows to wear gloves.'

'What do they think was done to the engines?'

'Water in the oil, they think, and probably sugar in the fuel – they found deposits of something sticky.' Gavin made an apologetic face. 'I'll need to be here a bit longer. An hour anyway, till Freya reports back.'

'I'll go and get tea, then wait outside again. No hurry.'

I was glad to get away, so that he couldn't read my face. I didn't go to the café; I made straight for the church and sat down in a pew, staring ahead at the curlicued cross that topped the wooden altar.

Busta House. Sugar. The first night of the holidays; Friday, the night I'd been babysitting Dawn and Peerie Charlie, while Vaila spent the night at Rainbow's. *I was just wondering if you were still going to do a helicopter search*, Rainbow had asked, and

336

the others had given her alarmed looks, as if she might be
going to give something away. *Sugar.* Peerie Charlie grousing.
Vaila took all the sugar. Bags and bags and bags of it. Vaila hadn't
wanted to help out at Busta, even though she was short of
money. Even the hoofprints I'd followed along the valley, when
we were looking for fox prints. I should have remembered that
the ponies that roamed the valley in summer were in their field
through the winter; I'd seen them there from the car. Vaila's
rubber boots, when I'd borrowed them, had smelled of horse.
They hadn't been there when I'd played trow, nor her snow
camouflage overalls; I'd had to borrow Inga's boots, and Charlie's white boiler suit. Vaila, Rainbow, Drew, John-Lowrie,
innocently playing cards when DS Peterson called.

I understood Vaila's anxiety now, and the changed face she'd
shown me on Saturday morning. Berwin should have been on
the raid with them. He'd done his disappearing act, and they'd
all thought he'd turn up that evening. *See you tomorrow.* I'd put
them on the spot when I'd asked them what they thought he
meant by that. But then he hadn't appeared, and they'd gone
ahead without him. Vaila had spent that night after the raid
thinking that harm really had come to him. Then, in the morning, he'd turned up alive after all, but not knowing what day it
was, or what he'd been doing. No wonder Drew had been so
insistent that one of them should go to the hospital with him.
They were terrified of what he might say. This wasn't a fun
prank with trowie footprints and a protest banner, this was serious, deliberate, expensive criminal damage. Water in the oil,
sugar in the fuel. Those engines would be done for.

I leaned back against the wall and thought it through. The
ride through the darkness. Those hoofprints would be gone
with the melted snow. They'd have tied the ponies up at the
last fence, out of sight of the farm above Kergord. If the ponies
were normally loose in the valley, them moving about wouldn't
have disturbed the people living there. They'd have checked

the diggers first, to make sure they really were locked. I remembered how the boys in our class used to swing over the multicourt fence every time a ball went out. Drew would be into that compound in seconds, to find the machines locked; not surprising. They'd have gone to the office and broken in. They'd thought that through: sticky-back plastic, a hammer. There might be prints on the plastic, if they'd handled it without gloves on at any time, but those could be anyone's: a shop assistant, a customer picking it up to examine, then deciding against it. The police couldn't convict on that. The smallest of them through the window, to get the keys. Back out, to do the damage. They'd have worn gloves for that. The keys replaced; back to the ponies, and home.

I thought about the green hills I'd grown up with, the unbroken skyline, the starlit nights without the flashing red turbine warnings that you saw all round the Norwegian coast. I thought of the birds who nested there, the raingeese and the whimbrels; the wild moorland where the only sound was the call of a whaup, not the thrumming of a hundred giant turbines. I thought of the Facebook posts I'd seen by people who'd moved away from their homes because they'd never been well since the turbines came.

I'd be on my ship soon, but Vaila and Rainbow, Drew and Berwin and John-Lowrie, they lived here. They wanted to stay and raise their children in the world they had now, not an industrial landscape. Twenty-five years meant their children, and mine, would be living with turbines until they left for university. Fifty years meant our grandchildren would. All legal attempts at protest had been steamrollered. I didn't blame them for taking direct action.

On the other hand, my older self pointed out, the contractors were just doing a job. Shetland Eco-Energy had hired them to dig roads. They weren't locals who cared one way or another. It was hard on them to have their plant destroyed. Their insurance would pay, but claw back the money in increased premiums. It wasn't right, what the teenagers had done.

All the same, I didn't want them to be caught. Sure, they'd not be sent to prison, they were all too young, but they might be sent to some sort of young offenders institution. They'd have a criminal record. No joining the armed forces: no Navy career for Drew, no police or civil service for Vaila or Rainbow. There would be major consequences, and not just for them. Their parents would be mortified. Protest was one thing; Inga was the first to shout out. Actual damage was different. She and Charlie would be determined that every penny of the repair cost would be paid back, whatever strain that put on the family, and I was sure the other parents would feel the same.

I saw their faces in my mind's eye: passionate Vaila, mercurial Drew, reliable John-Lowrie, animal-loving Rainbow. Berwin, who'd lost so much already. Young people with all their lives before them: school, exams, university, a career. I suspected Vaila would end up a teacher. Drew had his sights set on making captain. John-Lowrie would be the world's most trustworthy mechanic. Rainbow was an obvious vet. Berwin had once said he fancied being a doctor. They'd travel the world, or stay in Shetland and be part of the community. They'd be lovers and parents. Unless one of them decided to be a public martyr for the cause, nobody needed to know it was them.

Juliet had ended her life at only thirteen.

I needed to forget I knew this. I couldn't tell anyone, never, ever. Cross my heart and hope to die. Gavin might guess at Vaila, but if there was no evidence he wouldn't pursue her for a confession. Everybody else would be looking for an adult saboteur. Someone come up from south was always a handy scapegoat in Shetland. They wouldn't think of their own teenagers.

I was going back to sea. I'd be on the boat tomorrow, the

339

train on Friday, flying out from Glasgow on Saturday. On Sunday morning I'd be landing in Miami. By the time I came home again, I'd have forgotten. I'd make sure I forgot.

It was my last day. My leave had slipped away as swiftly as the fox retreating to his hills. Overnight, the snow had turned to rain. Cat came in with damp paws while we were having our in-bed cup of tea, and when I looked out the smooth snow had become white crescents in the hollows where it had lain deepest. The slope to the shore was green and sodden. The ditches glimmered with water; the sea was a dull, pale blue, and the view up to Brae was misted over with rain.

It would be sunny in Florida, with the light dancing on the water and on our ship's white sails.

'You're going,' Gavin said. He put an arm around me, and we stood looking out at the scudding catspaws on the water. 'I can feel it.' He made a little gesture with his free hand, and said a phrase in Gaelic, then reddened as he tried to translate it. 'Your heart's already away at sea, and your body's wearying to follow it.'

I slipped my hand around his waist and leaned my head against his shoulder. 'But once I'm there, a part of me will be longing to be here.' I took a deep breath and tried to make with the words. 'It's been good, being together. It's been easier than I feared it would be. I've been happy. I've felt at home.'

It was as near to true as I could say. His arm tightened on my shoulders. 'I wasn't sure how easy I'd find it either. I'm used to having my flat to myself. Being able to come home and just collapse after a hard day. Not eat if I don't feel like it. Not to have to talk to anyone, after a day of interviews.'

'But it's been okay, hasn't it?' I asked, suddenly anxious. 'You haven't minded having to eat, and talk?'

He shook his head. 'I've liked eating and talking with you very much.'

'Companionable,' I agreed.

We stood there for a moment longer. The otter slipped out from a holt somewhere on the point of Quiensetter and slid into the water.

'She's got cubs,' Gavin said. 'Listen, do you hear that whistling noise? They're on the shore, waiting for her to bring their breakfast.' His arm tightened on my shoulders, and he turned his face away from me, and spoke softly to the wind. 'Cass, *mo chridhe*, I know you couldn't have done the sabotage at the windfarm. You were playing trows with Peerie Charlie, then under Freya's eye, then with me. But I ken you're worrying about it.'

I should have known he'd know. 'I don't have any evidence,' I said slowly. I thought about a four-year-old telling me he'd seen his sister with bags of sugar, of missing rubber boots and white paper boiler suit. 'I don't think you'd find any even if I pointed you in the direction I suspect.' I turned to face him. 'I know it was wrong. I know it was the contractor who suffered, rather than Dad and the other people responsible. I think . . . I think I'd feel differently if it had been fair, if they'd asked the people who live here what they wanted, if there'd been a vote and the anti-windfarm folk had lost. Sabotage would be wrong then. But they, the people up the chain who gave permission, they made sure they didn't ask, because they knew they'd get the wrong answer. What can you do?'

'Lie down in front of diggers,' Gavin said. 'Chain yourself to their wheels. Build a shelter right in the way and live in it. Scream your cause to the heavens.'

'They tried to do that,' I said. 'Inga told me about it. They took it all the way to the Supreme Court, and they lost. There's no law to protect people. Where's the justice in that?'

He turned his head to kiss my cheek. 'Hey,' he said softly. 'I'm on your side for that one. My own ancestors were kept to run the farm, but the rest of the clan were cleared for sheep

341

grazing. I have a cousin in Canada who's so like me that we could use each other to shave by.'

My eyes dropped. I leaned my head against his. 'I don't want you to catch — ' I was about to say *them* — 'the person responsible.'

'I'll have to try,' Gavin said.

I sighed. 'I know.'

'But whoever it was wore gloves, and the largest size of used trainers, from a charity shop, maybe, to hide the real size of their feet. We managed to find a couple of trainer footprints among the machines. The drivers all wear steel toe-caps. If the person responsible doesn't play the martyr, and if it doesn't happen again, then he or she may well get away with it.' His voice hardened. 'If it keeps happening then we'll catch them.'

'I hope it won't,' I said. 'If all goes well with the Arctic fox, maybe it won't need to.' The thought cheered me. I slipped my hand into his. 'And it's only eight weeks I'll be away. March 8th, or thereby, once I get back from the Pacific. The middle of Lent.' I brightened. Eight weeks on, eight off. 'Time to get *Khalida* painted, and her mast up. All of April and the start of May to get her sailing.'

'I'll make sure,' Gavin said gravely, 'that I keep reminding Cat of his responsibilities as a sailing cat.'

Acknowledgements

As always, there are so many people to thank. First, foremost and always, my husband, Philip, for his constant support and encouragement. My agent, Teresa Chris, has also maintained my writing morale in this strange Covid year; she is always my fresh eye on a book when I've revised it until I can't see the wood for the trees, and her comments are percipient, practical and always gratefully received. My editor, Toby Jones, and his team at Headline, particularly Celine Kelly and publicist Emily Patience, are a joy to work with. Thank you to the two Karens here in Shetland: 'Bookshop Karen' and her staff at the Shetland Times Bookshop, and 'Library Karen' and her staff at the Shetland Library. It was a huge honour to be 'Shetland's most borrowed' two years running.

For this book particularly I'd like to thank the many people who helped me to get things right. Alex Dodge, of the Shetland Coastguard, helped me with details of a search for a missing person; Sergeant Victoria Duffy, of our police here in Shetland, helped me with administrative details. My former pupil Adam Mess not only gave me information on how to sabotage diggers, but trusted me not to go ahead and use it. Facebook is a wonderful resource: thank you to everyone of the *Wir Midder Tongue* page who responded enthusiastically when I asked for words, with a particular thanks to Barbara Fraser and Lorna Moncrieff for details of how to make sheep's head broth.

Naturally any errors are my own. Finally, thank you to the real Marvin Smith, who won the auction for being a character in 'the next Cass novel'.

Cass's dad's windfarm was a key element in the first novel, *Death on a Longship*, and I didn't mean to write about it again. That book was published ten years ago, and I was able to be more even-handed. The world has learned a lot about windfarms since then: yes, how good they can be as a source of clean energy, but also how far from green they are in terms of where the raw material comes from and how old turbine blades are disposed of, and the health problems they create in people living near them. Much more is also known about the importance of peat to our planet. The protests I've envisaged in this book were made impossible by Covid regulations, and in the last nine months the road scars have crawled inexorably up our hills. Now, when I go out for a sail, I can see the bulldozers on the skyline, and hear them rumble in the distance. In two years the view of hill and sky from our bedroom window will be turbines by day and flashing red lights at night.

Saddest of all, the windfarm debate has created bitter division within the community. A good number in Shetland feel it's our duty to the planet, and will bring money to the isles. I've tried to be even-handed and mention the benefits, but many people in Shetland feel, as I do, that this monstrous destruction has been imposed on us without real consultation, and against our wishes.

For that reason, this book is dedicated to the committee and members of the group Sustainable Shetland, who financed and fought a legal challenge to the Scottish Ministers and windfarm developers. The Shetland Islands Council didn't object to the plans (although almost 3,000 Shetland people signed a petition against the development), leaving the decision with the Scottish Government, so no public inquiry was held to allow local residents the chance to object. The legal reason for the challenge was to protect the breeding grounds of the rare whimbrel (apparently the people who live there don't count as needing protection). The Court of Sessions in Edinburgh initially found for Sustainable Shetland, then, on the developers' appeal, against them. The Supreme Court also found against them. I would like to express here my admiration for the determination and courage of these Sustainable Shetland officials and members, particularly those who were willing to face the lawyers of the Scottish Land Court in defence of their homeland. I just wish their challenge had succeeded.

Finally, and more cheerfully, in this strange year I haven't been able to do drama in the school, or join my fellow flute-learners at the Christmas service, or go to London to see my grandchildren. The pink-sailed Picos stayed in their shed at Brae all summer. I've missed being surrounded by young people, and consoled myself by writing about them. I hope that Cass's teenage fans here in Shetland and elsewhere enjoy this adventure.

A Note on Shetlan

Shetland has its own very distinctive language, *Shetlan* or *Shetlandic*, which derives from Old Norse and Old Scots. In *Death on a Longship*, Magnie's first words to Cass are, 'Cass, well, for the love of mercy. Norroway, at this season? Yea, yea, we'll find you a berth. Where are you?'

Written in west-side Shetlan (each district is slightly different), it would have looked like this: 'Cass, weel, fir da love o mercy. Norroway, at dis saeson? Yea, yea, we'll fin dee a bert. Quaur is du?'

Th becomes a *d* sound in *dis* (this), *da* (the), *dee* and *du* (originally thee and thou, now you), *wh* becomes *qu* (*quaur*, where), the vowel sounds are altered (well to *weel*, season to *saeson*, find to *fin*), the verbs are slightly different (quaur is du?) and the whole looks unintelligible to most folk from outwith Shetland, and *twartree* (a few) within it too.

So, rather than writing in the way my characters would speak, I've tried to catch the rhythm and some of the distinctive usages of Shetlan while keeping it intelligible to *soothmoothers*, or people who've come in by boat through the South Mouth of Bressay Sound into Lerwick, and by extension, anyone living south of Fair Isle.

There are also many Shetlan words that my characters would naturally use, and here, to help you, are *some o' dem*. No Shetland person would ever use the Scots *wee*; to them, something small would be *peerie*, or, if it was very small, *peerie mootie*. They'd *caa* sheep in a *park*, that is, herd them up in a field – *moorit* sheep, coloured black, brown, fawn. They'd take a *skiff* (a small rowing boat) out along the *banks* (cliffs) or on the *voe* (sea inlet), with the *tirricks* (Arctic terns) crying above them, and the *selkies* (seals) watching. Hungry folk are *black fanted* (because they've forgotten their *faerdie maet*, the snack that would have kept them going) and upset folk *greet* (cry). An older housewife like Jessie would have her *makkin* (knitting) *belt* buckled around her waist, and her *reestit* (smoke-dried) *mutton* hanging above the Rayburn. And finally . . . my favourite Shetland verb, which I didn't manage to work into this novel, but which is too good not to share: *to kettle*. As in: *Wir cat's just kettled. Four ketlings, twa strippet and twa black and quite*. I'll leave you to work that one out on your own . . . or, of course, you could consult Joanie Graham's *Shetland Dictionary*, if your local bookshop hasn't *joost selt* their last copy *dastreen*.

The diminutives Magnie (Magnus), Gibbie (Gilbert) and Charlie may also seem strange to non-Shetland ears. In a traditional country family (I can't speak for *toonie* Lerwick habits) the oldest son would often be called after his father or grandfather, and be distinguished from that father and grandfather, and probably a cousin or two as well, by his own version of their shared name. Or, of course, by a *Peerie* in front of it, which would stick for life, like the *eart kyent* (well-known) guitarist Peerie Willie Johnson, who reached his 80th birthday. There was also a patronymic system, which meant that a Peter's four sons, Peter, Andrew, John and Matthew, would all have the surname Peterson, and so would his son Peter's children. Andrew's children, however, would have the surname Anderson, John's would be Johnson, and Matthew's would be Matthewson. The Scots ministers stamped this out in the nineteenth century, but in one district you can have a lot of *folk* with the same surname, and so they're distinguished by their house name: *Magnie o' Strom, Peter o' da Knowe*.

Glossary

For those who like to look up unfamiliar words as they go, here's a glossary of Scots and Shetlan words.

aa: all
an aa: as well
aaber: able, energetic; an aaber skipper is a capable boat-captain
aabody: everybody
aawye: everywhere
in an aet: uneasy, agitated
ahint: behind
ain: own
amang: among
ammerswak: state of unrest or agitation
anyroad: anyway
ashet: large serving dish
auld: old
aye: always
bairn: child
ball (verb): throw out
banks: sea cliffs, or peatbanks, the slice of moor where peats are cast
bannock: flat triangular scone
birl, birling: paired spinning round in a dance

blinkie: torch

blootered: very drunk

blyde: pleased

boanie: pretty, good-looking

breeks: trousers

briggistanes: flagged stones at the door of a crofthouse

bruck: rubbish

caa: round up

canna: can't

clarted: thickly covered

cludgie: toilet

collieshang: disturbance, kerfuffle

cowp: capsize

cratur: creature

crofthouse: the long, low traditional house set in its own land

croog: to crouch down to

daander: to travel uncertainly or in a leisurely fashion

darrow: a hand fishing line

dastreen: yesterday evening

de-crofted: land that has been taken out of agricultural use, e.g. for a house site

dee: you; *du* is also you, depending on the grammar of the sentence – they're equivalent to thee and thou. Like French, you would only use dee or du to one friend; several people, or an adult if you're a younger person, would be you

denner: midday meal

deuk: duck

deukey-hole: pond for ducks

didna: didn't

dinna: don't

dip dee doon: sit yourself down

dis: this

doesna: doesn't

doon: down

dorts, taking the dorts: taking offence, sulking

drewie lines: a type of seaweed made of long strands

drummie: a bumble bee

du kens: you know

dyck, dyke: a wall, generally drystane, i.e. built without cement

eart: direction, *the eart o wind*

ee now: right now

eela: fishing, generally these days a competition

eident: always busy, industrious

everywye: everywhere

faersome: frightening

faither, usually faider: father

fanted: hungry, often black fanted, absolutely starving

folk: people

frae: from

gansey: a knitted jumper

gant: to yawn

geen: gone

gluff: fright

greff: the area in front of a peat bank

gret: cried

guid: good

guid kens: God knows

hadna: hadn't

hae: have

harled: exterior plaster using small stones

heid: head

hoosie: little house, usually for bairns

howk: to search among: I *howked* ida box o auld claes

ill vaandit: disagreeable, having unattractive manners; bad or awkward behaviour; also said of job badly done

isna: isn't

just: just

ken, kent: know, knew

keek: peep at

kirk: church

kirkyard: graveyard

kishie: wicker basket carried on the back, supported by a *kishie baand* around the forehead

knowe: hillock

lem: china

lichtsome: uplifting, cheerful, goodnatured

Lerook: Lerwick

likit: liked

lintie: skylark

lipper: a cheeky or harum-scarum child, generally affectionate

mad: annoyed

mair: more

makkin belt: a knitting belt with a padded oval, perforated for holding the 'wires' or knitting needles

mam: mum

mareel: sea phosphorescence, caused by plankton, which makes every wave break in a curl of gold sparks

meids: shore features to line up against each other to pinpoint a spot on the water

midder: mother

mind: remember

moorit: coloured brown or black, usually used of sheep

mooritoog: earwig

muckle: big – as in Muckle Roe, the big red island. Vikings were very literal in their names, and almost all Shetland names come from the Norse

muckle biscuit: large water biscuit, for putting cheese on

myrd: a good number and variety – a *myrd* o peerie things

na: no, or more emphatically, nall
needna: needn't
Norroway: the old Shetland pronunciation of Norway
o: of
oot: out
opstropolous: rowdy, boisterous
ower: over
park: fenced field
peat: brick-like lump of dried peat earth, used as fuel
peerie: small
peerie biscuit: small sweet biscuit
Peeriebreeks: affectionate name for a small thing, person
 or animal
perrnyimm: prim and proper
perskeet: prim, overly particular
piltick: a sea fish common in Shetland waters
pinnie: apron
postie: postman
puckles: small round balls, as in haily puckles
quen: when
redding up: tidying
redd up kin: get in touch with family – for example, a
 five-generations New Zealander might come to meet
 Shetland cousins still staying in the house his or her
 forebears had left
reestit mutton: wind-dried shanks of mutton
riggit: dressed, sometimes with the sense dressed-up
roadymen: men working on the roads
roog: a pile of peats
rummle: untidy scattering
Santie: Santa Claus
scaddy man's heids: sea urchins
scattald: common grazing land
scuppered: put paid to, done for

selkie: seal, or seal person who came ashore at night, cast his/her skin and became human

Setturday: Saturday

shalder: oystercatcher

sheeksing: chatting

sho: she

shoulda: should have, usually said shoulda

shouldna: shouldn't have

SIBC: Shetland Islands Broadcasting Company, the independent radio station

sjoamit: a white-wooled sheep, or figuratively, someone who has suffered a shock

skafe: squint

skerry: a rock in the sea

slester: a mess, generally involving a child and mud

smeegin: smirking, smiling mockingly, with a connotation of self-satisfaction

smoorikins: kisses

snicked: move a switch that makes a clicking noise

snippet: sharp-spoken

snyirked: made a squeaking or rattling noise

solan: gannet

somewye: somewhere

sooking up: sucking up

soothified: behaving like someone from outwith Shetland

spew: be sick

spewings: piles of sick

splatched: walked in a splashy way with wet feet, or in water

steekit mist: thick mist

sun-gaits: with the sun – it's bad luck to go against the sun, particularly walking around a church

swack: smart, fine

swee: to sting (of injury)

tak: take

tatties: potatoes

tay: tea, or meal eaten in the evening

tink: think

tirricks: Arctic terns

toorie: a knitted woolen cap

trauchle: trouble, bother

trigg: neat, orderly

trows: trolls

trunnie, making a trunnie: pulling a sulky face

tushker: L-shaped spade for cutting peat

twa: two

twartree: a small number, several

tulley: pocket knife

unken: unknown

vexed: sorry or sympathetic – 'I was that vexed to hear that'

vee-lined: lined with wood planking

voe: sea inlet

voehead: the landwards end of a sea inlet

waander: wander, or, metaphorically, waandert: not able to think straight

waar: seaweed

wasna: wasn't

wha's: who is

whatna: what

whit: what

whitteret: weasel

wi: with

wife: woman, not necessarily married

wir: we've – in Shetlan grammar, we are is sometimes we have

wir: our

wouldna: would not

yaird: enclosed area around or near the crofthouse

yoal: a traditional clinker-built six-oared rowing boat